Tl

Ally Sinclair grew up on the North Yorkshire coast and now lives with her husband in Worcestershire, at least until she can persuade him to give into her yearning to live somewhere nearer the sea. No kids, no pets. She sometimes manages to keep a pot plant alive. Briefly.

She has been writing professionally since 2013, and is also published as Alison May and, in collaboration, as Juliet Bell. Ally is a former Chair of the Romantic Novelists' Association, and currently works as an associate lecturer for the Open University.

Also by Ally Sinclair

A Season for Love
The Christmas Season

THE
Christmas Season

ALLY SINCLAIR

hera

First published in the United Kingdom in 2023 by

Hera Books
Unit 9 (Canelo), 5th Floor
Cargo Works, 1-2 Hatfields
London SE1 9PG
United Kingdom

A CIP catalogue record for this book is available from the British Library.

Print ISBN 978 1 80436 366 9
Ebook ISBN 978 1 80436 365 2

This book is a work of fiction. Names, characters, businesses, organizations, places and events are either the product of the author's imagination or are used fictitiously. Any resemblance to actual persons, living or dead, events or locales is entirely coincidental.

Look for more great books at www.herabooks.com

Printed and bound in Great Britain by Clays Ltd, Elcograf S.p.A.

I

MIX
Paper from
responsible sources
FSC® C018072
www.fsc.org

For Amy and Emma-Claire. Watching you both achieve your dreams inspires me every day to keep pursuing mine.

Happily Ever After...

Emma Love considered herself something of an expert on affairs of the heart. As the second generation in a family of professional matchmakers she knew more than a little about what sorts of people went together. Emma herself, for example, had had a number of very pleasant relationships with sensible, stable, thoughtful men, who complemented her own considered approach to life.

Which made the fact that she was standing at the front of a tiny chapel, presided over by a man in an Elvis costume, particularly unexpected. Across the aisle, Tom Knight, sexy, impulsive, professional gambler, winked at her. This was very much more his sort of thing than hers. She really didn't know how she'd been talked into this.

And then she looked to the front of the chapel and she knew they were in exactly the right place. In front of her, with Tom and Emma as their witnesses, Emma's brother and his bride shared their first kiss as man and wife, exactly seventy-two hours since they announced that they were engaged and precisely sixty-nine hours since the start of the champagne-fuelled conversation about whether you really could get married in Vegas straight away or if you needed to register and wait. Once the ball was rolling, it turned out that all you needed was Emma's ability to plan a trip, and Tom's ability to flash a credit card with no concern for the consequences, and away you went.

After the ceremony, Emma and Tom left the newlyweds to do their newlywed thing and walked back towards their hotel.

'I can't believe you've never been to Vegas before,' said Tom.

'How many times have you been?'

'Twice with my parents. Once with…' He didn't finish the sentence.

'You can say "with Jack".' Emma squeezed his hand. 'He's part of the person you are now.'

'I know.' Tom's voice was tight for a moment, before he smiled. 'Never been to a wedding here though. And, just think, that coulda been us.'

'Don't be silly.'

'I'm not being silly. We've been together as long as them.'

Technically that was true, give or take twenty-four hours, but Josh and Annie had been in love with one another since they were five years old. The fact that it had taken until they were in their thirties for the stars to align was simply bad luck.

'Don't worry. I'm only winding you up. When we get married…'

'When?'

He shrugged. 'I'm a natural optimist. When we get married, I will let you plan every detail months in advance. I will surrender myself to the spreadsheet.'

'I'll believe that when I see it.'

He clutched his chest in mock hurt. 'I mean it. And really, what greater love can there be than allowing your partner to reduce your grand romance to rows and columns?'

'You have to persuade me you're worth marrying first.'

He stopped. His hand in hers forced her to do the same. She turned towards him. He reached into his pocket. Emma's breath caught in her throat. He couldn't be going to… it really was too soon… not that she didn't love him… Emma's brain was doing the fastest analysis it could manage. She loved Tom. His impulsiveness and willingness to take a risk encouraged her to be a braver version of herself. And he was proving to be pretty much the only person on earth who could ever persuade her to take a day off. Of course she loved Tom, but their lives right now were going well. Would getting engaged change that or…

'Emma Love, will you…'

Was this really happening? She hadn't planned for it. She hadn't made a pro con list. They hadn't even lived together.

'Will you…' He lifted his hand towards her. 'Will you get yourself back to the hotel and get on with some of the sodding work I know you've been desperate to get back to all day?'

She shook her head, as he passed her the key card. 'Bastard.'

He pulled her close and kissed her hard. 'You really thought I was going to propose?'

'It's the sort of thing you would do.'

'Not until you're ready. I'm impulsive. I'm not in the business of steamrollering people I love.'

'What will you do if I go back?'

The man she'd first met at an online poker table raised an eyebrow. 'We're in Las Vegas. What do you think I'm gonna do?'

She kissed him again before he walked away. She really did want to get to work. They had four weeks before the official launch of the Christmas dating season, and her brother/business partner was now planning to be on honeymoon for one of those. Tom knew her better than she would ever admit. There was one thing that he didn't know though, one way she could still surprise him, one thing that, despite the lack of spreadsheets and lists and analysis, had become absolutely clear in a single moment. She yelled after him. 'Tom!'

He turned.

'If you had asked, I would have said yes.'

Chapter One

'So shall I talk you through what you missed?' Emma asked.

Josh's first day back in the 'office' (also known as the dining room) was precisely three weeks before the first event of the second Love's Love Social Season. The Season was very much Emma's baby. Her vision was for a string of social events, inspired by the social seasons of Jane Austen and Georgette Heyer, where eligible singletons could meet one another in real life and form lasting attachments based on attraction and compatibility rather than swiping right and hooking up.

The first Season had concluded less than three months earlier and had, Emma reassured herself, been something of a success. Her inbox was full of notes of thanks and invitations to joint housewarmings, and, thanks to Josh and Annie, they had already ticked off their first Season wedding. Which meant that the pressure to make the second time around even better was immense.

What Josh had missed, therefore, was a lot of hard work. She turned her laptop towards him.

'Actually there's something I need to talk to you about first,' he said.

Emma didn't bother to even try to keep the scowl off her face. 'Something important?'

'Yes. It's about Annie. We were talking while we were away about where we're going to live now we're Mr and Mrs.'

Oh. Of course. Annie spent pretty much every weekend at the house Emma shared with her stepbrother already, but during the week she'd been heading back to her flat which was much nearer the school she taught in. Obviously they'd live together now.

'So we were thinking, this place is big and Mum doesn't seem that bothered about selling it.'

Emma's mother had moved to Spain in the spring. Initially they'd agreed that Emma and Josh would live in the house until she was ready to sell, but she seemed perfectly happy in the apartment she'd rented and the money from her pension and Emma's stepdad's life insurance was keeping her going.

'You want to live here?' Emma knew she had no right to be affronted. This was Josh's family home every bit as much as it was hers. 'So I guess I'll have to find a place...'

'What?' Josh spluttered. 'No. Oh God. Don't tell Annie you thought that. She'd be horrified if she thought I was trying to chuck you out. I meant that it's big enough for all three of us, isn't it? And you know how much Annie loves the whole match-making thing. If she's here she can help out with the business?'

'Ok. Cool.'

'Really?'

'Really.' It was exactly how Love's Love had always worked. Emma's mum had started the business back in the days before the internet dominated the dating market, and some of Emma's earliest memories were sitting at the dining table watching her mother scour through her card index of potential matches for a new client. She'd earned her pocket money in the school holidays stuffing flyers through letterboxes and answering her mum's phones. Later, when they'd moved in with Josh and his dad, Trevor, the whole family had been roped into the business. The boundaries between professional and personal had never been closely observed. 'It sounds great. Tell Annie that my home is her home.'

'Thanks.'

Emma nodded. 'So can we get back to work now then?'

'Sure. What have I missed?'

She showed him her laptop screen. 'Ok. This is where we're up to.'

He scanned the list of confirmed events, venues and catering quotes. 'That's more than their original quote.' He tapped the screen on the catering price for the first event.

She had, if she was honest, been hoping – assuming – he wouldn't notice. 'They wanted to use a cheaper red for the mulled wine. I upgraded it.'

'Emma!'

'What? It's supposed to be classy.'

'It's hot wine with spices in it. Nobody will taste the difference. Change it back.'

Emma pursed her lips.

Her brother glared at her. 'What did we agree?'

He was referring to the agreement that she had insisted on drawing up when he'd invested in the Season and officially become her business partner. 'I'm responsible for event planning.'

'And I'm responsible for finances, and I am aiming for a situation where we actually make a profit and can afford to live.'

So there might have been one very small way in which the first Season hadn't been quite such a success. 'We broke even,' she muttered.

'Just. And only because you didn't pay yourself. Or me,' he added slightly more pointedly.

'Fine. I'll change the wine back.'

'Thank you.' He scanned down the rest of the list. 'This is great. Wow. How did you get that price?'

She checked the row he was pointing too. 'Fixed their events manager up with my hairdresser.'

'Excellent. That one's still a bit expensive. Don't suppose their boss is eligible and on the lookout?'

Emma was already ahead of him. 'Married with three kids,' she said. 'I checked.'

'Oh well, I'll have a look at the full quote and see what I can negotiate. Are you happy with all the events?'

Emma paused. She was happy that the plan she'd come up with was the best it could be.

Josh read her hesitation. 'I'll take that as a no.'

'It's the Regency thing.'

'What about it?'

The whole idea of the Season was inspired by a Regency social season. Emma had taken her cue from Jane Austen and Georgette Heyer and Julia Quinn and a million and one other stories and movies that she adored with all her heart. 'All the traditional Christmas stuff is Victorian,' she explained.

'Is that different?'

It was lucky for Josh that he was good with technology and finance, and that Emma's mum would yell at her if she fired him, because he would never have got a job with a dating agency based on his romantic soul.

'How about bookings?' he asked.

She moved to her registrations spreadsheet. They'd had a lot of good PR after the first Season and some excellent word of mouth, and, honestly, what single person wasn't hoping to meet a handsome duke all of their own? So bookings for the upcoming Festive Season were more than healthy. She scrolled down past the first few rows. Josh leaned over her and scrolled back. 'Emma!'

'Well, she was so disappointed at the end of the last one...'

'She upset your perfect run, is what you mean.'

Emma didn't dignify that with a response.

'We can't afford to give away freebies.'

'It's only one person.'

'Seriously Stilts?'

Josh had coined that nickname when they were teenagers and Emma still believed she might have another growth spurt coming. Emma had got stuck at 5 ft 1, and the nickname had stuck as well. He read down the spreadsheet. 'And what about these others?'

'Just a couple of friends. I thought she might feel better about coming back if she was with friends.'

Josh shook his head. 'You can't be everybody's fairy godmother.'

Well, why the hell not? And actually that was exactly what Emma's whole job was. She was there to help people find their happy ever after. Hope Lucas had been a rare failure at the end of the first dating Season, and Emma was determined that, this time, she would do whatever it took to ensure that Hope found her Prince Charming second time around.

She pulled Hope's profile from the previous Season up on her screen. Who was Hope Lucas's Prince Charming? According to her own declaration, she was looking for someone honest and open and ready to make a commitment. *Someone who won't back me into a corner.* That was an odd way of phrasing it, but overall the aspiration of a trustworthy, kind-hearted partner didn't seem like it ought to be beyond Emma's talents. Time for her to work some matchmaking magic.

Chapter Two

'I was not chatting her up.' Theo was indignant at the very suggestion, but Hope was more than familiar with her best friend's approach to women. That approach, so far as Hope could see, being: 'Here is a woman. I should probably have sex with her.'

'Good, cos actual members of my family are off limits.' Hope's father hosted a Halloween party every year, and seemed to invite everyone he'd ever met – Hope's mother excepted – and was also entirely chilled about any number of people he'd never met, and would never meet again, being dragged along in the wake of other guests. Theo's role was to be Hope's emotional support human and help her fend off interest from whatever chap her dad had run into at the races, or in the pub, and decided to bring along to meet his very eligible daughter. He wasn't supposed to get waylaid by attractive cousins making eyes at him. Although expecting anything else from Theo was like expecting water to flow uphill. Women gravitated towards him whether, according to Theo, he encouraged them to or not.

'She was like a second cousin or something. Doesn't count.'

'She knows my mum.' Hope shuddered. 'It counts.'

'Anyway I wasn't chatting her up,' Theo repeated.

Hope thought back. He hadn't actually seemed that interested, but somehow he had still managed to occupy all of the second cousin's attention for most of the evening. 'So what were you doing? Were you negging her or something?'

'Negging?'

His pretence at not knowing what she meant wasn't cutting any mustard. 'You know, making a girl feel bad so she'll be more needy.'

9

'Ugh.' Theo pulled a face. 'I do not neg.'

'So what was your plan?' Hope pulled her coat around her against the autumnal chill in the air. 'Why am I not doing a "taxi for one" home?'

'I walk you home loads.'

'Only when you strike out.'

'To strike out I would have to have been trying to pull. And I was not.'

'You always say that.'

'So why don't you believe me?' He did, almost, sound genuinely pained.

Hope had known him for too long to fall for that though. 'Because for a man who claims not to be trying you're never short of interest.'

Theo's voice was still tense. 'That's not by design.'

'Yeah. Right.' Theo must have crashed and burned. 'You can come back to mine and we'll have Marmitey toast and it'll make everything better. Ok?'

'Sounds perfect.' Then he stopped. 'Will Grace be there?'

'Well it's her house.' Hope's current abode was a house share with her twin cousins, who owned the house between them. Her live-in landladies were great in many ways, especially as they maintained a refreshingly relaxed attitude to Hope being late with the rent, which was, itself, gloriously low for the capital. 'Why do you care if Grace is there?'

'Well…'

He didn't need to finish the sentence. 'You didn't?' Of course he did. 'I said no family! What happened to not shitting too close to home?'

'It's not my home.'

'Well it is mine.'

'I came round to see you. It's not my fault if you're not there.'

'You are allowed to visit a house without shagging anyone, you know?'

'I never said we…' Theo's protest faltered when he saw the look on Hope's face. 'Well nothing would have happened if you'd been there.'

'So this is my fault.'

He grinned. 'Now you get it.'

It wasn't funny. 'You could have gone home.'

'I was in the moment. I panicked.'

'Well, anyway, you might be in luck. They're both out at a family wedding do tonight.'

'And you're not?'

'Their dad's side of the family.'

On arrival at the flat, Theo loitered in the hallway. 'What are you doing?' Hope asked.

'Waiting for you to check if the coast is clear.'

For goodness' sake. Hope called up the stairs, but there was no reply and no light on that she could see. 'You're fine. Just get in here.'

Theo followed Hope into the kitchen and filled the kettle while she set about making toast. They moved around each other seamlessly, in the grooves of a routine they'd perfected in the kitchen in halls as students and transplanted to houses and flats across the capital ever since. The patented Hope and Theo post-drinking hangover preventative pick-me-up. Marmitey toast and big mugs of tea consumed into the wee small hours until any and all alcohol must, unquestionably, have been either soaked up by carbs or diluted by tea sufficiently to pose no risk to morning health.

'What's this?' Theo picked up a cream envelope that was leaning on the elegant vase of dark red delphiniums and chocolate cosmos that Hope had arranged that morning. 'Addressed to you.'

It had the look of a high-class wedding or christening invitation. Great. Another day of politely smiling along as her friends ticked off life's milestones ahead of her. Another day of relying on Theo as her plus one, and batting away questions about whether she was seeing anybody. 'Open it.'

Theo did as he was told. 'Oooh. Freebies.'

'What?'

He held the contents of the letter up. There were four smaller envelopes, and a crisply folded sheet of heavy cream paper. Theo read the letter aloud.

> Dear Miss Lucas
>
> Thank you for attending our first social season. I was so sad that none of the matches you considered proved to be the start of a lasting relationship. I firmly believe that there is somebody out there for everyone, and I'd love for you to take a second chance on letting us find the one for you.
>
> Please find enclosed a complimentary pass for the upcoming Festive Season, along with three further passes to allow you to invite three single friends of your choosing.
>
> With very best wishes
>
> Emma Love

Theo fanned out the four envelopes. One was labelled, in neat calligraphy, *Miss Hope Lucas*, and the other three were blank. He pocketed one of the three blank envelopes.

'What do you want that for?'

Theo grinned. 'It's a whole gamut of single women? Right? Laid on for me.'

'You're not supposed to catch and release though.' Hope read from the letter. 'Lasting relationships – that's what it's all about.'

'Well, too late. I've bagsied it. You can't overrule a bagsy.'

Any continuation of the argument was curtailed by the sound of the front door opening and crashing closed again.

'Don't slam!' Grace Price shouted at her sister as she marched into the kitchen, her fifties-style dress swinging prettily above her patent Mary Janes. She stopped. 'Theo! Hi.'

'Hi Grace.'

Hope did her best to assess the atmosphere. It seemed more awkward than brimming with sexual tension or unfulfilled passion. Probably best to move things along. 'You're back early?'

'Yep. Long story.'

'What happened?'

'What do you think happened?'

Connie Price, Hope's second housemate, followed her sister into the kitchen. Her dyed purple hair was matted to the side of her face, and there was an impressively large plaster on her arm. 'It wasn't my fault.'

Hope sighed. She'd been hearing stories of how things weren't Connie's fault since they were tiny children and, somehow, Hope's Barbie doll had managed to get superglued to a wall.

'Like you shouldn't build a tower of champagne glasses if it's going to be that unstable.'

Grace shook her head. 'Most things are unstable if a fully grown adult crashes into them.'

'I was entertaining the children. That was a good thing.'

'Entertaining them by doing slides across the dance floor in her socks.'

'Well it sounds like it was an accident,' Hope conceded. A special, and entirely predictable Connie sort of an accident, admittedly.

'An accident that spilled champagne all over the bride,' Grace added.

'Oh dear.'

Connie slumped a little. 'It really was an accident. And you sorted her out.'

'Well I did my best to cheer her up.'

'Grace had like wet wipes and a sewing kit and...' Connie shrugged. 'That bag is like Mary Poppins land.'

'Anyway, by the time I'd calmed things down Connie was already outside waiting for an Uber.'

'Well I know where I'm not welcome.'

'I'll send her an apology note in the morning,' Grace suggested.

'Of course you will, Saint Grace,' muttered her sister.

'Anyway,' Theo interjected over the brewing row. 'Look what Hope got.'

He shoved the letter towards Connie, who turned the letter towards her on the worktop to read. 'The dating thing? I thought that had finished.'

'It did,' Theo explained. 'This is a new one. Christmas themed.'

'So what's the deal?'

'It's eight events, over about six or eight weeks,' Hope explained, again. She'd told Connie and Grace all of this the first time around and neither of them had expressed the slightest bit of interest. 'And you're supposed to be meeting people and forming attachments, like in a Jane Austen novel, you know?'

Connie fanned herself with the letter. 'Like "my my Mr Darcy what strong thighs you have" and all that bollocks?'

'Have you ever read Jane Austen?'

'I've seen the film. The one with the zombies and her out of *Downton Abbey*.'

'Right. It won't be like that.' Hope slid the two remaining envelopes away from Connie.

'Not so fast. Who are you planning to give those to?'

Honestly Hope wasn't sure. She worked for a local hospital trust, and didn't have that many friends outside work any more. Most of the work friends she did have were coupled up and she'd dragged the only one who wasn't along last time. She had, of course, instantly fallen in love. The Season worked. Only not for Hope. She eyed Connie's purple hair, nose ring and multiple tattoos. 'I'm not sure it's really your kind of thing.'

'Charlotte met a girl there, didn't she?'

'I didn't mean that.' The Season aimed to be fully inclusive. 'I meant…'

'What?' Connie's eyes narrowed.

'It's quite traditional.'

Wrong thing to say. Completely wrong. 'Oh, well in that case I'm definitely coming.'

One pass left, and no point thinking about who to give it to. Grace was already grabbing the letter out of her sister's hand. Where one twin went, the other was always determined not to miss out.

'It really doesn't sound like your sort of thing.'

'So you'd better believe I'm gonna be there,' Connie snapped back.

'And you'll be taking him?' Grace nodded at Theo without making eye contact.

Great. Theo had definitely made things more complicated than they needed to be there.

'Too right she will,' Theo confirmed.

'So you've got one pass left?' Grace smiled brightly at Hope.

And that made four of them, it seemed.

Chapter Three

The pleasure of your company is requested at a

Mulled Wine Reception

to mark the commencement of a special festive social season

The first event of the Festive Season was underway. They'd started last time with a champagne reception, but mulled wine set the festive tone much more. Emma loved buildings like this one with its cool stone frontage and sense of grandeur. So much of London's defining aesthetic dated from the early nineteenth century, from Marble Arch to Regent Street and Regent's Park, and Emma loved to bring her daters to places that at least felt as though they could have been part of a real Regency social season.

In mid-November the function room wasn't yet decorated for Christmas, and the weather outside was mild and damp, rather than providing the crisp winter chill Emma would have preferred. Inside, Emma had vetoed the venue's suggestion of putting the tree up before the first party. She wanted to build up towards their Christmassy finale, but there were wreaths of pine and holly and the cloths on the small standing tables around the room were an elegant evergreen shade.

Emma watched Josh greeting a group of new attendees. Oh, one of them was Hope Lucas. Emma should go and say hello, greet her properly.

'Josh knows what he's doing.' Tom appeared at her shoulder.

'What do you mean?'

'I mean you're watching him like an over-protective parent on the first day of kindergarten. He's fine. He's going to have a lovely day and if he wets himself you've packed a change of pants in his bag.'

She pursed her lips. 'I'm not watching him.'

'Yeah. You are.'

Yes. She was. She turned to face her boyfriend properly. 'You're supposed to be providing seasonal background music.'

'I am entitled to a fifteen-minute break.'

'You've only been playing for half an hour.'

He grinned. 'Well if you wanted constant music you should have gone with Josh's idea.'

Josh had vetoed Emma hiring a full band for the evening and insisted that downloading something appropriate and playing it from a tablet would be fine. He had no sense of style or grandeur at all. They'd compromised on having Tom to play the piano.

She sent Tom back to his position at the piano and scanned the room. A lot more people had registered in advance for this Season than for the initial run. That was good. That gave them a bit more financial certainty. It also meant that the scale of the job in front of Emma was apparent from the outset. So many people putting their trust in her to find them their happy ever after.

Josh joined her. 'Ready for your big speech?'

Of course she was ready. She pulled up her notes on her tablet for a final read-through. Emma's introductory talk was another chance to reiterate to the daters what made the Season special. She scanned through her bullet points one last time and stepped up to the microphone. She gave a nod to Tom, who closed the piece he was playing with a loud crescendo, breaking through the chit chat and highlighting the silence that followed.

'Good evening, everybody,' she began. She ran through her introduction smoothly and professionally. It was a pitch she'd been giving in one form or another for months now, since the very first time she brought the idea to her mother as her vision for the future of the family's dating agency business. The Season brought people together in an old-fashioned way. It eschewed the snap judgements of dating apps and social media, and encouraged people to get to know one another and form lasting attachments. To do that daters needed to take the time to listen and be willing to share parts of themselves with each other. 'We also recommend,' Emma continued, 'that you resist the urge to get, let me say, intimate with any of your fellow daters until you're confident that you've formed a real mutual connection. If this was a real Regency season then even spending time alone without a chaperone would be a scandal. We're not quite that strict. In fact, we do encourage you to meet up outside of our events to progress your courtships, but why not try to keep things in the Regency style – a promenade around the park, or a horse and carriage ride, rather than a belly full of Jägerbombs and a late-night kebab? We really do believe that if you slow down and think about courting the person you're attracted to then the Season is a chance to create a lasting bond. It's not about finding someone, anyone, who'll do for now, but about finding the one person who you might spend the rest of your life with. If you invest your time, and a bit of yourself, you could see the most wonderful outcome.'

Emma heard the murmur around the room and a couple of slightly nervous giggles. That was to be expected. She was talking sincerely about love and finding the one. It was natural for her very British audience to be half expecting a punchline.

'As we're nearing Christmas there will be a festive theme to our events this time, but please understand that the Season is open to people of all religions and none. At this time of year some of you might remember going to see a pantomime as children, and, whatever happens along the way, the ending to those stories is always a happy and a romantic one. So welcome to our version of that perfect fairytale. Our goal is that by the end of the Season you have all found your happily ever after.'

Emma stepped down from the stage and caught her stepbrother's eye. Josh nodded his approval. She just had to hope the room full of hopeful daters were equally on board.

–

Hope listened to the Christmas version of the speech she'd heard the last time she'd signed up for this thing. Despite her past disappointment, Emma was very convincing. Hope felt that little flicker of anticipation. Maybe this time...

'So what are we supposed to do now?' Theo asked.

'Mingle. Meet people. It's the first night. Try to get talking to somebody.'

'I'm talking to you.'

'Somebody you didn't arrive with. Your perfect fairytale princess might be in this very room.' Hope didn't have to look up to know exactly what face Theo was making. He'd been teasing her for being a romantic idiot since about twenty minutes after they first met. 'Anyway, go talk to people.'

Theo sighed.

'What's wrong? You're good at this. You can talk to anyone anywhere.'

It was true. It was Theo's superpower. It was what made him so good at his job in sales. His clients never felt like they were talking to a sales rep. They left thinking they'd had a lovely chat with a wonderful, handsome young man and told him all about their kids and their visit to their chiropractor and their upcoming choir recital and, entirely incidentally, also signed up for a brand new printing, scanning and photocopying solution for their office.

'Fine. If you want rid of me that badly.'

'I didn't mean...'

Theo shook his head as he walked away. 'Don't wanna be accused of cramping your style.'

The disappearance of the six-foot bloke from her side seemed to work like a beacon for the rest of the party. A tall, floppy-haired gentleman in blush red trousers was almost instantly in front of her. 'Giles,' he announced.

'Hope.'

'You hope?' The man frowned.

'What?'

'Sorry. Bit loud in here. What do you hope?'

Hope took a breath. 'No. I am Hope.'

Another smaller frown.

'Hope is my name.'

'I see. Sorry about that. I thought you were hoping for something.'

Hope shook her head. 'Well, beyond hoping to find Mr Right, like everyone else here tonight I guess.'

'Mr Wright? I've not met him.'

'No... I meant...'

He wasn't frowning this time.

'Right. You were joking.'

Hope laughed in a way she hoped sounded game, but probably came across more fake and verging on desperate.

Giles smiled. 'Shall we start again? Hello. I'm Giles.'

'I'm Hope.'

'Very jolly to meet you, Hope. So where do you hail from?'

'I live in east London, but I'm from Essex.' Hope braced herself for the inevitable incoming Essex girl joke.

'Really. Went to school with a chap whose parents had a place in Essex. Hatbury? Hatfield? Hatfield something or other? Anywhere round that way?'

'Not really.'

'Ah well. One never knows, does one? Doesn't hurt to ask.'

'No.'

'So Essex. Did you go to Park? That's where this chap's sisters went I think. Had hundreds of them.' Giles paused. 'Sisters that is.'

'No.' She had no doubt it would have been her mother's dream to send her daughter to the very expensive Park School. 'Just regular local comprehensive.'

'Right. Well good show. And now?'

'I work in a hospital.'

'A nurse. Top job. Well done you.'

'Actually, I'm in HR. Someone's gotta do it.'

'Quite. Quite.'

The conversation between them lulled. There was nothing objectively wrong with Giles. He was perfectly polite, clearly of excellent breeding – very much the sort of young man Hope's mother would be delighted to see her bring home, but… but what? Her heart said there was no spark, but wasn't she supposed to be breaking the pattern of the previous Season, which had been a string of perfectly pleasant men who didn't quite spark with Hope?

'So maybe I'll…' Giles nodded towards something in the middle distance and took a step away.

'Of course.'

So it wasn't just her. The feeling was mutual. Close, but absolutely no cigar. She looked around the room. There was a loosely formed group to her right. She could easily join them. It was the first night. People were supposed to be mingling and the group didn't look like a closely knit gaggle of old friends. Hope took a deep breath and stepped up.

—

Across the room, at least one of Hope's housemates lacked Hope's can-do attitude in social situations. In fact, Connie very definitely concluded that the party sucked. If the drinks weren't complimentary, and her very presence wasn't annoying her sister so splendidly, Connie would be out of there in a heartbeat. Everyone here was gussied up to the nines, but they were Grace people, not Connie people. Connie's uniform of black jeans and faux leather jacket were out of place. She doubted she could even find someone, in this room of perfect lip liner and stuffed suits, who she wanted to spend an evening with, let alone a lifetime.

Maybe she would be better off sneaking out early. She could go home, or go to the Lamb and seek out some of her actual friends. Connie drained her glass, set it down on one of those pointless tiny high tables that only exist for cocktail parties, and slunk out of the room before Grace could find her and tell her off for not staying the course, or whatever other holier than thou commandment her twin would think she was breaking today.

In the hallway she pressed the button for the lift and waited. One minute, two, three… no lift. Sod it. She set off down the stairs. Leaving was definitely the right call. Maybe she'd be better off abandoning the whole thing. It probably wasn't even too late for Hope to give the spare ticket to somebody else. She imagined her sister's response. *Another thing Connie didn't stick at.* And then she imagined her father's response to Grace's retelling of yet another Constance Price Failure (TM). He wouldn't even be disapproving. That was the worst of it. Expectations of Connie were so low that she aspired to achieving the heights of disappointing him.

So she wouldn't give up on the Season altogether. She'd come along. She'd show her face. She'd stay the course.

Just not tonight.

'Oh my God! I'm so sorry!'

Connie's body jolted into another one coming up the stairs. Instinctively she flailed and grabbed the stranger's hand to steady them both. The hand grabbed her back in response.

'So sorry.'

'Wasn't looking where I was going. My fault.'

'Not at all. I can barely walk in these things.' The stranger lifted a foot. She was wearing the most ridiculous high heels Connie had ever seen. She looked at Connie's boots. 'I thought I ought to dress to impress, but I am not used to heels at all. You had the right idea. I should have taken the lift.'

'I pressed the button,' Connie offered. 'But it didn't come.'

'Me too! We must have confused it!'

Aside from the terrible shoe choice, the woman was striking. Petite but athletic, with tanned shoulders visible in her sleeveless dress. Arms Michelle Obama's personal trainer would have been proud of, and bright copper hair chopped into the sort of short crop that demanded a beautiful face. And this face was more than beautiful. It was warm and hopeful, and Connie was caught for a second in its light.

'Were you here for the Season reception?' The woman frowned. 'Am I too late?'

'No. Yes. I mean…' Connie took a breath. 'I was here for that, but you're not too late. I skipped out early.'

'That bad?' The woman raised an eyebrow.

'Not really my thing.'

'That's a shame. You'll be at the next event though?'

Connie nodded mutely. She'd already let slip that she was leaving this event. Stupid. Too late to turn around and pretend that she too was just arriving, so she could follow the woman in front of her back into the party.

'Great. I'm Morgan by the way.'

'Connie.'

'Hello Connie.'

They stood for what seemed like far too long a time in silence on the stairs.

'Well I'd better get up to the party then.'

Connie nodded again.

Morgan smiled and leaned ever so slightly towards her. 'That means you'll need to let go of my hand.'

She was still holding on. There was no realistic possibility of Connie being able to turn back time and release Morgan's hand a clear sixty seconds ago, so she had no possible option other than to try her best to style it out. 'Oh, I thought you were still holding mine.'

'No.'

Of course not. Connie released her grip. Should have done that before trying to think of a stylish quip to ease the awkwardness. Now she'd failed to let go and failed to ease the awkwardness, and instead made the whole thing even weirder than it had been before. Great work.

Morgan moved past her, holding the hand rail as she tottered up the stairs in her heels.

'Maybe I'll see you next time,' Connie yelled after her.

Great, thought Connie. Shouting after a near-stranger on the stairs. Not looking needy at all.

Grace scanned the room for her sister. No sign of her. A sting of anxiety jabbed at her stomach. Was Connie ok? Grace told herself to breathe. Connie was an adult and, rationally, she was currently likely to be either bumming a ciggie off a waiter on a fire escape somewhere or she'd done a runner. Grace scanned the room one more time. Her gaze stopped abruptly when it reached the figure of the slim, athletic-looking redhead who had just come in. She was pretty. After a succession of thoroughly uninspiring small talk with entirely unsuitable people, Grace's evening was looking up.

'Oh for goodness' sake!'

The voice behind her was curt and male. She turned.

'What are you doing?' The man asking the question was tall and slender with neatly cropped blond hair. The sort of man who spent more on his suits than Grace earned in a month. The sort of man, Grace instantly judged, who would rarely take the same girl to his bed twice.

'What do you mean?'

He gestured. 'You were standing perfectly nicely over there, and then you walked two paces this way and stopped.'

'And?'

'And other people are attempting to get past.'

She peered behind him. 'By other people, you mean you.'

'I do.'

She stepped aside. 'Well don't let me stop you.'

The man stalked past. At least she'd managed to rule one person out from the sea of faces.

'What got his wotsit in a twizzle?'

This voice was softer, warmer. Grace turned. The face matched the voice. Friendly and smiling, with a flash of red hair cut short on top of her head. The woman from the doorway. 'I don't know.'

'Men, eh?' The woman rolled her eyes. 'I'm Morgan.'

Grace smiled. 'Grace.'

'Your face looks really familiar. Have we met before?'

Grace smiled again. 'Oh no. I definitely think I would have remembered that.'

–

At the other end of the beautifully festive function room, Hope was beginning to lose confidence that anything would be different for her this second time around. She smiled at the long story the dark-haired solicitor from Shepherd's Bush was telling her. Something to do with a terrible conveyancing mistake and a mad dash to stop a client collecting the keys on a property the seller turned out not to own. She wasn't honestly following that closely. She had smiled at a lot of stories she wasn't that interested in this evening. After Giles, who was increasingly looking like something of a catch, there'd been a bookkeeper from Clerkenwell, a goalkeeper from Clapham and an actual zookeeper from London Zoo. She'd have thought zookeeping, at least, would have been more interesting, but it turned out that his stories were mostly to do with shovelling shit. Literal shit. Maybe Hope was setting her standards too high but none of them had made her feel that rush of excitement inside, that feeling of anticipation.

The first time she'd met Simon it had felt like the room around them had disappeared. They'd been at a house party somewhere off campus during their first week of uni. Hope had resolved that at university she was going to be less of a wallflower and try to embrace the experience to the full, and meeting Theo at the very beginning had proved the perfect facilitator of that aim. Hence the party at the home of a third-year Theo had met in a bar, or maybe at the house of the friend of a third-year Theo had met in a bar. Hope wasn't sure. It didn't matter. All that had mattered to her that night was Simon.

A hand offering a glass appeared at her side. Theo. 'You look miles away. What were you thinking about?'

'Nothing.' Hope needed to push the past out of her mind. Tonight was about finding something new. 'What are you doing coming to hang out with me anyway? We're in a room full of single women keen to meet their Prince Charming.'

'Maybe I'm biding my time?'

'Well. I don't believe you're short of interest.' Theo never was. Women fell in love with him on an almost daily basis.

'I might have made a few new acquaintances.'

Even as he spoke, a short woman with long black hair braided down her back walked past and squeezed Theo's arm. 'Call me,' she mouthed.

'Typical,' Hope muttered. 'You're not taking her home then?'

'No! I thought this was supposed to be the opposite of that. The scary woman said it was about more than just getting lucky. Less drunk and desperate. More lasting affection.'

Hope wasn't sure about that. Less than two months to Christmas and a whole group of single Londoners all searching for their soulmate before the festive season descended. How many of the people here were truly desperate? Not for true love, necessarily, but to avoid another Christmas dinner explaining to parents, grandparents, aunts and uncles that no, there isn't anyone special at the moment, and yes, they are aware that they're not getting any younger. She wouldn't judge any of her co-participants for a little smidge of desperation to be coupled up before Santa arrived down the chimney.

'We are supposed to be meeting people though.' She turned her attention back to Theo. 'Meeting new people, not hanging out with people we're already mates with.'

'I like the people I'm already mates with.'

She rolled her eyes. 'Well we like you too. But you're not going to cop off with me are you? Or Grace.' She remembered. 'Not again at any rate. Or Connie.' Actually she hadn't seen Connie lately. Maybe her least sociable housemate was actually in amongst the throng somewhere meeting her soulmate.

Theo shrugged. 'I thought we weren't supposed to be copping off with anybody tonight. Look.' He checked the time on his phone. 'It's nearly midnight. If we stay much longer then the danger is that we do get drunk and silly and break all of the scary lady's rules.'

Hope would have been lying if she'd claimed that the idea of going home and getting into her pjs wasn't thoroughly appealing.

'Come on.'

'Taxi or bus?' Hope asked.

Theo rolled his eyes. 'Do you mean am I paying or are you?'

'You get commission. You're minted.'

'I am not minted.'

This was lies. Hope knew for a fact that Theo was well on the way to saving enough for the deposit to buy an actual flat, on his own, with no recourse to the bank of mum and dad. That meant that, amongst their group of friends, Theo was basically Bill Gates.

Hope threaded her arm through Theo's. 'It's cold, and the bus takes forever.'

'Fine.' Theo pulled his phone out and tapped the screen. 'Uber is four minutes away.'

'Thank you.' They wandered down the wide staircase. 'I'm not planning on making a habit of coming home with you though.'

'Of course not.' There was a hint of a laugh in his voice.

'I mean it,' Hope insisted. 'This time's going to be different. I'm going to find somebody.'

Theo slowed down. 'You know you don't have to, right? Like if you're not ready. After…'

'It's been ages. Of course I'm ready.'

Chapter Four

'What have you done to this?'

Grace's dad peered at the kitchen cupboard door that was currently hanging precariously from a single hinge.

'I didn't do anything to it,' she assured him.

'Right. What did your sister do to this?'

'It was fine when I went to bed one night and then the next day...' She pointed at the current state of affairs.

'Ah well. No problem. We'll have it fixed in a jiffy.'

'Thank you!' She sat at the kitchen table eating her overnight oats, while her dad waved his magic screwdriver at the cupboard door.

The comfortable calm was broken by Connie staggering into the kitchen. 'Coffee. Coffee and then toast,' she muttered. She stopped and stared at their father for a second, before turning to Grace. 'I told you I'd do that.'

'But then you didn't do it,' Grace pointed out. 'You also didn't replace the seal around the shower so it still drips into the hallway, and you didn't hang up the mirror I bought for the hallway.'

'Never said I'd do that. You can hang your own sodding mirror,' Connie muttered.

'I don't mind love. I can do those while I'm here.'

Grace smiled. Two birds with one stone. All the little jobs Connie promised to do, and then didn't, got sorted out and their dad got to feel useful.

'You don't have to.' Connie was jamming slices of bread into the toaster. 'I'll get to them. Apart from the mirror. She can do her own mirror.'

28

Grace rolled her eyes. Of course she could hang her own mirror, but if she did that their dad wouldn't have an excuse to pop round and he wouldn't feel useful and Grace wouldn't be able to make sure he was all right and eating properly.

'Didn't expect to see you this morning anyway.' Their dad was talking to Connie now. 'Not normally a fan of mornings.'

'I've got work,' Connie explained.

'Where are you now?'

'City farm.'

'I thought you were at that college place in Chelsea.'

'That finished.' Connie collected her toast and spread it liberally with butter and marmite. Grace's butter.

'I hope you're going to buy more bread and butter.'

'Whatever.'

Hope wandered into the kitchen. 'Oh. Hello Uncle Pete.'

'Morning love.'

'Hope has given us both free passes to this dating thing,' Grace announced.

'What dating thing?'

'It's called the Season,' Hope explained. 'It's based on a social season, like in Jane Austen. You go to a whole load of events in the hope of finding the love of your life.' She poured water from the kettle into her mug. 'It's silly.'

'Nothing silly about that. We all need someone to...' Grace's dad stopped slightly abruptly and looked from Connie to Grace and back again. 'And, anyway, you're both going?'

'Connie ducked out of the first event early,' Grace pointed out.

'It was boring.'

Grace drained her cup of mint matcha tea. 'Come on, Dad. You can't expect Connie to stay at a party all evening. It's like, so much commitment.' She smiled sweetly in the face of her sister's glare.

'Well to each their own.'

'I am committed.'

'Makes a change,' Grace muttered.

'Have you seen the scandal sheet?' Hope asked, trying to distract her cousins from their bubbling argument.

'The what?' Connie looked confused.

'Scandal sheet,' Grace repeated for her. 'It's… explain it to her, Hope.'

'It's like a newsletter thing for the Season. All the gossip and who's into who and stuff. Well, you know, as much as they can without everyone storming out in a huff. You should have it on the app.'

Grace opened the Season app that she'd installed before the first event, and tapped on the 'New Scandal…' notification. Most of the blurb was just welcoming them to the Season again and reiterating the importance of seeking a lasting connection rather than a quick fumble. Grace scrolled past that. She wasn't the quick fumble type anyway.

'What's it say?' Connie asked.

'You should have it on your own phone.'

Her sister shrugged. 'Didn't download the app yet.'

'And I thought you were so committed.'

'Gracie, don't tease your sister.' Their dad's voice cautioned her from inside the cupboard.

'Fine.' Grace scrolled further. 'Right. Here we go. *First up, let us blow our own trumpet for a success story from the first Season. We have just celebrated our very first Season wedding, between our own Prince of Matchmaking, Joshua Love, and Season dater, Annie Keer. And trust us, if Josh can find love, the Season can work for anyone!*'

'That's not true. Josh is cute,' Hope chipped in. 'And tall. And funny. If she couldn't fix him up she'd definitely be in the wrong job.'

'Anyway,' Grace read on. There was a bit about a red-trousered millionaire, which Hope gasped over.

'I talked to him. He never said he was a millionaire!'

Connie grinned. 'More interested now then?'

Hope shook her head. 'Still not sold on the red trousers.'

'What else is there?' Connie was managing a reasonable imitation of someone who was actually interested.

Grace read on silently. *This Season we are welcoming double-trouble. Which of our twins will win the race to find true love, and will the other be left lonely? Or is there enough love in the Season to make matches for two of a kind?* It was just a joke, but the sort of joke that Connie would get all Connie-ish about. 'Nothing.'

'What?' Now Connie was really interested.

'It's silly.'

'Give it here.' Connie snatched Grace's phone from her hand and read down, her expression distinctly unimpressed.

'It's not a competition anyway,' Grace offered.

'You only say that when you know you're gonna lose,' her sister shot back.

'You think?' For goodness' sake, Grace had been trying to be kind. Of course it was a competition, and of course Grace was going to win. 'Like you did so well last night. You didn't even make it to the end of the evening.'

'Right.' Their dad's voice cut through the moment of tension. 'Will you show me where you want this bloody mirror putting?'

—

Hope left her housemates bickering in the hallway and scuttled back to her room with her mug of tea. She knew that logically this was her home too, and Uncle Pete was lovely, but having him there always made her feel like she was intruding on a family moment.

She finished her tea, dressed quickly and headed out of the house, turning, without thinking, towards Columbia Road. The third great attraction of this houseshare – after the relatively low rent and Grace and Connie's relaxed attitude to when it got paid – was the proximity to Hope's absolute favourite part of London. She'd discovered it during her first term studying Accounting and Business at Queen Mary (not Hope's dream course, but definitely a sensible course for a conscientious girl with a brain) – Columbia Road Flower Market. There was an abundance of florist shops in the area anyway, but on Sundays the flower market descended and took over the street. Stall after stall of blooms and bouquets. It was Hope's personal idea of heaven.

She stopped by a stall selling bundles of carnations. Hope's favourite. Not the coolest choice, she knew, but symbolic of love and gratitude. And filled with memories. Her father had grown them, under glass initially and then in the full sun of the back garden at home. She remembered walking in the garden with him and being allowed to select a bloom for him to snip and pop into his buttonhole before church on a sunny summer morning. It was a memory from childhood that she clung to – proof that they had been happy at some point in some small way.

'All right Hope!'

A voice from behind the stall called out to her. She looked up and smiled. 'Hi Wes.'

Wesley had had a stall here since long before Hope had started visiting.

'You're here to stock up your shop? Right?'

'Not today. One day,' she told him.

He shook his head. 'Don't make me lose hope, Hope,' he told her.

She moved on. She wished, with hindsight, that she'd never fallen into conversation with Wesley and never told him – she counted, eight years ago now – that what she'd really love to do was run a florist shop, doing bouquets for weddings and arrangements for big fancy events. She'd even worked in a florist shop in the village, when she was a teenager. Every Saturday during A-levels she'd been there, holding the fort while her boss delivered displays and bouquets for weddings and parties. If she'd never told Wesley any of that, he wouldn't remind her, every time she came past his stall, that she was much more her mother's daughter than she would ever choose to believe.

Her phone rang in her pocket. Theo.

'What you up to?' he asked as soon as she answered.

'What do you think?'

He laughed. 'Fantasy shopping for imaginary bouquets.'

'Maybe.'

'So you're free for lunch then?'

'Sure.'

An hour later they were sitting opposite one another with a halloumi wrap and a plant-based burger on the table between them. If Hope hadn't been distracted by food, she might have taken a second to register who was calling when her phone trilled. 'Hello.'

'Hope, darling!'

Bugger. Theo raised a questioning eyebrow across the table.

'Hi Mum.'

Her best friend's face shifted into a mock grimace.

'I'm so glad I've finally caught you. I've been trying to ring you for days now.'

'Sorry. I've been busy. Work, you know.'

'Well no.' Her mother's tone was clipped and directly to the point as ever. 'I don't know, because you don't tell me, do you?'

'I'm telling you now.'

'Well.'

Hope's mother's *wells* could do the work of a thousand words. This well, Hope surmised, meant 'well, that's not good enough, and yet again there is a distance between us for which I hold you responsible'. Hope could see her standing in the hallway using the landline phone which still lived on a telephone table next to the door to the lounge. She had a mobile but it was only switched on when Hope's mother wished to make a call, and no amount of argument would persuade her to see the error of that approach.

Hope had been born when her mother was already in her forties – a wonderful surprise, she was always told, to a couple who had thought they were destined to be childless. Not wonderful enough, it turned out, to stop Hope's father from moving out the second Hope was out of the house and away at university. He swore to her that the two events weren't related but nothing could rid the situation of the stench of a deeply unhappy couple who had stayed together beyond their time for the sake of their only daughter.

33

'I have been really busy. You know what it's like coming into winter. The hospital's overrun and staffing is horrific and…'

'Well, that's not why I called anyway.'

'Right.' Of course it wasn't.

'I called to say I'm coming up to town next week. So if you're not too busy…'

'When?' Hope flicked through her mental calendar. Work, obviously Monday to Friday. Eight to five officially, but seven thirty to seven thirty if she was lucky at the moment. Evenings? She could try an evening.

'Tuesday to Thursday. It's with the Women's Guild. We're going to see *Les Misérables* on Wednesday night, but I shall be free during the day. Or until six p.m. on Thursday. I presume they do let you take time off from your work occasionally.'

'Well yeah.' Hope's natural defensiveness at the implied disapproval of her work schedule had robbed her of the opportunity to use work as an excuse. If she took part of Thursday off she could see her mother and have time to get ready for the Season event in the evening. 'Thursday afternoon then?'

'Very good.' Hope's mother slowly and deliberately read out the details of her hotel and instructed Hope to meet her there. Then she made Hope repeat the details and the time back to her to prove she had all the information.

'We could meet somewhere for coffee or lunch?' Hope suggested. It was pointless. There was no way Mother would venture out into London on her own.

'I don't think so. I'm sure they'll have a perfectly acceptable lounge at the hotel.' Her mother paused. 'And will you be bringing your young man?'

Now Hope pulled a face at Theo. 'I don't have a young man.'

Her mother sighed. 'Well you know who I mean. Young Theodore.'

Nobody called Theo that. Not least because it wasn't his name. His birth certificate said Theo, but Hope's mother could not abide an abbreviation, even one of her own imagining.

'Theo isn't my young man.'

Across the table, her friend clutched his chest like a man knifed through the heart.

'Yet you do insist on keeping him around,' her mother continued. 'How you think you'll find someone carrying on like that I do not know.'

Normally at this point Hope protested that she wasn't trying to find someone and she was perfectly happy on her own. But that wasn't true, was it? It was just as much a lie as if she caved to the pressure and pretended Theo was her boyfriend. He'd suggested it often enough. A cast iron plan to get her mother off her back about her lack of romantic prospects. Hope had always said no. Obviously. Right now the idea didn't seem quite as crazy. She ended the call, reassuring her mother, once again, that she knew where the hotel they were meeting in was and that she would be there at two p.m. sharp, and that she would take care on public transport. 'Why you don't get a car, I'll never understand,' her mother muttered.

'I don't need a car. I can walk to work from where I live.'

'You might be able to visit your mother a little more often if you did have a car.'

'I've got to go, Mum. Sorry. Busy busy. Byeeee.' Hope hung up. It wasn't her mother's fault she was unhappy. It wasn't her fault that Hope was such a disappointment. It was Hope's job to be the bright and happy and cheerful one in the relationship. She could do that, she told herself. And right now, she didn't have to do it for a whole week. So that was something.

'Denied once again,' Theo declared.

'Denied that we're an item because we're not an item,' Hope pointed out, entirely reasonably, in her opinion.

'Seriously – tell her we are, if it stops her going on.'

She wouldn't do that. Outright lying was a step too far. She'd accepted, she thought, that she and her mother were never going to be close, and there were elements of Hope's life in London that she omitted to mention when her mother called, but lying by omission somehow felt a degree more defensible than telling a direct untruth. 'Anyway, by Christmas I'm going to be with someone. Emma Love all but guaranteed it.'

'And here was me thinking we both crashed and burned last night,' Theo pointed out.

'I did not crash and burn. I...' She what? 'I just didn't meet anyone I had that spark with, you know?'

Theo didn't reply.

Hope stifled a laugh. 'Of course you don't know. You can spark with anything in a skirt.'

'That's not true.' Theo took a sip of his pint. 'Your mum's not so bad, you know.'

'Easy for you to say. She likes you.'

'Mums always do. I'm very presentable.'

'If only they knew the truth,' Hope joked. 'Anyway you don't hang around long enough to meet the parents.'

'I met Sophie's parents. And Andrea's. And Carly's. Her mum really liked me.'

Hope's reply was stopped by the grin on Theo's face.

'Like really really liked me,' he added.

'Ew. You didn't? Not with her mum?'

Theo grinned. 'We weren't exclusive. It wasn't cheating.'

'Did Carly know you weren't exclusive?'

Theo did look genuinely wounded at that. 'Yes. Of course she knew.'

Weirdly, despite his utter lack of sexual morals, Hope believed him. Theo was a player, but he was also scrupulously honest. He didn't promise anyone anything more than he was prepared to give. Which didn't mean women never thought they would be the one to change him, or save him, but did mean that however skewed Theo's moral compass was, there was always a moral compass in place.

'Don't you ever want to find the one?'

Theo made a show of chewing his burger, or playing for time as it was sometimes known.

'I don't know. Maybe that ship sailed for me.'

'What do you mean?' Ships sailing implied a missed opportunity, or one that got away. Hope thought back. Not Carly, clearly. Presumably not Carly's mum. Andrea had been fun for a while but she knew that the expiration of her visa had been met with more relief than regret. 'Sophie?'

Theo had met Sophie a couple of years ago, the Christmas before Hope and Simon broke up in the spring. They'd seemed solid for a while, well for about six months, which in Theo relationship terms was roughly a decade on anyone else's timescale.

He shook his head. 'No matter. Ancient history now.'

–

Emma held the shopping bags while Tom helped his mum into the stairlift at her three-storey home, and half listened while he pointed out, as he always did at this point, that if she sold this place, she could live in the absolute lap of luxury in a place with no stairs. It was a pointless conversation. Gloria had raised her son in this house, and loved and lost her husband in the house. She would never move and she would never sell.

'Tell him to stop going on at me, Emma.'

'Stop going on at her,' Emma dutifully parroted.

'Thank you.' Gloria turned her attention to her son. 'Emma understands. She's far too good for you, you know. I keep telling her.'

'I know you do.' Tom grinned. 'And you're right of course, but there's no need to keep reminding her.'

Once they'd got Gloria settled in her chair by the bay window of the big bedroom at the top of the house, Tom went to make tea. Emma was settling in for another round of being told how good she was to take him on when he reappeared, holding an envelope. 'What's this, Mum?'

His mother waved him away.

'It's from the hospital.'

'It's nothing.'

37

'Why are the hospital writing to you?'

'Oh, I'm old. Hospitals do nothing but write to old people. If you shake me I rattle with the number of pills I'm on.'

Gloria suffered, Emma knew, with severe arthritis, but she'd always assumed that there were other things that weren't discussed.

'You know I'm going to read it, don't you?' Tom was still focused on the letter.

'Well go on then.'

Tom opened the envelope and scanned the contents. 'Routine arthritis check-up,' he said.

Gloria smiled and leaned towards Emma. 'I don't leave the ones I don't want him to read lying on the kitchen counter.' She raised her voice towards her son. 'You were making tea, dear?'

Tom disappeared back to the kitchen.

'Now you tell me what you're up to, Miss Love. Tell me about all the wonderful matches you've made recently.'

'Well we've only just started the second Season, so no matches there yet.'

'I don't believe that. You must have fixed up the odd passing shop assistant or someone to keep your hand in.'

Emma laughed. 'Well I did notice that the waitress at lunchtime was making eyes at the bartender.'

'She was!' Gloria looked gleeful. 'We must go back there for lunch next weekend and see if we can stir the pot a little.'

'It's a good job you weren't a matchmaker when you were younger. We'd never have survived the competition.'

'Ah, I like to see young people happy.' The noise of conversation on the stairs caught their attention. 'Speaking of which…' Gloria added.

Gloria got through carers at a rate Emma could never understand for a woman who was nothing but sweetness and light to her personally. Tom reckoned she was cross with herself for getting old and needing help and sometimes that crossness spilled over. One carer who had managed to get through Gloria's non-existent sufferance for fools, though, was Hilly.

Emma stood to greet her. She adored Hilly. She'd even fixed her up with her boyfriend. Hilly hadn't even been an official attendee at the first Season.

Tom came through the door with a mug of tea for his mum. 'Kettle's still warm if you want one. We've got to head off though. Sundays with a workaholic.'

'I'm not a...' Emma's sentence stalled under the pressure of three pairs of eyes. 'It's a busy time at the moment. Second event of the new Season tonight.'

Emma and Tom headed downstairs and set off hand in hand towards the Tube. Her mind had already moved on to the things she had to get done in preparation for the next event. There was social media to schedule, emails to send, invoices to check. Invoices, obviously, were Josh's job, but still. Emma liked to have eyes on everything. 'So this afternoon, if you could sort out printing the seating plan that would be so great.'

Tom stopped. 'I wasn't planning on coming back to yours this afternoon.'

'What?' Emma thought back. To be fair, he'd never said that he was, but there was so much to get done.

'I'm recording a whole load of jingles tomorrow and I've barely looked at them. I've gotta go home and practise.' He grinned. 'Well at least open the attachment on the email.'

'Right. Yeah. Ok.' Emma thought ahead. 'So I'll see you during the week?'

He pulled her into a hug. 'Of course. I'll come to yours after work tomorrow?'

'Great. And you'll be at the actual ball?' The first ball of the Season was a big deal. The opening drinks reception set the tone but people were still nervy, getting used to the idea. The ball was where, hopefully, the romance started to kick in.

'Next Saturday?' Tom looked confused. 'I thought you had a band?'

'We do but...' In her mind, Emma had assumed Tom would be there for moral support and fetching and carrying.

'I told Eddie I'd go to the Vic with him. I figured you were working.'

'Right. Yeah. Of course.'

Tom frowned. 'Are you ok?'

Emma nodded.

'I mean I can change things round. It's just…'

Emma understood. The Vic was a London poker scene institution and one of Tom's regular stomping grounds in days gone by. 'When's the last time you played there?'

His gaze was fixed on the ground. 'Before. Eddie's been on at me to get back to it.'

'No. It's fine.' Of course it was fine. 'You go and play. Try not to lose the actual shirt off your back.'

'It's a social game. Nothing high stakes.' He stepped back slightly. 'You're sure you're ok?'

'Sure.'

'Like you knew I played poker when you got me?'

Emma laughed. Given that they'd met at an online poker table, she could hardly argue with that. And anyway that wasn't what was bothering her. Nothing was bothering her. Everything was absolutely fine. 'I just… nothing. It's fine. I'll see you tomorrow.'

Chapter Five

You are invited to a traditional
Stir-up Sunday evening

This was different from anything they'd tried before. Based on past experience, Emma liked events that encouraged mingling earlier in the Season, and only included seated events, where people were more likely to talk to a smaller group, later on, when attachments had started to form. But the Season was supposed to be an evocation of a Regency social season, and Emma's extensive research had revealed disappointingly few festive traditions with their roots prior to 1837. The Victorians had really done a number on Christmas, and while Emma would have to accept a certain amount of historical imprecision in her attempt to approximate a set of 'traditional' Christmas events and activities, the fact that Stir-up Sunday did seem to pre-date Queen V made it too good to pass up.

She'd attempted to mitigate the risk of attendees only talking to people they already knew by mixing up pre-existing friendship groups with newcomers, so, where possible, people would have the security of someone they knew – but weren't romantically inclined towards – close at hand, and the chance to get to know at least one potential suitor more deeply. And she'd grouped the daters in fours rather than pairing them off at this early stage. There was also a period for drinks and mingling at the end of the evening, so if anyone was grouped with people they didn't hit it off with at all, hopefully they'd have better luck later in the night.

'It's going to be fine.' Josh was standing at her shoulder. 'The cookery teacher texted. Delays on the Tube so I told her to hop in a cab and we'd cover it.'

Emma pulled a face of mock astonishment. 'You're paying for her taxi?'

'Well I thought about what it might cost me in limbs if I had to tell you that I'd said it didn't matter if she was a few minutes late.'

'At least a leg,' Emma told him.

'That's what I guessed. I mean it wouldn't have mattered would it? We'd have given everyone mulled wine and told them to mingle, and then you'd have done your bit about the history and meaning of this whole whatever it is and that would have filled the time before she got here anyway.'

Emma was convinced he only said these things to wind her up. Of course it mattered if the tutor was late. She was supposed to be here early, so Emma could walk her round and make sure the tables for the groups of daters were set up how she wanted them, and double check all the ingredients and the allergens list that Emma had sent out in advance and posted on the door – which to be fair would be triple checked as it had been checked twice already. Josh's *oh she'll rock up at some point and it'll probably be fine* approach was clearly insanity. She had also set aside time in her schedule to make sure the teacher understood the tone of the event and the history behind the whole idea.

Josh was still standing next to her. 'Anyway think of all the money we're saving not having sixpences to put in.'

The sixpence discussion had ranged over several days and taken in whether or not putting a coin in the pudding was a Victorian thing or earlier – Emma's research was not conclusive – whether you could even get silver sixpences any more – yes, you could – and whether the Season would be liable if somebody choked on a sixpence they'd put in the pudding themselves. In the end, Josh's insistence that they just needed to stop thinking about sixpences had won the day.

'And she's barely charging us anything for her time,' Josh continued.

Emma frowned, and then she remembered. 'Mum set her up with her second husband.'

'And her third.'

Emma's eyes widened. 'You mean Mum's first match didn't work out?' She wasn't proud of the fact that any hint of an Achilles' heel in her mother's matchmaking skills delighted her.

'Oh no. He was perfect apparently. He died. As did number three.' Josh paused. 'I don't think she's doing anything to them.'

Emma laughed. 'Maybe she tries out her more experimental recipes on them.'

Josh shrugged. 'She did ask if we had any thoughts on who the fourth Mr Cookery Teacher might be.'

'I'll bear that in mind.' Emma mentally flicked through her books for a mature gentleman with a strong constitution.

Their cookery instructor, Josie Baker, was deposited by her taxi in plenty of time for Emma to walk her round the room and listen to her coo with approval at the set-up. Chairs arranged around tables in groups of four, each with a large communal mixing bowl, a set of pre-weighed ingredients, and eight mini Christmas pudding pots. Ingredients had been tweaked for attendees with food allergies, and serendipitously there were four coeliac attendees, who seemed to break into two eminently suitable matches, so Emma had placed them together around their own table.

The evening was going to start with an introduction from Emma and then the actual stirring of the pudding, and then the puddings would be taken away by Josie and steamed overnight, ready to be served at the Season's Christmas dinner in a few weeks' time. Emma ran Josie through the traditions of stir-up Sunday one more time to make sure nothing was forgotten. 'They're not just making a pudding, you know. It has to be meaningful.'

The older woman nodded at her with an expression that could be seen as slightly weary. 'I know dear. You said.'

'Sorry. I like things to be just right.'

Josie Baker smiled more broadly. 'You really are your mother's daughter, aren't you?'

—

Hope scanned the seating chart at the door, hunting for her name.

'Miss Lucas!' Josh Love greeted her at the door. 'I believe you're down at the front. Middle table I think.'

Hope moved her attention to the relevant part of the plan and confirmed that Josh was correct. She was also seated with Theo. She sighed. What was the point of that? She was supposed to be here to meet new people she could form a connection with, not to hang out with a friend who'd held her hair while she puked way too many times to find her even passingly attractive any more. The two other names were ones she didn't recognise. Callum Welsh and Sadie Simpson. Hopefully Sadie would be distracting enough to keep Theo occupied and Callum would only have eyes for Hope. Try as she might though, she was already imagining Theo and whoever Callum turned out to be competing for Sadie's attention while Hope quietly stirred her pudding in a corner.

'Hiya.' Theo came up behind her and peered at the board. 'We're together.'

'Yep.'

He clutched his chest in mock pain. 'You could at least pretend to be pleased.'

'Well you don't want to spend the whole time with me either. I'll cramp your style.'

'Never.'

That was true, Hope supposed. Having a woman around to testify to Theo being, overall if you didn't look too closely, a good egg was probably more help than hindrance for him. 'Come on then.'

She led the way into the main room. It was a different place to the one they'd been to last time but shared the same high ceilings and elegant proportions. The Season only ever brought its daters to the most stylish and, if you squinted and ignored the power points and microphone jacks, plausibly Regency-era spaces.

There was already one person at their table. A young woman with thick, dark curly hair and deep brown eyes. She stood as Hope and Theo approached. 'Oh thank goodness! I thought I was going to be on my own. Can you imagine? Billy No Mates at a dating event.'

'Well we're very glad to be able to rescue you from that fate.' Theo held out a hand to greet the woman. Always the charmer.

'I'm Sadie.'

'Theo, and this is Hope.'

The woman frowned. 'You're here together.'

'Just friends,' Hope clarified quickly. She didn't want Sadie thinking she was competition for Theo's affections and focusing her energy on the elusive Callum.

The seats were arranged equidistant around a small round table. Hope took the chair opposite Sadie, putting Theo between them. Within the first two minutes he'd established that Sadie was a student, working towards becoming a barrister, and that her mother had bought her a membership to the Season as an early Christmas present. 'A present for her rather than me, I think. She's desperate to see me married off.' Sadie shrugged. 'She says that men don't like women who earn more than them, so I have to find someone now before I'm too successful.'

Theo laughed. 'Can you be too successful?'

'I don't think so.'

'Me neither. And I guess it shows her confidence in you, in a backwards sort of way. She has no doubt that you will be a glittering success.'

Sadie smiled. 'That's one way of looking at it.'

Hope was clearly the third wheel in that conversation, but a tall, tanned blond-haired man was approaching their table. Maybe the evening was looking up. Hope smiled in a way that she hoped said 'welcoming' rather than 'desperate'.

He stopped by the vacant seat. 'This must be me.'

A hint of an accent maybe? Hope greeted him. 'Hi. I'm Hope.'

Theo and Sadie broke off from their tête-à-tête to greet the newcomer, before huddling back together. Typical Theo, Hope thought. Finds a pretty girl and abandons the rest of the group.

She turned her attention to the newcomer, Callum. 'So you're Australian?'

He shook his head. 'Kiwi by birth.'

'Sorry! Is that a horrible faux pas? Like calling a Scotsman English?'

'I'm used to it. People always guess Australian, or sometimes South African. New Zealand is the poor forgotten cousin of the English-speaking nations. But actually I've lived in Oz since I was eight, so you were at least half right.'

Hope giggled. 'Well I'll be sure to remember it from now on. What's New Zealand like? I know nothing beyond what they showed in *The Lord of the Rings*.'

'Well it's very much like that, but fewer Hobbits.' Callum smiled a wide lazy grin.

Maybe the afternoon wasn't so bad after all.

Hope leaned in. 'So what brought you to London?'

–

'I don't understand why they've sat us together.' Connie had a face on her, as always. 'I mean I am definitely not going to cop off with you.'

'I bet there's a few straight men here who wouldn't object.' Grace wished she was joking. The number of men whose brain went instantly to a flashing neon sign that read 'THREESOME' the second Grace told them she had a twin sister was depressingly large.

'I thought the idea was lasting love, not pervy floor show.'

Grace ignored her. She was more interested in the third name on the plan for their table. Morgan Landy. That must be the Morgan she'd met at the first reception. The cute redhead with the Michelle Obama arms. Grace already had high hopes for their second meeting.

As they approached their table, halfway down the length of the hall, Grace could see that she was right. Morgan was already sitting at the furthest seat, currently alone, checking her phone in a classic 'trying to look like you're not freaking out at being stood up' way. Grace strode over to her, trying to wrap herself in confidence to make a good second impression. 'I think we're together.'

'Oh! Hello again. Con… Grace, isn't it?' Morgan's eyes slid past Grace to her sister and then back again. 'Oh.'

She'd started to say Connie, hadn't she? When had she met Connie? Connie had left the drinks reception about half an hour after they'd arrived. No point worrying about it. Even if Morgan hadn't met her already, she'd figure out this evening that they were sisters, so Grace would have to deal with The Connie Question at some point.

The Connie Question came up in all of Grace's relationships. It came, invariably, in one of two forms. The first, and an indisputable red flag, was the threesome suggestion. The second, thankfully more common option, was simply this.

'Oh my God. Are you sisters?' Morgan was acting out the scene in Grace's imagination beautifully. 'Twins?'

Grace nodded silently.

'But you're so…' Morgan at least had the good manners to leave the sentence unfinished. 'I mean yeah. I can see it in your faces.'

'But she's so pretty and I'm last night's leftovers that you didn't bother cleaning up?' Connie lacked her companions' social refinement.

Morgan blushed red, clashing for a second with her bright copper hair. 'No. I didn't mean – I meant, you look so different.'

Connie grinned at that. 'Yeah. Our mum used to dress us up matching. It was horrific.'

Grace didn't argue. She'd seen the photos of them as tiny matching toddlers though. She thought they were adorable.

'I believe I make four.' The voice behind Grace was smooth and masculine. The owner of the voice fulfilled the same brief. Tall, slim, short neat light hair, a slender face and bright blue eyes. He was wearing a perfectly tailored three-piece suit in dark grey with a deep red tie giving the only flash of colour. He looked familiar, presumably from the first event, but Grace couldn't place him. As he turned his body to sit down, she remembered. The bloke who'd yelled at her for getting in his way. Great. Maybe his ill nature would speak to Connie's natural grumpiness, and they'd both leave Grace and Morgan alone.

The new arrivals took their seats around the table. Grace was fighting to think of the perfect group conversation starter to put everyone at their ease, when the music dipped and Emma Love stepped up to the microphone at the front of the room.

–

Emma had prepared her welcome speech for the event carefully. And then she'd prepared it again when Annie, very politely, Tom, slightly less politely, and Josh, very rudely indeed, had reminded her that it was a dating event and not a history lecture. They were right of course. It was just a tiny bit frustrating to not be able to share all her excellent research into Regency Christmas traditions.

She did tell the gathering that Stir-up Sunday pre-dated most festive staples, which were Victorian inventions – thank you Prince Albert and Charles Dickens for that – and was a moment where families and communities would come together, not only to share in the making of the pudding for the festive meal, but also to make wishes for the year ahead. So this evening she was inviting people to come together as part of the Season community and make their own wishes, perhaps with a focus on the romantic, she suggested.

She stepped away from the microphone, Mrs Baker took her place and Emma took the chance to scan the room of daters. She was worried about this event. It put people into small groups too soon, and she didn't want to encourage matches of convenience that weren't right. Her mother would never have gone along with such a thing. It wasn't only about making a connection. It was about making the right connection.

She told herself to stop overthinking. She'd thought through the pros and cons of the event before she put it into the schedule. It felt traditional, and the activity was likely to get people talking about their hopes and dreams, which was a step up from the sort of small talk you could find in any bar in the city. And she'd grouped the daters carefully.

Her gaze moved across the front row. Hope Lucas. Emma's great white whale. Not that Hope was whale-like. She was friendly, and fun, and pretty, and down to earth. Matching Hope Lucas should be an absolute piece of cake, but Emma had already failed once. She looked across the other faces at Hope's table. Sadie Simpkins seemed like a good potential match for Hope's friend Theo. She was perky but not a pushover and seemed to have a good sense of humour, and step one in matching Hope this time around was definitely getting her away from Theo. Emma could recognise a comfort zone at a thousand paces and Theo Carter was Hope's, which meant that separating them needed some careful handling. She had decided against the short sharp shock of splitting them up today, and instead allowed them the safety blanket of being seated together, but with people who, Emma hoped, would be obviously better matches alongside them. The idea was that if Hope saw Theo hitting it off with someone, that would encourage Hope to turn her own attention to romance. Alongside Sadie for Theo, Callum Welsh was an excellent option for Hope. Well-travelled, adventurous, which would bring Hope out of herself, but also, from what Emma could glean, thoroughly decent and ready to make a commitment to the right person. Exactly how Hope herself had described her Prince Charming.

She moved her attention to other tables, reassuring herself that her seating plan was the best it could be. She could see potential couples hitting it off, and other groups interacting more as a four. That was fine at this stage. The Season was a marathon, not a sprint. That was, essentially, the whole point – to get past initial snap judgements and find something deeper, within a community. Happy ever after, Season-style, was more than two people meeting. It was the whole village Emma had created around that as well.

Her gaze paused on the twins. Almost unbelievable that they had sprung forth from the same DNA and the same upbringing. They were like a living answer to the question of 'nature versus nurture'. Only the answer turned out to be 'Actually, neither.'

Grace would be easy, Emma thought. She could match Grace a hundred times over. She was polite, friendly, well-presented, and eager to please. Nobody could object to Grace. Connie was… Connie was, perhaps, more of an acquired taste. But that was all right. Emma liked a challenge. One of their companions tonight was Morgan Landy. She was a conundrum. Emma could see her going for Grace very easily, but would they tire of one another over time? Emma couldn't help but feel that there was another layer to Morgan that she hadn't yet revealed.

And their fourth. Emma sighed at the fourth member of that group. He fell into the 'well you have to put him somewhere' category. Handsome, in a cool, slightly stand-offish sort of a way, but there was something there underneath the ice-cold exterior. A vulnerability perhaps? Her mother would have told her to work with that vulnerability. Emma sent up a silent prayer to the matchmaking gods for a dose of her mother's patience.

–

The man who made up their group of four hadn't even introduced himself before Connie asked him if he was only into women or if he played both ways. He pursed his lips slightly but didn't immediately reply.

'I'm pan, but I probably date more women and enbys,' Connie informed him, before pointing at Grace. 'She's more the other way round.'

'I date women,' Grace insisted. She shot a look towards Morgan.

'I usually say bi, but whatever,' said Morgan.

The man nodded. 'I see.'

'And what about you?' Grace asked pointedly. If everyone else was pinning their colours to the mast, why shouldn't he?

'I'm not really one for labels. So, will we need a sheet of paper to map out the possibilities?'

'Well for starters,' Connie deadpanned. 'I won't do Grace.'

The man looked from Connie's face over to her sister and back to Connie. 'I see.'

Well he seemed like a total dud. No chance Grace's interest would be taken up there. So was there even any point in Connie trying? Obviously Morgan was going to go for Grace. Why wouldn't she? Connie's twin sister was everything Connie wasn't. She was perky and upbeat and lived up to her name in every way. And she always got one up on Connie. Better marks in school. First place in cross country, barely breaking a sweat, the year that Connie pushed and scrabbled to finish in the top ten. Connie's life had been defined, in its entirety, by her sister's shadow. And now the Festive Season was going to be exactly the same.

Even Connie's coming out had ended up with her as second fiddle in her own life story. She'd planned it all and thought it through so carefully. She thought, well she hoped, her dad would be ok with who she was, but she also suspected it would be a little bit of a shock. Her dad was older and more traditional than the parents of most people her age, and, having lost his wife when the twins were still young, he had invested all of himself in their upbringing. Finding out that one of his little angels – even if it was definitely the lesser angel – was pansexual was going to be hard for him to reconcile. With all that in mind she'd decided to take him out to break the news, somewhere he felt comfortable but also somewhere where he'd be forced to stay calm and not blow up at her.

She'd gone back and forth on whether to invite Grace as well. With hindsight, of course, she should have talked to her dad on her own. No room with Grace in it was going to be a room where Connie was the centre of attention. But she had invited Grace and that was how she'd ended up at a corner table in the little pizzeria at the end of Dad's road listening to Grace tell them that she was really pleased Connie had organised this get-together because she had something she needed to tell them both.

Yes. Her sister had gazumped – gayzumped? – Connie's coming-out moment, leaving Connie to bleat, 'Well so am I!' while she watched her dad take her sister's hand and reassure her, with tearful eyes, that he was very proud of her and only wanted to see her happy.

That was Connie's pride and Connie's good wishes that Grace was stealing. 'I like girls too!' had been met with a slow shake of the head and a reminder that this was Grace's moment.

And that was the story of Connie's life. It was always Grace's moment.

'So what do you do, Connie?'

'Oh, different things. Mostly temping.'

Morgan smiled, and it didn't look like the *Poor Connie* smile that she was used to. 'That's cool. It gets boring doing the same thing all day every day. So where are you at the moment?'

'Oh. Between things. I finished somewhere on Friday.'

Grace failed to suppress a giggle. 'Tell her about the goat, Connie.'

'What goat?'

Fine. 'So I was working at the city farm in Hackney. Supposedly bookkeeping and admin, but it was a sort of "everyone mucks in" – literally – deal. And I might have kinda got knocked over by a goat.' She had absolutely, literally and definitely, been knocked over by a goat.

'In front of a whole school party. Into a pile of manure,' Grace added helpfully. 'It's on TikTok. Although it's mostly beeped out, so you can't hear what she says.'

'It wasn't my fault,' Connie tried to explain. 'That goat was a psychopath.'

Morgan frowned. 'Oh no. Are you ok?'

'I'm fine.'

'And they got rid of you because of that?'

'Not really.' Connie's manager had actually been very supportive, once he'd stopped laughing. 'I've got some shifts doing admin at a gas and electric company next week anyway. Time for a change.'

Connie leaned back, and let her sister lead the conversation. Grace was better at this stuff than her anyway. Grace was charming and presentable and all those other things that people liked. Connie watched Morgan as she shifted her attention to Grace. This was always going to be Connie's lot, wasn't it? Staring from the sidelines while the beautiful people fell in love.

—

The microphone at the front of the room crackled back into life, after the short lull following Emma's introduction.

'Good evening everybody. I'm Josie. I'm going to be talking you through the Christmas pudding making this evening. Shall we make a start?'

There was a volley of shouts of approval around the room.

'Excellent. So on your tables you all have a large mixing bowl, and a covered basket. It's time to open the basket!'

Grace did the honours for her group.

'Oh for goodness' sake,' the aggravatingly stand-offish man muttered. 'Is there a bar at this thing?'

'There's mulled wine cups.' Grace pointed towards the waiters circulating around the room.

Their fourth wheel shook his head. 'I'm not drinking a single mouthful more of that hot cough syrup. I'm going to find a proper drink.'

And then there were three. Grace smiled widely at Morgan. People like happy people, she reminded herself. A smile makes you look friendly. A smile is approachable. Across the table Connie was scowling at the basket full of ingredients.

'So what? We like whack all this in the bowl and mix it together?'

'I think you're supposed to wait for the instructions,' Grace cautioned.

'Seriously?' Connie was already tipping the contents of the flour bag into the bowl.

'I don't know if that goes first,' Grace stuttered.

Connie shrugged. 'All gets mixed in eventually, doesn't it?'

That wasn't the point. The point was that there was a right way of doing things that meant things worked out the way they were supposed to.

'Ok then. So we start by mixing together everything except for the butter,' the woman on stage announced. 'Everything is already weighed out for you, apart from the brandy.' She held up a mini bottle identical to the one in the basket on their table. 'Now usually we say a couple of tablespoons and you can do as you will with the rest.'

Grace winced as Connie tipped the whole bottle in. 'That's too much.'

'How about you Grace?' Morgan interrupted the dispute.

'I'm sorry?' Grace couldn't concentrate with Connie there disrupting everything.

'What do you do for work?'

'Oh, I'm a receptionist. Head Receptionist. Sort of Front of House manager really. At the Harker and Riley building.' Grace knew she was good at her job. Grace was indispensable. Everybody told her, from the cleaning crew to the chief executive. Nobody knew how they'd manage without Grace running the front desk.

Morgan frowned. 'The magazine people?'

'Magazines, digital content and the best in twenty-first-century information communications,' Grace told her.

'Right. I think they charged me twice for a magazine subscription.' Morgan grinned. She was even prettier when she smiled. 'You don't do subscriptions, do you?'

'Sorry. Not my department.'

'It was the gardening one,' Morgan continued. 'I never really read it anyway. Which kinda makes paying for it twice worse.'

'You like gardening? Our housemate is obsessed with flowers.' Which wasn't such a rich conversational ground as if Grace, herself, was obsessed with flowers, but it was something.

'I grow more veggies and fruit. I've got an allotment. I have a few flowers for colour though. Bulbs mostly.'

'I don't think I've done this right.' Connie pushed the bowl across the table to her sister.

Grace exchanged a look with Morgan. 'Don't worry, I'll sort it out,' she said.

It didn't actually look as though Connie had done anything wrong. She'd just lost patience long before the cake was properly mixed together. Being Connie, of course, she'd got cake mixture everywhere, making Grace's fingers sticky the second she touched the bowl. Grace stirred, and as she did so a tendril of hair worked its way loose from her hair band and swung in front of her face. She blew it out of the way once, and then twice, and then a third time. 'I'm sorry. Morgan, could you?'

She shook her head to swing the lock of hair out of her face. Morgan leaned forward and tucked it neatly behind Grace's ear. Her fingers were slightly rough, but warm and gentle. Grace glanced up at her and smiled.

–

By the time their ingredients were combined into the large mixing bowl they'd been given, Hope had learned more about the flora and fauna and history of both New Zealand and Australia than she would even have imagined wanting to know. Callum was easy company though – relaxed, chatty, laid-back. There was nothing not to like. Hope paused. On paper that had been true lots of times before, but somehow she'd never quite managed to get a romance off the ground. This time was going to be different though. Callum seemed nice and fun and he was definitely handsome. Why not now? Why not him?

Hope just needed Theo to co-operate by applying his considerable, well-practised charm to Sadie, and Hope's second attempt at the Season would be well on the way to going considerably better than the first.

Hope kicked Theo in the shin under the table and gave him a look that she hoped communicated the need for him to get in the game.

'Ow!'

Oh for goodness' sake. He was supposed to get in the game subtly.

Sadie leaned forward, concern on her face. 'Are you ok?'

'I'm fine,' Theo muttered.

'All right then.' A voice from the stage interrupted what Hope was willing to be a budding romance for her friend. 'Next it's time to stir! But there's more to Stir-up Sunday than stirring the pudding mix. I want each of you to take a turn, and as you stir you're supposed to make a wish.'

Emma stepped up and took the microphone from their cookery instructor. 'Making a wish is the central part of Stir-up Sunday. We're all here because we're hoping for love and romance, right?'

'Right,' Hope agreed enthusiastically. She wanted a relationship. She wanted a partner. She wanted there to be someone who was always on her side. She caught Theo staring at her. Hope looked away. No doubt he was horrified by all this talk of finding true love. Typical of him. He was a lone wolf, but at least he never pretended otherwise. It was blokes who promised the earth and still never called that she could do without.

'So maybe your wish will be for a lasting connection? Or for your perfect partner?' Emma laughed slightly at the microphone. 'But don't be too specific about that, ok? Too often we limit our options by creating the perfect man or woman in our heads, and never give anyone real the chance to match up.'

Hope didn't think she was doing that. She was open to possibilities. Too open probably. Across the table she watched Sadie stir the mix with her eyes screwed tightly shut. Was every person here really wishing for the same thing? A fairytale princess? A charming prince? Their very own happy ever after?

Callum went next, and then handed the spoon to Hope. 'Your go.'

She closed her eyes and pushed the spoon through the dense fruity mixture, letting the scent of fruit and brandy and childhood Christmasses fill her senses. She remembered the feeling of safety and warmth from when she was a little girl. Before her dad had left. Before Simon. Before life had tarnished a little bit of the magic of the festive season. *I wish...* for what exactly? All those things Emma had mentioned, of course, but what did she want specifically? *I wish to fall completely in love with no fear and no doubt.* The thought had crystallised before she had a chance to shut it down. It was an unreasonable wish. She knew that. She knew that there were always going to be worries, and that nothing was completely uncomplicated by fear. In her head she tried to qualify, to let the Christmas fairies know that she wasn't being entitled. She wanted a solid relationship. She wanted a kind and honest partner. She wanted someone who she felt reasonably sure of the majority of the time. In the silence inside her head, Hope's heart rebelled against her rational mind. Nobody wished, in the very depths of their soul, for someone they felt reasonably sure of the majority of the time. *I wish for love with no fear.*

She opened her eyes. The others around the table were staring at her. 'Hogging the wish-making a bit there!' Callum laughed.

'Sorry!' How long had she been lost in her thoughts? She handed the spoon on to Theo. 'Sorry.'

'Take all the time you need.'

'No. I'm done.'

She watched Theo take his turn. The polar opposite to her, of course. He didn't even close his eyes; a quick prod of the pudding mix and then done. He probably hadn't even bothered making a wish.

'So what now?' Callum held up one of the small ceramic bowls that were piled up in their basket. 'Into the bowls?'

'Yes.' There were eight individual-sized Christmas pudding bowls. The idea seemed to be that you would get to take one home and one would be served at the Festive Season Christmas meal in a few weeks' time.

'So did you have Christmas pudding like this down under?'

'We did. My dad's Scottish and he didn't move over there 'til he was nearly thirty so he always insisted on a *proper* Christmas dinner. I think most of my mates' families probably had something a bit more climate appropriate though.' Callum paused. 'My ex hated Christmas pudding, so I haven't had one for a few years now.'

'You were together a while?'

'Seven years. Split up in February.'

Nine months ago, give or take. That was ok. That wasn't worryingly recent.

'Of course we should have listened to all the warnings about a puppy being for life, not just for Christmas.'

'Sorry. What?'

'We got a dog, golden retriever – Bobbi – in December. So we're kinda stuck still being in touch.' He shrugged. 'Co-parenting.'

'Right.'

He pulled his phone out of his pocket and tapped to his camera reel. 'Here she is.' A young golden retriever sitting next to a petite brunette, followed by the same dog being walked by the same brunette, and then playing ball with the same brunette, on the beach with the brunette, in the park with the brunette, cuddled up on the sofa with the brunette… 'She's gorgeous. You see why I couldn't let her go.' He looked up and caught Hope's eye. 'The dog I mean.'

Hope leaned forward slightly. 'I should hope so.'

–

Connie couldn't begin to guess what Grace's wish was. Grace was perfect. Everything Grace touched turned out perfectly. She didn't need to wish. The universe was already smiling on her. Connie stirred the pudding and offered up her own silent prayer to whatever spirits of Christmas future might be listening. *I wish that someone would think I'm worth sticking with.*

'Are you going to tell me what you wished for?' Morgan asked. 'Or does that break the magic?'

'I don't think we're supposed to.' Saying it out loud would sound awful, wouldn't it? Needy and jealous and small. At least that would be how it came across to someone who hadn't walked in Connie's shoes.

Morgan smiled. 'Ok. We'll play by the rules then.' She started spooning mixture into the two small dishes in front of her. 'Do you want me to do yours?'

Grace leaned forward with her bowls. 'Yes please.'

Did Morgan hesitate ever so slightly? Connie told herself not to get her hopes up. If Grace had set her sights on Morgan, Connie would be better off moving on and finding someone else. If she really wanted to win there was only one thing she'd ever found that worked. She had to run a different race to her sister. There was something holding her here though. She pushed her bowls towards Morgan too. 'Oooh, and mine.' She could hear the simper in her voice. It sounded wrong. It sounded like Grace.

Across the table the fourth member of their party shook his head. Probably pity. Connie ignored him. Morgan started spooning mixture into Connie's two pudding dishes. She was doing Connie's first. Ha! It was the tiniest of victories, but it was probably all Connie was going to get.

'So what do you do, Morgan?' Grace asked the question. Connie should have asked Morgan about herself, shouldn't she? She wanted to know.

'I was wondering that,' she blurted out.

'I'm an artist.'

'Like as a job?' Grace asked.

'What sort of art?' Connie spoke at the same time.

'Yes, as a job. I do commissions and I teach a bit and I do a little bit of illustration for greetings cards and stuff like that. I'm trying to give that up though. It's a lot of time when I could be working on my own stuff.'

'So you draw? Or paint?' Connie followed up before Grace could reply.

'I'm a painter mostly. Acrylics. Sometimes watercolours if that works for the piece.'

'I'd love to see some of your work.' Grace again. Connie fought to keep the scowl off her face. She would also love to see some of Morgan's work. She couldn't say that now though. It would sound like she was copying.

'Well I've got a couple of pieces in a gallery in Bethnal Green at the moment. You're welcome to go along.' Morgan grinned. 'Even more welcome to put your money where your mouth is. They're way more likely to take more pieces if those ones sell after all.' She pulled her phone out of her pocket. 'Give me your number and I'll message you the details.'

Connie watched in silence as her sister tapped her number into Morgan's phone. Of course that was how this went. It was always going to be how this went. Better to move on and stop kidding herself things would ever be any different. 'Excuse me.'

She left the table and walked quickly out of the room. Where was she going? She didn't even have a plan. She'd left her bag on the back of the chair so she couldn't actually make a full escape, which was definitely her preferred option. It was fine. They'd almost finished the pudding making, so there'd be bar and mingling next. It would be easy enough to sneak back in, grab her bag and get away then. She just needed to wait out the next few minutes.

Connie leaned on the bannister that ran around the grand round stairwell in the middle of the building and looked down. It was the sort of long sweeping bannister that you couldn't help but imagine sliding down. At least Connie couldn't. It was the sort of thing Connie did. Inevitably she would break several priceless ornaments and probably at least one of her own bones when she did. She could picture Grace standing over her at the bottom of the stairs shaking her head and explaining to the gathered crowd that her sister had always been a bit of a loose cannon. She wouldn't actually say that this was why everyone liked Grace more, but everyone would know.

'You left your bag.' Morgan was standing behind her, holding Connie's tiny black rucksack. 'I thought you'd just gone to the loo but then you didn't come back, so I thought maybe you'd tried to make an escape. But you'd forgotten this. I didn't want you to end up standing in the hallway not knowing what to do.'

'That's not what I was doing,' Connie protested.

'So you were coming back?'

'Yeah.' Well probably. Maybe not. She had her phone and her keys. She could have texted Hope and asked her to pick up her bag, but she couldn't tell Morgan that. Morgan exuded an air of competence and capability. Not even able to walk out in a huff effectively wasn't the image Connie wanted to project.

'Right. Well, you won't need this then.' Morgan held the bag towards her.

Connie took it. 'Well since you brought it all this way.'

Morgan moved to lean on the rail alongside her. 'So you didn't ask, but like if you're interested you could always pop by my studio sometime. Like if you're interested in seeing what I paint.'

'You have a studio?'

'I do.' She laughed slightly. 'I mean I don't have a living room, or a dining room, or a spare bedroom, so don't get too excited. Basically my flat is one big room with a tiny kitchen and shower room next to it, and so I squashed a futon into one corner and I call the rest my studio.'

'So you're asking me back to your place.'

'Cool your jets. I'm inviting you to come see my studio. During daylight hours. While sober.'

'Ok.' Studio was still one up on gallery though, wasn't it? Studio was like the inner sanctum. 'I'd love to.'

'But we haven't finished the…' Grace spluttered after Morgan's disappearing back.

It was ridiculous. Connie'd had her little temper tantrum because she wasn't the centre of attention and people always ran after her. Morgan would learn. In the meantime it was sweet that she was so concerned though. Grace appreciated that – someone else taking a share of the responsibility for Connie's happiness would be so welcome.

'Don't do that.' The man who'd been a largely silent fourth member of their group sounded strangely disappointed.

Grace was gathering the eight dishes of pudding together and placing them neatly on the board in the basket, as per the instructions they had been given. 'I'm being helpful.'

'That isn't what I meant.'

She turned and looked at him properly. He was slim, fair haired and impeccably dressed. His suit jacket was placed over the back of his chair and his brilliant white shirt sleeves had been rolled up for the activity with an almost military precision. 'So what did you mean?'

'Why are you yelling after someone who is so very obviously not interested?'

He was wrong about that. She'd had a vibe with Morgan. Maybe Grace wouldn't be what she normally went for, but just because she was an artist didn't necessarily mean she was going to be more interested in someone cooler and more bohemian and more like… Grace shook her head. Connie wouldn't be interested in Morgan anyway. Connie was only here for the free parties and because Hope had had the temerity to suggest that it might not suit her. 'What do you know?'

'Perhaps not very much. What did you wish for?'

That was a simpler question. 'I didn't.'

He frowned. 'Why not?'

'Because wishes don't mean anything.' That sounded cold. 'I mean, you can wish for excitement or fun or passion, but then

62

you have to get on with life, don't you? There's things to do and people to take care of, and wishing doesn't change anything.'

'Are excitement and passion the things you would have wished for?'

Grace looked into his face expecting to see a hint of mockery or amusement. It wasn't there. He looked fascinated. It was the sort of look a person could lose themselves in. It was the sort of look that made her want to turn to see the more interesting person behind her.

She looked away. She wasn't going to answer his question. Like she'd said, it was irrelevant. You couldn't abandon responsibility and live your life for pleasure. She wasn't ready to let the previous conversation go anyway. 'What did you mean about Morgan?'

'Simply that I know the evidence of my own eyes. Our Titian-haired friend is not attracted to you. And you are either very stupid, very deep in denial, or you know that as well as I do.'

'I'm not stupid.'

'That's good to hear.'

'You don't know anything though.' She faced him properly. 'Blokes always think they know what women are thinking. Especially women who fancy women. You imagine we're all at it all the time.'

'On the contrary. What I have identified is that one particular woman has no interest in doing anything with you any of the time.' He leaned closer to her, so his breath was warm against Grace's neck. The proximity should have been over-familiar. Grace didn't think of herself as a touchy-feely tactile sort of a person. She air-kissed as far from the actual cheek as possible, and greeted friends with a nod rather than a hug. But this felt different. Not warm. Not cloying. Not at all friendly. She found herself leaning in.

'More fool her,' he said.

Chapter Six

The St Nicholas Night Ball was a big deal. The first two events had been fun curtain raisers, and Emma was quietly pleased with how her early instincts for who to sit with who had worked out at the Stir-up Sunday, but they were now five days away from the third event and then it would be the halfway mark and then the whole thing would be over before they knew it. Emma was determined that the ball would be perfect.

It would be grander than any of the events so far, and the black-tie dress code meant that the effort on the part of the daters was a little higher too. Emma, of course, had everything in hand. She had her team assembled, and she started from the top of the list.

'Right. Doors open at seven prompt, so we're going to work through everything up to that point.'

Josh had his own laptop open in front of him, with Annie craning her neck to see the screen. Tom was leaning back in his chair at the other side of the dining table.

'Ok. So I'll be arriving at the venue at three p.m. We have access to the room from three thirty p.m., which isn't ideal but Josh refused to pay for a whole day booking.'

'We don't need a whole day.'

'You say that, but we're lucky the other party is only lunch. If they had a day conference we wouldn't have got in until six.' The very notion brought a cold shudder over Emma's body.

'We've got three and a half hours. It's loads of time.'

It was not at all loads of time, but there was no point arguing. Not least because she'd already won. 'So Josh, you can park right behind the venue.' Emma pulled a visitor parking pass from her folder. 'Tom can't make it,' Emma paused. 'Which is fine, so Annie, are you ok helping out on the door?'

'Anything you need.'

Tom glanced up at the mention of his name and then went back to scrolling through his phone.

Emma walked Josh and Annie through the plans for the rest of the evening, with arrival times for the band, the caterer, the waiting staff and a thousand and one other little contingencies that were all built into Emma's minute-by-minute plan.

She'd moved on to discussing specific daters and matches that she wanted them to encourage when Tom gave a slightly dramatic throat clear. 'Sorry, but are we going to eat at all?'

For goodness' sake, it was only... Emma looked at the clock. It was quarter past eight. She'd told Tom to come round for food straight after work. That meant they'd been discussing the Season for nearly two hours.

'Sorry.' She pulled a face at him. 'This would be more interesting for you if you could come.'

'What would be really interesting though, would be dinner.'

'Yeah. Right.' Emma looked at her pile of papers. She still needed to run through the jobs she and Josh needed to tick off before they got to Saturday.

'We could pick this up in the morning,' Josh suggested. 'I mean we all need to eat. Look – you ring the Dragon, I'll drive down and pick it up.'

'I suppose we could discuss the rest over food.'

She caught the look her brother gave her boyfriend before his gaze landed back on Emma. 'Or tomorrow?' he suggested again.

'Fine.'

The tension in the air hadn't quite dissipated when Josh and Annie headed out to collect the takeaway. 'Do you want a beer or water or...?' Emma opened the fridge. They had milk. Thank goodness for Annie. 'A cup of tea?'

'I'll have a beer.'

She passed the bottle to her boyfriend and took one for herself. 'Sorry about all this. It would be more interesting for you if you could come.'

'He didn't reply straight away. When he did it was with the air of a man choosing his words carefully. 'Why would I be coming on Saturday though? I'm not looking for a date.' He hesitated. 'Am I?'

'I hope not.' So why would he be coming? 'But you could come to support me. There's so much to do. An extra pair of hands would be…'

'Ok.' He cut her off. 'Do you know how many live shows, piano bars, recitals and whatever I've played since we got together?'

Emma shook her head.

'Which is fine. Neither do I, to be honest. I do know how many you've been to.' He held up two fingers.

'I'm sorry. I'm really busy and…'

'Emma! That's not what I'm driving at. I'm a professional musician. Part of my job is playing backing music at venues and for bands and all that. I don't expect you to come every time. I don't even expect you to come most times. It's my work.' He looked over the selection of paperwork and technology still spread across the dining table. 'And this is your work.'

'It's more than just work.' Emma could hear the hurt in her own voice. The Season wasn't merely her job. It wasn't a side hustle or a chore to pay the rent. The Season was her baby. She'd poured her heart and soul into making it the best it could be. She was still pouring her heart and soul into making it the best it could be.

'Is it?'

'Yes.'

'Right. More important than spending time with the man you were talking about marrying a few weeks ago?'

'I didn't say that.'

He looked at the detritus of her work day spread across the table in front of them. 'You kinda did.'

'Wait.' They'd never had a row. They'd bickered, and they wound each other up almost continuously, but in three months together they hadn't yet had an actual argument. 'I don't want us to fall out.'

'Neither do I.'

And yet they were. The words, words which should have been conciliatory, were coming out with tension rather than kindness.

Tom continued. 'But I don't want to come to spend time with you and play second fiddle to a logistics meeting either.'

'You weren't second fiddle. You could have got involved.'

Tom's shoulders slumped. 'You know what? I might go and eat at home.'

'But Josh is bringing...'

'Yeah. Apologise to them for me. I'll see them another time.'

'But what about...?'

Tom was already in the doorway.

'What about what?'

Emma's phone rang in her hand. She glanced down.

'Do you need to get that?' Tom asked.

Unrecognised number, on her work phone. 'What's plus one?'

'What?'

'Plus one. The dialling code.'

'America.' His voice was ice.

Did she know anyone in America?

'I'm going to go.' Tom turned away.

'Wait.'

The door slammed shut.

Emma declined the call. She didn't know anyone in the US, did she? 'Tom...'

But he'd already gone. It was fine. All couples had rows. It didn't mean anything. He'd probably ring when he got home and he'd had a chance to cool down. If not then, then in the morning. Nothing to worry about at all.

Hope picked the cucumber out of her hospital canteen sandwich, and leaned back in her chair. When she'd started this job she'd told herself the weird mint green on the walls was cheerful, like having a blast of nature indoors. Now she wished it was the same sad grey and beige of the rest of the corridor. At least that was honest. At least that didn't raise expectations of finding any colour or joy in your work day.

Her phone buzzed in her bag. She fished it out and checked the message. Theo. Of course. It was way too soon for Callum to be calling. Even if he was interested – was Hope kidding herself to think that maybe he was – she assumed he would play it cool, knowing he would see her again next weekend at the ball.

Theo was suggesting curry and beer that evening. Yep. Hope was the girl guys texted at lunchtime on the day when they hadn't had a better offer for the evening. At least for Theo there was no pressure to dress up, or redo her make-up, or shave anything that wasn't visible from a hundred paces.

There was also no pressure, she told herself four hours later, as she ran from the bus stop towards Jaipur Palace, to be on time. Theo was already seated at a small table halfway down the length of the restaurant, the remnants of a plate of poppadoms in front of him. 'You ate all the poppadoms.'

'You were half an hour late.'

'I'm not that...' She checked her phone. She was precisely that late. 'Sorry. I got home and Grace was baking, and it's my turn to clean the kitchen this week,' according to the rota Grace made and Hope stuck to religiously and Connie barely looked at. 'So I hung around to help her clear up and then Connie had left her phone in there and it rang so I answered it and then I had to take a message cos I couldn't find her and...'

'Or you could have let Grace clean her own mess up and let Connie's phone go to voicemail.'

She shrugged. 'It was no bother.'

'They take advantage of you.'

'Grace doesn't.'

Theo shook his head. 'No. She just expects you to keep everything to her standard of pristine.'

'It's really cheap though.'

'It's not free though is it? You pay them to live there. You're not their maid.'

That wasn't fair. 'They charge me way less than they should. It's only fair that I do a bit extra around the place to make up for it.'

'One day you'll move out and those two will be lost,' Theo told her. 'Do either of them even know how to work their own dishwasher?'

'I'm sure they do.' Hope thought about it. Grace definitely did. Connie was more a 'rinse the same plate you used last time under the tap and hope for the best' person.

It wasn't a big deal though. 'It was Grace that organised getting the dishwasher. She made us all pay in ten pounds a week until we could afford it.' Hope strongly suspected Grace of paying Connie's third as well as her own.

They ordered food and another round of poppadoms. The waitress set them down with a half-smile in Theo's direction. 'I thought you'd been stood up,' she simpered. 'Never mind.'

'She was flirting with you?'

'What's it to you if she was?'

'Well nothing.' That wasn't the point. 'But she clearly thinks this is a date, which means she thinks she's flirting with you in front of your girlfriend.'

'But she's not.'

'But she thinks she is.'

'Ok, well feel free to be offended on my imaginary girlfriend's behalf.'

That wasn't quite right, but it was close enough. 'Fine. I will.'

The waitress reappeared with curries and rice and naans. Hope glowered at her, and this time she retreated with no comment.

'Happy now?' Theo asked.

'Much happier. Thank you.'

'So I did actually want to talk to you about something...' Theo started.

Hope's phone rang on the table between them. 'Sorry.'

Not a number she knew. She rejected the call. That always felt rude somehow, even though answering it would have been rude, in its own way, to Theo.

She apologised again. 'Sorry. What were you saying?'

'I was thinking about...'

A text popped up. *Wondered if you're free on Saturday? Would love to meet up.*

A second later another text.

This is Callum by the way. From Sunday.

Maybe it was time for Hope to feel a little more hopeful. Maybe the Festive Season would be the one. Maybe Callum would be the one. Her mind went to the blooms she would pick for her bouquet. She stopped herself. Maybe that was a little too hopeful. She pulled yet another apologetic face at Theo and texted back. *Would love to. Where do you want to meet?*

'Wow. An actual date.' Hope could feel herself smiling. 'How very 1998.'

'You were four in 1998. Who were you dating?'

'Grant Appleby. He proposed on the second day of school.'

Theo grinned. 'So will you have to tell this guy that your heart belongs to another?'

Fortunately not. 'He proposed to Jennie Hatton on the fourth day.'

'The cad!' gasped Theo.

'Well at least I'm free to go out with Callum.'

'The pudding guy?'

'Yep.'

'Cool. He seemed nice.'

'They always seem nice.'

The silence sat between them for a second. 'Well remember that it's ok to take things slow then. Don't let him pressure you.'

Theo's occasional over-protectiveness came from a good place. 'I know. I won't. What did you want to talk about anyway?'

He shook his head. 'Nothing that can't wait. Tell me about Callum. Where's he taking you?'

–

Emma checked another item off her to-do list. She now had zero unread emails. She had checked and forwarded all her invoices that were due in the next twenty-eight days to Josh for checking and payment. She had read a long item about feng shui online and dragged the dining table two feet across the room to create a better energy flow. She had thrown away her old hairdryer and the broken coffee cup that had been on the kitchen windowsill for the last fortnight, because, apparently, broken things discourage wealth from entering the home. She was googling home aquariums, apparently excellent for attracting wealth, when she finally stopped.

It was just possible that Emma was procrastinating.

She looked again at her to-do list, even though she was fully aware that there was only one item outstanding.

Call Tom.

It was two days since he'd left and two days that Emma had been failing to call him. She'd told herself, many many times, that if she just did this one more task before she called, he might call her in the meantime. But he hadn't, and there had always been just one more task.

All couples had rows. She knew that. She knew that one argument didn't have to mean anything. But one argument and then forty-eight hours without contact… Maybe that did mean something?

Maybe it meant that, for all that she was supposed to be the Queen of Hearts, Emma was actually no good at being in a relationship. Because whatever the problem was, it must be her. Tom had done all of this before, hadn't he? He'd had the perfect relationship. He'd proved that he was more than capable of being an excellent boyfriend, an excellent husband in fact. He could do this. The problem must be her.

Emma's laptop was still open in front of her. The temptation to do something that she'd never let herself do before was too strong. If she was all wrong, what did a relationship that was all right look like?

She opened Instagram and started to type into the search box. Jack Miller. She'd never searched for him before. She'd seen photos at Tom's flat, and Tom had never kept his past relationship secret. She knew the story of how they met, fell in love, and were parted by tragedy.

His page was still there. Could you get these things archived? How would you go about it? Tom had clearly either never tried or never got very far if he had. Jack was still there, smiling out at the world, captured in a few moments of perfect Instagrammable youth and joy.

Why was she even looking? She wasn't in competition with Jack. She understood that Tom could love Jack's memory and still love her. That all made perfect sense. It wasn't that.

'What should I do?' she whispered. 'What would you do?'

That was what she wanted to ask Jack. You know him. You've walked this path before me. Tell me what to do.

'Can I check the catering for...?' Josh's voice in the doorway interrupted her train of thought. Emma slammed her laptop closed. Josh frowned. 'What was that?'

'Nothing.'

'Nah. That was the laptop slam of shame. Porn or gambling?'

'Neither.'

He grinned. 'I know. It was Instagram. I saw. Who are you stalking?'

'Nobody.' Her brother just stared at her. 'Jack. Tom's husband.'

'You're stalking a dead guy?'

'I'm not stalking him.'

Josh plonked himself down next to her. 'Are you ok Stilts?'

'I'm fine.'

'And are you and Tom ok?'

'We're fine.'

'Actually fine? Or he stormed out in a mood on Monday and now you're googling his husband fine?'

Emma didn't reply. 'What do you want?'

'I just want you to ok the catering options for event four. We were low on vegetarian canapés at the ball.'

'Ok. I'll take another look.'

'Thank you.'

Emma added *Check catering event 4* to her to-do list. She would definitely call Tom straight after that.

Chapter Seven

Connie paced to the end of Morgan's street and then turned around and paced back. At the far corner she stopped and turned again. This time she would ring the bell. She'd made it as far as the door on her first pass, to be fair, so she wasn't a total wimp. Actually making her presence known had defeated her though.

She checked the street name and house number that Morgan had tapped into her phone. They hadn't changed. She was, still, very definitely in the right place. Ok. Time to do this.

Or was it? Of course they'd all had a drink at the Stir-up Sunday, so maybe Morgan was already regretting her decision to invite Connie over. Maybe she was hiding in her flat desperately hoping that Connie wouldn't show. Maybe she should call first. Or text. She couldn't text. Morgan had provided her address but no phone number. This was hell.

Connie gave herself a stern mental talking-to. The best approach to these things was always to go for it. She needed to walk right up to the door and ring the bell, and get the whole thing over with. If Morgan was dismayed to see her then at least she'd know, and she could get the hell out of here and never have to put herself through this again.

So she had to ring the bell. This time. She marched, with rather more purpose she hoped, up the street again, and turned towards Morgan's door. Which was already standing open. Morgan was leaning on the doorframe. 'I thought I should probably catch you this time round. I didn't want you stuck out there all day.'

Great. The actual worst of both worlds. Not only did she now have to find some level of charming delight in her soul, but she had to do it in front of a woman who absolutely, without question, knew that she was completely crazy.

'I thought I might be too early.'

Morgan shook her head.

'Right. Watch must have stopped.'

Morgan glanced down at Connie's arms. 'You're not wearing a watch.'

'No. Well that'll be why I didn't know the time then.' That made no sense. She risked a glance into Morgan's face, begging with her eyes that Morgan would let that particular moment of insanity pass.

'Right. I thought maybe you were one of those step count obsessives.'

That would have been a better explanation.

'Come in anyway. I'm still having breakfast.'

'See. I knew I was too early!'

Morgan laughed at that. Connie allowed herself to properly exhale. She wasn't stuck in a reception room full of silent waiters and women in impossible heels. She could be herself, well a version of herself. The version that didn't fall over goats or knock over champagne waterfalls.

She followed Morgan down what she took to be a communal hallway for the flats. The house was an older property, converted from a family home at some point in the distant past, Connie assumed. Morgan's flat-cum-studio was on the ground floor, and consisted of one big room where it looked as if two reception rooms had been knocked through. There was a futon pushed against the wall in the far corner, next to a small chest of drawers and a tiny bookcase, and a door half open to a kitchen. The rest of the room was given over entirely to Morgan's work. There was a draftsman's table at one side of the bay window at the front of the house and an easel at the other. A high stool with paint spattered up all four legs stood in front of the table. The shelves were stuffed with paints and brushes, and canvases were lined up against every wall. The dust sheet under the easel seemed like a fairly half-hearted attempt to keep the detritus off the wooden floors.

'It's a bit of a mess, isn't it?'

'It's…' Connie searched for the word. 'It's very artistic.'

'Yeah. It's a very artistic mess.' Morgan laughed. 'I tend to work on multiple things at the same time so there's always stuff piled up all over the shop.'

Connie wandered deeper into the space. Morgan's paintings were dreamy, mottled hazy colours that swam into one another. Pinks swirling into greys swirling into purples. Connie crouched down in front of a canvas leaning on the wall. 'This is beautiful.'

'Thank you.' Morgan moved to stand behind her. 'I can't really sell those ones. Bit old-fashioned. Not edgy enough for the art market. Not pretty enough for tourists.'

'I love it.'

'Look from over here.'

Connie stood and followed Morgan to the other side of the room. From a greater distance the swirls became more representative. 'It's a portrait?'

Morgan nodded. 'I started that one in a class. So it's of a model, not anyone I really know.'

'You've done portraits of people you know though?'

'I painted my ex. Quite a few times actually, but I could never quite capture them. That probably should have been a sign.'

'Of what?'

'I'm not sure. I think art's about seeing what's really there, so like maybe it meant I couldn't really see them, who they really were.' She stopped and took a sharp breath in. 'I'm not explaining this very well. I mean I could see them perfectly well, but I couldn't see what it was that made them them. That unique thing, you know?'

Connie did know. Connie had spent a long time trying to make herself unique.

'Like you and Grace.'

Grace. Great. She really did get everywhere.

'Same features. Same bone structure. Same eyes. Same skin tone. Same build. But like nobody could ever mistake you for each other, could they?'

'You'd be surprised.'

'Really?' Morgan did genuinely sound surprised. 'I guess those people weren't really looking. Or weren't really seeing.'

There was a moment. Connie thought there was a moment. Morgan was looking right at her, and Connie felt... exposed. She'd heard people talk about people – well blokes mostly – undressing them with their eyes and it sounded creepy and seedy, but this was something else. She felt as though Morgan was seeing parts of her she never showed to the world.

It was a moment. Connie stepped forward and moved her lips towards Morgan's.

And Morgan stepped back.

Oh God. Morgan stepped back.

Connie couldn't – wouldn't – raise her head. She didn't need to see the horror and disgust on Morgan's face. Of course she was repulsed. She had just been being friendly. She was probably trying to sell Connie a painting or something and she didn't want Connie going round to the fancy gallery she'd sent Grace to and embarrassing herself.

'I'm sorry.'

'No. You're fine.' Morgan was right at the other side of the room now. Connie risked looking up. 'I was going to say like, do you want a coffee or something?'

'No. I think I'll go. Things to do.' Connie started towards the door.

Morgan rushed after her. 'You don't need to go...'

Connie didn't slow when she hit the pavement. 'Lovely paintings,' she shouted back. 'Thanks for showing me.'

'Will I see you at the ball?' Morgan yelled the question as Connie set off down the street. 'Will you be at the ball tonight?'

Connie stopped. 'Yeah. Maybe. If I've got time.'

She strode away. Obviously she wasn't going to the ball. Grace could have Morgan. Connie would probably have to move away.

Far away. Chile maybe. Or New Zealand. It didn't matter, so long as it was a really long way away from here.

–

Not so far away, on the other side of the capital, Grace was also trying to nurture an interest in the arts. The gallery where Morgan was exhibiting was only a fifteen-minute walk from home, which meant that Grace had been able to wander by and recce the set-up already. Her goal was to look casual, so she'd waited until the weekend when she figured the space might be busier. She wasn't expecting Morgan to be there in person, but maybe she would. And being so local Grace would be able to style out an, 'Oh, I was passing and I remembered you mentioned this place…' coincidental meeting.

And if Morgan wasn't there, it would still be polite to be able to offer her some praise on her work this evening. Grace made her way into the gallery. It was a standard high street shop space, but decorated with pure white walls. There was a stairwell at the back that seemed to lead up to a second exhibition space. Grace strolled along one wall. She knew about art. Amongst other things, her employer produced an industry magazine aimed at the art world. So she didn't so much know about art, as know about the business of art, but she could throw together an opinion on Nazi art theft, or the prevalence of forgeries in major collections, in a heartbeat. She also knew that if you were trying to shift an Old Master the Saudis and Qataris were the people most likely to stump up top dollar, and the US and European markets had cooled a little on the traditional greats.

None of which, on reflection, was particularly relevant to a contemporary gallery in Shoreditch. It wasn't her sort of place. It was, she suspected, down at heel out of stylistic choice rather than a financial necessity. Grace felt simultaneously far too mundane and strangely overdressed in her yellow Boden coat. On the bright side, the staff were all far too cool to offer anything approaching service. Or perhaps they had simply identified that Grace was not going to make the sort of purchase that would give them a useful commission. Either way they left her free to look around on her own.

The first group of images she came to were cartoon or pop art inspired. Grace peered at the label. Not Morgan's. She moved on, past a sculpture made from mangled metalwork. The next set of paintings were landscapes, slightly more traditional in nature, slightly impressionistic. Still not Morgan's.

Grace moved towards the back of the gallery, as a volley of conversation broke out near the door. She glanced over and saw a tall, slim, fair-haired man being greeted like visiting royalty. She looked again. Shit. What was he doing here? Morgan hadn't invited him to see her work.

At the back of the gallery a short wall created a slightly separate bay. Grace ducked behind the wall out of sight, and moved to inspect the work in the furthest corner. The paintings here were abstract. Discordant colours burst onto the canvas in jarring shapes. Grace checked the label. Morgan Landy.

She took a small step back — far enough to get a new view of the painting, but not so far as to be visible from the rest of the gallery.

'I prefer her less fashionable work.' Grace turned towards the voice. Jon. The fourth member of their group from the Stir-up Sunday. 'So this is Morgan from last week. I should have realised.'

Grace tried to keep her tone casual. 'I thought I'd call in and see. She suggested that I might.'

'Not that you were hoping to run into the artist, at all?'

'Well what about you? She barely even spoke to you, and you're here.'

'I'm working.'

'Your work is wandering round modern art galleries on a Saturday morning.'

'Amongst other things. So what do you think?'

Grace stared at the nearest painting. 'I suppose it's pretty.'

Jon frowned. 'No. It's not. And you're not really looking. What does it make you think of?'

'I'm not sure.'

'All right. How does it make you feel?'

'Angry.'

He smiled ever so slightly. 'Better. One doesn't simply look at art with one's eyes, but with the heart as well. At least that's what I was taught. Now I'm mostly expected to look at the price tag, unfortunately.'

'Mr Rackham?' A young woman in black trousers and black polo neck was hovering a few feet away. 'We've got the work you wanted to see ready. It's upstairs.'

One quick curt nod. 'I'll be there presently.'

The polo neck scurried away.

'Her earlier work is softer, more open somehow. Out of step with the market though. It's a shame.' He looked at Grace. 'Always a shame when things aren't in sync.'

'What does that mean?'

'Well you're here, looking for her, and she's...' He looked around. 'Occupied elsewhere, I presume.'

'I wasn't looking for her.' Grace was not that needy.

He stepped towards her and leaned in. 'Well that is good to know. I shall see you this evening, Miss Price.'

–

Hope pulled her coat closed around her as she walked through the Queen Elizabeth entrance to Hyde Park. There was a new chill in the air, reminding her that Christmas was getting closer, and along with it the end of the Season. Six weeks and eight events seemed like a lot at the beginning but she was already conscious that time was slipping away.

She stopped at the foot of the statue of Achilles and checked her watch. She was early. The stars had aligned. The bus was on time and the journey had taken her a swift forty-three minutes rather than the hour she'd been expecting. So the fact that she'd been waiting ten minutes still didn't mean that he was late. It didn't mean that she'd been stood up. She told herself she wasn't about to be stood up. He'd contacted her. The day after they'd met. If he wasn't keen he simply wouldn't have bothered.

She checked her watch again. Still another six minutes before he was anything less than perfectly punctual.

Then she saw him, ambling through the gate and then jogging towards her. He was good looking. That was clear. He could have stepped off Bondi Beach and straight onto the streets of London. His time in the capital didn't seem to have dulled his natural sun-kissed charm one bit. 'I wasn't sure you'd show up,' he said.

'Why wouldn't I?'

'Oh, I don't know. Guy you've met once texts you the very next day suggesting a date. Thought I might have come on a bit strong.'

Hope stopped and pulled a face of mock indignation. 'This is a date? Well if you'd told me that...' She let her expression soften in the face of his obvious horror. 'I'm joking. I was flattered. I like it when people are direct.' That was too much, wasn't it? She downplayed the moment. 'Easier than second guessing everything.'

If he sensed something deeper behind the comment he didn't push her on it.

'Awesome. So I thought maybe a walk and then a stop for a drink somewhere?'

Hope nodded her agreement. They strolled deeper into the park, covering the standard first date topics. Hope learned that Callum had grown up in a small seaside town called Papamoa on the coast of New Zealand's North Island. It sounded idyllic. And then moved to Sydney when his mum got a job in Australia. His teenage years sounded like an Australian tourist ad cliché of backyard barbecues and weekends at the beach.

'So why did you leave?'

He grinned. 'Oh you know, the grass is always greener.'

'It sounds fairly perfect already.'

'I guess I wanted to travel when I was younger. I'd planned a year out after uni, but by then I was with my ex, and she was super career focused so it never really seemed like the right time.'

'Until...' Hope stopped. The end of that sentence was obviously 'until you broke up', which wasn't great as first date light and breezy chit chat.

'Until she ripped my heart out through my chest and stamped it into the gutter?'

'I wasn't going to put it like that.'

'It's ok. That's what happened. But yeah. Only contact now is when she sends me pictures of the dog. Anyway, within a fortnight I was on a plane.' He looked around. 'Never flown further than back to Christchurch to see my grandparents, and now I'm on the other side of the planet, so I guess all's well that ends well, you know.'

They had walked as far as the edge of the Serpentine, and they continued along the lakeside path.

'How about you?' Callum asked. 'What's your sad singleton story?'

Did Hope have a sad story? Not really. She'd been with someone and now she wasn't. That was all. 'Erm, kinda similar.' She giggled slightly too shrilly. 'I got together with someone at uni. That lasted until a couple of years ago and since then, I'm not sure. Life and work and everything kinda took over. So I wasn't really looking. And then my mother bought the Season thing for me in the summer, but I didn't find anyone so Emma gave me a freebie this time around.' That didn't exactly make her sound like a catch, did it? 'So sorry. You got last Season's rejects. I'm basically the sale rail at this point I think.'

'Then you're an absolute bargain.' He cringed at his own line. 'I'm sorry. That might have been unforgivable.'

Hope smiled. There was something more than a little endearing about Callum's direct approach to dating. 'I think I can forgive it.'

'I'm glad. So...' He gestured towards the building ahead of them at the end of the lake. 'Coffee? I'll buy you a flapjack. Or whatever you want. Or we could walk some more. What do you fancy?'

'I don't mind. Whatever you want to do.'

'I wouldn't mind a hot drink. I'm not really acclimatised to British winters yet.'

Hope let him lead the way into the cafe.

'I might have a hot chocolate. You wanna hot chocolate?'

Hope usually had a mocha, but this was a new start, possibly a… she didn't really dare think it… a new relationship, so why not do something different? 'Hot chocolate sounds great.'

Chapter Eight

You are cordially invited to a

St Nicholas Night ball.

Black tie.

'I don't know what black tie means,' Connie moaned.

Grace read from her phone screen, where she had saved the tab with all the relevant information from her extensive google planning session. 'For women black tie ideally means a longer dress, although on-the-knee or mid-calf lengths are increasingly acceptable. It doesn't need to be a full ball gown, but nothing too short or too revealing. In more contemporary settings a well-cut tailored trouser might pass muster, but do make sure you dress the look up with appropriate accessories and jewellery. Elegance is the order of the day, or rather, the evening!'

'I don't think I'm built elegant,' Connie complained, which was silly because she was built from the same stuff as Grace. Connie picked up a long black skirt from the floor. 'Will this do?'

'Not on its own. What do you normally wear with it?'

Connie shrugged. 'Like a T-shirt or something.'

'You can't wear a T-shirt to a black-tie ball.'

Grace unfolded herself from her seat on her sister's bed. 'Wait here.' It was typical Connie not to have her outfit ready, and to, apparently, not even have glanced at the dress code until an hour before the event. Grace, as always, would have to sort it out. She knocked on the door to Hope's bedroom.

'Yeah?'

Hope was standing in her bathrobe in front of the mirror door on her wardrobe, putting mascara on.

'Can I borrow your purple dress for Connie?'

'I wore it last week. It hasn't been in the wash yet.' Hope gestured towards the dress lying over the back of the chair next to her bed. 'I only wore it for a couple of hours though.'

'She'll be fine with that.' She'd have to be, and Connie only did her own laundry when there were no more pants to try. Grace grabbed the dress off the chair. 'Oh, and can I borrow your curling tongs?'

'On the dressing table.'

There wasn't anything else she needed from Hope right now. Grace carried her loot back to Connie's room. 'Right. Try this.'

The dress was long and form-fitting in a stretch fabric. The purple was close enough, Grace hoped, to Connie's preferred colour palette of black and used-to-be-black-before-I-washed-it, to not make her run a mile. The black and purple hair and the tattoos down both arms didn't scream 'elegant ball' and the dress was really more summer beach cover-up than evening gown, but it was full-length so technically the dress code was being adhered to. Connie pulled it on. As Grace had expected, the colour suited her. 'You look lovely.'

Her sister pulled a face.

'Fine.' Grace wondered if she could retract the compliment. 'You'll need shoes and make-up. And a bag.'

'Like a rucksack?'

Grace gave her sister another very hard look. 'Hope's got a black clutch. Go ask her if you can borrow it.'

Grace's own dress for the evening was dark blue satin with a wide circle skirt and slinky satin bodice with lace-thin spaghetti straps. Simple, stylish but a little bit sexy. Grace had done her preparation. She curled her hair, sprayed and shook down the curls.

She met Hope at the top of the stairs. She'd gone for a black lace high-necked dress that Grace had seen before. It suited Hope.

It was entirely demure, but the lace gave the impression of being something else entirely. It could be whatever the viewer decided it was. 'You look nice.'

Hope held up the small gold shoulder bag she was holding. 'Does this go? I lent Connie my black one.'

'It looks fine.' The black would have looked better, but Grace preferred to have two housemates who look acceptable than one who was on point and one who was sulking in her room and refusing to come out to play.

Hope's phone buzzed. 'Theo and the taxi are five minutes away,' she reported.

'Connie! Nearly time to go!'

Grace's sister trooped into the hallway. Along with Hope's clutch bag she'd added a pair of her own black boots, which had a tiny heel and a hint of Victoriana about them. Grace recognised them as Connie's most sensible shoes. She'd piled her hair on top of her head in a swirling black and purple bun. The overall effect was kind of cool. 'You do look great.'

'I feel stupid.'

Connie was simply her own worst enemy.

–

Hope tried to screen out the twins' bickering on the taxi ride to the party. Normally she could rely on Theo to change the subject and distract them from whatever fight they were having, but tonight he was being monosyllabic to the point of rudeness. 'What's up with you?'

'Nothing.'

Right. 'Are you looking forward to the ball?'

Theo shrugged.

'Well I am,' she told him.

He gave her a half-smile. 'Good for you. Date went well then?'

'Early days.'

'But you're not hiding in your room crying rather than coming out and seeing him again?'

Hope grinned. 'I am not.'

They walked in to the ballroom, which was decorated traditionally for Christmas, with one of the biggest Christmas trees Hope had ever seen right at the centre of the dance floor and garlands of holly and pine around the walls. Hope loved Christmas. No. Hope loved the idea of Christmas. She loved all this. The decorations and the celebrations and the anticipation. Actual Christmas was coloured by guilt towards whichever parent she felt she was abandoning each year, but this fantasy of Christmas that the Season was creating was beautiful.

And heading towards her, the moment she stepped through the door, was Callum. He was chatting to a tall dark-haired woman, but he broke away as soon as Hope came into his eyeline. That was nice. That would give anyone a little fillip of confidence. 'You look incredible.'

Good opener. Hope smiled. 'You don't look so bad yourself.' It was true. Callum scrubbed up impressively. He'd gone for a classic tuxedo but replaced the traditional bow tie with a thin black necktie. His floppy blond hair was gelled back from his face and the whole effect was a pleasing mash-up of James Bond meets surfer dude.

'Thank you. Borrowed this from my flatmate.'

'He goes to a lot of formal balls?'

'No. He moonlights as a doorman. I'm doing him out of a night's work by nicking the suit tonight.' Callum pulled a face. 'I did get it cleaned. Bouncer suits get a lot of...' He hesitated. 'Let's say fluids, on them.'

'Ew.'

'All clean now though.'

'I'm glad.'

'So, do you want a drink, or would you like to dance?' He paused. 'I mean assuming you wanna...' He pointed from her to himself. 'If you want to mingle, I get it.'

'Do you want to mingle?' The earth beneath Hope shifted slightly.

'Hell no. I want to spend the whole night with you.'

Straight to the point again. 'Ok.'

'So drinks or dancing first?'

The band was playing 'Have Yourself a Merry Little Christmas'. 'I don't mind. What do you think?'

'We could dance.'

'Ok.' She let him take her hand and lead her to the dance floor. The room was beautiful. Her dance partner was handsome. The music was charming. Hope even thought that she looked, in the grand scheme of things, better than ok. All was well. This was what she'd been hoping would happen right through the first Season. She wanted things to fall into place and feel easy.

'Sorry I'm not much of a dancer,' Callum whispered in her ear.

'That's ok. I think so long as we keep moving and don't fall over it's all good.'

He laughed. 'I can probably manage that.'

His hand was warm in the small of her back, his breath was soft against her neck, and as the tempo of the music changed she let him pull her a little closer. This was all exactly as it should be. The mood, the music, the man – all of them were just right.

She felt his body shift as he pulled slightly away from her. Hope looked up and into his face. He was going to kiss her. And why wouldn't he? It was a perfect moment, after all. Hope tilted her head and met his lips with her own.

–

Connie clung to her safe position next to the entrance, against the wall, as far from the dance floor as it was possible to be while still technically being considered an attendee at the ball. She couldn't face explaining to Grace why she wasn't coming, but she also very much didn't want to be here, so her plan was simple. One drink. Two at the absolute most. Stay in the corner, not talk to anyone, and then feign a headache and get Hope or Theo to tell Grace she'd gone home early feeling ill.

That didn't resolve the issue of Morgan and Grace inevitably falling head over heels in love and Connie having to move to Panama to avoid the horrendousness at family events. But that was a problem for another day. Right now, all she needed to do was keep her head down and get out of here as soon as she plausibly could.

'Hi.'

Of course the problem with her corner was that, although she'd hoped nobody could see her, it was also entirely useless as a vantage point to see who was heading towards her. Which meant she was blindsided by the one person she most definitely did not want to run into. Despite herself, Connie actually looked around in the hope of finding a hidden door, or unexpected teleportation device, that she could use as a means of escape.

'Hi!'

Right. Yes. She hadn't actually replied yet, had she?

'You know I can see you?'

'Yeah,' Connie nodded. 'Hi.'

Morgan smiled. 'Good. So I wanted to… you know, say hi.'

'Hi.'

'Hi,' Morgan repeated.

'Right. Well hi then.' This was horrible, and there was no obvious way of making it stop.

'I guess I just wanted to check you were ok. You ran out like you'd been shot this morning.'

'I'm fine.'

'Ok.' Morgan fell silent. 'Cos it seemed like you were upset.'

'I'm fine.'

'Right. So, do you want to dance or something?'

Connie did not dance. Connie was not a dancer. Connie didn't have whatever magic superpower it was that meant she could step onto a dance floor and move her limbs in time to music without looking like an idiot. And in a room like this that was magnified a thousand times. She was surrounded by elegant, confident people who were fully at ease. 'No. Thank you.'

'Right. Ok then. I hear you.' Morgan turned and walked away.

Connie stuck out her chin. That could have been worse. At least she hadn't made herself look even more of a fool, and that was all she could hope for now – to retain whatever shred of cool she was still clinging on to. Time to feign her headache.

She looked around for Hope or Theo. If she told one of them she was going, then she wouldn't have to face Grace, but could still avoid the row about how she'd snuck out without telling anybody and made them all worry. Hope was playing tonsil hockey with a blond guy in the middle of the dance floor, so probably wouldn't thank her housemate for the interruption. And she couldn't see Theo anywhere.

Sod it. She could text Grace once she was on the bus. Connie hurried out of the ballroom and out to the grand staircase that led down to the entrance way. Theo, it turned out, was not so hard to find after all. He was standing a few feet outside the door, staring back into the ballroom. Connie turned and followed his gaze. Well, obviously. 'When are you going to tell her?'

'Tell who what?'

Connie looked pointedly from Theo towards the clinch Hope was embraced in. 'Who do you think?'

'I have no idea what you mean.'

'Bollocks.'

'And I'm taking romance advice from a woman running away from a singles ball now, am I?'

'Fair point.'

'You are running away though?' Theo checked.

Connie nodded.

'Good call. I'll walk you to the bus stop.'

'I don't need you to.'

He folded his arms. 'Look. I don't know why you're running out early, but I'm guessing whatever the real reason is, your sister is going to get told you weren't feeling well or something?'

'Maybe.'

'Well then, if you're ill I should definitely at least walk you to the bus stop.' He glanced back towards the ballroom. 'Two birds, one stone.'

She followed Theo down the stairs. 'Grace told me what happened that night.'

'What night?'

'*That* night,' she emphasised. 'You and Grace.'

In front of her Theo shook his head. 'No comment,' he replied.

–

Grace probably ought to go and drag Connie back. She'd seen her, of course, sneaking out, and no doubt there'd be a message shortly saying that Connie felt sick or had a headache or some other entirely made-up ailment that Connie would expect her to believe. As if Grace wasn't always aware of what was happening with her sister, and hadn't watched the conversation with Morgan. She had no idea what had been said but it looked awkward and moments later, Connie had done her customary disappearing act.

She caught sight of Morgan at the bar and marched over. 'Where do you get off?'

'I'm sorry?'

'Where do you get off upsetting my sister?' That's my job, Grace added silently to herself.

'I didn't upset her. In fact she made it perfectly clear that she isn't the least bit interested in anything to do with me.' Morgan's reply was quiet, almost under her breath, like she was holding whatever she might be feeling far away from the surface.

That was not the point at all. Whether Connie was interested or not, Morgan had no right to upset her. Grace was the responsible one. Connie was the one that Grace was responsible for.

'Look, I don't want to fight with you over this…' Morgan started.

Grace paused. On the one hand neither did she, but on the other, 'Well don't mess with my sister then.'

Morgan moved away. That wasn't what Grace wanted either. She went to follow.

'Let her go.'

The hand on her stomach pulled Grace to a stop. Him. Again. 'Will you stop telling me what to do?'

'I will when you stop doing stupid things.'

'I wasn't doing...' What was she doing, actually? Going after Morgan to defend Connie or because she was still interested for herself? In this moment, she wasn't sure. 'It's none of your business if I was.'

'Ok.' He stepped back. 'Off you go. Make a fool of yourself.'

Morgan had disappeared from view. 'Well it's too late now.'

Grace tried to take another swig of her drink. It was empty. That was no good. 'I don't do stupid things anyway,' she told the interfering Mr... 'What's your name again?'

'Jon.'

'Jon what?'

'Rackham.'

That was right. That was what the simpering girl at the gallery had called him. The Interfering Mr Rackham. 'Well I don't do stupid things. I'm always very, very sensible.' She let him press a fresh glass into her hand. 'Everybody says so.' She took a sip. 'Are you trying to get me drunk?'

'Absolutely.'

So that was his game. 'I'm not going to sleep with you.'

'Well, you don't have to decide right now.'

'Nope. I don't fancy you.'

'That is disappointing news.'

Grace looked at him properly. Tall, slim, fair-haired, impeccably dressed in a tuxedo that Grace would bet good money wasn't rented for the evening. Older though. She didn't do older. 'I don't do older men,' she told him. 'Or women.'

'I'm not that much older.'

He might be telling the truth. He had smooth skin, even on the backs of his hands and his neck, which were usually a total giveaway.

'How old are you?' he asked.

'Twenty-seven.'

He smiled. 'So I'm a little older.'

'How much older?'

'Ten years. Give or take.'

So fifteen, Grace assumed. 'It's never gonna happen.'

He held his hands up in defeat. 'Very well.' He looked towards an empty table beyond the bar area, with two high stools. 'Why don't you sit down for a minute and tell me why you're so worked up?'

'I'm not worked up.'

'Then tell me why I might have misconstrued your calm for something else?'

Grace marched over to the table. As she wriggled her way onto a stool the wide circle skirt she was wearing sent the fabric puffing up in front of her. She smoothed it down. 'There's absolutely nothing to tell. I'm perfectly calm.'

'So why were you having such a contretemps with that perfectly nice lady?'

'She upset my sister.'

'I see. It was a twin loyalty thing? I understand that.'

'Really?' Grace didn't believe a word of it. She knew men like Jon. She saw them all day every day at work in their perfect suits with their expensively trimmed hair and subtle aftershave. She'd even been out with a couple of them. Loyalty hadn't been high on either of their agendas.

'Indeed.'

'The thing is, you see, Connie has like always done her own thing, which is fine and that, but it means everyone thinks she's the tough one.' Grace shook her head. She may even have jabbed at his chest to emphasise her definitely very good point. 'I'm the tough one.'

'I can believe that.'

'So I have to look out for her, don't I?' She watched Jon scan the room.

'So where is your wayward twin now?'

'She's gone home.'

'So maybe you could take the rest of the night off?' he suggested. 'I mean presumably you signed up for this because you were hoping to find your "perfect partner" as well?'

'Why'd you say it like that?'

'Like what?'

Grace mimicked his sarcastic tone. 'Perfect partner. Like you think it's stupid.'

'Not stupid. Perhaps a little naive.'

That didn't make sense. 'No. Because if you thought that...' Another chest jab for emphasis. Nice firm chest actually. '...you wouldn't be here, would you?'

'I am not here by choice.'

'Nope. You're a big fancy man. I don't think you'd let anyone tell you what to do.' Grace giggled. Of course – everybody had someone who could tell them what to do. 'Did your mum make you come?'

'No. My mother has no idea this is happening and she will never ever find out.'

She gave up. 'I don't get you.'

'Good. I am very happy to remain an enigma.' He smiled, a small tight smile that didn't actually make him look any happier.

Grace took another big gulp of her champagne and looked around. Jon was right. Connie was probably halfway to being safely tucked up in bed by now, and Morgan was nowhere to be seen. Maybe Grace really could be off the clock for a little while. No work in the morning. No plans until lunchtime, and she didn't even have to cook. It was their dad's birthday the following week so they were having one of their rare trips to the pub for Sunday lunch. For the next – she checked the time – fourteen hours she really could do whatever she liked. She didn't have to be responsible for anyone.

Grace could do whatever she wanted.

'What's that expression?' Jon was staring at her.

'What do you mean?'

'You looked, I'm not sure, a little lost maybe.'

Nobody had ever described Grace that way before. 'Don't be stupid.'

'I endeavour not to be.'

'I was just thinking about what to do.'

'When?'

'Right now.'

He moved ever so slightly closer to her. 'Well what do you want to do?'

She lunged, without thinking, pressing her lips onto Jon's before her brain had the chance to walk her through all the reasons this was a terrible idea. He stepped back. 'What are you doing?'

'Something stupid.'

'And you're sure you want to?'

'Yeah.' No. Obviously no, but she'd come this far, and the drink and the pure unexpected sexual need weren't going to let her stop now. 'Your place or mine?'

'I'm assuming your place is a horrid little shared house with damp on the ceiling.'

'So?'

'So my place.' He took her hand and led the dash to the lift, tapping his mobile screen quickly with the other hand. As soon as the doors were closed she pushed him back against the wall of the elevator and pressed her lips to his again. He responded hungrily, wrapping his arms around her waist and lifting her off her feet. The doors pinged open. He lowered her to the ground but kept his arm tight around Grace's body, stopping her from jumping away from him in case somebody saw.

'Tube or Uber?' Grace asked as they made their way out onto the street.

He scanned the road, presumably looking for a cab. Which was fine, so long as he didn't think Grace was paying for half of it.

A long black saloon car pulled up in front of them. Jon opened the back door. 'Get in.'

'What the fuck? I'm not getting in some sketchy car with you.'

Jon raised a perfectly sculpted eyebrow. 'Please don't refer to my driver as sketchy. He could take offence. Carl, can you reassure Miss Price that you're not going to dump her body in the Thames?'

''Course not,' the driver turned in his seat and addressed Grace through the open door. 'Thames is tidal, innit. You never know where someone'll wash up.'

'Not quite what I was hoping for, Carl.'

'Fine.' The driver hopped out of the car and walked round to hand Grace a card. *WhiteList Chauffeur Services*.

'You have a chauffeur?'

'Well I have a chauffeur service. So much more reliable than cabs, and I get work done on the ride, don't have to worry about parking.' He smiled. That wolfish edge had returned. 'Shall we?'

Grace jumped in. It was too late to try to look cool, as though she rode in chauffeur-driven cars all the time. She let her fingers spread over the soft dark grey leather of the seat. 'Nice.'

'Carl, close the screen, would you?'

'Of course, Mr Rackham.'

The tinted screen between the front of the car and the back-seat passengers slid closed. For a second the silence crackled between them. Jon didn't move. Grace cracked first, turning her head towards him and sliding along the seat to kiss him some more. He was an incredible kisser. Grace twisted her body and swung her leg over so she was straddling his thighs. She could feel his erection pressing into her leg. His hands moved behind her, easing the zip on the back of her dress down and then unhooking the clasp on her strapless bra. He slid the straps off her shoulders, letting her dress fall down, before pressing his palm to her breast, squeezing gently before moving to rub her nipple with the pad of his thumb. Grace gasped.

'The driver?' she whispered.

'Not really planning on inviting him.'

'Won't he see?'

'No.' Jon shifted slightly so she could see his face in the glow from the street lights as they drove. 'It's private. I promise.' He covered her breast with his hand. 'But we can stop until we get to my apartment, if you want.'

That would definitely be the sensible choice. Grace shook her head. His face dipped to her chest and she felt his lips close around her nipple. She gasped and her head flung back as his hand, freed from her chest, slid up her thigh, pushing the soft satin of her skirt up her leg to grip her arse.

How far was she prepared to go in the back of this car, with the driver just the other side of that flimsy screen? Jon's hand moved from her behind, and inched up her leg, thumb brushing the inside of her thigh. She should stop things before they went any further, before his hand moved any closer to...

'We're here.'

She realised, in a rush of disappointment, that the car was no longer moving.

'Shit. Sorry.'

Jon moved his head so he was looking straight into her face. 'No. I should have told him to drive around the block.'

He wriggled slightly beneath her.

'Right. Yes.' Grace shifted back onto the seat and tried to re-dress herself as quickly and as elegantly as possible. As soon as she was decent Jon opened his door, and a fraction of a second later, Grace's side door was swung open by the unseen hand of the chauffeur.

'Enjoy the rest of your evening, sir. Miss.'

Grace followed Jon towards the rather grand building in front of them. At the lift he stopped and took her hand, before tapping a code onto the console. The lift doors opened and they stepped in. Grace looked around.

'There aren't any buttons.'

'You programme the floor with the code outside. So only I can get up to the top floor. Well, and the cleaner. And the concierge service. And the chef, if I eat here.'

A chef? It didn't matter. Grace wasn't moving in with the guy. This was strictly a one-nighter. She wasn't interested in his cooking skills.

The lift doors slid opened straight onto the apartment. It was five-star hotel levels of tasteful – the sort of décor that didn't scream wealth, because that would be unspeakably vulgar, but rather whispered its luxury with a quiet reserve. Grace dragged Jon by the hand. 'Bedroom?' she demanded.

'Left and to the end of the corridor.'

He followed her silently down the corridor and let her pull him over to the bed. As soon their lips touched, everything became urgent all over again. Hands pulling at clothes, fumbling with belts and buttons and zippers, grabbing a condom from the night-stand drawer until finally Grace was able to sink down onto him, his hands gripping her hips. She screwed her eyes tight shut and moved against him harder and faster, searching for that last wave of pleasure to send her over the edge. And then it came and she soared just for a moment before floating back to herself.

Grace opened her eyes. Jon was watching her intently. She must look a sight. She could feel the sheen of sweat on her skin, and her face was probably the colour of beetroot. She manoeuvred her way off him and under a sheet as rapidly as she could, while he disappeared to the bathroom. By the time he came back she had the sheet neatly pulled up to her chest, and had run her fingers through her hair as well as she could manage. The colour of her face she could do nothing about without make-up.

'You don't need to cover up.'

Grace kept her sheet firmly in place.

'Up to you though.' He wandered, still completely naked, over to the window. Grace's horror deepened. Jon glanced back at her. 'Tinted glass. And we're on the top floor. The only people who are going to see up here are birds.'

'I should go.'

'You don't have to.' He slid into bed beside her. 'Sunday tomorrow. I presume that means no work.'

'Still.' Grace looked around. This was madness. She wasn't a naked in a penthouse sort of girl. She wasn't a naked sort of girl at all, generally speaking. Not until at least date four. And then she tended towards lights out and everyone's eyes firmly closed. None of this was her. 'I've got things to do in the morning.'

His finger traced a line up the outside of her thigh to her hip.

'I really have to go.'

He lifted his hand. 'And I'm not keeping you here.'

Grace scooched to the edge of the bed, holding the sheet around her as best she could. Her knickers were just out of reach on the floor. If she slid her bum to the very edge of the bed and stretched out her leg she could almost hook them with her big toe, and then it was just a question of bending at the knee and lifting her foot to her hand and knickers secured. She wriggled her way into her underwear and looked around for her bra.

It had come off in the car, but she'd put it back on for the walk inside. She thought back. She hadn't taken anything else off before she got to the bedroom, had she? She didn't think so, which meant that her bra must be… she traced the line from where her knickers had landed back to the door. No bra. She could see the edge of her dress where it was lying on the other side of the bed. So if her dress was over there, maybe her bra was… The mattress shifted beneath her as Jon jumped out of bed for the second time.

A moment later her bra was dangling in front of her from a long slim finger. 'I'm very tempted to chuck this across the room, just so I can see what level of acrobatics you're prepared to attempt to try and retrieve it without me seeing anything.' He stepped towards her, still holding her bra just inches out of reach. 'All of which I have already seen.'

'That was different.'

'How?'

It was objectively tricky to come up with a non-insane answer to that. It was different because so long as she got her kit back on right now and got out of here Grace could tell herself the whole thing was a one-off momentary aberration. 'Just give me my clothes.'

He handed her bra over, and stretched over the far side of the bed to pick up her dress. Grace clipped her bra on while he was looking the other way.

'I think your shoes must be in the hallway.'

'Thank you.' She had no choice but to stand up to put her dress on, but that was fine. Bra and knickers. She'd wear smaller bikinis on the beach. Well she wouldn't. But people did. She was twisting to reach the back zip when she felt his hand move hers out of the way and slowly pull the zip the full length of her back. She told herself his fingers hadn't lingered at all on the skin between her shoulder blades.

'Thank you. Again.' Grace stood. Jon was still sitting, naked and apparently entirely unconcerned by that fact, on the bed.

'Shall I call Carl to take you home?'

'It's fine. I can get the bus or...'

'Grace!'

'What?'

'Do you know where you are?'

She marched to the window. She'd lived in this city her whole life. They were high up, so not Westminster, but the view was strange. The only obvious landmarks were the river itself and the distinctive white dome of the O2. Normally she could anchor herself by finding St Paul's and Canary Wharf. Hold on. Where could you definitely not see Canary Wharf from? 'Somewhere round Canary Wharf.'

'Very impressive.'

'So I'll be fine.' She checked the time. Ten to one. Jubilee line and overground would still be running.

'I have no doubt of it, but Carl will have you home much quicker and much more comfortably. And it would put my mind at rest.'

Don't look a gift horse in the mouth Grace, she told herself. 'Well thank you.'

Jon tapped his phone screen. 'You don't even have to tell me where home is if you don't want to. Tell Carl and then tell him to forget where he dropped you. The car will be outside in five minutes.' Jon hopped off the bed and pulled his dress trousers and shirt back on. 'Let me walk you down.'

'You don't have to.'

'I know.'

The ride down in the lift must have taken at least ten times longer than the ride up. The ride up had passed in a blur. Every second of the journey down seemed to extend into an unfillable silence. Grace stared straight ahead for as long as she could before the urge to sneak a glance at Jon overtook her. He was maintaining the straight-ahead gaze rather better than her. Grace took the moment to look at him properly. There was something austere about him now, a coolness that seemed to hold him slightly separate from the world around him. 'This isn't going to happen again,' she told him.

'Really?' He didn't turn his head towards her.

'Really. It was a one-off. I don't do things like this.'

Now he turned to look at her. 'Although apparently you do.'

'No. Not normally. It's bad enough that I'm a notch on your bedpost. I'm not going to be making a habit of it.'

Jon pulled a face. 'You seem to be assuming that I do do things like this.'

Well obviously he did. Grace had very much been there while he was doing them.

The lift doors slid open and they stepped into the cool empty lobby.

'Well thank you for a lovely evening.'

There was a hint of a laugh in his gaze. 'Lovely?'

It wasn't the right word. Obviously. 'Well you know.'

'Off you go then.'

Grace hadn't left.

His fingers closed around her wrist and her body moved, of its own volition it seemed, to press against his. He bent his lips towards hers, and Grace felt herself lift her face to meet him. He stopped, millimetres, moments, short of exploding her world open with another intoxicating kiss. 'Goodnight Grace.'

He stepped back, his hand released her, and he strode back to the elevator. Grace stood completely still and completely alone. The moment should have passed the second he stepped away. The bubble should have popped. Instead it felt as though there was a tie between them that was pulling tauter and tauter until eventually it would snap her back into his orbit.

But no. This whole night had been a terrible, drunken mistake. She would go home. She would deal with the hangover that would inevitably take over her morning, and she would never think about Jon Rackham again.

Chapter Nine

It was nearly one a.m. when Emma and Annie collected their coats and headed out to meet Josh, who was bringing the car round from the tiny staff parking area at the back of the building. Emma checked her phone. No messages.

'Emma!'

Annie was clearly trying to ask her a question. 'Sorry. Miles away.'

'Yeah. I noticed. Were you happy with how it went tonight?'

'Mmmm,' Emma nodded.

'I thought the sugar plum fairy getting it on with the juggler was a surprise,' Annie added.

'Yeah…' Emma's brain finally caught up. 'What?'

'Just checking if you were paying attention.'

'Of course I am. And anyway, the ginger chap who looks a bit like Prince Harry is a juggler so…'

'Right.' Her sister-in-law looked sceptical. 'What do you make of the twins?'

Emma dragged her wandering attention back to the evening's ball. She'd seen both the Price sisters in conversation with Morgan Landy, who was, by Emma's estimation, one of the catches of the whole Season. Clever, creative, funny, pretty and ready for a relationship. But Morgan ended the evening dancing with what seemed like a revolving door of suitors. 'Connie, the one with purple hair, hardly put anything down on her profile.' Emma thought about that. 'I'm not sure if that's because she's here under duress, or if she doesn't like to share.' She considered her sister-in-law. 'Maybe at the next event you could make them your special project?'

'What do you mean?'

'See if you can get to know a bit more about Connie.' Emma paused. On the surface Grace was easier to match. She was more polished, certainly, but there was something – a brittleness to her sheen of confidence. 'About both of them actually,' she added. 'I'm not quite sure who they're supposed to be with at all.'

'I'll do my best sleuthing,' giggled Annie.

'Annie Keer undercover,' joked Emma.

'Actually it's Annie Love now.'

Of course. Why hadn't Emma registered that? 'Josh never said whether you were changing your name.'

'I know it's a bit old-fashioned but we got married so quickly it sort of felt like it solidified it, if you know what I mean.' She grinned. 'And it is such a cool name. You don't mind me being Ms Love as well, do you?'

'Not Mrs?'

'Well, it was either share a name with you or with your mum, and I really like your mum. I do. It's just…'

'She's terrifying,' Emma helped her out.

'Absolutely terrifying. I couldn't cope with picturing her every time one of the kids called out my name.'

'I'm delighted for you to be the newest Love.' Emma checked herself. She really was delighted. She put an arm out and squeezed her sister-in-law around the shoulders. 'Like you're properly part of the family.'

'Brilliant.' Annie beamed. 'Where on earth is Josh? It's freezing out here.'

Emma checked her phone again. No message from Josh. Or anyone else.

'Tom hasn't called then?'

'That wasn't why I was looking.'

'Sure. And that's not why you've been looking all week?'

'Have I been that bad?'

Annie pulled a face. 'Well you haven't been quite at the top of your game.'

It was ridiculous. One falling-out with a chap and she fell to pieces. 'I haven't heard from him since he walked out on Monday.'

'And have you called him?'

Emma stared at her feet. 'No.' She didn't need to look up to know what look Annie was giving her. 'Do you think I should?'

'Well it might be more effective than staring at your phone and willing it to ring.'

—

Emma stuck with the staring at her phone and willing it to ring plan all the way home in the car. If she called him, what would she even say? She was sorry. Was she sorry? She wasn't sorry for loving her work, and he'd known that about her when he signed up. It was possible that trying to combine a date with a Season planning meeting wasn't entirely romantic, but it was how relationships worked, wasn't it? Look at how easily Annie had slotted into the family team.

It was nearly two a.m. by the time she was alone in her room. If Tom had been playing at the Vic there was every chance he'd still be up. He might even still be playing. No reason not to call him right now. Emma's finger hovered over the call button.

Maybe it was too late? He was already pissed off with her, without her waking him up.

She flipped her laptop open on her knee and clicked onto her favourite online poker site instead. She'd met Tom online playing poker and chatted to him for weeks before realising that her online crush and her real-life nemesis were one and the same person. She told herself that she wasn't logging on in the hope that he'd be online, because he wouldn't be. He was playing at the casino tonight. He'd hardly come home and log straight on to play online, would he?

She clicked through to the private table Tom usually played at, telling herself it was just out of habit. The second she clicked to join the table the message popped up.

Hi Queenie.

He was there. Emma's stomach leapt. What was she supposed to say? What should she have said any one of the hundred times she'd decided to call him during the week and then wimped out at the final moment?

I kept nearly calling you this week. Tom's message appeared before Emma had decided what to say. That made things easier.

Same, she replied.

What would you have said?

Damn him. Emma should have asked first. The ball was definitely in her court now. What would she have said? It was complicated, but at the same time very simple indeed. *Sorry*, she typed.

The chat box was silent for a moment, before Tom's reply came though. *Same.*

Emma felt herself release the breath she hadn't realised she was holding. Tom was still typing. *I know how important the business is to you. I know you're busy. I was being a dick.*

No, you weren't... She typed and deleted and typed again. *You were just...* Delete. Still not right. It wasn't him she wanted to say something about. *I don't think I'm a very good girlfriend.* She hit enter before she could take it back and waited for a reply.

You're great. I think we're both a bit out of practice.

That was probably fair. *So what now then?*

Come round here. During the week? We probably need to talk.

Yeah. They probably did. They set a date and played a couple of hands of poker without chatting much more. Tom won, which definitely implied that Emma was off her game, and then he logged off while he was still ahead, which suggested he wasn't feeling entirely himself either.

Emma checked her email. One new message to her business address. She scanned the subject and the first two lines. *Exciting opportunity... once in a lifetime... New York.* Ugh. Spam. Emma hit delete.

Chapter Ten

It wasn't that Grace didn't sleep. It was that she never slept so deeply that she wouldn't be woken up by the slightest noise. If someone else in the house was awake, then so was Grace. This morning Grace could hear Hope moving around downstairs. Normally that set Sunday off on a positive note, at least. Hope being up and about often meant croissants or scrambled eggs or some other sort of goody would be waiting for Grace in the kitchen when she got up, along with a bunch of fresh flowers beautifully arranged on the kitchen table.

They hadn't known they were getting a live-in domestic goddess when Hope moved in to the third bedroom, but Hope diligently cooked and cleaned and generally sorted out the house. It would have been churlish to be annoyed by that, so Grace had decided that she wasn't. She was used to being the person who took care of things, but that didn't mean she always needed to do it.

But today she wished her perfectly perky cousin had decided to take a morning off. Today Grace wanted quiet and solitude and for the feeling that something was hammering on her actual brain to go away. There was a sharp knock on her bedroom door.

'I'm putting a dark load on. Shall I put your stuff in too?'

'No thank you.'

'I don't mind. It'll save you doing it.'

'No.' Grace didn't mean to shout. She took a deep breath in and forced herself to moderate her tone. 'No thank you. It's fine.'

She heard Hope move away. Grace checked the time on her phone. Half past ten. She'd been in bed nine hours but hadn't slept more than one. Every time she closed her eyes her mind bombarded her with the feeling of Jon Rackham's lips on her breasts, his fingers digging into her skin, him deep inside her.

Grace sat up in bed and pulled her knees up to her chest under the duvet. Grace knew what she wanted in life. She wanted a good job where she knew she was indispensable. She wanted to be able to watch out for her dad and for Connie. And yeah, she did want a relationship, but not a relationship with a man like Jon. Grace wanted someone warm and nurturing. Someone who would be a good parent. Someone who would fit into her life. Jon was none of those things. Jon was cool and stiff – all hard edges and silent secrets.

Last night had been an aberration. She'd clearly drunk more than she'd intended. Those silent white-shirted waiters constantly filling your glass were a danger. It shouldn't be allowed. It was their fault that the whole... her mind struggled to find the right term... the whole *incident* had occurred.

Grace still had her eyes screwed tight closed. Maybe she could go back to sleep. Maybe if she lay really really still the day wouldn't happen at all and she could drift away into sleep, and then sleep and sleep and sleep until it felt like last night was nothing more than a slightly unnerving, inappropriate dream. Like the time she'd had a kinky dream about their old next-door neighbour and not been able to look him in the eye for the next six months.

She was woken by another sharp knock at the door, but this knocker didn't wait for a reply before wandering in. 'What you doing still in bed?' Connie opened Grace's curtains, and tugged at the corner of the duvet. No use. Grace had that bad boy properly secured under her leg. 'Are you ill or something?'

Grace did not get ill. 'I'm fine,' she muttered.

'Good. Then get the fuck up. We're due at lunch in less than an hour.'

That couldn't be right. 'It's only half ten.'

'It's quarter past twelve.' How? Grace must have gone back to sleep at some point. 'And it'll take us twenty minutes to get there if we're lucky. You told me that.'

That was true. Grace had been very clear about how they needed to go out at twelve thirty so they wouldn't be late. 'I must have overslept.'

'Ya think?'

Grace rubbed her eyes and tried to focus on her sister. Connie was already dressed. If Grace wasn't mistaken she'd even brushed her hair. 'You look nice.'

'Well it's his birthday, innit? Thought I'd make an effort. Unlike some people.'

Right. Grace needed to get her act together. The inside of her mouth tasted like death. She reached her hand to her head. As she feared her hair had formed an unkempt ball on top of her skull. And she must, somehow, reek of sex. 'I need a shower.'

'Well you've got fifteen minutes, if we're sticking to your schedule.'

Seventeen minutes later Grace was showered and dressed, with her unwashed hair scraped back into a clip as best she could. She still looked a mess, but at least she no longer smelled a mess.

She slumped into the seat next to her sister on the bus. Connie was staring out of the window. 'So what happened to you last night?'

'Nothing.' Grace snapped her reply.

Her sister turned towards her. 'Yeah. Right.'

'I went to the ball, had a nice time, came home.' *Had a nice time* was covering an awful lot of territory in that sentence.

'No prizes for guessing who you had a nice time with.'

'I don't know what you mean.' For the first time in the conversation Grace was being genuine. She hadn't said or done anything in front of Connie that would give the slightest impression she was interested in Jon, had she? Because she wasn't interested in Jon. Obviously. He was an aberration.

Connie took a deep breath in. 'Look. I'm saying it's fine. I might have liked her to start with but she's clearly more into you and that's fine. Go for it. It's cool.'

'What?'

'You are really not with it this morning, are you?'

'Sorry. Must have drunk more than I thought.'

'I'm just saying, with Morgan, it's fine. I wasn't that into her.'

Morgan. Right. Of course. She was what Grace wanted, wasn't she? Pretty. Together. Direct. It wasn't that simple though. 'I thought you liked her?'

'Nah. You know, I don't think I'm really up for finding the one.' Connie didn't meet her eye. 'Not really me is it? Long-term commitment?'

They arrived at the pub five minutes early, despite Grace's tardiness getting out of bed. That was testament to the value of setting a schedule which allowed time for things to go slightly wrong. She told the barman they had a table booked for Price and followed a waitress through into the restaurant area. The table was set for four. 'Oh, there's only three of us.'

The girl frowned. 'Four.'

'No. One, two...' Grace pointed from herself to her sister. 'And our dad. That's all of us.'

'Fella phoned this morning. Was booked for three, but could he change it to four?'

Grace gave up arguing. They were almost certainly sat at some other family's table but that would become clear when they turned up and then she could try to explain again to the dim-witted waitress child.

'Girls!'

Grace stood and hugged her dad. 'They seem to think there's four of us. I tried to explain.'

'Ah, yes. Well that will be because there are four of us.' He paused. 'I wanted to do this with both of you here and I thought, well, why not today? Best not to put these things off.'

'Put what off?'

'Well love, you know that I loved your mother very much, don't you?'

'Of course. We know you miss her,' Grace agreed. Connie was silent alongside her. What was he building up to?

'But it's been twelve years, and at some point we've all got to move on haven't we? I mean I've seen you girls right, I think. Set you up with the house. It's time for me to move on with my life now.'

'What are you talking about?'

'For Pete's sake, Pete, get to the point.' For the first time Grace registered the presence of a short round woman standing behind her father. She had the sort of figure that meant her boobs greeted you sometime before her face. 'I'm Jackie. Your dad and I are seeing one another.'

Grace looked from her dad to the stranger and back again. None of this made sense. Her dad didn't see people. Her dad read his paper and went to work and went to the shop and fixed Grace and Connie's washing machine for them, and once a fortnight Grace and Connie went over to see him and Grace cooked them a proper lunch. 'How? When?'

'Online,' her dad muttered.

'I swiped right on him.'

'You…' Grace stared at her dad again. 'You're on Tinder?'

'Well not any more I hope,' said Jackie.

'Just for a couple of months a while back. Tamsin at work went on it after her divorce, and I thought why not?'

'Right.'

'Well shall we?' Her dad and this Jackie woman sat down and started considering the menu. The babble of whether they were having a starter and whether if they did that would spoil their pudding and maybe they could share a pudding competed for Grace's attention with the swirl of thoughts in her head. The only thing cutting through all that noise was the aggressive silence emanating from the seat beside her. 'Are you ok, Connie?' Grace whispered.

Her sister gave the tiniest little shake of her head.

Jackie mused that she might have the prawns to start. What were tiger prawns? Were they the same as king prawns or were they the massive ones? Grace's dad said he thought king prawns

III

were the massive ones, but he wasn't really sure. Jackie didn't think she'd fancy them if they were going to come with the heads still on.

'Did you meet other people off Tinder?' Connie finally broke her ominous quiet.

'A couple. And then Jackie.'

Grace's dad wondered what the soup was. They always said soup of the day and then you had to ask the waitress and half the time they had no idea anyway and they had to go and ask, and then you felt bad if it was something you didn't fancy after they'd gone to all that trouble.

'So how long ago did you meet?' Connie again.

'A couple of months.'

'About five months.' Jackie answered at the same time, and then shot Grace's father a look. 'Or it might have been a bit less,' she added.

'Right. And you're mentioning it now.'

Grace tried to shoot her sister a look. A look that said, 'be nice, it's his birthday, we can talk about this when we get home.' The expression on Connie's face suggested she wasn't getting the message.

'However long, when you know you know, don't you?' Grace's dad squeezed Jackie's hand. 'Oh, the soup's up on the blackboard. Carrot and coriander.'

'You don't like coriander,' Connie pointed out.

'Oh nonsense,' Jackie told him. 'You had coriander in that thing at Sally's and said it wasn't so bad.'

Grace could see how tightly her sister was gripping her menu. 'He doesn't really like anything spicy.'

Jackie frowned. Grace saw the look she shot across the table and she saw her dad give a tiny shake of his head.

'I'm getting a bit more of a taste for it lately. I don't like too much heat but spice without too much chilli I'm quite coming round to. Jackie does a big curry sometimes with the leftovers from the roast.'

The group fell silent, as though the image of Jackie getting in amongst Grace's leftovers had crossed an unspoken line somehow.

'So tell us what you've been up to, Grace,' Jackie broke the silence. 'Your dad tells me you two've signed up for this big dating thing.'

Grace bristled slightly at the idea of them discussing her private life, but pushed the feeling away. It was her dad's birthday. They were going to have a nice time. 'We got a freebie. It's not a big deal.'

'So you haven't met anyone who took your fancy yet?'

The remembrance of Jon's breath on her neck sent a shiver right through her body. 'Not really,' she replied.

'That's a shame. Still time though?'

'Well, there is this one woman.' Grace didn't take her eyes off Jackie, gauging her reaction. None. So that was another thing that had already been discussed. 'Morgan. She's an artist. She invited me to her show.'

–

Connie pushed her chair away from the table. This was too much. She didn't care if she was being rude. They were being rude. That woman was being rude, turning up here without any sort of warning or respect. Their dad didn't need bringing out of himself and encouraging to try new things. He was perfectly happy as he was.

She didn't say anything as she stood and walked away from the table. She could hear her dad's voice asking where she was going, and then, inevitably, the sound of footsteps following her. Grace caught her at the entrance. 'Where are you going?'

Connie shook her head.

'We're here for Dad's birthday.'

'With some stranger.'

'Well not a stranger to Dad, obviously.'

'Stop pretending you're not bothered.'

Grace folded her arms. 'Well I'm a bit taken aback, but what were you expecting? That he'd be single forever?'

That wasn't it at all. That was the total opposite of it. Connie pushed the heavy wooden door open.

'You can't go!' her sister insisted. 'I won't come after you.'

'I'm not asking you to.'

'Good, because at least one of us has to go and be polite and eat lunch like an adult.'

'Fine. Have a nice lunch.' And Connie was out into the street, walking as briskly as she could away from the pub. At the corner she slowed ever so slightly. She glanced, quickly and surreptitiously, back towards the pub, but Grace really hadn't followed her. That was fine. She hadn't been relying on her sister coming after her and making everything all right again. She slowed a little more.

She'd only been gone a few minutes. She could walk back in, say she'd felt sick or something, and carry on with the meal. Everyone would know it was an invention, of course, but they'd probably go along with it to keep everything nice and friendly. Connie hesitated. That was what Grace would do. The thought of that almost made her laugh. It wasn't what Grace would do. Grace would never be in this situation. Grace was not the type to storm out and cause a scene.

It was the right thing to do though. She could be good. She could smile and nod and tell them, like she'd planned, about the turgid job at the energy company that was looking like being made permanent. Her dad would pat her hand and tell her he was proud of her settling down.

And yet, Connie's feet wouldn't turn her around and walk her back to the pub. Connie's feet were on the same autopilot they'd adopted when she'd run away from Morgan's place after her humiliation there. All Connie's feet wanted was to be a million miles away from here. Away from perfect Grace being the perfect daughter. Away from her dad and that woman pawing all over him.

Connie hadn't decided where she was going, but her feet already knew. It would be another black mark against her name in comparison to perfect Grace, but it was what she needed. It was where she'd always been heading from the moment she pushed her chair back and stood up from the table.

So instead of turning round and going back to lunch, or even walking to the bus stop and making her way back home, she headed for the Tube and meandered her way through the changes to get the shiny new purple line to Manor Park and then she made the fifteen-minute walk to the City of London cemetery.

The grave she was looking for was beyond the modern crematorium, in the shade of the line of trees at the furthest end of the graveyard. She normally only came here four times a year – her own birthday, Christmas, her mum's birthday and the anniversary of the day her mum had died – but the last few days had left something open and raw in the middle of her. Connie needed her mum.

Dad had insisted on a traditional burial rather than a cremation. He'd said that was what was right and proper and that it was important to have a place to come and pay respects. So far as Connie was aware he didn't come here though, not recently, not since Connie and Grace had moved out, she didn't think. And Grace never came, but she never had. Dwelling on the past wasn't Grace's way.

Connie sat cross-legged on the slightly damp earth at the foot of her mother's plot. If her mum was really here she would know what to do. Her mum had been that sort of mother. Not bossy or over-involved but always there ready to spring into action if she was needed. She was always ready to talk and to listen and to provide soft squidgy hugs and big mugs of hot chocolate. Connie summoned the feeling of being pressed against her in a cuddle, and of her mum brushing her hair back out of her face when she put her to bed at night. She remembered her mum telling her that it was ok not to be like Grace, to not be someone who never got anything wrong and never put a foot out of line. Her mum made her feel like being Connie was all right too.

Sometimes when she came she talked to her mum. She told her what was going on in her life and what annoying thing Grace had done now and she imagined her mum rolling her eyes and telling Connie to let Grace be Grace and concentrate on being the best Connie she could be. Connie closed her eyes and tried to picture her mother's face, but she couldn't quite focus on any individual part. Her mum was a haze of warmth and light shining down on her – perfect, and filled with the memories of love, reassuring her that she was right exactly as she was.

Connie's phoned buzzed in her pocket. A new scandal sheet from the Season. Hope had persuaded her to install the app. Apparently she couldn't claim to be taking it seriously if she didn't. But of course she wasn't taking it seriously at all. She wasn't built for forming lasting connections. She was built to be a rebound fling or a drunken one-nighter.

She tapped on the notification. It would be something to tell her mum about at least. The first paragraph made her slam her phone down. *At the start of the Season we talked about the possibility of double romance for two dating sisters. Now perhaps one of them is going to take the crown as the Season's diamond. Or perhaps, if she's not the diamond herself, she might be about to snag the interest of another diamond. One green-fingered artist has been turning heads across our opening events. Perhaps she's the diamond our sparkling twin is destined to catch?*

Of course Grace would be the darling of the whole damn thing, and of course she was going to ride off into the sunset with Morgan. Whatever comfort her mother might have been able to offer if she was still here was no use to Connie now. The best Connie she could be wasn't good enough. Connie couldn't hold down a job. She couldn't afford rent, so she was stuck living literally, as well as figuratively, in her sister's shadow. She couldn't find a partner who would hang around for more than a minute. And when she did like someone she ballsed it right up by coming on too strong.

No. Not by coming on too strong. That was denial speaking. The stupid scandal sheet thing made that clear. No amount of softly softly was going to win Morgan over to being interested in Connie. It wasn't the approach that was the problem. It was her. All those years of unconditional love that her mother had poured into Connie's heart were wrong. Well-intentioned, of course, but still wrong. Connie wasn't enough as she was. Her mum had been kind, but maybe, when all else was said and done, her mum had also been wrong.

Chapter Eleven

Emma wandered into the living room. She was ready for her 'date' with Tom, but somehow nerves were bubbling over. She was hoping Annie would tell her she looked fine. Better than fine. Great.

'You look great. Where are you going?' Annie was nothing if not reliable in her enthusiastic loveliness.

'Just to Tom's.'

'Doesn't she look lovely?' What hadn't been in Emma's mental picture of the scene where her sister-in-law helpfully bolstered her confidence was a room full of people. A room, in fact, full of former clients.

Annie had joined the first Season herself, but she hadn't come alone. Her two close friends, Jane and Lydia, had joined her and, one way or another, they'd both found their happy endings as a result of it. Jane's happy ending, Charlotte, was also currently in Emma's living room. Annie looked, momentarily, anguished. 'You don't mind that I've got people round?'

'Of course not. Your house too,' Emma reminded her.

Annie nodded a little uncertainly.

'Seriously. It's your house too. And I'm going out anyway.' She looked around. 'Where's Josh?'

Lydia raised a wine glass. 'Josh is bringing us food.'

'Will's not with you?' Emma asked. Technically Will hadn't been registered for the Season, but Lydia had met him when he was working behind the bar at the first ball, so Emma still counted them as a Season dating success.

'He's back at the family pile. His dad's sick.' She frowned slightly. 'Like no one's really saying how sick, but I don't think he'd have gone back there if it wasn't pretty much it.'

A hush fell over the room. 'I'm sorry,' Emma said.

'Yeah. They didn't get on but still. I'm going up there at the weekend.' Lydia took a big gulp of wine. 'Lots of changes coming up for Hot Viscount.'

Of course. Aside from being lovely and working behind Emma's bar, Will was also the eldest, indeed only, son of an earl. 'Right, so he'll be...'

'The Earl of Hanborough.'

'Shit,' Annie gulped. 'And what does that make you?'

Lydia shrugged. 'Nowt. I'm nothing. I'm just some girl.'

'Unless he asks you to marry him,' Jane chipped in.

Lydia gave her friend a very definite look. 'Don't even joke about it. Lady Hanborough.' She stuck her nose in the air. 'I can't see it. Can you?'

Emma smiled. 'Well stranger things have happened.'

Annie nodded vigorously. 'And love always finds a way.'

Emma left them shouting down Lydia's vociferous objections to the imagined likelihood of her marrying an earl. *Love always finds a way*. That was what she preached. If only it was as straightforward to do as it was to say.

–

'So where are you taking me?' It was Tuesday evening – the only evening that week that neither Tom nor Emma was working – and Tom had come to meet her from the Tube.

'Actually, if you don't mind, I thought we could stay in. I've been in bars and clubs the last five nights. I cannot do another night of cheesy piano music fighting with people talking too loud.'

'You play the piano music!'

'Yeah, but I play what they tell me to.' He grinned. 'The money's been very welcome, but not my most artistically fulfilling work.'

'So what are we going to do at your place?'

'Well, eat for starters,' he grinned. 'And for main course and pudding actually. I'm going to cook. That's the plan anyway.'

'Really?'

'Really.'

'Well I'm not going to turn that down.' Tom had been very keen, over the last three and a half months, to tell Emma that he was an excellent cook, but so far the chances to put this claim to the test had been limited to pancakes, and some emergency assistance with Josh and Emma's well-intentioned but utterly ineffectual attempt to make Annie a birthday cake, and that assistance had largely boiled down to firmly telling them to start again and then sending Emma to the shop to buy new ingredients.

They walked the two streets back to his flat. The aroma of cooking hit Emma as soon as Tom opened the door. 'Ok. That smells promising.'

'I'm glad you think so.' She followed him through to the tiny kitchen and leaned on the doorframe to watch him work. 'Help yourself to wine. There's white in the fridge or red on the table.'

Emma poured two glasses of white, and set one on the worktop next to Tom's chopping board.

'I don't have a starter. There's posh crisps though, if you're hungry while you're waiting.'

'I'm ok.' It was strangely restful watching him slice and dice, so long as she ignored the mass of unspoken serious talk that was swirling between them. 'That's some proper knife skills.'

'Grew up with two chefs didn't I?' Emma knew that, of course. Both Tom's parents had worked as private chefs for wealthy clients, travelling the world to work before they settled down with their much longed-for son. 'My mum taught me this when I was way too young to be using a knife, but she said it was much safer that I learn to do it properly than that I blundered in when I was a teenager with no clue and cut a finger off.' He held up both his hands. 'And ten fingers still, so she must have done something right.'

He threw the sliced vegetables into a sizzling hot wok with chilli and onion and garlic. 'Ok. Aromatic pork with sticky rice and stir-fried vegetables.'

They sat squeezed around two sides of the tiny table that was pushed up against the wall of the living room. 'This is delicious. I'd sort of stopped believing you when you said you could cook.'

Tom smiled. 'Would I lie to you?' The question could have been meant in jest but there was a weight to the words that suggested something else behind them.

'No. I don't think you would.'

'I haven't cooked for anyone, apart from my mum, since Jack. We used to have friends over all the time but… I don't know. It never seems worth it just for me, and it's like… this is going to sound really wanky.'

'I'll humour you,' Emma reassured him.

'Cooking for friends, or for someone you love, is an act of love. It's probably in my head, but I always feel like if I'm just going through the motions it won't taste right.'

'So I should take the fact that this is delicious as a compliment.'

He took a deep breath in. 'Absolutely. It's like playing piano. I can do it, like the last few nights in the restaurant, but it's just fingers on keys, pay check in pocket. If I'm not really feeling it, it's never going to be great music.'

'I used to feel like that about work.'

'What?' Tom frowned. 'I thought you were an incurable work-aholic.'

Now they were moving into more delicate territory.

'I am. Sorry.'

'I did kinda know what I was signing up for.'

She shook her head. 'It's not just work though. It's who I am. Before I worked for Love's Love I was fine. I did other jobs, but it was just work. As soon as Mum let me come into the business it's been my whole life. And the Season was like… is like… it's my baby.'

'And I basically told you your baby was getting on my tits?'

'You didn't say that.'

He grinned slightly. 'Well not out loud.'

'Doing this, running the Season — it's exactly what I wanted. I wrote the whole business plan and persuaded Mum, and then Josh invested his own money, and now Annie's involved as well. And we're not even paying her, but I think Josh would like to and I bet if we offered her a job she'd quit teaching and take it. And that's how it's always been in our family. Mum was a matchmaker, and then she met Josh's dad and he was an office manager, and he had no interest in dating or any of it, but she dragged him in.' She couldn't quite put it into words. Yes. She could. 'I'm Emma Love junior. I sell people the idea of happy ever after, and in my family happy ever after is this mix of work and business and personal and family. There are no boundaries.'

Her boyfriend took a deep breath in. 'I have my own career, and I like my independence. I don't want to be subsumed into your life.'

'I understand that.'

'Do you? Cos it sounds like you think I'm rejecting you.'

Emma told her clients that communication was the heart of a healthy relationship. So hard to put into practice though. 'Are you?' she whispered.

'Never.' He twisted in his chair and lifted the fork she was still clutching out of her fingers so he could wrap her hand in his. 'I love you. I never thought I would get to say that to someone again, and it blows my mind that I get to say it to someone as incredible as you. I love you. I'm not going to stop loving you, but I don't want to be slotted in to a neat hole in your life.'

That was fair. 'I don't want that either.'

'Honestly?'

'Well honestly it might be easier, but I fell in love with you. I don't want to bend you so hard that you break.'

He pressed his lips to her hand. 'So what now?'

'I have absolutely no idea.' And that was what was freaking her out. 'I've always known what I want. And I'm the Queen of Happy Ever After. I should be able to make my own work without all this mess.'

Tom looked like a man swallowing back a laugh.

'What?'

'The mess is making it work, I think. We fall out, we talk, we make up, we try something different. I love you. You love me. The rest is all up for grabs.'

Emma pursed her lips. 'That sounds like an awful lot of uncertainty.'

'I love you. You love me,' he repeated. 'Two massive certainties right there.'

That was true.

'What if you tell me what the really important bits of the Season are, the most stressful bits, and I'll try to come to those?'

She nodded. That was reasonable. 'And what if that doesn't work for us?'

'Then we'll try something else.' He leaned towards her and rested his forehead against hers. 'We've always got the Vegas plan to fall back on.'

Emma finally smiled. 'Get married and damn the consequences?'

'Always an option.'

'You're mad.'

'But you also knew what you were signing up for,' he reminded her.

'You said that we fall out, we talk and then we make up.'

'I did.'

'So how does the making up work?'

'Why Miss Love, I do believe you're propositioning me,' he laughed.

That wasn't right. This wasn't a moment for laughter. Emma was deadly serious. 'Take me to bed.'

'Right now?'

'Right now.'

He took it slowly and Emma was very happy to follow his lead, to not be in charge, to not be the person having to make the decisions and be responsible for everyone else being ok. Instead she luxuriated in Tom's attention as he unbuttoned her silky shirt and pushed the fabric off her shoulders. Gradually she found herself meeting his intensity with her own, as thoughts of work and responsibility drifted away and he pulled her into this moment. She wrapped her legs around his now naked torso and pulled him to her.

Afterwards, they lay together in a mass of warmth and sweat tangled limbs. 'Thank you.'

'What for?'

What for? 'Everything. For not letting me break us.'

He kissed the top of her shoulder. 'You weren't going to break us.'

She might have been. 'I think I got so tied up with what I thought all this relationship stuff was supposed to look like that I lost sight of you. I want you to be you.'

'Good.'

'I've never felt like this before.'

'Like what?'

She stared up at the ceiling, so she couldn't see him watching her face as she spoke. The words were enough. Who knew how much else her face would give away? 'Like I loved somebody enough that I want to make a space for them, rather than them slotting in.'

'How to tell me you've never been in love before, without saying you've never been in love before.'

'Maybe.' Emma's previous relationships had been pleasant, friendly, fun, but she'd never felt like she could drown in the depth of emotion involved.

'Is that part of why you've been freaking out?'

Was it? It definitely ought to be. 'Only when you're not around.'

He pulled himself up on one elbow so she couldn't avoid his gaze. 'What do you mean?'

'It's like I said before. I sell happy ever after, don't I? But like, what does that mean? I guess I'd always pictured a wedding and children and buying a place with someone.'

'Ok.'

'But...' She tailed off. But what?

'But what?' Typical. 'You don't want to get married and have children with me?'

'It's not that.'

'Cos, once again, you have already agreed to marry me.'

'What happens in Vegas doesn't really count.'

'Don't tell Josh and Annie that.' He pulled her closer into his arms. 'Explain yourself then.'

'It's not that I don't want all that with you. It's that that picture doesn't feel solid any more. Like I can't picture the future.' Emma had always been able to picture her future. She would run Love's Love and make it the most successful dating company in the capital. She would find her own One and they would become part of that empire, and at some point there would be children. She'd always assumed she would be a mother one day. But then Tom happened. 'I guess I always thought when I fell in love it would be like my mum and Trevor. Or even Josh and Annie. The new person would fit in with what I wanted. Like I don't think Trevor ever wanted to be a partner in a matchmaking business, but my mum was such a force of nature and he ended up doing so much to support her that he became her right-hand man. And Annie's the same. Josh will have her officially working for us as soon as our profits allow. But you're different.'

'Sorry. I don't really want to be a matchmaker. I'd be terrible at it. I'd keep telling people how painful and tortuous love can be.'

'Yeah. Not the image we're really trying to project.'

'I'd tell them the good bits too.'

Emma shook her head. 'I fell in love with a musician and a gambler. I don't want you to change who you are to fit in with me. It's like I always knew what my life was going to look like, but now I can't just fit you into what I want, can I? Cos you're real and complicated and I love you and I want you to have what you want too.'

'And what do I want?'

'Actually I don't know.'

'Oh. I was hoping you might, cos I don't have a clue.' He took a breath. 'Honestly I think I got used to not planning ahead.'

'I know. I understand.' Tom had been married long before he met Emma to the man he'd thought would be the one and only love of his life. Jack. Jack had died suddenly and horribly, and Tom's life had stopped.

'For a long time I couldn't imagine the future at all.'

'And now?' she asked quietly, tentatively. The answer was too important, important enough that part of her wondered if she wanted to know at all.

'Now I can't imagine a future without you in it, but beyond that I have no clue.'

'Me neither.' She rolled to face him properly, lifting her leg over his hip. 'So what do we do?'

'I guess we love each other and see what comes.'

'No plan.'

'We make the plan up as we go.' He kissed her. 'Does that freak you out? Would you prefer it if we made a spreadsheet?'

'Honestly yes,' she admitted. 'But I don't want to force you into a hole you don't fit in.'

'Dirty.'

'That's not what I meant and you know that's not what I meant.'

'Sorry.'

'I want to be with you for the rest of my life.'

She saw the flash of anguish on his face.

'Or for as long as we're given. So yeah, I'm in. We love each other and see where that takes us.'

'Deal. I'm in. All in.'

'All in,' she confirmed.

No plan. That was fine. Emma didn't need a plan. It would be crazy to need to pin down the next fifty years right now. Of course she didn't need that. The next week or two, maybe a month, six months, perhaps a year, that would be quite comforting enough.

Chapter Twelve

Hope arrived at her mother's hotel at 3.33 p.m. and was greeted with a weary, 'So glad you could finally make it.'

Her mother had already ordered tea for two, so Hope ignored the fact that she would have preferred a cappuccino and sipped her over-stewed tea.

'So what are the rest of your group doing today?'

Hope's mother pursed her lips. 'Shopping I believe.'

'You didn't want to go with them?'

'Well what do I need?'

'I don't know. You could get something just for fun.'

Hope's mother didn't reply.

'Like a Christmas jumper or something? That would be jolly?'

'Why would I want a jumper I can only wear once a year darling?'

'I dunno.'

Hope's mother was from the school of buying little and infrequently. Garments of higher quality lasted longer and small tears and wear could be mended. There was nothing there that Hope could, logically, disagree with.

'So Theodore couldn't join us?'

Hope hadn't asked him. She was wishing, within five minutes of being in her mother's company, that she had. For reasons Hope had never been able to fully understand, her mother found Theo charming. 'I think he was working.'

'You don't value that boy.'

'We're just friends.' For the five millionth time.

'And yet I don't see you with anyone else on your arm. Not since Simon.'

'Actually I'm kind of seeing someone.' Hope snapped the words out before she could stop herself. That wasn't how this worked. Her mother lived in a compartment over there. Hope's real life in London was over here. So long as the two never met, they never had to have an actual conversation about what had happened with Simon, who her mother had clearly thought was very suitable indeed, and Hope never had to take any potential new beau home.

'Kind of? Please try to be precise, darling. Imprecise language smacks of imprecise thought.'

'Sorry,' muttered Hope.

'And does this kind of someone have a name?'

She was stuck now. 'Callum. But it's very early days.'

'I'm sure. Callum.' Hope's mother repeated the name. 'Scottish I hope?'

'Actually he's from Australia, well New Zealand originally. I think his dad's Scottish though.'

Hope's mother's expression tightened. 'Gosh. How exotic.'

The conversation lulled. This was what Hope most associated with visits to her mother since her dad moved out. The silence. The wracking of her brain for something to say. The feeling that all of this should be somehow easier. She found her attention wandering. The Christmas tree in the corner was plastic and too small for the space. There was a tiny vase on each table with a single plastic holly sprig. They gave the whole room a slightly sad air. Fresh displays, something small and unscented for the tables, and then a feature arrangement of seasonal blooms in the foyer would be so much better. For December she'd have poinsettia, and a really generous wreath on the door. It could be so bright and warm and inviting.

'These are rather sad, don't you think?' Hope's mother gestured towards the vase, demonstrating a rare moment of being in sync with her daughter's own thoughts.

'Yeah. Not the most inspiring.'

'You used to bring me home lovely flowers.'

'When I worked for Julie?' Hope had loved that Saturday job.

'No. Well yes, but I meant when you were tiny. Every time you went out with…' The familiar catch in her mother's voice was still there. 'With your father, you'd come back with a handful of daisies and buttercups, and even dandelions, to present to me. And you'd insist they went in a proper vase on the windowsill with water in to keep them nice.'

'I don't remember that.'

Hope's mother shook her head. 'No. Well I suppose it was a long time ago.'

They eked out the next hour with a stilted conversation about Hope's work – as much as she was prepared to volunteer at least – and her mother's life in the village. So far as Hope could see nothing had changed there for years. 'So you came to London with your women's group? Is that the church women's group?'

Her mother nodded. 'Although it's not what it was. The new chairwoman has had this big thing about encouraging younger people to join. I remember when I was the younger people. We did salsa dancing last week.'

From the tone Hope gleaned that this wasn't a good thing.

Around them the hotel lounge suddenly got busier. First one woman wandered in, and then two more behind her, and then another two, and then three, and then a whole gaggle.

'Miriam!' A grey-haired woman with a streak of pink through her bobbed hair came over to them. 'You missed a great morning.' She turned to Hope. 'You must be Miriam's daughter. We said she could bring you too, but I think she wanted you all to herself.' The stranger beamed at Hope. 'Mother daughter time. We all need it don't we? My youngest, Kaley, moved out last month and I'm beside myself. Not that I'm not proud of her. She's gone to Oxford, would you believe? I don't know where she gets it from. I was never a bookworm and her dad can only read until his finger gets sore, if you know what I mean. But she's as bright as a button. History of Art she's doing. And her brother went two years ago. He's in Canada now, so it's just me and Gavin round the house. Not a clue what to do with ourselves. This trip has been a godsend. I can't even tell you.' The woman paused. 'What am I going on about? I'm Evie.'

'Hi.' Hope greeted her new friend, about whom she felt she now knew more than she knew about her own mother. 'I'm sure you'll get used to it. And she'll be home for Christmas before you know it.'

'Quite right. And in the meantime I get to make the most of not having anyone to pick up after. Well apart from Gav, and he can pick up after himself. Now we've got afternoon tea booked before we have to get off. You'll join us, won't you Hope?'

Hope made her excuses. She had places to do and people to go and all that sort of stuff, but she couldn't help but look back from the entryway to the hotel. Her mother in amongst a whole group of women in the same boat – women who'd raised families in all sorts of different circumstances, coming together to have fun and support one another. And yet Hope's mother walked stiffly into the dining room, alone in the centre of the crowd.

Outside on the street, Hope pulled out her phone. Could she call Callum now? She was seeing him tonight, and she'd seen him twice during the week. He seemed genuinely keen, but would calling him look needy? She could be needy. It was one of the things that had always wound Simon up.

She took a breath. Everything had wound Simon up. The fact that he told her repeatedly that she was too needy and she needed to chill out didn't make him right. It didn't make him wrong either though.

She scrolled past Callum's number and called Theo instead. Theo knew her mother of old so she wouldn't have to go through that round of explanation. And Theo never moaned at her for calling or texting too often.

'Hi!'

'I just saw my mum. And she wheeled out the fact that I'm seeing...'

'Sorry Hope. I can't talk at the moment.'

Hope stopped. Theo could always talk. Even in the middle of work, he was always up for pretending she was a potential sales lead when his boss came by, and then reverting to gossip the moment they were out of earshot. 'Oh. Sorry.'

'No need to be sorry. I'm in the middle of something. Hold on.' She heard Theo's muffled voice talking to whoever he was with but couldn't make out what he was saying. He must have put his hand over the receiver. 'Sorry.'

'It's fine. I'd have thought whoever you pulled last night would be long gone by now.'

'It's not like that.'

'Right.'

'Look. Sorry. I do have to go. Shall I pick you up in an Uber again tonight?'

'Actually I'm going with Callum.'

'Sure. Right. Well I'll see you there then.'

And Theo was gone, back to whatever, or whoever, he was finding so much more interesting than Hope.

Chapter Thirteen

The pleasure of your company is requested at

an evening of

ice skating and festive nibbles

'Ok. This is very cool,' Josh conceded.

He'd been entirely unconvinced by Emma's pitch for rooftop ice skating, but she was, of course, entirely correct in her belief that this was the perfect romantic setting. There were views of the night sky across the city, and you could see the lights of Canary Wharf on one side, the Tower of London on another and the river on a third. And ice skating. Seriously, could there be a more perfect date activity? Lots of opportunities for hand holding and supportive arms around one another, but also a brisk enough form of transport to be able to speed away from a less welcome admirer. There was a bar in the corner of the roof garden – serving mulled wine and Baileys hot chocolates as well as more traditional bar fare – and around the edge of the skating rink there were fairy-lit pods and benches with warm snuggly blankets. Emma was half-minded to come back on a regular public session and bring Tom.

There was a strong nip of cold in the air. 'It's definitely getting colder,' Emma said. 'I wish it would snow.'

'Yeah. I think that might be beyond even your organisational ability.'

She refused to concede the point. Snow was more likely in January or February than December but, according to her research, snow fell on average on two of December's thirty-one days, so why not today, when it would add such a pleasing festive sparkle and nobody would be worried about falling over in their high heels.

'It's not very Regency though, is it?' he pointed out. 'And I thought you were all about the historical accuracy.'

Her brother would have to try harder than that if he was going to find a chink in Emma's event planning armour. 'Actually ice skating is entirely Regency. The last great frost fair was in 1814.'

'The last great what now?'

'Frost fair. Market stalls and games and…' Emma smiled as she emphasised her point. 'And ice skating on the frozen Thames.'

'You couldn't get snow, and you couldn't arrange for the river to freeze? You must be losing your touch.'

Emma shot him a look.

'I'm kidding. You do actually seem like your head is back in the game tonight.'

'What's that mean?' Emma's head was never not in the game.

'It means I assume you've made up with Tom.'

Emma had definitely preferred it when her step-bro was fully clueless about affairs of the heart. She'd clearly been teaching him to observe too well. 'Was I that out of it?'

'A little preoccupied maybe.' He looked again round the venue. 'This all looks good, and it's the halfway point as well, isn't it? How do you think it's going?'

How was it going? From a business perspective, pretty well. Their numbers were up from last time and they were still getting strong positive PR and social media buzz. Everyone really did love a love story. But that wasn't the reason they were doing this, was it? What mattered was the daters and finding every single person their perfect happy ever after. 'Ok. I'd like a few more of them to be forming more solid attachments by now though, if I'm honest.'

'So how do we put a hand on the scales tonight?'

'Tricky.' This was one of the most free-form events of the whole Season. The mood was informal, so the chances for Emma to place people next to others who she thought might be perfect for them were more limited. Not non-existent though. 'We can do a bit of "have you met…" And then next up it's the Christmas meal, so we need to start thinking about who to put with who for that.'

Emma checked her watch. 'Apart from that, make sure nobody is on their own, and try to encourage people to skate.' That was the worrying part of the evening. What if everyone just stood around the edge of the ice rink looking nervous?

'They'll skate. It'll be fine.'

'Right. Nearly showtime.' They moved to the welcome desk they'd set up between the stairs and lift that would bring daters onto the roof. In front of them were piles of individual cards which functioned as tokens to collect skates and complimentary drinks. Each card was decorated with a holly and heart motif that Emma had designed for the festive Season. They looked good. The whole rooftop looked good. The strains of 'Winter Wonderland' were wafting gently across the space. Emma pulled her coat tighter around her body. She felt a little shot of the magic that was supposed to be what this Season was all about. Love. Christmas. Snuggling up close to someone on a winter's night. Hopefully the daters would feel it too.

The lift doors swung open and the first daters arrived. Emma and Josh greeted people and handed out cards and instructions for where to collect ice skates and drinks, and offered strong reassurances that it was totally acceptable for adults to use one of the penguin balance aids if they needed to.

Hope Lucas was one of the first to arrive, hand in hand with Callum Welsh. Emma was coming around to that match. On paper Hope had always seemed like she should be easy to match. She was pretty and friendly and seemed good fun as well as having an obvious caring side. That was part of the reason Emma had failed to set her up during the first Season. She'd never been on Emma's list of potential problems to solve. She seemed like the sort of person who wouldn't be short of interest. And thinking back, she hadn't been, had she? But nothing had quite stuck. Callum seemed to be making a better show of things so far at least.

The rest of Hope's friendship group were still proving harder to place. Emma still thought her pick of Sadie, who had been seated with Theo at the Stir-up Sunday evening, was a good match. She wondered if she could press that point a little more, or whether that would simply be doubling down on a failed instinct. And the twins. The twins.

Think of the devil and he shall appear. The Price twins seemed, rather distressingly, to follow the same rule. Or one of them at least. 'Grace?'

Emma could hear the hint of doubt in her brother's voice, but yes, this was Grace. 'No Connie this evening?'

Grace's face tensed up. 'We're not joined at the hip.'

'No. Of course not.' Josh handed over Grace's card for the evening, and pulled a face at Emma as Grace walked away. 'Good luck matching that one.'

Emma laughed. 'She's the easy one,' she muttered.

—

Hope was a terrible skater. She'd been skating a total of one previous time in her life, when she was thirteen years old. She'd fallen over eight times in ten minutes and then sat at the side for the rest of the night.

Callum had never been skating in his life, but he'd grown up surfing and paddleboarding and skateboarding and seemed to have the sense of balance of a tightrope walker as a result. Hope let him lead her onto the ice, skating backwards and holding her hands. 'You're doing great.'

'Only cos you're holding me up!'

'That's ok.' He slowed so that she was right up against his body. 'I'm not going to let go.'

He moved so that he was skating alongside her, one arm wrapped tight around her waist, the other hand holding hers in front of his body. 'Follow me.'

'How can you be so good at this first time?' It was genuinely infuriating.

'I dunno. You just have to not fall over.'

'Right. Thanks. That's helpful.'

'And you haven't fallen over, have you?'

'Because you're holding me up.'

He loosened his grip ever so slightly.

'That wasn't an invitation to let go!'

'You're ok. I've still got you.'

Hope was unconvinced. 'You're going to do the dad with the bike thing, aren't you?'

'The what?'

'You know when you're learning to ride a bike and your dad says he'll hold on to you but then he lets go and you're supposed to magically realise that you're doing it all on your own.'

'I wasn't going to do that.' The laugh in his voice told a different story.

'Good. Cos when my dad did that I fell off immediately and had to go to A and E.'

'You ended up in the hospital?'

'Broke my arm in two places.'

'I will definitely keep hold of you.'

'You don't fancy a night in the hospital?'

He slowed, and steered them to the barrier at the side of the rink, easing them both to a stop. 'Actually, oh man, I was going to try to do this in like a cool way, but both my housemates are out tonight. I was going to ask if you wanted to come back to mine.'

Right. Well of course. Why not? If you counted the pudding making and the ball, this was the fifth date.

'Like say if you don't want to, but I feel like we have…' He grinned. 'What is it the bossy lady says? "Formed a genuine connection"?'

Hope nodded. Callum was fun and kind and seriously handsome and he was, perhaps, exactly what she needed. He was direct about how he felt. He didn't obfuscate or make her guess what was going through his head. He liked her and he said so. And now he wanted to sleep with her and he said so. It was simple. Simple was exactly what Hope needed after... she shut down the thought. There'd been blokes who'd been interested since Simon, but Callum was the first one who seemed like he might be here for more than just a good time. 'Ok,' she said.

'Ok?'

'Yeah. I'd like that.' It was cold and her skates were pinching her feet, and the warmth of Callum's body inches from hers felt good.

'Great.' He grinned. 'Sorry if this is too forward, but do you wanna make a move? Like I know we only just got here but I'd really like to have you all to myself.'

Direct. Clear about what he wanted. What else could Hope ask for? 'Yeah. Let's get out of here.'

–

Grace started her evening at the bar. It gave her a vantage point to look around and see who else was here. Not that she was looking for anybody particular. Well Hope and Theo obviously. But nobody else.

She would skate later. She could, of course, skate perfectly well. She hadn't been skating for years though. She remembered going skating for the very first time at Christmas with Connie and their mum. Dad had insisted on watching from the side, clutching a styrofoam cup of tea and grumbling about the cold. She remembered skating holding Connie's hand with her mum shouting at them to take care and look after one another.

She'd tried to do that this week, hadn't she? Connie was still all but refusing to come out of her room. She emerged about once a day and got some cereal from the kitchen and then vanished again. Grace had told her that she'd feel better if she put proper clothes on and had a shower and called the temp agency to find some new work.

Connie didn't seem to pay attention to any of it.

And she'd ignored Grace entirely when she'd knocked on her door and asked if she was coming this evening. Grace told herself she couldn't be expected to sort everything out, all the time. She didn't believe it.

'Hi.'

She hadn't seen Morgan approaching. She looked ridiculously cute, bundled up in a thick cowl-necked jumper under her jacket. The last time Grace had seen her she'd yelled at the poor woman for upsetting Connie.

'Hi,' Grace whispered.

'Look, about what happened at the ball. I didn't mean to upset anyone.' Morgan looked around. 'Is Connie here?'

Grace shook her head. 'She's in a bit of a funk actually.'

'And you blame me for that?'

Another shake of the head, which was half a lie. She partly blamed Morgan for it, but she mostly blamed the appearance of Jackie. Even then though, Connie could get into one of her moods for any reason at all. And often for, it seemed to Grace, no reason at all. 'I shouldn't have had a go at you. Sorry.'

Morgan smiled. 'That's ok. It was sweet actually. You're protective of her.'

'Yeah, well she's not as tough as she looks.'

'And you are?'

Grace laughed. 'Oh, I'm way, way tougher than Connie looks.'

Morgan smiled again. Any tension between them after Grace's outburst seemed to have thawed. 'So, are you skating?'

Grace put her cup down and nodded. 'I will if you will.'

Morgan pulled a face. 'I haven't skated for years. I'll probably fall on my arse in thirty seconds flat.'

'Don't worry. I'll look after you.' They pulled on skates and slipped their own shoes into the alcoves along the wall of the roof terrace.

Their first steps onto the ice were tentative, but Grace quickly found her feet. 'Come on. Hold my hand if you want.'

She reached her hand out to Morgan, who grasped it tightly between both of hers.

'You're fine,' Grace reassured her. 'Keep your bum over your feet.'

'Well obviously,' Morgan deadpanned.

'But it's not obvious. If you feel your feet going away from you your instinct is to put your weight backwards to try to slow down, and then you end up with your feet going one way and your body weight going the other, and before you know it you're bum down on the ice. If you feel your feet getting away from you, shift your weight forward so that your centre of gravity stays over your feet.'

'If you say so.'

'Trust me. So long as you keep your bum above your feet you will never fall over.'

Slowly Morgan got more confident, and soon they were skating hand in hand, laughing at the sensation of moving freely over the ice. Grace focused on the feeling in her body, on the comfort of Morgan's hand in hers. This was what the Season promised, wasn't it? Not a fiery attraction that would inevitably burn out as inexplicably as it arose. Morgan was the sort of person who could offer her something more than that.

'Thank you,' Morgan had to shout slightly to be heard over the babble of voices from the other skaters.

'What for?'

'For looking after me. I would have been far too nervous to have a go on my own.'

'That's ok.' It really was. It felt good to be looking out for somebody who appreciated it.

They made another couple of circuits round the ice, before making their way to the edge of the rink. 'So we could get a drink?' Grace suggested.

Morgan's eyes flicked towards the exit. Grace told herself not to read anything into that.

'Or something to eat?'

'Maybe in a bit.' Grace's disappointment must have shown on her face. 'Don't look like that. I just need to...' Morgan glanced around again. 'Find the loos.'

'Right. Of course.' Not a rejection at all then. Grace relaxed slightly. Everything was going perfectly well.

'Having fun?'

The voice close to her ear made Grace's whole body tense. She took a big step to the side and turned to face Mr Rackham. 'Yes. Thank you.'

'And you can't think of anything that would be more fun?'

'I'm having a very pleasant time here.' She'd been working, all week, on absolutely not thinking about that one night. Not even a whole night. Those few hours. It was a question of self-discipline.

'Pleasant?' He pulled a face. 'That sounds terrible.'

'What do you want?'

He grabbed her hand and pulled her around the side of the bar. At least that's what Grace told herself he did. In reality his grip on her fingers was light. She could have dropped his hand and walked away, but she didn't. She followed him to the more secluded corner, out of view, she thought, of the rest of the party.

And then his lips were on hers, hard and urgent, fingers digging into her sides. Grace's body responded, taking the controls away from her brain and pressing itself against him, opening her mouth slightly in response to his probing tongue. His hand made its way to her waist, under the jacket she was wearing and then under the soft sweater she had on beneath, until it made contact with skin. She gasped like she'd been shocked.

Her brain continued to fire objections at her body. They were in a public place. Jon Rackham was not the sort of person she wanted to be with. This was not the sort of thing Grace did. This was definitely not the sort of thing Grace was looking for.

She pushed him back, two hands on his chest. He took a second to catch his breath.

'This isn't what I want,' she told him, ignoring the disbelieving arch in his eyebrow. 'I want something sensible. I want pleasant.'

'Very well.' Jon turned to walk away, and then stopped and turned back, pulling a gold-edged card from his pocket. 'For when you stop lying to yourself.'

He thrust the card into her hands. A name and a mobile number, nothing as classless as a company name or a job title.

'I'm not lying…' Grace stuttered.

'Call me. We could do something…' He smiled. 'Pleasant.'

'I'm sorry.' It was best to be honest. 'I don't want to go on a date with you.'

He really was walking away this time. He turned back. 'I wasn't planning on taking you to the pictures and then walking you politely to a cab.'

'What does that mean?'

He closed the gap between them one more time, leaning close to her ear. 'I don't want to date you, Grace. I want to fuck you. And I think, if you're honest, you want to fuck me too.'

—

Emma thrust her glass of lemonade towards the barman. Nobody was listening. 'Pop a shot of vodka in there please,' she whispered. Normally she absolutely did not drink on duty. She often had a glass of what looked like champagne in her hand to make the guests feel like she was there with them, rather than on the clock, but it was invariably actually elderflower or sparkling apple juice. Just a part of the image. Tonight she allowed herself an exception. She needed a moment, and a stiff drink, to help her process what she'd just witnessed.

Grace Price and Jon Rackham would not have been on her Festive Season bingo card. They wouldn't have been on anybody's. Clearly Emma only had herself to blame. She had seated them together at Stir-up Sunday, but that was more out of desperation, and lack of obviously better matches, than romantic expectation. To be entirely honest, she'd sort of suspected Jon would have abandoned the whole thing by now. She brought up his registration profile on her tablet.

Twelve years older than Grace. Not a deal-breaker. Some forty-year-olds were still children at heart and Grace had a hint of an older soul about her. She scrolled down. One answer jumped

142

out at her. One of Emma's mother's most hated dating red flags. Under *when did your last relationship end?* Jon Rackham had left a blank box. Which meant what? That his last relationship hadn't ended, or that there was no last relationship? Emma had no evidence to suggest he had a wife or girlfriend squirrelled away somewhere. Surely if that was the case he'd simply lie about it. There was no indent on his ring finger and he didn't carry the air of a man who was worried about being seen. The Season had over two hundred attendees – surely the risk of one of them recognising him as the nice man who picks up little Jocasta from nursery would be too high. Jon didn't strike her as the kind of man who would take that sort of risk.

Nonetheless, perhaps it wouldn't hurt to repeat her pre-Season social media trawl for evidence of a significant other on the scene. Emma scrolled down to the organisers' notes on his profile. The red flag started waving a little harder. According to Josh's research, Jon Rackham had no Facebook profile, no Twitter account, no Instagram and no LinkedIn. The sort of men who thought them-selves too high-powered to bother with Facebook or Instagram always had LinkedIn. But Jon had nothing. So far as the internet was concerned he was a ghost.

No reason to freak out yet. Maybe he was just private. Although if he wasn't hiding a secret wife on a Facebook account under some other name, the other possible implication of that skipped question was also something that would have set Emma Love senior's nerves on edge. Emma could hear her mother's voice in her head right now. 'Lord save us from forty-year-old men who've never had a relationship.'

Emma remembered telling her mum not to be judgemental. There were lots of reasons someone might be single later in life. Her mother had agreed with that, but in her mind the reasons were a straight fifty-fifty split between overbearing mother and the man in question actually being the devil. She couldn't picture Jon as a man tied to his mother's apron strings. So what was it? Secret wife or actually the devil?

'A double of whatever the least festive thing you have is, mate.'

The voice ordering at the bar next to her pulled Emma out of her reflection on Mr Rackham, and reminded her that she had one hundred and ninety-nine other clients to worry about as well. Theo Carter was accepting the whisky that was being put down in front of him.

She was about to spark up a conversation when a woman appeared at Theo's side. Sadie Simpkins. She was the woman Emma had paired him with for Stir-up Sunday. She turned slightly away so it was less obvious that she was paying close attention.

'Theo!' Sadie was clearly delighted to see him.

'Hi again.'

'Have you skated yet?'

Theo shook his head. 'I've just been hanging out, chatting to people.'

Sadie moved closer. 'We haven't had a chance to catch up lately.'

'No. That is true...' Emma continued to watch from the corner of her eye. Theo's body language shifted, as though a decision had been made. 'I'm sorry. I'm not feeling that great. I think I'm just going to get one more drink and then head off.'

Sadie's expression brightened.

'Alone,' Theo clarified.

Emma fought to keep the wince off her face as Sadie slunk away, and made a mental note to find her someone perfect at the next event. She moved along the bar towards Theo. 'You're not having a good time?'

He turned. 'It's fine. Nobody I know is still here though.'

'I thought Grace was...' Emma didn't finish the explanation of what she thought Grace was doing.

'Said she wasn't feeling well a few minutes ago.'

Noted.

'And Connie never showed up.'

'And Hope?'

'Think she left early,' he muttered.

Emma knew full well that Hope had left early, arms wrapped around Callum Welsh. That, at least, was looking like an increasingly firm match.

'Well, the idea is rather that you try to meet new people. Or at least the right new person.'

'I'm not really interested in meeting someone new.' He held the glass up to the bartender. 'Another of those.'

The barman shot Emma a quick look. He had strict instructions to cut people off if they were at risk of getting too pissed. It wasn't the tone of the Season, and next to an expanse of ice the size of half a football pitch on top of a roof, it was also a health and safety nightmare. Emma nodded her approval in this case though. She had no idea, really, what Theo was looking for in a partner, that Sadie, and everyone else he'd met so far, hadn't been able to offer, and in vino veritas and all that.

He downed the second whisky as briskly as the first. Emma surreptitiously indicated her approval for one more.

'Last one mate,' the barman smiled. 'Don't want anyone to crack their head on the ice. Know what I mean?'

Theo didn't answer, which meant he didn't argue. That was probably good enough in the circumstances. 'So if you aren't interested in meeting someone new, why did you come to the Season?'

'Hope.'

'Well hope is a good starting place for romance.'

Theo's brow furrowed. 'No. Hope's started a romance.' He waved a hand towards the exit. 'With surf boy.'

Emma's brain caught up. 'Yes. Sorry. You came because of Hope. Because she had the free pass.'

'Yeah. Because of Hope,' he agreed.

'But you must have been thinking that you might meet someone yourself as well?'

Theo jabbed a finger on the bar. 'Told you. Don't want to meet someone. Met someone already.'

'I see. You've already met someone, before you came to the Season.'

Theo nodded.

'So why come here?'

He was staring at her now, like she was the idiot. 'Hope…
Hoped…' He was slurring ever so slightly. 'Hoped to get over
her maybe.'

So Emma was fighting against the allure of the one who
got away. Unrequited love was one of the matchmaker's biggest
nemeses, because it was always perfect in the smitten person's
imagination. No real flesh and blood human Emma put in front
of them would ever match up. Emma thought back through the
registration forms. Who was Theo's last significant other? Sophie
Something?

'So why didn't things work out?' she asked.

'Timing.' He laughed slightly as he said it.

'Right. So have you told her what you want?'

Theo shook his head. 'She's with someone else now.' He
turned to face Emma properly and smiled. 'So nothing doing
there I'm afraid, Miss Matchmaker.'

'But you're here? So maybe part of you does want to move on,'
Emma pointed out.

'So what do you suggest?' Theo seemed to have pulled himself
together and was bestowing the full beam of his dark-eyed attention on Emma now. 'Give me the benefit of your professional
expertise.'

'Well maybe if you try to adopt a bit more of an open mind as
a starting point?'

'You really think that's all it takes?'

'Well it's a starting point. Come on,' Emma could hear that she
was pleading slightly. 'Matchmaking is what I do. At least let me
try. Come along to the rest of the Season and give me a chance
to find you the perfect person.'

'I don't think…'

Emma was determined. 'I mean your friends will be coming,
so you're probably going to tag along anyway. At least give things
a fair chance while you're here.'

The pitch was so ridiculous that Theo actually smiled. 'Fine. I will try to adopt an open mind.'

'Thank you.'

'It won't work though.'

'Open mind,' she cautioned.

'I'll try,' he promised, which was probably the best she was going to get.

'That's all I ask.' Emma smiled to herself as Theo wended his slightly inebriated way towards the exit. And, without any warning, fat white flakes started to fall from the sky around her.

She watched her brother shaking his head in disbelief by the welcome desk and laughed. Across the rooftop couples were looking up to the sky and snuggling in close for warmth in a perfect romantic scene. She raised a silent thanks to the dating gods. Of course she could make it snow.

Chapter Fourteen

'Hopey!'

The voice stopped her in her tracks as she rushed out of the hospital the following evening. 'Dad?' She turned and found herself wrapped up in a huge cigar-smoke-scented embrace. 'What are you doing here?'

'I can't drop in on my favourite girl?'

'I thought you were away.'

'I was for a bit. Carlisle. And then Newcastle, and then up to Edinburgh.'

'Doing what?'

He shrugged. 'Bit of this. Bit of that.'

Hope was hazy on the details of her father's current employment. After twenty apparently uneventful years married to Hope's mum, moving from one administrative job to the next, he now seemed to be in a different city every time he called his daughter. 'How long are you back for?'

'Couple of months at least. Tina's getting hacked off with me buggering off all the time.' Tina was her dad's current partner, or to borrow Hope's mother's terminology 'the floozy' he'd taken up with a suspiciously short amount of time after he'd moved out of the marital home. 'And I thought, while I'm in the area what better than to take my little girl out for dinner?'

'Oh. I'm supposed to be meeting someone.'

'Well tell Theo you can see him anytime.'

'It's not Theo.'

Her father pulled a face of mock horror and placed the back of his hand to her forehead. 'Another friend?' Her silence sent his play acting into overdrive. 'A young man?'

'Maybe.'

'Well in that case I definitely won't keep you. Hold on.' He pulled a handful of business cards from his pocket and rifled through them. 'Here you go. That's the right number. You call me and we'll get together when you don't have more exciting fish to fillet.'

'I will.' Hope hugged her dad. 'And give my love to Tina.'

'Of course. You should come over while I'm home.'

'Is it safe?'

Her dad laughed. 'What could you possibly mean?'

'I mean is she still in her tarantula phase?'

'One tarantula, securely confined to quarters when guests come. And she's moved on anyway. Pottery is the thing now. I'm surprised she hasn't sent you an ash tray.'

'I don't smoke.'

'Neither does she. Doesn't stop her making three or four of the things a week though.'

Hope waved her dad off with promises to call and arrange something the very next day, and then dashed down the path outside the hospital and round the corner to the Hospital Inn. That wasn't actually the pub's name. It had been years ago but the current management had tried to distance their hostelry from associations with backless nighties and penicillin-resistant infection. Nevertheless, the Hospital Inn was still what half the customers called it. The other half were so used to wandering the hundred yards from ward to bar at the end of a shift that they simply called this place Outpatients.

Callum was already three quarters of the way down a pint at a small table next to the door. Hope babbled out her apologies and swiftly secured him a second pint along with a double gin and tonic for herself. 'I'm so sorry. It was a crazy day.'

'That's ok.' Callum grinned. 'So what do you want to do tonight?'

'I don't mind. What do you fancy?'

'Well this is kinda touristy and you might not wanna, but on my way down here someone gave me a flyer for this.' He pulled a scrunched-up sheet of A5 from his pocket. *Jack the Ripper Walking Tour.*

Hope kept the frown off her face. One of the few things she really disliked about living on the edge of Whitechapel was the steady stream of Ripper tourism she had to pick her way through. *What are you doing?* she wanted to yell. *You're in one of the most vibrant cities in the world and you're most excited about a dead serial killer.*

'Thought it might be interesting,' Callum added. 'And if we get scared it'll be an excuse to stay nice and close.'

That part didn't sound so bad. 'All right then.'

They checked the time and the meeting point on the flyer and decided to grab something to eat first. So an hour later, stuffed full of chips, they were outside Aldgate tube ready to be led around London on the path of Jack the Ripper. The tour was actually much less toe-curling than Hope had expected. The guide was impressively knowledgeable and talked widely about the social and economic realities of life in Victorian London and focused more on the lives of the Ripper's victims than the more lurid details of their deaths.

And it was nice to have Callum's arm around her shoulders as a protectorate against terrors from long ago.

'You weren't really into that, were you?' Callum's first question when the tour group finally dispersed suggested she hadn't made as good a pretence of enjoying the tour as she'd hoped.

'Sorry. Not really my thing. It was more interesting than I thought it would be.'

'Why didn't you say so? You should have said if you didn't fancy it.'

This was a talk they were going to have to have. Hope hadn't planned to have it this early and she hadn't planned to have it standing outside a microbrewery on a back street in east London. She turned to face him. She could talk about this. She wasn't ashamed. 'My last boyfriend. I told you I was with him right through uni and we broke up about three years ago?'

'Yeah?'

'Well he was…' The words were sitting there in her brain. They sounded so lame though. 'He was kinda… He liked to be in control of things.'

She saw his expression change. 'How do you mean?'

'It wasn't awful.' Why was she saying that? 'He wasn't like violent or anything. More that I just… I don't know. Sort of lost confidence in what I want.'

'So like a…' He hesitated. 'A coercive control kinda thing.'

'Yeah. I guess.' That was what the counsellor she'd seen had called it. Those weren't Hope's words though. Simon hadn't controlled her. He hadn't had to. He'd stripped her confidence so far away that there was nothing to control. She'd been turned into a blank space on which he could paint the girlfriend he wanted. 'I lost who I was a bit for a while.' She smiled brightly. 'It was a while ago now. I guess I'm out of the habit of thinking about what I want.'

'Thanks for telling me.' He pulled her closer. 'I'm glad you did. And you know, whatever you want, I want you to tell me.'

'I'll try.'

'Ok. So do you want to come back to mine? Zack's there but he'll be gaming in his room so you won't have to do the whole meeting the friends thing if you don't wanna.'

Hope nodded. 'I'd love to. And I'll even risk meeting the mythical Zack.'

–

Connie lay on her bed and scrolled through the latest scandal sheet on her phone. It opened with a litany of past Season successes. The previously jilted groom who'd found true love with a woman whose heart was made to care for those around her, the midwife and the schoolmistress expecting the Season's first baby and another schoolmistress who'd apparently snagged herself an actual peer of the realm. Next they moved on to the developing romances of the Festive Season. *Will hope finally be fulfilled with a beau from a faraway land? Everyone at Season HQ is rooting for this romance…* Connie rolled her eyes and read on, and rapidly wished she hadn't. *An unexpected connection seems to have come to fruition for one of our tempting twins. Might a happy ending that's full of grace be on the horizon?* Of course Grace was getting lucky. Why wouldn't she be? Morgan was bound to go for the prettier, perkier sister.

Connie swung her feet onto the floor and made her way to the stairs. She stopped. She could hear the voices downstairs. Grace chatting animatedly, as if Grace ever chatted any other way, and then the second voice, deeper and gruffer. Dad. She listened as hard as she could, straining to hear if there was a third voice in the kitchen. Had That Woman come with him?

You didn't even give her a chance. Grace's voice wasn't just in the kitchen. It was also inside Connie's head, parroting the things Grace had been saying all week, and the thing Connie was determined to deny. That Woman was the enemy. The confidence with which she'd walked into their lives. She didn't even have the grace to apologise, for… *For what?* Grace would have asked. For anything, Connie mentally replied.

She couldn't hear anyone else downstairs though. Maybe it was only Dad. Maybe – a shot of hope sprang through Connie's mind – maybe he'd come around to say sorry for bringing the horrendous woman along and to explain now that he'd had an inexplicable momentary loss of sense and got sucked in to whatever-she-was-called's evil clutches, but had, of course, now seen the light and would never go on another date again.

Connie swung her legs out of bed and padded barefoot onto the landing as quietly as she could manage. The voices were clearer now. Definitely only two of them. Grace and Dad. Connie could go down there and join them and it would be like normal. Dad would be fixing something, probably whether it was broken or not – he did so like to be useful – and Grace would be making tea and offering biscuits and slices of whatever cake Hope had made recently. Connie could slip in and join them.

She edged towards the stairs and made it down the first two steps before she heard her name.

'You know what's Connie's like.' That was Grace. Of course it was Grace. Grace always had an opinion on whatever Connie did.

'Don't talk about your sister like that.' Good for Dad. Grace shouldn't talk about Connie any way.

She edged down another stair.

'I have tried to talk to her though.'

'I know love. I appreciate that.' Their dad paused. 'I knew she might not be best pleased, but I didn't think she'd…'

'Storm out like a spoilt teenager.'

'Gracie!'

'Just saying it like it is.'

That wasn't fair. Connie waited for her dad to defend her, to admit that he'd been in the wrong, that he had no business bringing some loud, brash woman to replace their gentle, warm-hearted mother. Her father said nothing.

'I think she thinks you're replacing Mum.'

Connie lowered herself to take a seat on the stairs. Eavesdroppers never hear good of themselves. Wasn't that the old adage? What the saying didn't specify though was that eavesdroppers did definitely hear stuff, so there were pros as well as cons. She waited, in the growing silence, for her dad's reply.

'Your mum died fifteen years ago, love.'

'I know.'

'And I know it was horrible for you girls, but it wasn't fun for me either, and…' Connie could picture her dad sipping his tea and looking out of the window, as if he was distancing himself from the heavy emotion in the room. 'And I tried my best for both of you.'

'Of course you did. You were…' Grace tailed off. That wasn't like her. Had Dad shushed her?

'But that meant that I didn't really get to grieve her myself, not until you two moved out and started living your own lives. I waited ten years to grieve her.'

'Oh Dad. I…'

'It's all right, love. You girls came first. But now I've had my time thinking about what I've lost and it's time for me to move on. I'm not even fifty yet. I could have another forty years. What does Connie want? For me to shrivel up so she can keep someone who's been gone half her life alive?'

'No… well…' Connie could hear the strain in her sister's voice. 'Maybe you could have given us a warning before you brought her to lunch though.'

'Yeah. I probably should have done that. Let Connie get used to the idea.'

'I am sorry she was like that. I'll try to talk to her again.'

'It's not up to you to make everything all right love.'

'I don't mind. I think if I talk to her again then…' Grace was jabbering now, talking nineteen to the dozen.

'Love, you don't have to do anything. If Connie wants to come and talk to me about things she knows where I am.' She heard a mug being set down on the table. 'I assume she's hiding upstairs at the moment?'

'I don't know. I think she might have gone out.' Grace was lying. Grace knew full well that Connie had barely left her room since The Lunch with the Devil Woman. That couldn't last. She'd binned off the billings department at the energy company without a second thought but she would need to earn some money soon. Downstairs Grace was still talking. 'I am really sorry, you know, for how she behaved.'

'You don't have to apologise for your sister.'

Grace actually laughed at that. 'Well sometimes I do.'

Connie ought to go down there and give them a piece of her mind. How dare they talk about her like that? She had every right to be utterly furious with them. She ought to march right in there and let them know that she'd heard it all. That would wipe the smug smiles off their faces.

Connie didn't move from her spot at the top of the stairs. She tried to picture wiping the smiles off their faces, but the image wouldn't come into her mind. Even when Grace had laughed, it hadn't actually sounded for one second like either of them were smiling. Her dad wasn't making jokes at her expense. He didn't sound jubilant. He sounded sad. So very very sad.

And Connie had made him sad. And Grace was having to apologise for her. Again. She knew she was the family screw-up. That was her role and it was one she fulfilled with ease. She wasn't like Grace. She couldn't hold down a nice sensible job. She didn't have nice sensible relationships. She tried the best she could, but Connie had always been aware that she was, somehow innately, the bad twin. She'd never thought about how that affected the people she was supposed to love though. She'd never thought that she might make her dad sad and worried. She'd always thought that Grace was interfering and bossy, but never thought for one second that she felt responsible for Connie's messes and lived a life of constantly apologising and trying to make things right. Connie was the root of all of this. Something had to change. Someone had to change.

She couldn't quite believe what she was contemplating. It went against everything that she was. It broke all her self-imposed rules, but the sadness in her dad's voice and the weariness in her sister's layered themselves in her mind over the image of Morgan's horrified face when Connie had tried to kiss her. All of them telling Connie that she wasn't good enough. She needed to be better.

She'd already tied herself in knots over what to do about Morgan. Option one: bin off the Season. That was the easiest option. Nobody would be surprised. She was Connie. She was expected to mess up and flake out. But then what happened? Grace and Morgan would get closer, and Connie would end up in peach taffeta, playing the reluctant bridesmaid at their fabulous lesbian wedding, with both the brides stressing out about how Connie was going to mess everything up this time.

Option two: move to Panama immediately. She spoke Spanish to a solid B at GCSE level, and beyond establishing that that was totally the relevant language the only other thing Connie knew about Panama was that it was a really really long way away. She could avoid her dad and his new ladyfriend entirely legitimately based on the excuse of living on the other side of the planet. The awkward conversation she could see looming in her future would never have to occur. She could send a postcard. *Sorry I overreacted. Hope you have a nice life. Lots of love Connie xxx* Unfortunately the very appealing distance was matched by the very unappealing cost of flights. Panama was, sadly, off the table.

Option three: front up to her dad and to the rest of the Season as she was. Try to be nice to the devil woman and try to understand her dad's point of view. Deal with the knife of pain in her belly at the idea of her mother being left behind. Deal with the fact that Morgan clearly wasn't into her like an adult, and move on. Connie almost laughed out loud at the very notion.

Which only left option four. The nuclear option. An option that two short weeks ago she would never have imagined she would have considered. And now here she was. Finally she stood up and padded back across the upstairs landing and knocked on Hope's door.

'Come in.'

She pushed the door open. Hope's room was spotlessly clean and neat. She really was the dream lodger. Hope herself was sitting on her bed with her laptop on her knee. She closed the computer and set it aside, giving Connie her full attention.

'I need your help with something,' Connie said.

—

'Have you seen this email?' Josh leaned over and waved his tablet under her nose. 'Came to the info@ account. Says they've already emailed you direct though.'

Emma glanced at the screen. *From Nelton@loveUSA.com.* She'd seen that email address before. She thought back. 'Oh, that's just some spam thing. Delete it.'

Josh shook his head and tapped the screen a couple of times before holding it out to her again. 'I don't think so.'

His tablet was now showing the webpage of Love USA, which proudly proclaimed itself to be North America's largest match-making service. The page he'd opened was the *Meet our team* section. And there she was – Nina Elton, Vice-President for Service Development.

Emma tapped back to the email and read it properly. 'So they're interested in the Season?'

'Sounds like it.' Josh was grinning. 'We're going global.'

'Don't get excited. Probably we'll reply and never hear from her again, and in six months' time they'll have exactly the same thing on their website like it was entirely their idea.'

'So sceptical.'

Emma shrugged. This idea she'd had was good, but having a series of parties wasn't exactly patentable. There was nothing much she could do to protect them from the risk of other people ripping them off. All she could do was try to make their versions of the Season good enough that nobody in London would think it was worth muscling in.

'Well I'm going to reply.'

'Fine. But don't tell her how to do it all. Make her do her own work at least.'

'I'm going to thank her for her interest and see what she says.'

'Whatever. Even if it is legit, she's not going to answer 'til Monday anyway.'

His tablet pinged with an incoming email less than three minutes later. 'Well what do you know? We have ourselves a video call with the New York office.'

'A what now?' Emma was not video call ready.

'Not until next week. Wednesday. Noon.'

'Noon here? That's like stupid o'clock in New York.'

'She's clearly very keen.'

'What do they even want to talk to us about?'

Josh read aloud. 'The possibility of licensing the Season to Love USA for roll-out in New York City initially, with an option to develop the brand across North America.'

'Woah.'

'I know.' He grinned. 'We're going to be rich. Rich I tell you!'

'Don't get excited. It won't come to anything.'

'When did you get so downbeat?' Josh looked over the table in front of her. 'And why on earth can you not do this on a spreadsheet?'

'It's not the same.' In front of her Emma had the names of every single dater who had signed up for the Festive Season, all written out on individual slips of paper, and she was moving them around, trying to work out the perfect seating arrangement for the upcoming Christmas lunch. An arrangement that gave the budding couples she already approved of a chance to spend the evening getting closer without too many likely temptations around them, while also putting the still single daters next to prospects Emma had identified for them.

The names in front of her right now were giving her the most grief. Grace and Connie Price. It was fairly obvious that they had both been interested in Morgan Landy. It was less clear whether Morgan was still interested in either of them. Emma feared Morgan might be tiring of both sisters. She could stick all three of them together and let the chips fall where they may, but that risked a literal punch-up in the middle of her elegant luncheon, and that wasn't really the romantic, peace-to-the-world sort of vibe she was aiming to create. She could put one of them with Morgan, but that probably increased the risk of a major fight breaking out. So maybe neither of them with Morgan, but where should she put them instead? Not together. That seemed clear. She was sure she had plenty of blokes on her books who would love to be seated with twins at a dating event, but that was also not the tone of the party.

She looked at the third and fourth slips of paper in her 'Problem' pile. Jon Rackham and Theo Carter. Another two she couldn't place at all. Theo had been personable and polite and charming and she would have thought she could match him with half the women on her books, but she hadn't seen him settle into conversation with the same person twice at any of the events so far, and since their impromptu chat at the bar she finally understood why. He was living in hope of a sudden change of heart from an ex who got away.

Emma went to her dwindling pile of still unattached straight women. She had no doubt that at least half of them would find Theo utterly infatuating if he was prepared to make an effort. She put one name on either side of Theo on her seating plan. She could put massive troughs of eligible water in front of that particular horse. What he did next, would have to be up to him.

She turned her attention back to Jon Rackham. Jon had been another mystery solved at the ice-skating event. She paused. Actually not solved. If anything her questions about Jon were multiplying faster than she was answering them. In a million years she would never have put him with Grace Price. And yet, there they were, snogging like horny teenagers behind a mini Christmas tree.

She brought his profile up on her tablet screen once more, and read through in full. That worrying lack of response about his last relationship still jumped out, but what else? He listed his profession as 'Sales and Financial Services', which was gloriously vague, but from the cut of his suits and the slick black saloon car she'd seen drop him off at events, she was going to guess that he wasn't a deputy branch manager for HSBC. He had listed no hobbies or interests, and under *Other Information* it said, 'I'm looking for someone who'll see past the front I put up. I'm sensitive and very caring, even if I don't always let it show. Jon needs to find someone he trusts enough to let in.'

Emma kicked herself for not noticing that before. They'd started writing 'I...' but had slipped up and typed 'Jon...' later on. He hadn't filled this in himself. At first she thought he'd got his PA to fill the form in for him, but that felt off. Emma read again. This had been written by somebody who cared about him. So someone thought enough of Jon to want him to be happy, to the point of taking matters into their own hands. Maybe that meant she shouldn't dismiss him too quickly.

She looked at her pile of challenging daters. Her mother wouldn't have been so negative, would she? Emma Love senior had started her dating agency from scratch and had always been adamant that there was someone for everybody.

Emma needed to find the right somebody for Jon. Was that Grace? Grace was measured, calm. Even seeing her getting hot and bothered at the ice skating hadn't quite broken Emma's mental image of a fundamentally cautious, sensible soul. So what did Jon need? Someone like Grace but with a bit more of an edge. Emma laughed at her own stupidity. Could the answer be that simple? She still wasn't sure.

She spread the slips of paper out in front of her and started again. Nearly an hour later she was basically back where she started.

Josh wandered back into the room, this time followed by his wife. 'You're still doing this?'

Emma thrust the four remaining slips of paper at her brother. 'These ones don't fit anywhere.'

Annie took the slips off him, and scanned the neatly arranged names spread across the table, and then put two slips down in each of the remaining gaps.

Emma frowned. It was pretty much the arrangement she'd come up with before she started second guessing herself. 'You think her there?'

Annie nodded.

'Next to?' Emma held up the relevant name.

'Yeah. I mean I don't think they're right for each other.'

'Don't you?' Emma had been thinking that pair was a potential match.

'No, but I think they need to work that out for themselves?'

Emma didn't generally favour people working things out for themselves. She much preferred it when she was able to line things up neatly in advance, but in this case, maybe Annie was right. Maybe sometimes you had to let people find their own path. Even if that meant going down the wrong route first. And, then again, maybe Emma was right. Maybe these were the right matches. In which case the plan was even more of a success. 'Ok. Seating plan done.'

Chapter Fifteen

The pleasure of your company is requested at

a traditional Christmas Luncheon

For the Christmas lunch Emma was aiming to dial the level of festive ambience up to eleven. In addition to the background music, and the room decorations, today she had tables set for a banquet and laid with rich red and gold cloths. The napkin holders were decorated with holly sprigs. She looked around and she was pleased.

The lunch also marked a return to Emma's most regular venue, which made the set-up part of the day less stressful than going to a new place for the first time. Nonetheless, once she'd taken the Events Manager, Harriet, to one side and pointed out that one of the tables had clearly been partially set by someone who didn't know left from right, Emma felt a lot better.

'You know she leaves mistakes like that so you've got something to find,' Josh informed her.

'Don't be ridiculous.'

'I mean if I was her, that's what I'd do. If you don't find anything wrong, you keep looking until you do. Much easier to let you find something straight away.'

Emma pursed her lips and watched Harriet relaying the table. If she was honest with herself, Josh's suggestion was exactly what Emma would do in Harriet's position as well. Damn. Now she'd have to walk the room again to find the real thing that inevitably wasn't quite right.

Annie bustled into the room and almost walked right into her. 'Would you believe two of the dispensers in the ladies' were out of hand soap? I'll ask Harriet to refill them.'

Emma watched her sister-in-law go. She turned to Josh. 'You and your dad totally shared a type, didn't you?'

'What do you mean?'

'She's more like my mum than I am.' Emma paused. 'She wasn't like that when I met her.' The Annie who had come along to the Season in the summer wouldn't have said boo to even a very small non-threatening goose.

'She was when I met her.' Josh and Annie had been friends since primary school, but had fallen out of touch since Josh moved areas in his teens. 'I think life knocked it out of her a bit. It's really good to see her being more Annie again.'

Emma checked the clock. 'Right. Nearly time to open the doors. You know who you have to keep an eye on.'

'We're on it,' Josh confirmed. 'If it looks like kicking off, Annie and I will take out a twin each.'

Emma laughed. 'Good man. Right. Let's do this then.'

–

Hope scanned the seating chart. She hadn't stayed at Callum's last night because he'd been working until the early hours, so she'd arrived with Theo instead. He leaned over and pointed at her name. 'There you are.'

Hope caught Theo's name out of the corner of her eye. She was at table one, and he was at table twenty. Those didn't sound close together. 'And there's you.'

'Oh.' Theo sounded seriously nonplussed.

'Well we can't hang out together the whole time. You're supposed to be trying to meet someone too.' As she said it Hope heard the slightest catch in her own voice. Of course Theo wouldn't find someone. Theo wasn't the type to settle down and do long term.

'Yeah. Sure.' He nodded. 'I was hoping to have a chat with you about something.'

She moved away from the seating chart and collected two glasses of champagne from the waiter at the door. 'Well you can chat to me now. We're a bit early for sitting down.'

'Right. So I was in Columbia Road a couple of weeks back.'

Hope gasped in mock outrage. 'You didn't go to the flower market without me?'

'I wouldn't dare. No. It was during the week. I was on my way to a meeting with…' He trailed off. 'Anyway, I noticed that there's a unit to let.'

Why was he telling her this?

'And like don't be mad at me, but I might have called the agent and asked her to send over the details.'

'What for?' Hope was holding her voice calm and steady.

'For you to look at.' He spread his hands wide. 'It was your dream, and I figured it couldn't hurt to look. Right?'

He was wrong about that. It could hurt to look. It could hurt very much.

'Well it looks great, and the rent is way lower than they were saying.'

'What?'

Theo looked blank.

'What do you mean "lower than they were saying"?'

'Right. Yeah. So I went to see it, and there's a few issues, like it needs decorating, and there's a broken pane of glass in the door, and the previous people have left a load of crap behind. Nothing major you know, just hassle for them to sort out, so I got them to agree that if you…' He stopped himself. 'If someone took it as was they'd lower the rent for the first year.'

'Why?'

'What do you mean why? Because it's your dream.'

That wasn't right. Years ago maybe. During college, she'd talked the hind legs off anyone who'd listen, which was mostly Theo as it turned out, about how one day she'd have a flower shop and she'd do amazing artistic floristry. 'That was years ago.'

'How often do you go to the flower market?'

'That's not the point.'

'I kinda think it is the point, Hope. You want to do this. You've always wanted to do this. It is not impossible for you to do this.'

'I've got a job.'

'And there's nothing to stop you having a different one.'

She told herself he meant well. 'I don't know anything about running a business.'

'You have a degree in running a business.'

'The theory. But that's all big corporate stuff. I don't know anything about small business. Like permits. I bet you have to have permits.'

'Probably. Which you can google and will be on the council website.' Theo sighed deeply. 'Just come and look at it.'

'No.'

'Why not?'

He was really pushing his luck now. Hope and Theo very rarely, if ever, fell out, but this was a point where Hope had to draw a line. 'Because I don't want to.'

'Yes. You do,' he replied.

'Hey there!' Callum's laid-back greeting cut through the ice that was rapidly descending between them. 'I think we're at table one.'

'Yeah.' Hope grabbed his hand. 'Better go find our spot.'

—

The Price sisters were still downstairs in the lounge. Grace had insisted that they needed to talk before they had to deal with company. Connie didn't quite see why frankly. At least her sister was fulsome in her praise for Connie's new look. With Hope's help she'd managed to rid her hair of the purple and bring it back to a rather sedate dark brown. She'd borrowed a knee-length emerald green dress and even put on high heels. Well, high for her. Compared to the things Grace managed to stride around on they were practically orthopaedic, but Connie felt like she was tottering on stilts. Hope had also done her make-up for her, assuring her that a neutral palette complemented her eyes and her skin. The overall effect was… Connie caught a glance at herself in the mirror above the bar. What was the phrase for when robots looked slightly too human? The uncanny valley. That was it. Connie looked, to her own assessment, like a mid-quality AI version of her sister.

'I'm sort of wondering why…' Grace stuttered. 'And why you didn't ask me? I could have helped you know.' She eyed Connie's hair. 'Like that maybe needed lightening a whole lot more first.'

'I wanted to do something for myself.'

Grace didn't look wholly convinced. 'You need to talk to Dad as well. He was really upset after his birthday.'

Connie knew that. And she would. She definitely would, as soon as she'd had time to practise being this new, improved version of Connie who wasn't destined to disappoint him at every turn, but she wouldn't be doing it because Grace said she had to. 'We should head up,' Connie pointed out. 'We don't want to miss lunch.'

She followed her sister up the stairs, and then did her level best to hide her relief that they weren't seated together. She wasn't sure she had the strength for a whole afternoon of Grace questioning her new look and lecturing her about her obligations to their father.

'Grace! You've changed your…' Joshua Love greeted them enthusiastically and failed utterly to hide his double take when he saw Grace standing behind her. 'Sorry. Connie! You look great. My apologies.'

That was new. Connie had had all her hair cut off for the first time when she was six years old and she'd come home from school and cried on her mother about how everybody confused her with Grace, but somehow never seemed to confuse Grace with Connie. Rather than tell her not to be so silly or not to let it get to her, Connie's mum had agreed to her request to make herself look as different as possible from her sister. So from a pixie

166

cut in primary school to purple streaks at twenty-seven, Connie was unused to being mistaken for her sister.

Behind her Grace laughed. 'We're identical again, Connie!' she squealed.

Not quite. Hope had suggested going blonde but Connie had vetoed that. There were some lines she was never going to cross.

'I'd better find my seat.' She stalked away from her sister. A few people were already seated at tables, but most of the daters were still milling around, standing in small groups and sipping champagne.

'Nice hair Grace,' commented one total stranger as she passed.

'I'm Connie,' she muttered.

The second time she corrected them again. By the third time she nodded politely.

Eventually she found her place and glanced at the name cards either side of hers. *Julian Gatesby*. Not a clue. Sounded posh. Connie wasn't sure she did posh. And *Jon Rackham*. That one rang a bell.

'Oh my goodness. What have you done to yourself?' The voice provided an instant reminder. The arrogant dick from Stir-up Sunday.

'I'm not Grace,' she muttered.

He rolled his eyes. 'Well obviously not. What happened to the purple?'

'I fancied something different.'

'You had something different. This is something…' He didn't even try to keep the disdain out of his voice. 'Rather drearily the same.'

'Well I'm sorry you disapprove.'

He sat down next to her. 'I neither care one way nor the other. I am a little surprised. You seemed like the sister who'd already worked out who she was.'

Well how very wrong a person can be, thought Connie. 'No. Grace is the sorted one. She's always got all her ducks in a row.'

He pulled a face. 'How very boring for her. Oh, that's not what you're aspiring to, is it? Conformity and predictability?'

Connie felt her sisterly hackles rising. 'Grace isn't predictable.'

He didn't meet her eye for a second. 'Indeed not. I apologise.'

'Thank you.'

He leaned back in his seat. 'You must tell me what inspired,' he gestured towards her hair and outfit, 'all this? New job perhaps?'

Connie shook her head. 'I'm doing mystery shopping. Anyone can be a shopper.'

'Up to a point.'

'I thought we were supposed to be spending the evening in conversation with real romantic prospects?' Connie complained.

'Do I take that to imply you're not interested in me?'

Of course not. Connie checked herself. Was she? Nope. Definitely no. Not so much as a flicker of a spark. This was so much easier than talking to Morgan. Maybe she should form a relationship with someone she didn't fancy at all, so she could continue to be confident Connie. 'I'm afraid not. But I don't think you're interested in me either, are you?'

'Oh absolutely not.' He paused. 'Which is interesting I suppose.'

'Why?'

'No reason.' He lifted his glass towards a passing waiter. 'Shall we get moderately inebriated and enjoy the free dinner then?'

Connie found herself smiling. 'You're on.'

—

Grace knew she should be very happy indeed about how the lunch was playing out. The atmosphere was beautiful. The ambience was elegant and sophisticated but still warm and festive. She was at the opposite side of the room from Jon Rackham, which took a whole lot of complication out of the equation. And she was right next to Morgan, which was, obviously, exactly where she wanted to be. Everything was as it ought to be.

Morgan was already standing next to their table, glass of champagne in hand. She looked beautiful. That was new. Grace thought of her as cute and pretty for sure, but tonight she looked stunning. She'd gelled her short hair back from her face and was wearing a plain black column dress. It was the sort of unattainable beauty that Grace would normally have shied away from. 'You look…' Grace couldn't find the word. 'You look great. Different.'

'Thanks. I think I might have overdone it a bit. It's been a bit of a week. I sort of felt like being someone else tonight, if you know what I mean.'

Grace didn't know at all. It was like seeing Connie's new look all over again. What was wrong with people? You were who you were. You couldn't just decide to be someone else.

'Like playing dress-up when I was a kid.' Morgan smiled. 'I wish I had a wig. Something ridiculous. Blue spikes or something.'

'That might rather draw attention,' Grace suggested.

'Yeah, but different attention. Not like attention on me.' Morgan shrugged. 'Hard to explain.'

The change in Morgan poked at something in Grace's gut. Morgan wasn't supposed to be confused or confusing. Morgan was simple, and that was what Grace had decided she wanted.

'Good evening, and season's greetings everyone. If you would like to take your seats, our first course is about to be served.'

Emma's voice from the front of the room saved Grace from having to delve further into what was troubling Morgan. The rest of the group were relative strangers to Grace. Faces she recognised but nobody she had got to know as yet. And she wouldn't be wasting time getting to know them tonight. She'd chosen her genuine connection. Whatever was troubling Morgan wasn't going to be allowed to knock things off track.

Morgan picked up the menu card. 'Giant champagne and lemon prawn vol-au-vent,' she read. 'Like a twist on a prawn cocktail. I guess they're doing like Christmas dinner classics?'

'Sounds like it.'

'Oh, unless you're vegetarian.'

'No.' Grace tried to think of something further to share.

'I'm pescatarian,' Morgan said, barely chipping the silence between them. 'So I eat fish.'

169

'Sure.'

Grace dipped her head politely to one side to allow the waiter to place her plate in front of her. The silence extended as they both took their first bites. That was fine, wasn't it? You couldn't eat and talk at the same time. But you couldn't let the silence extend too far either. 'So how are things going with your paintings? I happened to be passing the gallery you mentioned.' Was that casual enough? 'I thought your stuff was great.'

'Oh. Thank you. Not going that well to be honest though. They sold one, but that was the only real interest. I have to go and collect the rest next week.' She took a sip of champagne. 'No prizes for guessing where the crisis of confidence that made me do this...' She pointed at her hair. '...came from.'

'I liked them. They were very...' Grace had been onto Amazon and bought a book on art appreciation since her gallery visit. She wasn't going to fail to make a good match through lack of preparation. '...I thought the use of colour was evocative of the early impressionists.'

'Really? What did you think of the choice of scale?'

Scale? The book Grace had read talked about grand epic-sized pieces and about miniatures. Morgan's work was what? Sort of normal-sized.

'I thought it was great. You know, really...' Grace held her hands up in front of her to the size of the canvases she'd seen. 'Really well-scaled.'

'Thanks.'

'We publish *Art Today* where I work.' Grace steered them onto more confident territory. She was good at work. She knew what she was doing there.

'Not really my thing. That's more Old Masters isn't it?'

'Yeah.'

A silence fell between them. Grace told herself that was fine. Comfortable silence, no pressure to make chit chat – that could be a good thing, couldn't it?

Next to her, Morgan took a very deep breath in. 'Look Grace. I like you.'

'Great.' Grace waited for the fizz in her stomach to come.

'No. Not great. I mean…' Morgan took a big swig of champagne. 'I mean I like you, like in a friendly way, but I don't like *like* you, if you know what I mean.'

'Right.' Grace knew exactly what she meant. 'You're just not that into me.'

'Sorry. I mean you seem really nice, and you're really pretty and I'm sure lots of people here definitely do fancy you. It's not you…'

Grace held her hand up. There was never any need to finish that particular sentence. 'I get it.'

'Like, I like you, but there's no stomach flip. Is there?'

Grace opened her mouth to argue. Of course there was a spark. They were both attractive and intelligent; why wouldn't there be a spark? And if there wasn't then Grace could damn well make one. Just wishing for happy ever after wasn't how it worked. Sometimes you had to be prepared to put some work in. Grace could make this sparky, if that was what Morgan wanted.

'I hope you don't mind me being blunt.'

'It's not that. I just…' She just what? She was feeling piqued. She was frustrated. A spark wasn't what made a relationship. A spark was terrifying. A spark was something that you couldn't control, but a spark was what Morgan wanted. Could she really begrudge her wanting that frisson, that moment of electricity when nothing outside of that single moment, that flame between you and another human soul, could touch you? Grace hadn't felt that with Morgan. Until a few weeks ago, Grace hadn't felt that with anyone. 'Blunt is good, I guess.'

'I'm sorry.' Morgan did look slightly stricken. 'I've spent a long time learning to trust my feelings. I can tend to blurt them out a bit. Are you ok?'

Was she? The emotion that hit Grace, unexpectedly but with the force of a thousand romantic sparks, wasn't hurt or sadness, or even anger. It was relief. She smiled at Morgan. One thing she could do honestly, was reassure her. 'Yeah. I'm fine.'

'I mean what did he think he was doing? Getting details of a bloody shop without telling me, without even asking if I was interested.' Hope jabbed the air with her fork. 'And then he even went to see it. I'm lucky he hadn't forged my signature on the lease.'

Callum frowned. 'He hasn't though, has he?'

'No.' That wasn't the point. The fork jabbing resumed. 'It's presumptuous and rude and thoughtless. And he should know...' That was the crux of it. 'He should know better than anyone.'

Callum turned his chair all the way to face her properly. 'Hope! What should he know?'

'Why I don't like being pushed into stuff.'

He nodded immediately. 'Cos of your ex?'

'Yeah. Theo was there. He saw how I was...' She shook her head. The state of Hope at the end of her last relationship was not a topic for lunchtime chit chat. 'He's supposed to be my best mate.'

'Maybe it was well-intentioned?'

'You're too nice.'

'Nah. I'm just trying to cheer you up.'

'That's sweet. I can't believe he'd try to push me into this.'

Callum took her hand. 'How about we make a deal? I'll never try to make you do anything you don't want to.'

'Thank you.'

'So what if you put Theo out of your mind, stop waving cutlery at me like an offensive weapon and we enjoy the rest of the day?'

That was exactly what she needed. She didn't need bullying or cajoling. She needed someone who supported her and let her be. 'Sounds perfect,' she whispered.

Emma surveyed the room from her vantage point in the corner. The main course had been served and was now being cleared away from the first tables. Generally conversation seemed to be flowing, and there was a pleasing amount of 'accidental' arm touching going on. She scanned the room for people who were alone, people not turned towards either of their neighbours.

Unsurprisingly Grace and Morgan were deep in conversation. Slightly more surprisingly Jon and Connie were too. Maybe Emma needed to give herself more credit. Maybe love was going to blossom after all. She sought out Theo Carter. The young woman to his left was making a valiant effort to chat to him, but Theo himself looked disengaged. Emma frowned. That wouldn't do. That wouldn't do at all.

While she was watching Theo pushed his chair back from the table and stood up. Emma followed him towards the exit. 'Where are you going?'

'Do you usually follow your clients to the toilet?'

Emma gestured back across the dining room. 'The toilets are that way.'

He sighed. 'You got me. I'm heading home. Look, you gave it a fair crack but...'

'Wait!'

Theo slowed down enough for her to catch him at the top of the steps.

'At least promise me you'll come to the next event. You've...' She stopped herself. She was going to say he'd paid already, but actually Theo hadn't paid anything. 'You've come this far,' she finished, which even to Emma's ear was pretty lame.

'Why do you care? I only came to keep Hope company. She was your project and she's love's young dream now.'

'I care because you're still a client and it's my job.' And one day I'm going to achieve my perfect run, she added in her head.

'Fine. If it means you won't chase me down the street, I'll promise to come to the next thing.'

'Good.' Emma would have to be satisfied with that. 'Thank you.'

She marched back into the dining room. Pudding bowls were being cleared. The logistics of making sure everyone got their individual pudding from Stir-up Sunday had been a right pain, but Emma had persevered, despite Josh's repeated insistence that nobody would know whose pudding they were eating, so long as they got the right label. Not the point. Not the point at all.

Most of the daters were still settled in their seats, waiting for coffee or another drink and mints. Emma wanted them to linger over the meal. The sit-down lunch was a chance for real conversation, one to one. A couple of clients were on the move though. Morgan Landy had made it out of the door before Emma could catch her, leaving Grace flying solo again. And Connie Price also looked like she was making a move. Emma was quicker than her. 'Heading off?'

'Yeah,' said Connie. 'I've got somewhere to be this afternoon.'

Emma didn't believe it for a second. 'It looked like you and Jon were getting on well?'

'Yeah.' Connie sounded surprised. 'He's not so bad once you get under the serious business face. Not my type, but maybe he'll find someone.'

Not Connie's type. Damn. Emma looked back across the room. That meant Theo Carter, Connie and Grace, Morgan and Jon were all still utterly uncoupled. Her positive mood slumped. She made her way out through the side door and sat down on the back staircase, and pulled her phone out of her bag.

'Hey. How's it going?'

'Terribly.'

Tom sighed on the end of the line. 'I'm sure that's not true.'

'It is. None of the people I was worried about are any nearer to finding the one. I ended up chasing one of them halfway out the building to convince him to come back.'

Her boyfriend laughed.

'It's not funny.'

'It's a bit funny.'

'You're supposed to be making me feel better.' She paused. 'Sorry. I'm not supposed to be dumping my work on you.'

'It's fine. I wanna be the person you ring when you need to unload.'

She smoothed her skirt over her knees. 'It's no good. None of them are any closer to happy ever after. What am I going to do?'

'Don't give up.'

'I did literally have to chase one of them down the stairs to persuade him not to give up on the whole thing.'

'Well that sounds familiar.'

And so it did. The last client Emma had run after in an attempt, an attempt which had at the time seemed all but futile, to persuade him not to give up on love, was Tom himself.

'And I stuck around,' he reminded her.

'Yeah, but I don't think I can sleep with everyone who clearly has no hope of finding anyone else, can I?'

'Ooof,' her boyfriend let out a gasp of mock offence. 'Like a knife to the heart. Seriously though, I was only there to keep Mum happy. If you can change my mind, there's hope for anyone.'

'You really think so?'

'In matters of romance, you're the best of the best. You've got this.'

'Thanks.' For a moment her professional confidence had wavered. 'I needed the pep talk.'

'Always happy to oblige.' He was quiet a second.

Emma filled the silence. 'I'll be done here in an hour or so if you want to do something.'

'Erm… I've got stuff on later.'

'Sure.' Why wouldn't he? 'No problem. Maybe during the week.'

Another silence. 'This week isn't great. Can we catch up after next weekend?'

'So Monday evening? You could come to me?'

'Sure.' He fell quiet again. 'You don't mind?'

'Of course not. Are you ok?' Something in his voice told her he wasn't.

'I'm fine. Just a bit preoccupied.'

'And you're coming to the craft thing next Saturday?'

'My keyboard skills will be at your disposal.'

'Thank you. I didn't want to impose, but all our regular musicians have Christmas events and concerts and…'

'It's fine.' His voice remained tense.

'And you're really ok?'

'Really. You'd better get back to work. I'll see you next week.'

'Bye then…' But he'd already hung up the phone.

–

Morgan had eaten a polite amount of her dessert and then made her excuses, claiming a busy work day and a need to clean up her studio before she got into things tomorrow. Grace had let her leave. Morgan was right. There was no romantic spark there, and however much Grace might have tried to convince her that a spark could grow, they'd have been starting from a position of both wondering if there was something more exciting out there.

'You're on your own too?'

Grace didn't need to turn her head to recognise the voice. 'I thought you were engrossed with Connie.'

'I was. She's ever such good fun, your sister.'

Way to choose your words. Fun. Connie was the wild one. Sure, she was the moody disruptive one too, but she was fun. Grace wasn't fun.

Jon slid into the vacant seat next to her. 'Not as much fun as you though.'

Grace noticed that Morgan hadn't finished her champagne. She tipped the leftovers into her glass. 'I'm not fun.'

'I beg to differ.' He leaned in close to her, as he always seemed to, so she could feel his breath on her ear. 'Shall we get out of here?'

'I don't do one-night stands.'

'Well you couldn't if you wanted to. It's the middle of the afternoon.'

'What happened with us was a mistake.'

He raised an eyebrow. 'Was it?'

'Of course it was.'

'Why?'

'Because…' He was exasperating. 'Because I don't do casual sex.'

'You definitely do.'

'Well that one time. Not normally. We're supposed to be here looking for a relationship, not…' She closed her eyes without thinking about it to block out his closeness. It didn't help. Everything they'd done together was there playing on a loop inside her head.

'And is there anyone here you want to start a relationship with?'

'Well I haven't met everyone yet.'

'Of those you have met?'

Grace shook her head.

'So tell me, what is the perfect relationship that none of the several hundred people on offer today can't provide?'

That was a stupid question. Everyone knew what a perfect relationship was. You dated a while and then moved in and then engagement, marriage, nice house somewhere out of the capital and then children. Most people thought two, but Grace thought three. Two could be intense.

'What are you thinking?' Jon asked. 'Two point four kids. Roses round the front door. White picket fence?'

'No. Not exactly.' But wasn't that what everyone wanted really? 'So what do you want then? If you don't want that?'

'I want to take you to bed.'

'And then what?'

He frowned again. 'Why does there have to be a then?'

'Because that's how time works.'

'Fine. And then nothing. I don't want to find the love of my life. I'm not offering a relationship. I do not want to be anybody's boyfriend. I do not want to meet your friends or your parents. I do not want to go to to…' He actually grimaced at the

177

word. '…IKEA with you on a wet bank holiday and talk about bookcases.' He stopped and looked up, meeting her gaze. 'I do want to have sex with you, possibly quite a lot of sex. On the simple basis that we've done it before and I enjoyed it very much. And it seemed as though you did as well.'

'That's not how relationships work,' Grace protested again.

'And I'm not offering a relationship.'

Grace told herself she wasn't tempted. This wasn't her. 'Just sex.'

'Well, sex. Never say *just* sex.'

He leaned towards her again, this time as if to kiss her. Grace would move away. Of course she would move away. But then he stopped, a fraction away from pressing his mouth to hers. Grace's lips parted involuntarily.

Jon moved back. 'Well I'm going to go. You're very welcome to come too.'

Grace watched him move away, waiting for him to slow down or look back. He didn't. Oh for goodness' sake. She grabbed her bag and walked as briskly as she could manage without in any way giving the impression that she was running after a man.

She caught up with Jon as he stepped out of the lift and she arrived, slightly flustered and pink in the face, at the bottom of the stairs. If he was surprised to see her he gave no indication of it. 'The car will be here in a moment.'

Chapter Sixteen

It was the same driver as the last time. 'Miss Price.'

'Does he have to remember the names of all your conquests?'

'Don't use that word.'

'What word?'

'Conquest. It makes it sound as though you're a poor innocent victim of my wiles, rather than a willing partner.'

'I didn't mean…'

'Good.' They didn't speak for the rest of the journey. Jon tapped away on his phone, leaving Grace to watch the city roll by outside the window until they finally pulled up outside the building she'd visited before.

Carl opened the door for her to step out, and Jon took her arm and led the way inside. She was expecting… what? The last time they had been insatiable. He hadn't been able to take his hands off her. Grace waited until they were inside the apartment until she couldn't wait any longer. If he wasn't going to make a move, then why shouldn't she?

She grabbed his belt and started working it free. Jon's hand closed over hers, calmly moved it away, and stepped back. 'Drink?'

'I thought we weren't doing that?' she challenged.

'I said I didn't want a relationship. I didn't say I couldn't be civil. We've got all afternoon.'

Grace followed him to the kitchen and accepted the glass of wine he offered her, pointedly ignoring his wince as she necked a big old gulp. Jon swirled his glass and sniffed. Grace laughed.

'What?' he asked.

'I've never seen anyone actually do that.'

His face cracked into a rare smile. 'My mother was a wine merchant. Old habits I suppose.'

'My mother was teetotal.'

Now he did look horrified.

'She wasn't well. Drink messed with her medication I think.' At least that was what Grace had always assumed.

Despite his insistence that he'd invited her here for one reason only, Jon didn't seem in any great hurry to get on with things. Grace took a moment to take in her surroundings. The kitchen opened on to a huge open-plan dining and living space with floor-to-ceiling windows and views across the Thames. Everything in the room was elegant, from the pale cream of the seating to the inky blues of the art hanging on the otherwise bare wall. It was beautiful. It also gave the apartment the air of a very high-class hotel. It was tasteful, but somehow impersonal.

'Where's all your stuff?'

'What do you mean?' Jon looked around. 'This is my stuff.'

'But like books, and music, and junk mail, and you know…' Grace tried to think what detritus filled their house. Hope was pretty obsessive about getting rid of actual rubbish, but there was still a healthy level of lived-in clutter. 'Like, you know, the stuff you buy and then don't quite know where to put.'

Jon frowned. 'Why would I buy something without a use or a place for it?'

Now Grace was horrified. 'Because buying stuff is fun. Like, do you never go on Amazon to find a book and then accidentally add a garden parasol and a kettle bell to your basket?'

'No garden, and the building has a very well-equipped gym downstairs.'

'Of course it does.' Grace moved to the window. If she lived here, to be fair, she wouldn't be worrying about art on the walls or personal touches inside. She'd spend the whole time right here, looking at this view. 'I love London.'

'You grew up here?'

Grace nodded. She'd never understood people who came to the city and found it overwhelming or cold. It was really an interconnected mass of a hundred tiny villages and different town centres, each bleeding into the next. 'What about you?'

Jon shook his head. 'No. I ran away to the big city the very first chance I had though.'

Grace opened her mouth to ask another question, but Jon's hand removing the wine glass from her own stopped her. He set her glass down and slid his arm back around her body, pulling her against him and pressing his lips to her neck. It seemed the time for small talk was over. Something about this slower, more languid approach was putting Grace on edge though. When everything was a frenzy she hadn't had a chance to stop and think, and now that she did, it felt as though she ought to be doing more. There was no hiding the fact that Jon was hugely sexually confident. Grace had a growing worry that she ought to be doing something more to please him, to show him that she was willing to get on with things if that was what he wanted.

Grace levered herself out from under him and stood up. 'Shall we get on with it?'

Jon retrieved his wine glass from the glass side table and took a seat in front of the window.

She stopped in the doorway. 'What are you doing?'

'I'm sorry, but I don't consider "shall we get on with it?" to qualify as foreplay. And, as I said, we've got all day. I'm presuming you don't have anywhere else to be?'

'No, but I thought...'

'We agreed I wasn't your boyfriend. We did not agree on a schedule.' His expression softened slightly. 'Sit down. Drink your wine. Take your shoes off before you put your feet on the sofa.'

'Yes sir,' Grace deadpanned.

Jon shot an eyebrow up. 'Sir?'

'Not in a sexy way.'

'Let me be the judge of that.'

Grace kicked off her shoes and took the seat next to him. She wasn't used to feeling unsettled on a... her mind wanted to say date, but that definitely wasn't what this was. She wasn't used to feeling unsettled with the people she dated. Lately, before the Season, she seemed to mostly go out with well-groomed young men, the sort of men who came in and out of the building where she sat behind reception all day, for meetings and interviews and to generally make their way in the world. Men who had moved through their post-university wild phase and were at the point of looking for a nice young girl to bring home to their parents. Men who were looking to settle down – and yet none of them ever had. Or at least, Grace had never settled down with any of them.

Jon lifted his head. 'What are you thinking about?'

'Nothing.'

'Bollocks. You were miles away. I want you in the room.'

'Sorry.'

'I shall have to work harder on keeping your attention.'

Jon moved to kneel in front of her. And then, without breaking eye contact for a second, he pushed her skirt up her thighs and ran his hand up her leg until her reached the soft cotton of her knickers. He slid a finger under the elastic at each hip. Grace raised her bum from the sofa to allow him to pull her underwear away. He lifted her foot and placed one leg over his shoulder and then kissed his way from her ankle, up her calf, across the ticklish spot at the back of her knee, and moved up higher still, where his pace slowed to a languid lick, as he nuzzled every inch of her inner thigh. Grace should definitely be doing something a bit more interactive now. He'd hardly be impressed by her just lying back and letting him do all the work. She tried to angle her body up to pull his lips to her face, but he raised a hand to her torso, holding her back in her seat.

'I don't want…'

Immediately he stopped. 'Don't want what?'

'I don't… I'm not really into…' She gestured towards his lips. There was something about a man taking this much time over her that put her on edge. It gave her the feeling that she was taking up too much attention.

He leaned back on his heels. 'What don't you like about it?'

'I don't know.' She looked away. 'It feels a bit selfish.'

'What?'

'Like I ought to be doing something for you.'

His expression was one of genuine confusion. 'We're not conducting a business negotiation.'

'But like, I should be trying to make you...' Her voice trailed off. 'You know.'

'And this is also not a race to the finish line.' He kneeled back on his heels. 'How about this? For the remainder of the day I give you full dispensation to do nothing, to think for not one second of anyone's pleasure but your own.'

'But...'

'But nothing. I am entirely happy, and it is entirely my concern if I find that I'm not.' He raised a sceptical eyebrow, and bent his lips to her thigh. 'Now do you really not like that?' he asked.

'I don't know.'

'I love it,' he continued. 'I love the feeling of giving someone that much pleasure, of being completely focused on making another human being lose themselves entirely. It's as if you are completely in their service, and completely in control all at the same time.'

Grace's heartbeat moved up a notch.

'If you let me, I would love to run my tongue all the way up...' His finger traced a line up her thigh, and brushed across the triangle of neatly trimmed hair, before trailing down and stopping right on the edge of her. And then, very slowly, excruciatingly slowly, he moved his hand so his thumb was brushing against her. 'I want to hear you gasp. I want to make you beg me to keep going. I want my lips pressed against you while you come so hard you forget your own name.' He lifted his hand. 'But if you want me to stop...'

She should want him to stop. She should walk away right now. She should commit to the next chinless wonder who asked her out to dinner and get on with the life plan that led to the nice house out of the city and the three, not two, children and... and... and... 'Don't stop.'

Afterwards, after he'd done everything he'd described, and then, finally, taken her to bed, and done most of it again, Jon lifted his head on his hand and looked at her with the same cool gaze he always seemed to adopt. Half disinterested, half amused. 'So might you have enjoyed that after all?'

'I might.'

'Good. But, I have to say, this new discovery does not reflect well on your previous sexual partners.'

Grace wasn't thinking about them. She wasn't thinking about anything. She was spent. Actually spent. There was no thought in her head. Sex with Jon had left her fizzing with energy and utterly numb all at the same time.

'You look exhausted.'

'Gotta go home. Need sleep.'

Jon smiled. 'You can sleep here.'

'No. Girlfriends stay over. Whatever this is, people don't stay the night.'

'Grace, it's not even eight in the evening. Have a nap. When you wake up Carl can take you home.'

She frowned. She definitely wasn't going to stay the night. Neither of them wanted that. But lying in bed, on the most ridiculous… 'What's the thread count of these sheets?'

'I have no idea.'

It was high. She was sure of that. Anyway… lying in bed, on the most ridiculous sheets, every single muscle in her body relaxed and overwhelmed, the thought of closing her eyes for a minute or two was too good to resist. 'Just a nap,' she murmured.

–

When she opened her eyes it took a second to orient herself. Unfamiliar sheets. Window on the wrong side of the bed. Sounds coming from down the hall. Unfamiliar sheets. Stupidly high thread count. Grace sat up and located her phone in her bag next to the bed.

8.43.

She must only have been asleep an hour. Not even that. Light was streaming in at the window. No. There was no way she'd have slept through Jon coming to bed and then getting up again.

'You're awake.' Jon was fully dressed, in formal shirt and trousers. Shit.

'I'm late for work.' Grace jumped out of bed. Where was her dress? Could she wear that for work? If she threw it on right now and ran to the Tube, she'd still be what? Well over an hour late. And even if she could get away with last night's dress, her hair was... she put a hand to her head, and had a flashback to Jon coming all over... her hair definitely needed washing. 'Shit.'

'You work for Harker and Riley?'

Grace nodded.

'Building by London Bridge?'

Another nod.

Jon pulled his phone from his pocket. 'Call Genevieve Riley.'

'What are you doing?'

Jon held up a finger to silence her. 'Gen, good morning. Sorry to ring so early... Yes. Great. It's just that I wasn't sure who to call? I'm with one of your employees. Grace Price. Receptionist...'

'Head Receptionist,' Grace muttered.

'...at the H and R building. Yes. Well she's been taken ill. I wondered if you could pass the message along.' He nodded. 'Thank you. Oh no. Nothing serious I don't think, but she does need to stay in bed today.' Another pause. 'Oh yes. Of course we can discuss that. How old is she? Gosh. It seems like no time at all since we were ordering christening gifts. So sweet sixteen?' He frowned. 'Taylor Swift? Right. No. Let me see what I can do. I'll get back to you.' He hung up the phone. 'There you go. Genevieve Riley's office will contact your boss and tell him you're not coming in today.'

She ought to be cross with him for taking over, but she didn't have the energy to pretend she wasn't relieved. 'How do you know Genevieve Riley?'

Jon shrugged. 'She's a client.'

'What do you actually do?'

Another shrug. 'Various things. And you're a receptionist?'

'Head Receptionist,' she repeated.

'I apologise. Tricky job. Keeping smiling when everyone wants something different from you?'

Grace nodded. 'Yeah. People usually say "*just* a receptionist".' Her tone challenged him to try it.

'No. No. The right first impression is everything.' He looked her slowly up and down.

Grace pulled the duvet higher to cover herself. The feeling of being seen made her suddenly want to hide. She changed the subject. 'I'm sorry I fell asleep.'

'It's fine. I didn't want to wake you. You looked like you needed the rest. I'm afraid I do have work to do, even more work now I've talked to Genevieve, so make yourself at home. Shower through there.' He pointed out the smoked glass door at the far side of the bedroom. 'Towels in the cabinet. Coffee in the kitchen.'

'Thank you. I'll be out of your hair in no time. Sorry.'

'No rush.' He moved to the bed and leaned down to kiss her, hard and passionate.

Grace was coming out of the shower, wrapped in one of the huge fluffy towels she'd found, when she heard the second voice.

'Why don't you have a tree?'

'What? I just…'

'Fine. I'll leave it on the bed.'

'Wait!' That was Jon. 'I can take it.'

Whoever he was talking to, he was too slow. The bedroom door swung open and a woman carrying a large gift-wrapped box appeared. A short blonde woman, in a three-quarter-length puffer coat, who seemed quite at home until she stopped and stared, open-mouthed, at Grace's hurried attempts to secure her towel.

A man who didn't want a relationship. A man who disclosed precious little about his personal life. A man whose city apartment was devoid of personal touches. How on earth could Grace have been so blind? A man, she now realised, with a wife and kids squirrelled away somewhere in the countryside.

The woman stared from Grace to Jon and back again. Grace braced for the fury that was clearly about to come her way. The only option open to her was to get her defence in first. 'I didn't know.'

The woman frowned.

'I didn't know,' Grace repeated. It was all she could think of to say. Her only other thought was that she had to get out of here. She had to get far away from Jon and his... his what? Wife? Girlfriend? Grace picked up her clothes with as much dignity as she could muster. And then she stopped. Why should she be the one who was embarrassed?

With a firm grip on her towel, she turned back. 'You should probably know that he's signed up for a whole dating agency thing.'

The woman beamed. 'And that's where he met you? Oh, brilliant!' She turned in the doorway and shouted over her shoulder. 'You went? To the Season?'

Jon joined her in the doorway, his face pinched and tight. 'I did.'

'I never thought you'd actually go.'

'But he's telling people he's single,' Grace pointed out. Was that true? Grace wasn't actually sure it had ever been discussed, but she'd met him at a dating event. That definitely strongly implied single.

'He... what?' The woman's face creased, first into a frown and then a smile. As was becoming the norm in the time she spent with Jon, Grace felt as though she was half a step behind. 'Put the girl out of her misery, sweetie.'

'Sarah, Grace. Grace, Sarah. My sister-in-law.'

Oh.

'I was married to his brother,' the stranger, Sarah apparently, quickly added. She smiled at Grace. 'So Grace, tell me all…'

Her enquiry was firmly cut off by Jon taking the woman by the elbow and steering her out of the door. 'Why don't we leave Grace to get dressed?'

'I'll make her a cup of tea,' Grace heard. 'Would you like a cup of tea, Grace?'

She was honestly absolutely parched. 'Yes, please.'

Grace hurriedly put on in yesterday's dress and tights, which were ridiculously over the top for a Monday morning cup of tea. Jon must have a sweatshirt or jumper or something she could put on for warmth and to lessen the general walk of shame look of her cocktail frock. She opened a wardrobe and had to stifle a giggle of shock. A row of white shirts, all identical, all perfectly pressed, all still in the covers in which, she assumed, they'd been returned from the dry cleaners. Another row of dark trousers, similarly pristine, and then jackets. She opened a drawer. Underwear neatly rolled in perfect rows. The man did not appear to own a single item of casual wear. She opened the final drawer. Finally! Sportswear. Two pairs of navy blue shorts. Two pairs of navy blue running pants. Five breathable T-shirts. No hoodie? No sweatshirt? She gave up. She'd be cold, but at least Grace wouldn't get the blame for messing up whatever anally retentive laundry system he had going on here.

She checked herself in front of the mirror, before making her way through to the kitchen. She would have to do.

Sarah was still chuntering at Jon's poor hospitality. She looked up when Grace came in. 'Has he even offered you breakfast?'

'It's fine.'

'I told her to help herself,' Jon insisted without looking up from the laptop that was open in front of him.

'Only to coffee,' Grace corrected.

He didn't reply.

'Let me get you something.'

'It's fine. I should get going.'

'Not a chance.' Sarah was dropping teabags into mugs. 'Milk? Sugar?'

'Just milk.'

'And you are not going anywhere until you've given me all the gossip. I never meet any of Jon's...' she hesitated. 'Friends. He always tells me he doesn't have any...' Another arch pause. 'Friends.'

'I have friends.'

Sarah mouthed, 'He doesn't,' at Grace. 'So why don't we go into the snug and leave Grumpy to his work?'

Grace followed Sarah to the other side of the living space and through a door she hadn't tried before. The smaller reception room was lined with bookcases full to overflowing with hardbacks. 'Does he buy these by the metre?' joked Grace.

'You wash your mouth out,' Sarah laughed. 'I can't imagine him ever considering something so uncultured.' She took a seat at one of the sofas in the middle of the room, and waited for Grace to join her. 'So, how did you meet?'

'Oh, erm, we're both doing this dating thing.' Grace shook her head. 'It's silly.'

Sarah squealed. 'The Season! You're doing the Season. Oh my God, I will never let him live this down.'

'What do you mean?'

Sarah grinned. 'I may have bullied him into signing up. Not bullied. Encouraged. Persuaded.' She paused. 'No. Actually not even bullied. I didn't tell him 'til after I signed him up.' She smiled. 'And now here you are.'

'We really are just friends.'

'Mmmm hmmm.'

'Really.'

'You were coming out of his en suite shower at nine in the morning.'

So clearly not just friends. 'It's not serious.'

'Oh God.' Sarah slumped back in her chair. 'Did he give you the "I'm not interested in being anyone's boyfriend" speech?'

'No,' Grace lied. She wasn't sure why. Acknowledging it felt disloyal somehow.

'Course he didn't. Ugh. That man is his own worst enemy.'

'So you're married to Jon's brother?' Grace dived for a change of subject.

'Yes. No. I was.' She took a long sip of tea. 'Sorry. You'd think I'd be better at explaining it by now wouldn't you? He died. My husband. Jon's brother. Matt. Four years ago. He was in the army so I'd had years of that worry in the back of my mind, and then he came back from Afghanistan all in one piece and got knocked off his bike near Hackney Marshes.'

'I'm so sorry.'

'It's all right. I didn't talk about him to anyone except Jon for a long time. It's nice to be able to say his name without bursting into tears. And lots of people have it worse than us. I get his army pension and Jon's been so kind.' Sarah leaned forward. 'Matt's parents were never that keen on me to be honest. Not the sort of girl they imagined their son with. Jon always stood up for us. He's a better man than he gives himself credit for.'

Grace was about to ask what that meant when the man himself appeared in the doorway. 'I thought you had lots of things to do,' he said pointedly to his sister-in-law.

'Fine. I'll leave you to your...' She looked from Jon to Grace and back again. 'Whatever this is. But you must come to dinner, the pair of you. I could invite your parents as well.' She smiled at Jon. 'They always say they want to see the grandchildren more, and the two of you being there would be the perfect distraction from how much they hate me!'

'No thank you.' Jon's tone was definite.

'But I haven't got all the gossip out of Grace yet.'

'And now you've missed your chance.'

He ushered Sarah, very much against her will, out of the apartment.

'I'm sorry about that.'

'It's fine. She seems nice.'

'She is. And you thought she was what? My secret wife?'

'No.' Grace couldn't meet his eye. 'I mean, I don't know.'

'Well for the record I'm offended both that you think I would tell such a predictable lie, and also at the slur on my organisational abilities.'

'What?'

'I told you I wasn't looking for a relationship. That preference does rather rule out having a wife.' The chill in his voice didn't quite match the hint of laughter in his gaze. 'And if I was secretly married I would ensure that there was absolutely no risk of you running into her.'

Grace shook her head. Teasing Jon she could deal with. 'I must have had a moment of insanity. What sort of woman would want to tie herself to you anyway?' As soon as the question left her lips she heard it. 'I didn't mean tie, like tied, like tied up, like you know.'

The hint of amusement in his voice reached his lips. 'Shame.'

Grace refused to get drawn in. 'She told me about your brother.'

'I see.'

'I'm sorry. I can't imagine what that must be like. I mean Connie does my head in but...' It really was unimaginable. Connie was a pain in the butt, but she was Grace's pain in the butt. She tethered Grace to the earth somehow.

'It's fine.'

'No. It's not.'

Jon's face had resumed the cool distant expression that said don't come any closer. 'Well it was a long time ago now. I really do need to work. You're welcome to stay so long as you're quiet, or I can call Carl to take you home.'

She was being dismissed. Grace folded her arms. 'It's fine. I can get the Tube perfectly well.'

Chapter Seventeen

The impeccably dressed woman on the other end of the video call was tapping her ear in the universally recognised gesture for 'I can't hear you'.

'Oh bugger,' muttered Emma, and tapped the unmute button. 'I think I'm muted. Can you hear me now?'

'I can hear you now. I think you were muted.'

Emma nodded. 'Sorry.'

'That's just fine.' Nina Elton in person was perfectly made up, dressed in a red tailored top, lips and nails painted scarlet to match. 'I am so excited to be talking to you.'

Emma smoothed down her shirt, so as not to show a single crease on camera, and tried to make her face look as excited as she was definitely supposed to feel. 'Yeah. Totally. It's great.'

'Now you know how much we love what you're doing. My assistant read about it on your *Evening Standard* website, and simply could not sleep until they'd brought it to me. It's so right for this moment. Such a wonderful synergy.'

'Thank you.'

'Every girl in New York is desperate for her Mr Darcy. Or her perfect Regency duke, if you know what I mean?'

Emma knew exactly what she meant.

'And we're suckers for that English accent. It just evokes a more proper way of doing things. You understand what I'm saying?'

Emma did. She felt herself preening slightly at the recognition. She had created something that this stranger from the other side of the world was excited by. 'Well, even over here the appeal of a bygone age is strong.'

Emma thought back to when she'd first conceived the idea of a brand new social season. 'The idea of falling in love in person never goes out of fashion.'

'You are so right. "Never out of fashion." I'm noting that down right now, Emma. So shall we talk next steps? We would love to bring the Season to the US. Starting in New York, and then who knows? Rolling out to LA, Chicago, San Francisco, Seattle, Dallas. The sky's the limit.'

'Right, well, what do you want to know?'

'Straight to the point. I love it,' the woman laughed. 'What I want to know is your price.'

'What? Well…' Emma had thought this was going to be a nice chat to share ideas and then thank you very kindly and the glamorous American would go to do her own thing. She hadn't been expecting to be offered actual money.

'How much to license the idea for the US market? And then of course your remuneration on top of that. There'll be a relocation package obviously, in addition to whatever salary you require.'

Emma opened and shut her mouth a couple of times. What was happening?

'I think you might have gone on mute again, sweetie.'

'No. Sorry. I was a little bit taken aback.'

'Of course. I know what you Brits are like when it comes to talking about money. What do you say I tell you what we were thinking and you can let me know whether we're in the right ball park?'

'Sure.'

Nina Elton said a number.

'I'm sorry. Can you say that again?'

Emma had heard her correctly.

'That's in dollars of course.'

'Of course.' Dollars, pounds, Macedonian denars – it made no difference. It was a really really big number. Bigger than Emma knew what to do with, anyway.

Nina was still talking, breaking down the headline figure into an annual licence and Emma's own remuneration package. 'So obviously your package could be renegotiated at the end of the first Season. We understand you might not want to stay stateside forever. I'm sure you've got a love of your own back there?'

She did. Of course.

'Anyway, having you here to steer the inaugural ship is worth every last cent for us. So what do you say?'

Emma realised she was doing the goldfish thing again. 'I think I might need to call you back.'

Josh was in the kitchen when Emma finished the call. 'How did it go?'

'She wants to give us silly money to license the idea of the Season, and she wants to pay me to move to New York to run it for her.' Emma sank onto a chair at the kitchen table.

Her brother stared at her. 'That's incredible. We should celebrate. We should go out. Or wait… I know…' He opened the fridge and pulled out a bottle of champagne. 'This was supposed to be for Annie for our two-month anniversary but I can get another.'

'It's the middle of the day.'

'So what? It's the middle of an amazing day.' He opened the fizz and poured two glasses. 'Seriously, Stilts, this is incredible. You totally deserve it.' He raised his glass. 'To you. To all the money and to New York City!'

'To New York City,' Emma muttered through her daze and took a sip.

'What are we celebrating?' said Tom. Tom was here. Of course Tom was here. She'd left him upstairs, apparently dealing with emails, but probably actually playing poker online. She'd told him she had a call.

'We…' Josh started.

'It's Josh and Annie's two month-iversary.'

'Their what?' asked Tom.

'Since the wedding,' Josh chipped in. 'Two whole months.'

'But Annie's not here.' Tom frowned. 'And it isn't. That's next week.'

'No. Right. That's why it doesn't matter that Annie isn't here. We're rehearsing.'

'Rehearsing drinking champagne?'

Emma wasn't sure whether her boyfriend or her brother was currently the most confused by her behaviour. She gave Josh a look which she hoped communicated that this was a delicate stage in her relationship with Tom and they'd found a nice equilibrium, partly based on Emma trying not to be quite such an unrepentant workaholic, and the America thing was still more likely to turn out to be a pipe dream rather than anything concrete, so why rock the boat for no good reason? She didn't think he really got it.

'We're trying the champagne. It's from the caterer, for the final ball, but it's a different one to what we've had before so we wanted to try it. And then Josh thought we shouldn't spring an experimental champagne on Annie on her actual anniversary.'

'Heaven forbid,' said Tom.

'Right. So we're just trying it now.' Emma smiled, like everything she'd said made perfect sense. 'Do you want to try some?'

He glanced at the clock. 'Sure. Why not? I do think you two are getting madder though. I mean it's too late for Annie. She signed a contract, but you know, I could still...'

He gestured towards the door.

'Don't even think about it,' Emma laughed.

–

Hope didn't need to look at her phone to know who the message was from. It would be Theo. Like the previous fifteen messages he'd sent in the three days since they'd talked at the Season Christmas meal. And the three voicemails he'd left. And the one time that he'd come round to the house and Hope had told Grace to tell him she was out.

But she did look anyway.

'Theo again?' Callum asked.

'Sorry. I'll put it away.' They were sitting in the corner of the coffee shop in the hospital foyer. Hope looked around. 'Sorry I don't have time for a proper lunch break either.'

Callum grinned. 'It's fine. No pressure. I know it must be horrific at this time of year.'

Flu season was always the worst time in the hospital, but recently it felt like all the times were the worst time. Everyone was stressed. Everyone was getting sick. Staff were coming to HR with problems. Management were coming to HR expecting her to make all the staff problems go away. She was exhausted. 'Always busy,' she muttered. 'I could do without my supposed best friend putting all this extra stuff on me. I've told him I'm not interested.'

Callum took her hand. 'And that's all you can do. He shouldn't be pressuring you like this.'

Back in her office Hope moved numbers into columns and papers from one tray to another. The only small highlight was seeing Charlotte's official notification of her request for parental leave in her inbox. A new baby. That was something to look forward to at least.

Who would her and Callum's babies look like? She shook her head at the thought. Hugely premature. They'd only been dating a few weeks. They hadn't even said the L word yet. They would, Hope thought. Callum wasn't the type to drag his heels and pretend something was casual when it obviously wasn't.

Her phone pinged again.

Please call me. I'm sorry. Can we talk?

Three days was nothing, but three days was also the longest Hope had gone without at least messaging Theo since she'd met him on the first day of freshers' week eleven years ago. They were an odd couple – *we're not a couple*, added the voice in her head – precisely because they weren't a couple and had never had so much as a flirtation in that direction. People asked sometimes and Theo fell into a horrified silence. They were so close that most of their mutual friends refused, absolutely, to believe that there had never even been so much as a moment between them.

But there hadn't.

Unless you counted, Hope smiled at the memory, unless you counted that very first evening. Freshers' week, in the students' union bar. She'd already met Theo, who had a room down the corridor from her in halls and had cropped up again at registration for her actual course. And they'd been dancing – not couply dancing, but crazy drunk eighteen-year-old dancing, her and Theo and about half the university from the way she remembered it. Everyone else had sort of drifted in and out of the circle but she and Theo had stayed all night, and then they'd walked back to their rooms and there'd been a fraction of a second where she'd thought he was going to kiss her, but he hadn't, and she remembered thinking, 'That's ok. We've got the whole three years.'

And of course the very next day, they'd gone to a party and met Simon. Simon Wooller, who was handsome and charming and ever so slightly lost, and Hope had made it her mission to save him.

And it was all for the best. Not the Simon part necessarily, but that she and Theo had never, because it meant that she'd gained a friend. A best friend. She sighed. However pissed off with him she was, you couldn't not talk to your best friend for more than a few days. She tapped a reply.

I'm pissed off with you.

He replied almost instantly. *I know. Can we talk? I can come over tonight?*

Callum was working. She didn't have any plans beyond a ready meal for one and bad TV, and she was desperate not to spend another evening stuck in the office. *Ok. See you about 6.15?*

It was ten past six when Hope turned the corner towards home and saw Theo pacing the pavement outside. She stifled a laugh. It was not like him to be on edge. But then, they'd never really fallen out before. Perhaps this was just what he was like without her. Utterly unable to cope.

'Hi.'

He stopped pacing at the sound of her voice. 'Hi. I'm sorry.'

'You're forgiven.' Because of course he was forgiven. The number of times he'd held her hair while she puked, or run interference with her mother when Hope couldn't cope with her any more, bought him a certain amount of messing-up allowance. And the shop was a sweet idea, in its own wrong-headed way. 'I know you were trying to be nice.'

'No. I'm not sorry for that.'

'What?'

'I'm sorry I didn't do this before.'

'What are you talking about?'

Theo took hold of her arm and led the way down the street.

'What are you doing?' Hope screeched.

'What I should have done to start with. Come on.' He released her arm and took her hand. He clearly wasn't actually going to force her to go anywhere, but had definitely decided on making it as tricky as possible for her to refuse. 'Look. I can't make you do anything, but seriously, just come and look.'

'Look at what?' Oh. Of course. They turned into Columbia Road. 'I already said no.'

'Just look. That's all I ask.' He stopped. 'The agent gave me the key on the promise that I would return it first thing this morning, and take her daughter's phone number, which was a little bit creepy. So please don't make all the effort I went to charming her go to waste. Just look. If you still hate it then I will never mention the idea of a shop or flowers or changing career again.'

'Fine. But only to make you shut up. And I'm retracting my forgiveness.'

'Maybe putting it on hold?' He still had hold of her hand. 'Come on.'

The shop in question was tiny, and looked even tinier because of the rubbish left behind by the previous occupant. The front was currently painted in a desperately unlovely shade of green which was peeling around the window, and part of the door was covered over with chipboard. Even in the darkness of the winter evening, Hope could see that it needed a lot of TLC.

Theo pushed the door open and led her inside, fumbling for a light switch. The space was small but functional. The shop itself would be barely big enough for two customers once the place was filled with blooms and foliage. At the back, there was a nasty vinyl-covered counter with a section that lifted up, like the end of a bar in a pub, to allow the staff to move from the back of house to the front. Behind the counter was a door to another room, larger than the first, where, presumably, additional flowers and equipment could be stored and the work of making up bouquets and displays could take place. 'So what do you think?'

What did it matter what Hope thought? The idea of running her own business, of working with flowers, was nothing more than a dream. It wasn't something she was actually going to do. And certainly not right now. She had enough on her plate with work, and her mother who wasn't getting any younger, and she was with Callum now. She hadn't even discussed the idea of quitting her job with him. 'It's fine.'

She saw Theo's shoulders slump a little.

'Imagine though,' he said. 'You behind the counter. Maybe an assistant making bouquets in the back?' He moved to the front of the shop. 'Maybe a couple of chairs here for consultations, you know, when brides come in or whatever?'

Well that was silly. 'Not enough space, and you want all your best blooms in the window. No.' Hope looked around. 'What you'd do, is you'd take out that partition.' She pointed to the wall dividing the shop space from the back room. 'And put the counter at the side, and then you could have your work space and shop space all as one. The customers would be able to see the bouquets and things you were making and that might inspire them when they were choosing, and then you could have a proper space for consultations, not cramped in the corner. You see?'

She caught the hint of a smile on Theo's lips.

'I'm still mad with you.'

'I know.'

'Do you?' He should know. He should know better than anybody. 'I don't like feeling pressured.'

'I know.' He looked around. 'That's why I thought so hard about this.' He took a deep breath. 'That's why I think so hard every time I ask you to do something.'

Hope hadn't known that. 'Don't be silly. I'm fine, mostly. It's just when I feel like people are trying to make me do something I don't want to do.'

'I wouldn't do that.'

Hope turned around, pointedly looking at the vacant shop they were standing in.

'This isn't me trying to make you do something you don't want to.' He sounded defeated. 'This was me trying to make you do something you do want to do.'

Hope shook her head. 'Not any more.'

'Fine. You came. You looked. That was all I was asking.' Theo stepped towards the door. 'Come on. I'll buy you a drink and we can talk about other things.'

Hope should have been turning to follow him. He'd admitted defeat. He was letting the whole thing go. That was what she wanted, wasn't it?

But now she was standing in the shop, she could see it. She'd have the seasonal flowers by the window. In fact, in time, she wondered if they could take the window out and put in floor to ceiling glass that she could open all the way during summer. That would probably be expensive, so at first she'd have to make do with fabulous displays of colour and joy in the window, and then the back part of the shop would have examples of the sorts of bouquets and artistic displays she could offer. And then there was the counter. The horrid vinyl thing would go obviously. She wondered if she could find a reclaimed antique replacement somewhere. That would be incredible.

'Hope!' Theo's voice broke through her thoughts, followed by his hand on her shoulder. 'Hope, are you ok?'

'I'm fine.'

'You're not fine. You're crying.'

She was. She hadn't noticed it start, but now she couldn't make it stop.

'I'm sorry. I shouldn't have pushed this.' Theo's arms wrapped around her. 'Come here.'

She let him hug her and waited for the calm to descend, but none was forthcoming. Instead she sobbed big, ugly gulping tears into her best friend's shoulder. 'I thought I was better,' she sobbed.

Theo stood back slightly and cupped her face in his hands, rubbing her tears away with his thumbs. 'What do you mean?'

'I thought I was better after Simon, but I'm still so fucking scared.'

'I know.'

'How do you know? I didn't know.'

Theo smiled at her. 'I know you. Lately you stay in your lane, even if it's not making you happy. That's why I did all this. I thought if you remembered how passionate you used to be about this stuff it might bring the spark back.' He looked down at her teary face. 'I may have misjudged that part a bit.'

Hope stood back and wiped her face on the back of her sleeve. 'No. I think you got it perfect. I didn't know I wasn't happy already.' She managed a snotty, red-faced smile. 'It was a bit of a shock.'

She looked around the shop again. She needed to think about this. She needed to make a list of pros and cons and discuss it with Callum and check the lease properly and get quotes for the work that needed doing and... 'Do you really think I can afford it?'

'It's been empty for ages, so the landlord is prepared to drop the rent quite a bit, and if we did as much of the work ourselves as we can, yeah. I think probably.'

'We?'

'What?'

'You said if *we* did the work...'

Theo nodded. 'Of course.'

It was possible. It was crazy, but it might be possible.

'So do you want to do this?'

Hope took a deep breath in. 'Well it needs a lot of work, and I need to think about the money, and…'

'Hope, do you want to do this?'

'I think I do.'

Hope's phone pinged in her pocket. She checked the message. That was weird. 'Dad. Sorry. I thought I was supposed to be going there tomorrow, but apparently there's a whole moussaka in the oven and they're wondering where I am.'

'You'd better go. Wait. Am I allowed to tell the agent you're interested?'

'Yes. You win. I'm interested.'

Hope jogged to the bus stop. She was still in work clothes, but given the confused nature of the invite, that would have to do.

Forty minutes later she was being greeted by the smell of home-cooked food and a hug which pressed her vigorously into Tina's generously proportioned bosom. 'Your dad swears he told you today. Thanks for rushing over. I don't know what I'd have done with all this food.'

Hope didn't point out that she was only one extra person and did not necessitate Tina's habitual catering for an army. 'Well I'm here now. Sorry I didn't get a chance to get changed after work.'

'Oh you look lovely, sweetheart. Doesn't she look lovely?'

Hope's dad was opening wine. 'Always a stunner. Theo not with you tonight?'

'I didn't think you invited him,' Hope argued. 'And I told you I was seeing someone.'

'You did?' Her father looked blank.

'I did.'

'Ignore him. He doesn't remember anything apart from his golf scores these days.'

'You're playing golf?' Golf seemed like the sort of thing her mother would entirely approve of, and therefore also the sort of thing her dad would run away from.

'There's a club down the road. Good bunch of chaps. A round and a pint. Can't say better than that, can you?'

'Just the one pint?' Tina queried.

Hope's dad grinned. 'Well one or two. I'm easing into my retirement, love. It's time to start enjoying life.'

Tina shook her head. Did she look a little tired? 'What have you been doing up to now?'

Her dad passed Hope a glass of wine. 'Well you can always find ways to enjoy life more.'

Over dinner conversation moved to Hope's life. She told them about Callum, the headlines at least. New Zealander, kind, funny, very sweet on Hope, and handsome – eagerly confirmed by Tina after inspection of the photos on Hope's phone. 'You'll have to bring him next time, love,' her stepmum said. 'The more the merrier. We'll miss your Theo though.'

'I'm still friends with Theo. We were never a couple.'

'Yeah. That's what you always said anyway.'

'It's true.' Hope protested. 'Anyway…' She decided it was time to move on from her love life. 'Anyway, I have other news.' It was a good idea to practise saying this out loud here, to an audience she was confident would be fully supportive, before she had to tell her mother. 'I might be leaving my job and opening a florist shop. Finally!'

Her dad laughed and then stopped abruptly. 'Oh. You're serious.'

Hope's certainty wobbled a little. 'Well, yeah. I mean it's not definite yet. I might not.'

'No. Nothing wrong with dreaming though.'

Her dad had always been a dreamer. That was why Hope was telling him first. She knew how her mother would be. Thin-lipped. Disapproving. Absolutely certain that staying in her nice, reliable, stressful, overwhelming, exhausting job was a much better idea.

'It is my dream,' Hope confirmed. 'And Theo found this empty shop, and it's small at the moment but there's a space in the back that I could use, and maybe even knock through, and, yeah. It could work I think.'

'Well that sounds wonderful,' Tina chipped in. 'Doesn't it, love?'

Hope's dad nodded. 'If that's what you want, love.'

It was what she wanted. Wasn't it?

'Risky in this economy,' he added.

Hope pushed down the sense of deflation at her dad's reaction. He was just concerned for her. That was good. That was nice. It didn't mean he wasn't excited really. The thought of telling her mother took on an even darker hue. If her father was concerned about the risk her mother would doubtless react as if she'd set fire to her life savings and moved into a crack den.

'So what else have you been up to?' her dad said. 'Tell us more about this feller of yours.'

So Hope explained about the Season and how they'd met, and that reminded her. 'Oh, there's a family thing as part of it.' She checked the details on her phone. 'Carol singing and mulled wine. You'll come, won't you?'

Which meant that she wouldn't be able to invite her mother, because she would never agree to be in the same room as Dad anyway. Much, much easier this way.

—

It was nearly half past nine when Hope got home. Connie was sitting in the kitchen, eating nachos, drinking tea and scrolling her phone. She looked up. 'You're not Grace.'

'Neither are you,' Hope pointed out. 'Were you waiting for her?'

'Not really. I got back from work and she's out. She didn't say she was going out.'

Hope frowned. 'Why were you at work so late?'

'New job. Theatre box office. Open 'til after the interval.'

'Right.' Hope definitely wasn't keeping track any more. 'What happened to the mystery shopping?'

'Just not my thing,' Connie explained. 'And did you know that she never came home on Sunday night?'

'Who?'

'Grace.'

Of course. Nobody was as close a monitor of either twin's movements as their sister.

'I think her and Morgan are doing it.'

Hope caught a whiff of something that definitely wasn't tea. 'Are you drinking wine from a mug?'

'Maybe.'

Hope wondered if an intervention was required. That seemed more like Grace's area though. 'Why are you doing that?'

'Because we didn't have any beer. Or whisky.' Connie shrugged. 'I think it was yours.'

'That's fine.' Hope added wine to her mental shopping list. 'I meant why from a mug? We own wine glasses.'

Connie pulled a face. 'They're right at the back of the cupboard.'

That was a fair point. She pulled her attention back to Connie's earlier point. 'I don't think they are.'

'Who are?'

'Grace and Morgan are. Doing it.'

'You saw what the scandal sheet said about Grace.'

That didn't mean anything. 'Morgan left really early on Sunday,' Hope explained. 'About the same time as you.'

Connie looked up. 'Did she?'

'Yeah. I saw her going when I went to the loo, and you when I was on the way back I think. Grace was definitely still there after that.'

'Ooooh. So where did she go? And where is she now? Did she hook up with someone?'

Hope thought back. 'Not that I saw.'

'She's definitely banging someone.'

'Is that your twin sixth sense talking?'

'Ew! No. We don't have psychic orgasms. That would be...' Connie pulled a face. 'Just ew. But she's out now and she hasn't told either of us and she didn't come back on Sunday. She pulled.'

It certainly sounded that way. 'Well good for her.' Hope found the half empty bottle of white in the fridge and filled her own mug. 'And it's not Morgan.'

Connie half-smiled. 'I blew my shot there anyway.'

'How come?'

'She wasn't into me.'

Yep. That would do it. 'Sorry.'

'Have you read the new scandal sheet?'

Hope shook her head. It had arrived while she was at her dad's and she'd intended to read it on the bus, but instead she'd scrolled through TikTok and then Instagram and wasted another thirty minutes of her life.

Connie tapped her phone into life. 'It's mostly the usual stuff. Past successes. Did you know she got someone together with the venue manager last time around?'

Hope nodded. Robbie and Harriet. She remembered them.

'And there's a love across the social divide with that red trouser chap you binned off the first night and some eco hippy chick.'

'Fair enough. He wasn't awful. He just didn't...' Didn't what? Didn't set Hope's heart aflutter somehow.

'And then this bit...' Connie paused. 'Listen. *After weeks of twin trouble, the denizens of the festive Season would be forgiven for thinking they really are now seeing double, as one twin has proved inconstant and changed her signature look to something rather more graceful.* They're saying I look like Grace.'

'I thought that was the idea.'

Connie pouted, which, if anything, made her look even more like her sister. 'No. Well... no. Not like Grace exactly. Just, I don't know, just less like me.' She paused.

Hope opened her mouth to tell Connie she was just fine as herself, but her cousin closed her down.

'Anyway, listen to this next bit. *We are ready to crown the festive Season's most eligible bachelor. Blessed with hope, grace and constance from the moment he walked in to our very first reception, he's yet to be blessed with the perfect match. If you want to snap up one of the prizes of the Season time is running short, and we don't think this heartsick hero will be single for too much longer...'* She looked up. 'That's Theo! Cos of the Hope, Grace and...' she pulled a face at her real name, 'Constance thing.'

'Yeah. I got it.'

Connie grinned. 'The most eligible bachelor.'

'Apparently.'

'Oh come on. He's your best mate. You must think he has some attractive qualities.'

Well obviously Theo had a surfeit of them. He was handsome and clever and funny and he genuinely did take an interest in everyone he met. Hope teased that that interest was largely in whether he could get them in to bed, but that was just teasing. He charmed people simply by listening to them as if they were the very centre of his world. Theo loved everyone, which was probably why he never committed to just one someone.

'Did he track you down tonight? He was loitering outside like a spare part when I came home before.'

'He did, and we made up.'

'Good. He was starting to unnerve the neighbours. Much easier if we can let him back in the house.'

'And then I went to my dad's.'

'How is the Wayward Uncle?'

'He's not wayward. He's living in Poplar with Tina. He's very settled.'

'Sorry. That was what Mum used to call him.'

Hope didn't take issue with that, but as lies went it wasn't a very good one. Hope's parents had still been together when Auntie Eve died, so she would have had no reason to refer to her sister's husband as wayward. 'Well, he's fine. How about your dad?'

Connie's expression tightened. 'Haven't spoken to him yet.'

'Oh Con. Tell me again. What actually happened?'

She listened to the story of the birthday lunch gone wrong. She'd heard it before, of course, but that was mostly at volume and mostly from Grace, who was seriously unimpressed with her sister's behaviour. Connie's version was more hesitant. 'I know I was out of order. I know I need to get myself together.' She gestured at her neat brown hair. 'That's kinda what this was all about. I know I need to do better.'

'Did your dad say that?'

'Not exactly. I know it's silly to freak out at him seeing someone new. I do know that.'

Hope sipped her mug wine. 'Then tell him that.'

–

It was too late in the evening to go round there now. Not that there would be any point. Her dad had sounded so disappointed in her, but also so utterly unsurprised. What could Connie say to undo that? And anyway, if he was that upset he could come to her, couldn't he?

Her thoughts were interrupted by the sound of the front door opening. 'Grace?' she called out.

A second later her sister appeared in the kitchen. 'Mug wine? Pour me one.'

'So where have you been?' Hope stood and grabbed a clean mug. 'Connie thinks you've pulled.'

'What?'

'She thinks you're banging someone from the Season and that's where you were tonight.'

'No!' Grace sat down next to Hope and sipped her wine. 'I've been at Dad's actually.'

'How's he?' Connie asked.

'He's ok.' Grace paused. 'Actually he's upset. As you'd know if you'd been to see him recently.'

'I was going to…'

'But?'

'But I didn't.' It felt like something irreparable had changed. In her mind 'Mum and Dad' were still a single unit. Dad wasn't supposed to move on. 'Was she there?'

'She's called Jackie. And yes, she was.'

'All happy families then. You and Dad and her.'

Grace looked pained. Connie's stomach tightened.

'I invited them to the family evening thing. The carol singing for the Season.' Grace looked at her. 'I thought it might help to spend some time all together.'

That was the sort of thought that made perfect sense to Grace. She would absolutely believe that if she could get everyone together and they all adopted a positive attitude everything would be all right. That's why Dad didn't talk about Grace in the sad, baffled tone he used for Connie.

'Great. Lots of fun hanging out with all the people who are pissed off with me.'

'They're not pissed off with you,' Grace insisted. 'Not really. If you went round and said sorry it would all be ok.'

That was what Grace would do. At least in principle. In reality Grace would never storm out on anyone in a sulk and so would never have been in this position in the first place. Connie downed the rest of her wine. 'Right then.'

'I didn't mean now.'

'Well you've just come from there, so they must still be up.'

Grace pursed her lips. 'Well yes, but...'

'But what?' Sensible, mature Grace would wait until morning, but tonight Connie was fuelled by Dutch courage and had a sense of purpose that the cold light of day could easily strip away. She put down her mug and marched into the hallway.

She heard Grace's voice as she slammed the front door. 'I didn't mean now...'

But now it was. The strength of her resolve carried her most of the twenty-five-minute walk to her dad's place, before she started to slow at the end of his street. Maybe he'd already have gone to bed. Maybe it was better to wait until tomorrow. Maybe she could text him. Or email. Email was good. She could really put down what she needed to say in an email.

She told herself again that he might already have gone to bed, but her feet kept moving her forward until she could see

209

quite clearly the light blazing from the front room window of the garden flat her dad called home.

Connie knocked, quietly, quietly enough that he might not hear, but Connie would still be able to tell herself that she had tried. A second later she heard footsteps in the hallway. Not quiet enough, it turned out. The door swung open.

'Oh.' She shouldn't be surprised. Of course the woman might be here. She was enough of a fixture to be introduced to the children. Why shouldn't she be here at half past ten on a Tuesday night?

'Grace?' Jackie frowned.

'Connie.'

'Right. Well, shall I get your dad?'

'Yes. Please.' Connie changed her mind as the Jackie woman turned away. 'Wait. I need to say this to you as well.' Deep breath time. Big girl pants time. Being a better Connie time. 'I'm sorry for how I behaved at lunch.'

'Ok. Well good. I'm sure your dad'll be pleased to hear that. Come in then.' She followed Jackie down the hallway and into the front lounge. Her dad was sitting exactly as Connie always pictured him, on the end of the settee with the best view of the telly, bottle of beer on the table in front of him, staring determinedly at the local news, as if the strength of his concentration would deal automatically with any pressing issues of the day.

He looked up. 'Connie, love?' Her dad gave her a slightly wary look. 'Did Grace send you?'

Connie shook her head. 'Well, sort of.'

'She's come to say her sorrys.'

Then let me bloody say them, she thought. Connie glanced around the room and then focused back on her dad. He wasn't actually quite exactly as she pictured him. The beer wasn't a traditional ale, but something fancy looking with… Connie stared… a slice of lime shoved into the neck. And his shirt was tucked into his jeans rather than hanging loose over his beer gut, his beer gut that seemed noticeably smaller than Connie remembered.

Connie took a seat at the other side of the room, in the chair that, in their old house, she'd always thought of as 'her mum's spot'. Jackie collected a second bottle of beer from the side table next to Connie's chair and took a seat on the settee. Right. This was going to be a whole group activity, was it? Connie inhaled.

'Would you leave us a minute, love?'

Connie swallowed the wave of relief. 'No. It's ok. I should say sorry to both of you. I was rude. I'm sorry.'

Jackie's closed expression broke instantly. 'Oh, that's all right, love. I told him he shouldn't do it like that. He should have rung you before, given you a chance to get used to the idea, or introduced me in a big group so you could see I wasn't the wicked witch of the west before you found out he'd installed me here.'

What now? 'You're living here?'

'Ah. Right.' Jackie shot her partner a look.

'Well not so much living...' Connie's father stuttered. 'Staying. You've still got your own place, haven't you?'

'Well only because there's another three months on the tenancy.'

'Yes. I mean that's part of it.' Connie's dad wasn't making eye contact with either of the women in the room.

Connie heard her own voice as if it was coming from a stranger's mouth. 'I'm sure you'll be very happy.' She looked around. Even though their dad had moved after Grace and Connie left the family home, everything had sort of stayed the same. The same furniture, laid out in the same way. He sat in the same chair and drank the same beer and read the same paper and watched the same TV. And now there was lime in his beer bottle, and a *Mirror* and a celebrity gossip mag on the coffee table. 'I should go. It's late. You'll be wanting to...' She couldn't say 'get to bed', not about her dad and his new girlfriend. 'Anyway, I should go.'

Her dad followed her out into the hallway. 'I'll come by. Grace asked me to look at your shower drain.'

'And we're coming to your dating thing, aren't we?' Jackie added.

Connie smiled as brightly as she could manage. 'Great. That'll be great.'

Chapter Eighteen

You are invited to an afternoon of

traditional Christmas crafts

It was possible that the sixth event was Emma's favourite of the whole Festive Season. The venue alone had almost made her do a little happy dance when she'd discovered it. A short walk from Borough Market – the downstairs space was a multi-vendor retail space. At least that's what the website said. That description did no justice at all to the plethora of beautiful stalls selling art and handmade crafts.

Upstairs was even more magical. The first-floor event space ran the full length of the converted warehouse, with exposed brick walls and a high vaulted ceiling. Today there was an enormous Christmas tree at the centre of the room and the scent of pine in the air, and all around the edges local crafters, including many of the stallholders from the store downstairs, had set up tables where daters could try different crafts to make their own tree decorations to add to the central tree. It had all the elements of a good dating event. The crafts would anchor people to a particular space and provide a focus for conversation, but there was enough going on that people could still circulate and mingle, if they hadn't yet found their One.

Annie had set up the welcome table. Emma scoured it for something she could improve. Nothing. Annie was really irrit-atingly good at this. Emma set off to walk the room one last time before the daters arrived. If her sister-in-law hadn't left anything amiss, then someone else definitely would have.

And she could easily have guessed who. The discarded Starbucks cup next to the keyboard in the corner suggested that, despite his agreement to help out this time, her own darling boyfriend wasn't really entering into the aesthetic Emma was going for. She went and collected a red-and-green holly-patterned china mug from the box discreetly hidden under the welcome table and decanted his rapidly cooling coffee.

'Are you tidying me up?'

'We're creating an ambience.' She pointed at the keyboard. 'Very much what you're here for.'

'I know. I know. No death metal.'

'Can you play death metal with one person and a piano?'

He grinned. 'Do you really want to piss me off enough to find out?'

'I do not. Traditional and Christmassy please.'

Her instruction was greeted with a mock salute, as she moved away. She turned back. 'And thank you for doing this. I know it's a bit of an imposition.' She wanted background music and the musician she'd booked had come down with flu. Asking Tom had felt like a breach of their new understanding that she couldn't expect him to simply slot into her life.

'It's fine, honestly.' He grinned. 'You pay. I play.'

Emma started looking over the stalls. Josie Baker, who had helped them with the pudding making, was here again, with boxes and boxes of mini gingerbread shapes ready for decorating. 'Found me a new chap yet sweetie?' she asked.

Emma gave Tom a very pointed look. 'This one might be going spare if he's not careful.'

Josie gave Emma's partner an openly appraising look. 'Very nice. Don't mind if I do.'

Tom grinned. 'Sorted. I'm running away with Josie. She can bake, you know.'

Emma left them to their flirtation, and checked the rest of the stalls. There was glass fusing, felt craft, ceramic painting, origami, and countless other options to create your own Christmas decorations. She stopped next to the pottery table which was being overseen by an earnest-looking man in his late thirties. 'I'm sorry they won't be able to take these home today.'

'That's ok. Having something to come back and collect together gives them an excuse to meet up later.'

'So that's the whole idea of this? It's a dating thing?' The man smiled slightly apologetically. 'I'm a bit hazy on the details. Josie told me I was doing it. You don't really argue with Josie.'

Emma could imagine. 'Yeah. It's a whole series of events, like a mini social season, like in Jane Austen. The idea is that people get to know one another over time and form a lasting attachment rather than just swiping and hooking up, you know?'

The man nodded. 'Sounds wonderful. I might have gone for something like that if I was younger.'

He couldn't be more than forty. 'You're not exactly over the hill?'

'No. I think my romance days are past. I lost someone.' He clapped his hands together. 'Sorry. You don't want to hear my sad story.'

Emma checked the clock above the stairwell. She had ten minutes, and thanks to Josie and Annie's attentions the room was all set and ready to go. 'Tell me.'

'Oh well, I was engaged. Ten years ago now. It was…' He gave a slightly awkward little laugh and pushed his glasses up the ridge of his nose. 'It was everything that it should be. I knew the night I met her that she was the woman I was going to marry. But not to be.'

'I'm sorry. She left?'

'She was taken. Cancer. They didn't catch it 'til it was far too late. She was young, you see, so nobody even thought it was a risk. We planned to marry, even right up to the end. There was a chapel at the hospice, but no. Not enough time even for that as it turned out.'

'I'm so sorry.' There was nothing more Emma could say.

'Better, I'm told, to have loved and lost.' He clapped his hands together again. 'And it's true. I wouldn't swap a single moment I had with her even to avoid the pain at the end.'

'What was her name?'

'Candi.'

'She sounds wonderful.'

'She was spectacular.'

Emma probably ought to leave it at that, but she was a match-maker. It wasn't just what she did. It was who she was. 'Would she want you to be single forever though?'

'Well she did say if I met someone new too quickly she would haunt us both.'

Emma laughed. Candi sounded like a woman after her own heart. 'Ten years though?'

The man looked away. 'I don't know. Who could match her?'

'It's not about matching what you had before. It's about being open to something new.' Emma pulled a business card from her pocket and slid it across the table. 'Think about it.'

Annie appeared at her shoulder. 'Ok to open the doors?'

It was a minute early, but everything seemed to be in place. Emma nodded, and took her place at the welcome table. Within a few minutes the room was full of people wandering around and cooing over the different activities. Josh and Annie were thrusting room plans into their hands as they arrived along with drinks tokens.

Emma left them to it and made her way to the far end of the room to ensure that people were circulating all the way around and not getting caught up with the first few activities and missing out on the rest. She took a moment to observe. There were a growing number of settled couples now. Hope Lucas had been well and truly ticked off Emma's to-do list. Callum was showing every sign of being a keeper. Right now, they were together, heads bent over Josie's gingerbread decorating stand.

The rest of Hope's group was still a worry. Grace clearly couldn't keep her hands off Jon Rackham, but was that a match? Or was it just sex? Emma pursed her lips. No sex before a genuine attachment was one of her core Season rules, but in practical terms, entirely unenforceable. If you put a group of single people, actively looking for love, together in a room with alcohol and tell them not to shag, someone will always view that as a challenge.

Emma had liked Morgan Landy for Grace. They both seemed fundamentally sensible and level-headed people, but Morgan had that additional creativity that might encourage Grace to loosen up a fraction. Jon didn't have that. He was all sharp edges and uncomfortable corners.

Theo Carter walked in. Emma watched his progress around the room. He exchanged greetings and hugs with every second person he passed. Everyone he spoke to was pleased to see him, eager to extend the conversation, but he didn't linger with anyone. She watched him make it past the Christmas tree and then stop. She followed her gaze with his own, and found Hope, giggling next to Callum.

Right. There were only three events left. Now was the time for Emma to put a very definite hand on the scales, and separate Theo from the comfort zone that hanging out with his best mate provided. She strode over to Theo and greeted him like a much beloved, but long lost, friend. 'Just the man I was looking for.'

She took him, firmly, by the elbow, and led him over to the origami table. The elegant American woman carefully folding paper on her own was, Emma checked her memory, a legal secretary. Raised in Houston, but her dad was British. Moved to London for university and never left. She was fun, clever, ridiculously beautiful. Emma tapped her on the shoulder. 'Have you met Theo?'

Emma stood back, far enough for it not to look as though she was hovering, and observed. Theo was charming, friendly, asking questions about Texas and working in law. The woman was starting to flirt a little. Emma started to relax, and was about to step away when Theo shook the woman by the hand, stood up and left the table.

'What are you doing?' Emma was straight after him.

'Nothing.'

'She was interested.'

Theo sighed. 'I don't know. Didn't you think her hair was a bit strangely shiny?'

'I don't even know what that would mean.'

An hour later, Emma had established that every still-single woman in the room had met Theo, and they pretty much all adored him. He was not a man short of options. He was a man who was absolutely refusing to play along though.

'What was wrong with her?'

'Weird laugh,' he muttered.

'Right. And the one before her. Gabi?'

'I dunno. Didn't you think she looked a bit too much like that film star?'

'Which film star?'

'You know, Scarlet Thingy. *Black Widow*, but without the ginger wig.'

'Scarlett Johansson? She's gorgeous. Basically you think that woman is too beautiful.'

Theo shook his head. 'She looks fine, but don't you think it would be weird? Constantly catching yourself thinking your date is out of *The Avengers*?'

'No. I think that would be fine. I also think she doesn't even look that much like her and you are coming up with excuses to reject every single person you meet.'

He folded his arms. 'They're not excuses. You want to know why I'm not attracted to these people, and I'm telling you.'

Emma looked around. 'You're deciding not to be attracted because you're hung up on your ex. But she's with someone else and you missed your chance,' she hissed. She wouldn't normally talk like this to a client, but it was time for some very tough love. Theo could have his pick of the women here, but he was trapping himself by his refusal to see sense. 'You need to move on, I'm afraid.'

Theo stepped back.

Emma was losing him. 'I mean that if you want something to change, then you need to try doing something different.'

He hadn't walked away.

'You can't carry on like this indefinitely, can you? Look around. People are making real connections here. There's no reason you can't do the same.'

He still hadn't walked away, but his expression had the aura of a particularly angry thunder cloud.

'I am trying to help,' Emma concluded.

'Well thank you for your advice.' This time he did stride away. She'd pushed her luck too far.

Emma took a breath. Tom was playing piano a few metres away. She went over. 'Can you play and talk?'

'So long as you don't use big words. What was that about?' he asked. 'Clients storming off doesn't seem super romantic.'

'He's hung up on someone who's not into him. He won't see it though.'

'Poor git.'

Emma managed half a laugh.

'You're sure this other person's not into him?'

'Well she's with someone else, so…'

'Is she with them or *with* them?'

'What's that mean?'

He shot her a look. 'You know what that means.'

She did. 'Well I've never met her, so I guess I'm not sure. I'm not in the business of breaking people up though. He needs to move on.'

'Not that easy though, is it? I'd still be in love with you if you were with someone else. You can't just turn love off.' Tom shrugged as much as a person playing 'Winter Wonderland' could. 'Maybe not everybody gets a second bite of the cherry?'

–

Hope thought she was doing pretty well at the biscuit decorating. Her gingerbread candy cane had an impressively neat array of red and white icing stripes along its length. Callum's snowman looked like it had been run over by a truck. 'That's terrible,' she giggled.

'It's harder than it looks.'

She pointed at her perfect candy cane. 'Is it though? Is it really?'

'Show off,' he grinned.

'So, erm...' Hope told herself that what she was about to say would be ok. 'I invited my dad and my stepmum to the family thing. So...'

Callum put down his snowman. 'So I'm going to meet the parents?'

'Yeah. Well my dad. Not my mum. Like, if we really try you might never have to meet my mum.'

'She can't be that bad.'

'She's not.' And she wasn't. Not bad exactly, just better contained in her own compartment. Hope could cope with the world and she could cope with her mother. It was when she had to mediate between the two that everything fell apart. 'She can be a bit prickly. And her and my dad in the same room is never a good idea, so let's take them one at a time.' The doubt that gnawed permanently at her tummy was still there. Less, but it was still there. 'You're sure you don't mind? Like if it's too soon, please say.'

'Hope! It's fine. I'm looking forward to it. I'll be my most charming.'

'Ok. If you're sure?'

'I'm sure.' He set his biscuit down. 'Do you want to try something else?'

Hope nodded her agreement. There were so many stalls to choose between. She slid her hand in Callum's as they looked around.

'So it looks like I might have the keys to the shop this week. Theo thinks we should start clearing it out this week.'

Callum's brow was furrowed in concentration on his remedial snowman efforts. 'Does he? And what do you think?'

'Well I guess it needs doing, so...'

He hesitated. 'Do you need to be the one doing it though? I mean, look, it's your call, but you'd never mentioned any of this stuff before – the flowers or wanting your own business or whatever. And you've got a perfectly decent job. I don't want Theo pushing you into stuff.'

'He's not.' Was he? He was, at least a bit. And Hope could see that it was well-intentioned, but it was still pushing. 'I mean a bit, but for the right reasons.'

'You don't need to do this. I mean you haven't signed the lease yet, have you?'

'Thursday.' She'd booked a whole day off work especially.

'Ok so, just make sure you're not making this whole massive life change because of Theo.'

'There you are!' And as if talking about him could summon the man himself Theo appeared at her side. 'Have you made a wreath yet?'

'What?'

'A wreath. Come on. They've got ivy and holly and pine...' he shrugged. 'Pine bits and berries and all that stuff. You'll love it.'

Hope found herself hesitating. A month, or even a few days ago, she probably would have loved it, but right now she was frozen to the spot. She felt herself gripping Callum's hand even tighter.

'Hey, what's up?'

'Nothing.'

Callum nodded. 'Cool. Do you want to do this wreath thing then? Show us your skills!'

'Ok,' she agreed, because why wouldn't she? She couldn't be a florist who was scared of making a wreath.

A group of four stood up just as they were nearing the table, leaving space for all three of them to sit down together. Hope would far rather have been doing this on her own in the back room of her own little shop with nobody else around. What if she'd lost the knack? What if the whole idea of making a dream into a life really was a horrible mistake?

The girl running the stall explained that there was foam already wired into a circle shape and that everything else was really up to them. Hope barely listened. She could see all that for herself. She took in the range of foliage and colour spread across the table in front of her and then, all in an instant, she could see the finished wreath in her mind. She could picture precisely how the different foliage would intertwine and form the perfect backdrop for the bright red berry clusters she would weave between them. Just for a second the room around her drifted away.

'Hope says she's signing the lease this week.' Callum was talking to Theo. Hope let the voices drift beyond her, as her fingers started to place the pine branches around the circle. She heard snippets of discussions of skips and costs but, just for the moment, she didn't care. All she wanted was to lose herself in creating the perfect wreath. This was absolutely what she loved. Theo had been right all along.

—

'Why have you got such a face on you?'

Connie shook her head. 'I don't have a face on me.'

'You do. You've looked like that the whole way here.'

'Well if I've got a face on me, so do you. It's the same face.' Connie fell back on her favourite childhood taunt for whenever her sister accused her of looking miserable. 'However I look, you do too.'

Grace pouted. Now she really did look miserable.

'I don't know what the point of this is. There's no one I'm into.'

'You were into Morgan.'

Connie hadn't given her sister the full chapter and verse on her spectacular crash and burn. 'And it's perfectly clear that she likes you better.' She folded her arms. 'Which I'm fine with.'

'You don't sound fine with it.'

'Well I am.' Connie was perfectly aware that her tone of voice was very much that of a sulky fifteen-year-old. 'Honestly.'

'Yeah. Right.' Grace didn't look as pleased with the news that Morgan was all hers as she ought have to been. 'I'm not sure she's right for me anyway.'

What?

'You know, I'm not sure if there's a spark.'

Connie was really pissed off now. She'd handed the woman to Grace on a platter and now her sister didn't want her. It was like every childhood argument replayed. Connie wanted to do colouring, so instantly Grace wanted the colouring pens and she couldn't possibly share with Connie because Connie didn't put the tops back on right and the pens got all dried out and ruined. And Grace would win the fight – Grace always won the fight – and immediately decide she wanted to play with Barbies after all.

'Anyway, we're here now,' Grace pointed out. 'And there's still three more events. You could at least enter into the spirit of things. Who knows who you might meet?'

Connie grimaced.

'Seriously, Connie. You look pretty now, and everyone here is trying to meet someone. At least try.'

'Fine.'

'Good.' Grace peeled away to look at the nearest craft table. Connie moved on. She wasn't going to do any sort of artistic activity with Grace. Whatever Grace created would be pretty and dainty and exactly in line with the instructions provided. Connie would, inevitably, end up with glue on her dress and in her hair and glitter stuck to one eyebrow and a horrid sticky mess of a creation that looked like it had been done by a five-year-old and which even that five-year-old's mother would accidentally lose at the earliest opportunity.

She made her way deeper into the room, looking for something she could do that looked easy enough for even her not to embarrass herself, while also not running into Morgan, avoiding her sister, and, she supposed, if she was really going to enter into the spirit of the thing like Grace wanted, finding true love. It was a lot to look for in a craft table.

Too much as it turned out, because she'd lost focus on the key requirement of 'not running into Morgan'. There she was, head bent over a piece of glass alongside a tall, cropped-haired Asian woman who was holding up her creation for Morgan's approval. They looked good together. They both had the same elegance that Connie would simply never achieve, however much she dressed herself up in Grace's clothes.

She dropped her head and walked briskly on.

'Connie!'

Not briskly enough. She turned back. Morgan had left her partner and was making her way over to Connie.

'Hi.'

'Hi.'

'I didn't get a chance to see you at the lunch,' said Morgan.

'No. Well, you looked like you were having a nice time with Grace anyway.'

Morgan frowned. 'With Grace? Yeah. I mean she's nice. You know that we're not…'

Connie did know that. Her sister had made that very clear. 'Why not?'

'What?'

'What's wrong with her?'

She watched Morgan's mouth open and then close and open again. 'There's nothing wrong with her.'

'No. Good. You could do a lot worse than Grace. She's smart, and she tries really hard to make everyone happy and yes, she can be a bit…' What was the word for it? '…a bit Graceish, but that's because she cares about everything.'

'Yeah. Right. I mean, like I said, there's nothing wrong with her.'

So they were agreed. 'Good.'

The silence hung between them for a moment, before Connie broke it. 'I mean I didn't leave you for Grace for you to just—'

'I'm sorry. What?'

'What?'

'You *left me* for Grace?'

'Well I mean, you weren't into me, so...'

'So you left me for your sister. Like half a plate of cold chips, or a top you're not quite sure about.'

'I didn't mean...'

'I got exactly what you meant. What the fuck, Connie?'

This wasn't how she'd wanted this conversation to go. She'd told herself she didn't want to have this conversation at all, and assumed that if she did it would involve her showing how utterly unconcerned she was over Morgan being with Grace. This new reality where Morgan was angry with her was spikier and more complicated than anything she'd imagined. 'I meant, you know, she liked you and you obviously didn't like me, and...'

'I obviously didn't like you?' Now Morgan looked confused. 'What do you mean?'

'You know what I mean.'

'You mean I didn't kiss you?' Morgan stepped back. 'Like if I'm not going to give you at least a snog in the first ten minutes you're out of there? For fuck's sake Connie, you're worse than most men.'

That wasn't right. That wasn't how it had been. She had done the brave thing and put herself out there and been rejected. She was the one who had the right to be pissed off. 'It wasn't like that.'

'It kinda seems like it was.'

Connie didn't reply. Was it like that?

'Wait.' Morgan was staring at her again. 'Is that why you did all this?'

'All what?'

'This weird Grace cosplay thing you've got going on. You think I rejected you so now you're a whole different person?'

Another question Connie wouldn't answer. 'I just fancied a change.'

Morgan shook her head. 'I don't know what's going on with you and your sister, but right now I have no interest in being

225

the shiny new toy you're fighting over. There's nothing going on between me and Grace. I thought you and me... I dunno. I thought maybe, but then you stormed out and you didn't even message to say you were ok. I was worried about you. I thought I'd done something.'

'Didn't want to hang around where I wasn't wanted.' Connie could hear the moody teenager in her voice again.

'It wasn't like that.'

'It seemed like that.'

Morgan stepped back slightly. 'Look, we've all got baggage. I've got pretty much a whole luggage carousel's worth myself, which is maybe why I don't like to rush into things until I've got to know someone.'

That made sense. 'I get that.'

'It doesn't seem like you do. And honestly Connie, I can't be doing with all this. Like change your hair, I get that. But this? This isn't you, is it? You look more like...'

She didn't need to spell it out again. Connie knew exactly who she looked like.

'I'm just, I don't know.' Morgan took a deep breath in. 'I'm at a point where I'm ready, you know, for something real, something that might last. Something that might turn into living together, getting married, all that stuff further down the line, but I also know that it's taken me a really really long time to get to this point. I've learned to love myself and all that crap. I don't think I can risk all that on someone who doesn't know who they are. Sorry.'

Connie couldn't reply.

'Shit. That was a really long speech to give someone you haven't even been on a real date with, wasn't it?'

'Yeah.'

'I overshare when I like people. Sorry.'

Connie had been hit by a lot of emotion. Her brain grasped onto the most recent part. 'You like me?'

'I do. I did, but I can't make you like yourself. I think, at the moment, I need someone who's already done that work. I am sorry.'

Connie had no choice but to let her walk away.

–

Grace didn't need to look around to know who was standing immediately behind her. The scent of him was imprinted on her brain. It evoked sex in the same way that wax crayons evoked childhood or the smell of a wood burner made you want to snuggle up and drink hot chocolate. She refused to allow herself to look round, focusing all her energy on the ceramic Christmas tree in front of her.

'That's very neat,' he whispered.

'Thank you.'

'Was it a compliment?'

Of course neat was a compliment.

'You're not tempted to paint outside the lines occasionally?'

'Don't be ridiculous.'

He laughed behind her. His laugh was unexpectedly deep and warm and Grace realised that she hadn't heard it very often before.

'You have a nice laugh.'

He didn't reply. That did it. The silence drew Grace's attention behind her and she looked around. His face had settled into the slightly pinched expression he wore so much of the time. 'You should laugh more often,' she told him.

'Maybe.'

She handed her perfectly neat Christmas tree to the lady behind the stall and took a ticket with the number she would need to collect it in a few days' time after firing, and turned her full attention to Jon. 'So what crafts have you tried?'

'I'm not really the crafty type. And I don't have a Christmas tree so I don't really need decorations for one, do I?'

'You should have a Christmas tree. It's not Christmas without a tree.' Grace remembered decorating the tree when she was little.

Her mum had always had beautiful glass decorations and Grace had always been so careful with them. She hadn't thought about that for years.

'What are you thinking about?'

'Nothing.' She took in his outfit. Three-piece suit, perfectly polished shoes and silk tie. He really didn't look ready to get his hands dirty at all. 'You're not really dressed for this, are you?'

'I came straight from work.'

She remembered the lines of perfectly pressed shirts in his wardrobe. 'Do you even own casual clothes?'

'I like to be well-presented.' He looked around. 'Why don't we get out of here?'

His fingers danced at her waist, pulling her inexorably closer to him. No. Grace wasn't kidding herself any longer that she wasn't going home with him, but it was going to be on her terms. 'No. I am a crafty person, and I've only tried one thing, so you have to do at least one activity with me before we go.'

'I thought we had discussed this.'

Grace glanced around. There was space at the pottery table. 'We definitely never discussed clay Christmas decorations.'

'I meant, I thought we discussed that this is not a relationship.'

'We did. I agree. Whatever this is, you are not my boyfriend. But I don't think making a pottery angel is going to risk changing that.' She smiled her sweetest, most Graceish, smile. 'And that's the deal. No pottery angel. No sex.'

His expression eased a little. 'And what do I get if I make a whole pottery nativity?'

This was a moment where Grace could come up with something sexy and dangerous to whisper in his ear, but they were in the middle of a room full of people and her sister was just over there and her cousin and her boyfriend were at the other side of the room and Grace wasn't the talking dirty sort and...

He smiled. 'I do enjoy it when you go all prim and tongue-tied.'

Grace could feel her cheeks starting to redden. It was ridiculous. He'd seen her naked. He'd heard her beg. He'd heard her screaming his name. And she was still embarrassed to admit that she wanted him. 'Pottery first,' she muttered.

His pottery angel was impressively well constructed as it turned out, and was swiftly followed by a pottery shepherd and a pottery lamb. Grace found herself watching his long fingers press the clay together around the mould, and smooth down the slip-lined edges.

Her own attempt at a set of three kings was much less tidy. Jon glanced over. 'Oh dear.'

'I can't concentrate with you there.'

He pulled a face of mock outrage. 'I am simply sitting here finishing my shepherd. Like you wanted.'

He was right. Technically. He was just sitting there. But he was sitting there with his jacket off, and his shirt sleeves rolled up over strong, lightly tanned forearms. He was sitting there with one thigh resting against hers, sending heat through her whole body. His gaze kept flicking over to her, making her feel naked and exposed.

He set his lamb down on the board in front of him. 'I mean if you would prefer to abandon this and find some other entertainment…'

She'd set a boundary. She wasn't just going to fall into his bed again. Obviously she was going to fall into his bed, but that wasn't going to be the sum total of her day. 'Stop looking at me.'

'Ok.' There was a hint of that deep, warm laugh in his voice. 'I'll concentrate on glazing these then, shall I?'

'Yes. You do your thing. And I'll do mine.'

'And then?'

Fine. 'And then we can get out of here.'

Grace had never left a single project, work task, or even piece of childhood homework, as shoddily finished as those poor clay magi. Within twenty minutes she was diving into the back of the sleek black car that appeared, on Jon's command, and muttering a greeting to Carl. Carl was definitely not getting a fair impression of Grace's social life.

The drive should have been twenty minutes, but heavy traffic pushed it to thirty. Thirty minutes of restraint. Thirty minutes of Jon detailing exactly what he was going to do with her when they were inside. Thirty minutes of her trying to get things moving and Jon demurring. 'Anticipation is half the fun,' he whispered.

'Anticipation is the worst.'

'No patience,' he teased.

Eventually they were inside the apartment. Finally, now she could have him, but every move she made was skilfully parried, as he forced her to go slower, take longer. Every item of clothing that was removed was done so inch by inch, delicately, languorously, agonisingly.

When he finally relented and slid himself into her Grace came almost excruciatingly quickly, clinging to his shoulders and gasping with pleasure. And afterwards, she lay back in the warmth of her delight, and rode the wave of calming ecstasy as he teased and caressed her with his fingertips.

'See,' he whispered. 'Anticipation is everything.'

'Maybe.' She picked her phone up from the floor next to the bed. 'I guess I'd better get going then.'

'As ever, you don't have to.'

Grace shook her head. 'And, as ever, isn't hanging around afterwards girlfriend behaviour?'

'And leaving the second the deed is done is hooker behaviour. You're not on the clock, are you?'

'No!'

'Well then,' he swung his legs out of bed. 'I shall order food. Have you eaten?'

'Not since breakfast.'

He handed her his phone with a menu from a very smart Japanese restaurant on the screen.

'This place is well fancy. They don't deliver.'

Jon raised a single eyebrow. 'Tell me what you want.'

Nowhere on the menu was a single price listed. If you had to ask, Grace assumed, you probably couldn't afford it. 'Is it tiny portions and you have to have some toast when you get in to fill up?'

'It's fine dining.'

It wasn't what Grace felt like. And with Jon there was nothing to lose by, just for a few hours, not bothering to pretend. 'I want a pizza. A massive one with plastic cheese.'

'You can have an authentic Neapolitan-style pizza with buffalo mozzarella.'

Grace sensed an argument she wasn't going to win. 'But a massive one?'

'Absolutely huge,' he promised.

'And I can eat it in bed from the box?'

He narrowed his eyes. 'Do you do that at home?'

Of course she didn't. 'I have to wash the sheets at home.' She smiled. 'You probably have like a whole laundry service thing. You don't even care.'

'I have a housekeeper.'

'And she washes your sheets?'

'Well there always seem to be clean sheets, so one assumes so.'

The pizza had green stuff on top of the cheese and tomato and the ham seemed to be parma rather than the factory-reconstituted variety, but it was absolutely enormous, so Grace did not complain. 'I really like not being your girlfriend,' she announced.

'Good.'

'It's like, if you were a new boyfriend, or even a potential boyfriend, I'd have to arrange myself all sexy and get the sheet so it covered up any fat bits, and I'd have been straight in the bathroom to redo my make-up after we…' She waved a hand towards the crumped sheets. 'But you're not, so it doesn't matter, does it?'

'You're thinking about all that every time you go to bed with someone?'

Grace nodded.

'Even with women?'

Another nod. It was actually worse than that though. It wasn't only with people she slept with. It was all the time. Grace liked things to be just so, so nobody around her would ever be upset or perturbed. Grace chewed her pizza and didn't respond. 'This pizza is good. Aren't you having any?'

She offered him the box, and he took a single slice – the smallest slice available, she noticed – rolled it neatly in a way she'd only seen done before on her school trip to Rome, and ate it from one end of the roll.

'I don't get you.'

'What do you mean?'

What did she mean? The shirts. The suit at the craft fair. The single slice of pizza, efficiently consumed. 'You're so controlled.'

He grinned. 'I like control.'

'I noticed.' But that wasn't it. 'It's not the same sort of control though, is it? When we…' Another wave towards the messed-up sheets.

'When we fuck,' he offered.

'Yeah. That.' She caught his smirk at her prudishness. 'When we do that, you can be feral.'

He laughed.

'You're so in the moment and so full of…' Her voice dropped. 'Passion. But as soon as we're done everything is cool again. I can't work out which is the real you.'

'Do people have to be just one thing?'

Well, essentially, yes. Grace was graceful. She was precise. She was nice. She was kind. She made everyone happy. That was who Grace was. Connie was the rebel. Grace was the good girl. That was her thing. 'I'm just one thing.'

He shook his head.

'What does that mean?'

'It means I disagree. What one thing are you?'

'I'm…' She couldn't say it. She couldn't say *I'm a good girl* out loud to the man who had seen her abandon all sense in his bed so many times. Not least because he would take it as an invitation. 'Well, like Connie is the one who messes up.'

232

'Right. So you're Little Miss Perfect?'

'No.'

That constantly teasing eyebrow raised again.

'I try to be good.'

'So this is what? Time off? To eat pizza in bed and get screwed into next week?'

'This is…' She couldn't finish that sentence. Being with Jon was something… it was something new, something different to anything she'd had before. 'I don't know. I like it though.'

Jon reached over and lifted the pizza box off her lap and discarded it onto the floor, before bending his head to hers and finding her lips. The sex, the inevitable sex, was unlike any they'd had before, slow but purposeful, no build-up, other than the kiss, before she was straddling him and pushing down onto his sheathed length, so they sat face to face, torso to torso, lip to lip, his arms encircling her body and supporting her as she moved against him. Grace had never felt like this. What was it? What was happening to her? He buried his face into her neck as he came inside her. Grace felt his breath on her and his body against her. It was just sex. She didn't… That was the deal. They weren't a couple.

Yet, there were words in the back of Grace's mind, fighting to be let out. Words that said more than that she liked it here. Words that said that he was wrong about this being time off from her real life. Words that said this could be her real life. The words took form and danced onto her tongue. They were words that wanted to be said out loud.

No commitment. That was what she'd agreed. She pushed herself off him and staggered back. 'I have to go.'

He stared at her, still discombobulated from his orgasm. 'What?'

'I really have to go.'

She grabbed underwear and clothes and flung them on. She found her bra after her T-shirt and stuffed it in a pocket. It didn't matter. All that mattered was getting out of here before she ruined everything. Jon was still lying on the bed. 'You don't have to…'

'I do.' She dashed into the hallway and found her boots next to the door. Who was that girl who'd politely removed her shoes before coming inside for an afternoon of passion? What level of self-control had that girl been exercising? What universe had she been living in?

She had dragged her second boot on and was fumbling with the door lock when he caught up with her. 'Are you all right, Grace?'

'I'm fine.'

He leaned past her, filling her senses with the scent of him and of sex, and flicked the lock open. 'You are welcome to stay longer.'

'I have to go.'

His hand landed in the small of her back, burning even through three layers of clothes. 'Why?'

'So that I don't tell you that I love you.'

Fuck.

The words she didn't want to say hung in the air between them. 'I didn't say...'

He stepped back. His face closed tight once again. 'No.'

She ran out of the door. Stupid stupid hope made her pause by the lift, willing it to come more slowly, daring to think that he might come after her, and do something, or say something, that would make this better. That he felt the same. That he'd been scared to admit his feelings. That Grace was the one woman for whom he could change his ways.

But he didn't. Of course he didn't. He'd been nothing but entirely honest about what this was. It wasn't the start of a grand affair. It wasn't a relationship. It was sex and occasional laughs and even more occasional pizzas. It was Grace who'd messed up. It was Grace who'd played outside their own set of rules.

Chapter Nineteen

Emma was getting used to the bustle of a full house since Annie moved in. It was good. It reminded her of when Trevor was still alive and Mum was still here and they would have a constant stream of friends – often grateful couples her mum had brought together – calling in. Today Tom was here, along with Josh and Annie, and also Annie's friend Lydia and her... 'Hot barman!' Emma exclaimed. 'Sorry!'

'That's ok.' Will March rolled his eyes. 'I'm getting used to it.'

'It's not right though.' Emma was a stickler for the proper etiquette. 'You're a Hot Earl now?' Then she caught herself again. He was the earl because his father had passed away. 'And I'm very sorry for your loss.'

'Thank you. And just Will really is fine.'

Next to him his girlfriend shook her head and squeezed Will's arm. 'You'll always be Hot Viscount to me babe. Anyway.' She nudged her hot viscount in the ribs. 'It was actually you that he came to see.'

'Right.' Will nodded. 'Yes.'

That was surprising. People generally only came to see Emma if they were single and desperate, in which case they didn't usually bring their current partner along with them. 'What can I do for you?'

'Right. Well, I am the earl now, which is ridiculous and it doesn't mean anything, and I just want...'

'Will!' Lydia interrupted the flow of class guilt.

'Sorry. Erm, thing is, it comes with this huge estate.'

'Massive,' Lydia confirmed. 'He's got huge tracts of land,' she sniggered.

'Ah, well no. That's very much the point. Not rich. Not really. Big house. Big estate. No cash, so we need to either sell some of those...' He shot Lydia a look. 'Huge tracts of land, or find a way to make the estate pay. So we're kind of looking at everything.' He counted the plans off on his fingers. 'Holiday cottages. Opening to the public more. Making a proper farm shop, tea room, and doing events.'

'Which is where you come in,' Lydia added.

'It's Cotswolds isn't it?' Emma shook her head. 'Too far out of London for a Season event.'

'But what about a whole Season?' asked Will. 'Weekends with overnight stays. It would have to be smaller than the London ones cos of providing accommodation, but it's an idea?'

Emma thought about it. A more exclusive Season would mean a higher price and would probably attract a certain type of customer, but a higher price could mean... She turned to Josh, who was listening silently. 'What do you think?'

'We'd be able to charge more. We'd have to if it was smaller, but that could mean more profit. And you'd have a captive audience. Much more chance to steer them towards the right people.'

'You can't just lock them in a country house and see who hooks up,' Tom pointed out. 'You'll need stuff for them to do.'

'Bracing country walks. Clay pigeon shooting. Cookery classes. Archery?' Will suggested.

'Axe throwing?' Lydia added.

'Well we might need to slim down the number of offensive-weapon-based activities?' said Emma.

Lydia shrugged. 'Dunno. Last two standing get to shag works for me.'

Tom's phone rang. He frowned at the screen, before going into the hallway. 'Excuse me.'

Emma's mind was racing. A series of weekends with a smaller group could work, and being hosted by an actual earl definitely added a bit of an old-fashioned romantic sheen to the proceedings.

'What about America?' That was Josh.

Emma didn't know.

'What about America?' Will asked.

'Emma's been asked to go to New York and launch the Season over there.'

'Oh my God!' Lydia's jaw dropped. 'You won't want his old draughty house then will you?'

'Nothing's decided yet,' Emma protested.

'Yeah, but you're going to go,' Josh said. 'Why wouldn't you go?'

The door to the living room opened. Emma waited for Tom to ask who wouldn't go where, and then she'd have to come clean and explain what she should have explained weeks ago, but he didn't say anything. Emma went to her boyfriend. 'What's wrong?'

'That was Hilly. My mum's in hospital. They think she's had a stroke.'

–

By Wednesday Grace's week had fallen into a definite pattern. At night she went to bed and stared at the ceiling, but instead of worrying about Connie and Dad and a thousand and one other things, she spent the hours desperately trying to think of ways to turn back time so that she could choose not to accidentally tell Jon that she was in love with him. And then after eight hours of that she got out of bed and went to work and tried not to jump every time somebody in a well-fitted suit came through the door, because, obviously, none of them were him. Because he wasn't going to walk into her place of employment and declare his undying affection, and Grace simply had to tell herself, constantly, that this was never going to happen. And then she went home and went to bed and started the cycle again.

When she left work on Wednesday, after three nights with barely any sleep, she resolved that she had to do something different. Marching across London and bursting into his flat and telling him she'd misspoken and she'd meant to say that she was in love with pizza or Anton Du Beke or the chimes of Big Ben didn't seem like a workable option. Not least because every time she played out that scenario in her mind she stalled at the moment where she tried to picture his response. It wasn't that she couldn't picture it. It was that she could, all too easily. The arch of his eyebrow. The disdain on his face. The disappointment that she had not only done something so pedestrian as fall in love, but had also been idiot enough to think he would entertain her denial of the fact.

So she wouldn't do that. But she needed to do something. Something that would change the rhythm of the day. Something that would help her look herself in the eye in front of the mirror once again. Which was how she came to be getting off the Tube at Manor Park and taking a walk she both barely remembered and, at the same time, could never forget, to the City of London cemetery. She knew that Connie came here quite often and she knew that she disapproved of the fact that Grace didn't, but Connie's relationship with their mum had been easy and filled with shared jokes and mutual understanding. Grace hadn't entirely had that. She'd loved her mum, and she'd known, somewhere deep inside, that her mum loved her, but she'd never quite escaped the feeling that her mother had admired Connie rather more.

The grave was neatly tended with fresh flowers in the holder by the headstone. Was that Connie's doing? Grace pulled her coat around her. She'd pictured herself sitting down on the grass and telling her mother all her troubles, but, of course, the grass was cold and in the shade of this corner the morning's frost had never quite fully thawed. And, even though there was nobody around to hear, it felt silly to talk out loud when no one was there. Grace stared at the headstone in silence.

What would her mother have said? Her mother had said that antiseptic cream was magic and scared all the badness away. She'd said that if you listened really hard after the rain you could hear the pixies under the earth sucking the water in through their straws.

She'd said that the sky was held up with sky hooks and that when you went on an aeroplane you might see them if you looked out of the window really hard.

None of which seemed desperately helpful right now. The truth was, Grace realised, she had no idea what her mother would say about any of this. About falling in love. About having your first orgasm with someone else in the room at the age of twenty-seven. About feeling like you needed someone so much that you want to burrow under their skin to get closer to them. She'd lost her mum at twelve years old. She knew what she thought about grazed knees and first periods and how to cope when you'd cut your own fringe and it was far far too short. On real grown-up stuff, Grace had nothing.

Footsteps coming closer disturbed her train of thought. Not that it mattered. However much she wanted some divine sign that her mum was watching over her and all would be all right, there was nothing for her here.

Grace kept her head bowed to let the footsteps make their way past to their own private communion with the dead, but they stopped. 'What are you doing here?'

Grace looked up. 'Why shouldn't I be here? She was my mum too.' That sounded shorter and meaner than she intended. She saw her sister's bottom lip quiver. 'I meant... She was my mum. I can come here.'

'But you don't come here.'

That was fair. 'I had stuff on my mind.'

—

Connie was confused. Grace was not the sort to have stuff on her mind. Grace made plans and executed them and everything came up roses. Grace did not suffer from an excess of inner turmoil. 'What sort of stuff?'

'It doesn't matter.'

'Did you come to talk to Mum about it?'

Grace nodded.

'Did it help?'

'I didn't talk to her. Felt stupid.' Grace turned to face her properly. 'And I don't know what she'd say about any of this. I don't know what she'd be like now. I can't...' Connie realised her sister was crying. 'I can't picture what she'd be like now. How she'd deal with us being grown up.'

'I think she'd be just the same.'

'How?'

'I dunno. Making up stories to explain things. Trying to stop us killing each other. Trying not to let me see that you're Dad's favourite.'

'I'm not Dad's favourite.'

'You so are.' Why would Grace even bother denying it?

'Well you were Mum's favourite.'

That was ridiculous. 'Mum didn't have a favourite.'

'If you say so. What are you doing here?'

'Same I guess. I came to talk to her about the whole Season thing. I messed it up.'

Grace wiped her face on her glove. 'So did I.'

'How?' Connie couldn't imagine Grace messing anything up. Grace was destined to meet a perfect partner and have a perfect home with their perfect children.

'I accidentally told somebody I loved them.'

Right. There was a lot to unpick in that sentence – too many questions to ask in one breath. Connie's brain alighted on the least important detail. 'Accidentally?'

'Yep. It just came out. Didn't mean it to. Didn't mean to love him actually. All a horrible accident.'

'And this someone didn't say they loved you too?'

'No.'

'I'm sorry.'

'It's ok. I knew he wouldn't. He told me he wasn't looking for a relationship. I thought I could handle that. Couldn't handle it.'

The most important detail finally dragged itself to the forefront of Connie's mind. 'Who?'

'You'll laugh at me.'

Now she really needed to know. 'Who?'

'Jon. Jon Rackham.'

'The fancy chap?'

'Yeah.'

Well that was unexpected. 'I didn't even know you'd seen him, like apart from at the Season stuff.'

'Seen him. Shagged him. Shagged him again. And again. And again. And again…'

'Shit.'

'Yeah.' Grace shrugged. 'The sex was good. So, you know, that's something. Even if it won't be happening again because I messed up everything.'

Connie took a step forward and put an experimental arm around her sister. 'I think Mum would say that everything happens for a reason, and that even if something doesn't work out we get to learn something from the experience that we take forward into life.'

'Would she?'

Connie nodded with a confidence she didn't entirely feel. 'Something like that. Definitely. So what did you learn?'

'Honestly?'

'Of course.'

'Honestly, it was mostly about what stuff makes me come.'

Connie stepped back. 'Ok. I take it back. Not honestly. Make some shit up.'

'Fine. Maybe I learned that I need something more than I usually let myself have.'

'Wow. That sounds deep.' Connie took her sister's arm. 'I think Mum would have been dead proud of that.'

'Maybe.' Grace was silent a second. 'Why did you come here tonight?'

'No reason.'

'I told you mine. It's your turn.'

They started to walk back towards the gate. Connie took a deep breath. 'I messed things up with Morgan. I came on too strong.'

'Did you tell her you were in love with her before you'd technically even had a date?'

'No.'

Grace squeezed her arm. 'Then how bad can it be? Really?'

Connie honestly didn't know any more. At the time Morgan's horror when Connie had tried to kiss her had, without a doubt, been the worst possible thing that could have happened. But now it seemed like what happened next had been a thousand times worse. Connie had run. She hadn't stayed and apologised and listened to whatever Morgan might have said next. Things had got a tiny bit difficult and she'd run away.

'What did you do after you'd said you loved him?'

'I got the hell out of there.'

'Do you think you should have stayed to see what he did next?'

Connie's sister didn't reply for a moment. When she did it was about something else entirely. 'Do you want to see what I got you for Christmas?'

Connie's eyes widened. 'It's not Christmas yet,' she pointed out in mock horror.

'I know but...' Grace got her phone out of her pocket and scrolled to a picture. The image was of a painting, with flashes of purple and black overlayered with softer swirls of white. 'The photo doesn't really do it justice.'

'Is this Morgan's?'

'It's new. I saw it on her website, and I dunno. It made me think of you.' She stopped. 'Not think of you. It felt like you.'

Connie stared at the image. It was messy, but somehow coherent. 'So basically chaos?' she asked.

'Chaotic but still right. Beautiful.'

Connie didn't quite know what to say. She slid her arm through her sister's. 'I haven't got you anything.'

'Rainbow jumper dress. Gap website. I'll send you a link,' Grace replied.

'Thank you. Seriously, Grace, thank you.'

They walked through the cemetery together. 'Why don't we get a Christmas tree?' Grace asked.

'For the house? I dunno. We never have.'

'Mum always used to get a proper tree,' Grace reminded her.

'Oh God,' Connie gasped. 'Those glass ornaments. I broke so many of those.'

And her sister laughed. 'It didn't matter though. It was all part of Christmas.'

Chapter Twenty

Hope weighed the sledgehammer tentatively in her hand and eyed the partition wall that divided the current shop space from the back work room. 'Are you sure about this?'

'It's just partition,' Theo promised her.

'Absolutely sure,' Callum confirmed.

'The ceiling won't fall down?'

'Definitely not.' Her boyfriend was adamant. 'But I can do it if you don't want to.'

'Let Hope do it,' Theo countered. 'It's her project. And this is the fun bit. The start of your grand vision. Go on.'

Hope lifted the sledgehammer and swung it towards the sad stained wall and slammed a jagged hole straight through. Callum and Theo both cheered as she swung again. Within a few minutes there was a clear view from the front of the shop right the way to the very back. Hope stopped and stared. This was really hers. She was actually making it happen. Theo was beaming next to her, and Callum had already started taking debris out to the skip, which was, as Theo had promised, ridiculously cheap as a result of a favour from a friend of a friend of a… he'd stopped explaining at that point. *Of a girl he'd slept with*, presumably.

'I should take some of this stuff out.' Hope put down the hammer and started gathering up detritus into the wheelbarrow Uncle Pete had provided.

Callum was leaning on the skip outside, looking up and down the street. 'It's a nice street.'

'You should see it on a Sunday. All of this is market stalls.' She pointed at the front of the shop. 'When I can afford it, I'll get this changed so it opens right up and we can have a table selling right onto the street on market days.'

'Sounds cool. Did you tell your work you're leaving yet?'

'I will. In January. There's work to do here before I can open, so I figure if I can keep earning while we do that, it'll be better.'

'We?'

She stopped. She'd been thinking of her and Theo, not her and Callum. Which was simply force of habit. Theo had been her stand-in significant other for so long. It was bound to take a minute to get used to thinking of someone else first. 'Yeah. I mean if you want to help.'

'Sure. So long as I get a go with that sledgehammer.'

They made their way back inside. Theo was on the phone. Hope frowned. Theo was on Hope's phone. He mouthed an exaggerated 'I'm sorry' in her direction, before he spoke into the handset. 'Yeah. She's here now Mrs Lucas. Yes. Yes. Lovely to talk to you too. I'll hand you over. Here you go. Yeah. Yes. Bye.'

He thrust the phone at Hope, ignoring her rapidly shaking head. 'Hi Mum.'

'Hello dear. Where on earth are you? Theodore…'

'Theo,' Hope corrected.

'…was being quite mysterious. I don't know what on earth got into him.'

'Right. Yeah. I'm…' What? I'm in the shop I've leased on a whim so I can jack in my perfectly sensible job and become a florist. She could imagine how that would go down with her mother. But what else could she say? 'I'm actually at my new business.' She continued quickly, leaving no space for objections from the other end of the line. 'It's a little shop. It's going to be a florist, but lots of work to do before I open so I haven't given up work or anything yet.'

'A shop?' Her mother sounded surprised rather than outraged. That was probably the shock.

'Yes. Just a small one. Remember how I used to want to have a floristry business. My own shop.'

'I do. And I remember your weekend job with Julie in the village when you were doing A-levels.'

'Right. Yeah.' Something deep inside Hope desperately wanted to pipe up that the new shop wouldn't interfere with her studies.

'Well, marvellous. It's about time you took the plunge. I assume you have enough money to get things off the ground.'

Hope wasn't sure how to reply. 'I mean it's still a bit of a risk.'

'A calculated risk though?'

It was. Theo had been convinced enough for both of them that the maths stacked up, but Hope had still spent every free moment of the last two weeks writing a business plan and working out a budget for the business and then a personal budget for her to pare her expenses down to the absolute minimum. 'It's tight, but if I'm careful about what stock I buy and concentrate on getting some wedding business to build up word of mouth I think I can make it work.'

'Well good luck to you then. I shall have to come to town when you open to have a look.'

'That would be nice.' At least it was a nice idea. Her mother hardly ever came to London though, and never on her own. 'You don't have to.'

'I'd like to,' her mother replied.

Hope pushed the comparison with her father's reaction to the news out of her mind. Her dad was always on her side. Of course he was. He didn't need to say so.

Her mother was still talking on the other end of the line. 'Of course I'll see you before then.'

'Christmas. Definitely.' Hope could barely believe that was less than a week away.

'And tomorrow.'

Tomorrow? Tomorrow was the family carolling event. Tomorrow was when Callum was supposed to meet her dad and stepmum. Hope looked up and straight into Theo's guilt-struck face. 'Tomorrow?' she whimpered.

'At this family evening. Theodore said you must have forgotten to ask me.'

'Sorry, sorry, sorry, sorry, sorry…' her best friend whispered in her direction.

'Right. Yeah. I thought I mentioned it.' Hope improvised. 'Erm, you might not want to come though. Dad and Tina are coming.'

There was a silence on the end of the line. Hope's heart cracked a little bit. This was her fault. She should have asked her mother first. She could imagine her, standing by the landline phone in her hallway, alone. 'Well of course you have if it's a family day. I'm sure that won't be a problem. I can be civil if he can, after all. Send me the details on the email.'

'Ok.'

Hope ended the call and glared at Theo.

'I'm so sorry. Callum said something about meeting the parents…'

'You keep me out of this.'

'…And I assumed you'd already invited her.'

'I invited my dad,' Hope hissed.

'Yeah. I figured that out. I am so sorry. I will run interference. I will keep them as far apart from one another as it is possible to be.' He clapped Callum on the shoulder. 'We both will, won't we?'

'Sure. They can't be that bad though. And it's only one day.'

Hope shook her head. 'They literally haven't been in the same room since my dad left.'

'And that was?'

'Fourteen years ago. They haven't spoken, seen one another, emailed, exchanged smoke signals, anything other than via solicitors over the actual divorce.' Hope's fist clenched up at her side.

Theo picked up the sledgehammer. 'Do you wanna knock some more wall down?' He smiled as encouragingly as he could manage. 'It might help.'

The respite room at the care home was decorated in a resolutely cheerful shade of yellow, and there was a pretty floral-patterned cover on the duvet, and a pot plant on the tiny ledge by the window. Someone had clearly tried really hard to make the place feel warm and welcoming and like something more than it was.

Emma watched, feeling utterly useless, as Tom and a carer helped his mum from the wheelchair and into the single brown armchair in front of the window. The stroke they'd been worried about was not as serious as initially feared. A TIA, the doctor had said, and a fall. Recovery should be good, but Gloria looked somehow smaller than she had a week before. The care home was a temporary measure, Tom had told her.

Gloria looked out of the window at the rather drab patch of gravel outside. An empty bird feeder hung from a rusting metal stand. The carer stepped back. 'I'll let you get settled in. I think there's some stuff for you to sign at reception.'

Tom nodded. 'Are you ok here?'

Emma squeezed his hand. 'We'll be fine.' She pulled a folding plastic chair over to sit next to Tom's mum. 'It's only for a few weeks. Just until you can manage to move around a little bit.'

Gloria fixed her with a watery stare. 'I think we all know that isn't true dear.'

'Don't say that.'

'Somebody needs to. I'm going to be in this place until the end, aren't I?'

Emma looked around. 'We don't know that, and however long you're here, we'll make it nice. We'll get some of your things. Your pictures and maybe even some of your furniture. We'll make it feel like home.'

'You're a good girl. How has he been though, our boy, this last couple of weeks? It's the worst possible time for this to have happened.'

'Just before Christmas?'

Gloria moved, awkwardly, to look Emma in the face. 'No. I meant with it being just past Jack's birthday. Things get a bit dark for him round this time of year.'

'Right. Yeah.' Emma nodded, as though this wasn't new information at all. 'Of course. I think he's ok.'

'And he's got you now. You're good for him. And I wouldn't want to think I was leaving him with nobody.'

Emma's breath caught in her throat. Gloria was a lot older than her own mother. Tom had been adopted, so his mum and dad had come to parenthood slightly later in life. But Emma couldn't imagine being in this situation with her own mother, which was silly really. Everyone got old – well, not everyone, but getting old was the better of the available options. One day it would be her mum in this chair, and then her. She took Gloria's hand. 'You're not going anywhere. Not any time soon. It was a very minor stroke.' She grinned. 'Barely even a stroke. You'll be back to your crosswords and your chess games and God knows what else in no time.'

Gloria looked down towards her left hand, sitting awkwardly on her lap. 'I'm not sure I'll be writing any answers in the crossword soon.'

'Well you can get someone to write them in for you.' She hoped she sounded more confident than she felt. 'Where there's a will there's a way.'

'Maybe.' Gloria looked back out at the limited view beyond the window. 'So long as Tom's not going to be on his own though. Whatever comes will come. That's my mind at rest at least.'

The older woman's eyes drifted closed, and Emma put a blanket over her knees. Tom came back and leaned over his mum.

'She's tired I think,' said Emma.

He nodded. 'I'll come back tomorrow.'

They walked hand in hand out to the car park, and climbed into Tom's rusting Polo. He didn't start the engine.

'How are you doing?'

'I'm ok. Just, I don't know. When Jack died I thought that was the worst. You know, to have someone go that suddenly, but this…' He looked back towards the home. 'It's a different sort of worst. It's like we've turned onto a path that only ends one way.'

'I know what you mean, but this is just respite at the moment. With physio she could improve a lot, and then…'

'And then the next thing, and the next thing. She's frail, Em. And the fight's gone. I can see it.'

Emma could see it too. 'We'll make whatever comes next the best we can. I told her we'd bring some of her stuff from home to make the room a bit more, well a bit less…'

'Like heaven's waiting room?'

'Yeah.'

'That's a good idea.' He lifted her hand from her lap and pressed it to his lips. 'Thank you.'

'What for?'

'Everything. This week. Coming to the hospital and making me eat and keeping me moving forward.'

'That's ok. It's part of the deal, isn't it?'

'I guess so. Doesn't mean I can't tell you I appreciate it though.'

'It's nice to be appreciated.' She took a deep breath in. 'Your mum told me it was Jack's birthday last week.'

Tom didn't meet her eye. 'Week before.'

'The week you said you were too busy to see me.'

He nodded. 'I'm sorry.'

'You could have told me.'

'I know. It wasn't you. It's… I don't know exactly… I'm not sure I even understand.'

She twisted in her seat to look at her partner. 'How do you mean?'

'I love you. You make me really happy, and I am so glad, but then I still miss Jack and that can still make me sad.'

'That's ok. Love doesn't just stop.'

Tom shook his head. 'That's not it though. Like last week, I was sad, but I don't think I was quite as sad as last year and that, somehow, was a million times worse. Like if I'm heartbroken over him, I feel guilty because I've got you and you're wonderful and

I know I'm lucky, but then if I'm not heartbroken I feel so much more guilty because I loved him.' His voice cracked. 'And it's not fair at all that I'm still here and he's not. So whatever I feel is wrong.'

Emma squeezed his hand. 'No. Whatever you feel is exactly right. I love you. Jack loved you. I didn't know him, but speaking on behalf of the people who love you, I promise you it's ok. However you're feeling, it's ok.'

'Thank you. And sorry. I should have said something to you, but I just wanted to hide away for a bit.'

'Well next time you need to hide away, maybe tell me you're hiding away?'

He nodded and cleared his throat, forcing the moment to pass. 'Anyway, onward. You're working tomorrow, right?'

Emma nodded. She'd had to leave Josh and Annie with far more of the preparation for the family day than she was comfortable with, but this week Tom had come first. Before the Season. Before work. Before the abstract possibility of finding love for someone else, she'd had the real practical graft of loving the person right here in front of her.

'Ok. So I'll collect some stuff from the house for her tomorrow, and then will I see you on Saturday?'

Emma ran through her mental calendar. She had two more events, including tomorrow, and it was now only four days until Christmas. The final ball was on Christmas Eve. She was just about on top of the Season side of things, but with Gloria's illness Christmas itself had got away from her. 'I probably should do some Christmas shopping.'

'Shit. Haven't really thought about Christmas.'

The silence sat between them for a moment.

'I usually go to Mum's. I cook for both of us. I guess…' He looked towards the concrete box of the care home in front of them. 'I guess that won't be happening.'

'Why don't you come to mine? Josh and Annie will be there I think.' Emma thought through the arrangements Annie had babbled at her. 'I think they're going to Annie's mum's to open presents in the morning and have a mince pie with her and Duncan, but then we're having Christmas dinner in the evening. Maybe with Jane and Charlotte. And Lydia.'

'And the Hot Earl?'

'I guess so. You're very welcome. And we could come and see your mum during the day?' Emma thought it through. 'It's a lot of people though. We can hole up in your flat if you prefer. Or you can do your own thing. I don't mind.'

'Where do you want to be?'

'Annie and Josh are going to cook.' Emma had never thought she would say this. 'I think I quite want to sit on the sofa and let them do everything around me. And I'd like it even better if you were there too.'

'Ok. That's a plan then.'

'Good. Your mum will be happy you're not going to be on your own.'

'What did she say in there?'

'She just worries about you. If something happens to her she wants to know that you won't be left alone.'

'And what did you tell her?'

'That after she goes I'm fleecing you for the inheritance and doing a runner.'

'She'd probably approve of that.' Tom managed a laugh.

'I told her you wouldn't be alone.' Emma stroked her finger down the side of his face. 'And I meant it.'

And you lied, the voice in her head reminded her. You're going to America. Emma told the voice in her head to bloody well be quiet. He was facing the possibility of losing his mum while the wound of losing his husband still had the power to hurt him some more. She couldn't tell him that he might be about to lose her too. Not today.

Chapter Twenty-one

You are invited,

along with your closest friends and family,

to an evening of wassailing

Grace read out the details from the Season members' website as the Uber carried her and her sister across the capital.

'What's wassailing?' her sister asked.

'Dunno. Think it's like drunk carol singing.'

Connie pulled a face. 'That doesn't sound particularly romantic. Read the rest.'

Grace read aloud. '*Family involvement is at the heart of the idea of a Regency-inspired programme to find love. In a Regency social season, parents would have been instrumental in making a match for their children. We don't expect that, but we are encouraging you to make a lasting attachment that will endure beyond the end of the Festive Season. With that in mind, this is an opportunity to introduce your potential partner to your family, or found-family, and see how they fit into your life outside the Season.*'

'So you're going to introduce Jon Rackham to Dad then?'

'Jon is not my potential partner.' The more she kept telling herself that, the more chance she might learn to accept it.

'Noooo. He's just the dude you're in love with,' Connie pointed out. 'What would him and Dad even talk about? Like what does he even do?'

'What about you? You don't have a likely candidate to thrust in front of Dad either.'

'Don't change the subject.'

Sometimes Grace genuinely wished she didn't have anyone in her life who knew her strategies for avoiding unwanted questions as well as Connie.

'What does Jon do?'

'I don't know,' Grace admitted.

'What?' Connie's face was a picture. 'So you've been to his flat and shagged his brains out multiple times but you've never asked what he does for a living.'

'I asked.'

'And he said?'

'Nothing specific,' she muttered.

'Great. You're shagging a mobster. Or a hitman.' Connie grinned. 'Or a spy. Like one of those Cambridge University gentleman spy types.'

Grace frowned. Actually she could totally see that. 'I don't think he's a spy.'

'You don't think.'

All of this was irrelevant. 'Anyway, he's not a potential partner. Let's go, see Dad, make nice with the wicked stepmother...'

'Grace!'

'What?'

'I thought you said she wasn't wicked.'

'She's got him doing Pilates. It's weird.' Grace was open to seeing the best in Jackie, the best being that Dad seemed to be happy, but forty-nine-year-old men with bald spots and beer guts taking up Pilates was tantamount to midlife crisis territory. 'But she's not actually wicked I don't think. Just a bit...' What was Jackie?

'Loud.'

'Yeah.' Grace couldn't really disagree. 'So long as Dad's happy though?'

'Yeah. I know.'

Her sister didn't sound fully convinced, but she wasn't arguing so Grace took it as a win.

Jackie's loudness was in evidence within a few seconds of them hopping out of the Uber and making their way through the large iron gates into the gardens beyond. Mulled wine was already flowing and Jackie's voice carried across the terrace enthusiastically declaring everything she came across to be charming and lovely and wonderful.

Grace caught her sister by the elbow, before she could even attempt a disappearing act, and steered her towards the voice. 'Girls!' Jackie was hard to miss in her cerise pink puffer jacket and purple bobble hat. And she spotted them as soon as they were within view. 'Look Pete. It's the girls.'

Grace exchanged a look with her sister. It was so tempting to swap names, especially with Connie's new look, but with their dad there they'd never get away with it. 'I'm Grace,' she offered helpfully. 'We'll have to start wearing name badges.'

'Grace.' Jackie looked slightly uncertainly from one face to the other. 'Right. You are so very alike.'

'Identical,' deadpanned Connie.

'We're not really though,' Grace added. 'I'm blonder. And I've got a scar on the back of my left knee.'

'Well I can't very well be peering at that every time you come round.'

'I've got a pierced nipple and a dagger tattooed on my arse cheek,' Connie added.

Jackie pursed her lips. 'That's worse than the knee thing. Now Pete, don't just stand there. Fetch us some mulled wine. And song sheets for the girls.' She seemed genuinely excited. 'We're going to be carol singing you know. Now it says on the sheet that we will be doing some religious ones, but not just religious and if you're non-Christian and you want to sit those out that's absolutely fine. Are you girls Christian?'

'Erm...' Grace glanced at Connie who shrugged. 'I think we're sort of nothingy really.'

'Right. Well you'll not be offended by "Away in a Manger" then.'

Both twins shook their heads.

'Good stuff. Now do you have anybody you need to introduce to your dad tonight? The email thing said it was a chance for us to meet anyone you'd formed a thingummy with.'

Both twins shook their heads again.

'That's a shame.' Jackie looked around the rapidly filling garden. 'Nobody at all out of all these people?'

'Just unlucky in love, I guess,' Grace offered.

'Oh well. You'll both find a decent fella eventually.' She stopped. 'Or lass.'

'Mmm hmm.' Grace was rapidly coming to see the appeal of Connie's 'just run away' approach to awkward situations.

'You do right, keeping your options open. I tried it with a girl once when I was in nursing school. Didn't take to it. Shame though. The idea of having a woman around the whole time is much more appealing really.'

Thankfully their father returned with a tray of cups of mulled wine.

'They haven't met anyone special,' Jackie informed him. 'Not that it matters. It'll give us time to get to know one another a bit more won't it?'

Grace wondered if, given that she already knew about Jackie's same-sex experimentation phase in college, there was really that much more left to get to know.

'Hi.' The whole group turned towards the voice. It was Morgan, bundled up in a bright blue wool coat and thick black scarf. She really was very pretty. Slightly serious, slightly earnest, and no spark at all, Grace now accepted. Not even a flicker. And Morgan hadn't changed, so the difference must be inside Grace herself. 'Connie, I was wondering if we could have a little chat?'

Grace watched her sister follow Morgan to the other side of the garden.

'Who was that?' her dad asked.

Jackie shot Grace a look. 'I'm guessing that was one of the nobodies that we don't need to meet?'

Connie and Morgan found a bench around the bottom of a tree trunk in one corner of the garden and squeezed in next to one another. 'Was that your mum?'

'No. My mum died when I was twelve.'

Morgan's face creased up in embarrassment. 'Oh God. I'm sorry. I think I knew that.'

'It's ok. That was my dad's new girlfriend.'

'Well she seems nice?' There was no hiding the tone of question in Morgan's voice.

'She seems to make my dad happy,' said Connie. 'And that's good.'

'Yeah. Nice that they both wanted to come today.'

It was. Connie glanced around. 'Who did you bring?'

'Right. Yeah. I didn't invite anyone.'

'Ok.' Nobody at all? That seemed surprising. The blurb from Emma was very clear that close friends or anyone that you viewed as family were more than welcome. They weren't taking DNA swabs at the gate.

'Yeah. You're probably wondering why.'

'A little bit.'

'Right. So I went no contact with my parents about eighteen months ago. They were...' Morgan swallowed. 'They weren't good people. I've got a brother who's older, but he left when he was sixteen and I haven't heard from him since. I started looking for him, but honestly, I don't know if he's still in London, or the UK, or even...' She shook her head.

'Shit. Sorry.' Connie was a long, long way out of her depth here. She was the girl who'd lost her mum when she was a child. The worst thing that could happen had actually happened to her. She was the person people offered the sympathetic shoulder squeeze to. She wasn't the shoulder squeezer. 'You don't have to tell me.'

'I will. If you want to hear.' Morgan looked around. 'But not today. Not here.'

'Ok.'

'Before I went no contact, I was engaged. To Elliot. When I told them about my parents though they went and confronted them.'

'What happened?'

'Nothing. My parents told them I was unstable and had a tendency to make things up, and they believed them. They came home and told me that I needed help, and that I needed to stop saying such horrible things about such good respectable people.'

'I believe you.'

'What?'

Morgan was staring right into Connie's face. Whatever she said next absolutely had to be the right thing. 'I don't know what exactly it is you want to tell me, but whatever it is, I believe you. I will believe you. I already believe you.'

'Thank you.' So quiet it was barely more than a breath on the breeze. Morgan exhaled hard. 'Thank you.' She looked around. 'I love gardens in winter. One day I hope I can get a proper garden flat. I love it.'

'Or a whole house?' Connie suggested.

'In London? As an artist?' Morgan laughed a little. 'Anyway, I wanted to tell you at least something, so you might understand why I don't rush into things. But at the same time I wanted to tell you because I still think this might be something. I know it was barely anything, but I keep thinking about you. Silly really.'

'It's not silly.'

'It's not like me at all,' Morgan continued. 'But I'm not looking for a big declaration of love or anything like that. I just wanted you to know that I can't do this at any pace other than my own. I'm sorry. I've worked so hard to get to here. I paint. I have an allotment. I create things and I grow things and I live as simply as I can and any time I have any spare cash at all I spend it on therapy. Doing the Season and taking the step to try to meet someone, is the most extravagant thing I've done, well ever really, and I chose this because they said it was all about taking things slowly. And right now slow and simple is how things have to be. The idea of bringing someone else into my life is scary, and it would probably be easier to give up on the idea of having that spark but...' She looked at Connie.

'You think we have a spark?'

'I do, but I really can't rush into anything. Even if I want to, I can't.' She smoothed her jeans down. 'So yeah, that's what I wanted to say. I'd like to see what might happen, but it has to be slow.'

'I...' Connie started.

Morgan held up a hand to quiet her. 'You don't have to reply now. You know where I live. If I'm not there I'll be at the allotments opposite Highgate Library. That's it. That's my whole life. Think about it.' She smiled. 'Don't rush. Take your time.'

–

Hope was in hell. Actual literal hell. Her hope that her parents would take up positions at opposite sides of the garden and leave the largest possible no man's land between them were dashed the moment her dad arrived and marched right up to her mother and attempted to kiss her on both cheeks. 'Miri! Long time no see.'

Miriam Lucas took a definite step backwards. 'Indeed.'

'You remember Tina.'

Hope's mother's gaze shifted to Hope's stepmum. 'No. Actually I don't believe I do.' She was frowning.

Of course her mother remembered Tina. She'd never lessened in her dislike for the horrid little shop girl Hope's dad had been having it away with, even all these years later. 'Tina you say?'

'That's right. Now I know from Hope what you think, but I want to tell you straight that nothing happened between me and Tony 'til long after you'd split up. I'd hate for you to think I was that sort of woman.'

'Tina?' Hope's mother asked again.

'Yes.'

'That's not short for anything?'

Tina shook her head.

'Very well then.' It wasn't clear from that response whether Hope's mother believed Tina's protests or not, but it did seem that that part of the conversation was over.

Hope scoured her surroundings for moral support. Or immoral support. Any sort of support really would do at this point. Theo? Everyone liked Theo, but, of course, despite his promises to run interference, he was nowhere to be seen.

A shock of blond hair heading her way caught her attention. Was this better or worse? It was the moment of truth anyway. She raised her hand in a wave, as he approached. 'So everyone, this is Callum.' She took his hand. 'Callum, this is my mum and dad, and Dad's partner Tina.'

'G'day all.' He grinned. 'What is it with this country and doing stuff outside in the depths of winter?'

'You're Aussie aren't you?' Hope's dad stepped forward and pumped Callum's free hand vigorously.

'Kiwi, but lived in Oz most of my life.'

'Good stuff. Are you a cricket man?' Hope felt the grip on her hand loosen as Callum was drawn into conversation with her dad. Hope hung back next to her mum. She'd never hear the end of it if her mother thought she'd been abandoned in favour of her father at the family day.

'So how long is he in London for?'

'I'm not sure.'

'But there'll be visas and such like.'

Would there? 'I'm not sure. His dad's Scottish so he might have dual nationality, I guess.'

'But you don't know?'

'We haven't talked about it yet.'

Her mother gave a small nod.

Hope felt her hackles rise. 'We will. It's early days.'

'I didn't say a thing.'

But I could feel you thinking it, thought Hope.

'He seems very personable.'

'He is.' Callum had the sort of easy personality that got along with everyone.

'Simon was very personable,' her mother added.

'Simon isn't around any more.'

'No. Quite. For the best, I'm sure.' Her mother paused, as if weighing her next thought. 'Your father too. Very personable. Everyone would agree.'

Hope did agree. Her dad and Callum certainly shared an ease, a sort of laid-back charm. She watched them joking together, with Tina leaning against her dad. That was exactly how she'd imagined some future boyfriend fitting in with her family. Charming Tina, joking with her dad, and with her mum, what? There was no breaking through her reserve. The best you could hope for was to avoid outright public disapproval.

Her mother was looking around. 'Will Theodore be here tonight?'

'Theo,' muttered Hope. 'And he was supposed to be. Yeah.'

'I hope you've thanked him for all the help with the shop.'

'Yeah.' Had she? Helping was just sort of what Theo did. 'Callum's been helping as well.'

'Well that's nice of him.'

Hope searched for a change of subject. Nothing safe presented itself, so she went for dangerous, but one step removed from Hope herself. 'You didn't have to pretend you don't remember Tina? She knows you know about...' Hope had never actually acknowledged that she knew about this too, despite years of her mother's insinuations. 'Well about the affair.'

'Affairs.'

'What?'

'Affairs plural. And I did indeed know, but not one of the ones I was aware of involved her. When I heard he was with her someone so soon after we separated I simply assumed it was the same girl.' She looked at Tina. 'Apparently not. I wonder how many he's had since.'

Hope knew her dad had had an affair, but he'd had an affair with Tina because Hope's mum was cold and judgemental and sucked the joy out of the house, and it had only been Tina and they'd been together ever since. So it wasn't even really an affair sort of an affair. 'He's with Tina now. Why would you say that?'

Her mother pursed her lips. 'I know you idolise your father, dear. And that's all right. That's something that I've had to learn to accept, but however he might be as a father, surely at your age, you can see that he might not have been the most wonderful of husbands.'

That was ridiculous. Hope's dad had worked hard right up until Hope had gone to university. The fact that they lived relatively austere lives was down to her mother's refusal to spend a penny more than she absolutely had to. 'He worked hard for us.'

'And he gambled even harder. And bought drinks for everyone. And made half the girls in the village fall in love with him. He was everyone's best friend, but he was not a good husband.'

'But…'

'But what?'

'But he's changed.'

'Perhaps. I'm sorry, Hope.' Her mother frowned. 'I really did think you knew. I mean, you saw it, what men like that can do.'

'What do you mean?'

'Well, your Simon. Did he ever change?'

Simon was different. Simon wasn't like Hope's dad. Simon was charming… Hope looked at her father. Ok, well, charming didn't mean anything. He'd controlled Hope by taking over the money. Hope remembered her mother counting out coppers on the kitchen table to give Hope her school dinner money. Simon had cut Hope off from her mates. Only Theo had had the determination to stay the course. Hope remembered her mother alone amongst her ladies' group, not sure quite how to connect with the people who would, in a heartbeat, have been her friends.

'Simon was very…' Her mother hesitated. 'Personable too.'

'Dad is nothing like Simon.'

'Well, not exactly like. No two people are ever exactly alike, are they?'

Her mother had no idea. 'Dad's fun. You knocked all the joy out of him.'

'That's enough.' Her mother stormed away from the group. Hope marched after her. Her mother stopped and turned. 'I think it's time you heard some home truths. You're right. Your father was marvellous fun. Throwing his cash around in the pub and at the bookies. I couldn't afford to be such fun because I was too busy scraping together whatever was left to keep you fed and clothed.'

No. Hope shook her head. Her dad was lovely, easy-going, the life and soul... she didn't have to listen to this. 'Dad is nothing like Simon. If you knew what Simon was really like.'

'Charming?' her mother asked. 'So much fun in company, which feels off because if he was so charming and so much fun, where did all your friends go?'

How did her mother knew she felt like that? 'You adored him.'

'And what would have happened if I'd said anything else?'

'What do you mean?'

'I mean that if that young man had thought, even for a moment, that I might say a word against him, he would have poisoned you against me.' Hope's mother's face was tight. 'Which probably wouldn't have taken much.'

'I didn't know.' Hope tried to think back. She thought she had clarity about a lot of what happened with Simon now, but specific memories and realisations still had the power to shock her. 'I didn't really know who I was by the end,' she admitted.

Her mother gave a small nod. 'But you did end it. That's the main thing. I'm very proud of that. I wasn't that brave.'

'Dad wasn't the same.' She was still clinging on to that. 'And even if he was, it's different with Tina.'

'I hope so. For her sake.'

'And Callum's not like Simon,' Hope added. 'Just cos he's sociable. I mean, that's a good thing. I can't let what happened before stop me from ever trusting anyone again.'

'Again, you are the brave one. I rather shut up shop after your father.'

Hope did understand that. Without Theo cajoling and persuading her to get out and live her life she could very easily have done the same. 'Maybe I should introduce you to Emma, who runs all this. See if she can find you a match?'

'I don't think so darling.' Her mother looked utterly horrified at the suggestion. 'Perhaps I'll start by taking up one of the invitations to coffee that the women's group keep throwing at me.'

Hope was surprised to find herself welling up. 'I think that's a really good idea.'

'Oh. Here's your Theodore.'

Theo kissed Hope's mother on the cheek. 'Mrs L! How are you?'

'Very well thank you. I've just met Hope's young man.'

'A great pleasure I'm sure.' Theo threw his arm over Hope's shoulder and gave her a squeeze nobody else would have perceived. 'I'm so sorry I'm late,' he whispered, before he turned back to her mum. 'Now, has she told you about the shop? You have to come and see it. Hope is going to do such amazing things.'

–

It was nearly time for the actual singing to begin. Josh had been absolutely dead set against this particular event idea, so Emma was making mental notes of all the excited comments she heard as she walked around the garden. The general consensus seemed to be that nobody had had a good singsong in years and that you couldn't beat an old-fashioned carol, could you? Emma told herself not to be smug, but frankly it was tricky when you were this damn good at your job.

Family groups were huddled around prospective couples, and she'd even seen Connie Price and Morgan Landy deep in conversation. Perhaps Emma was about to grab victory from the jaws of defeat on that match. She stopped when a stranger caught her eye. The woman was in her thirties or early forties and she was sitting alone on a bench next to the building, with a little boy, no more than six or seven, playing on the ground in front of her and an even smaller boy asleep with his head resting on her lap. She wasn't a dater, so she must be somebody's family. So why was she here alone?

'Hi. I'm Emma. I'm the organiser. Are you ok there?'

'I'm supposed to be here. I've got the email thing.'

'Oh no. It's fine. I wondered if you were with someone.'

'Yeah. Well no.' The woman looked around. 'Jon. My brother-in-law. It was actually my idea to send him on this whole thing, and he did invite me to this a few weeks ago, but I texted yesterday to confirm and he never replied. And he's not answering his phone. I was hoping he might turn up here.'

'I haven't seen him tonight. Sorry.' Emma wasn't sure what else to say. 'I hope he's ok.'

'Oh, I'm sure he's alive and kicking somewhere. He's being a dick, is what he is.'

The little boy playing alongside Emma gasped. 'You said a bad word, Mummy.'

The woman rolled her eyes. 'Sorry darling. He's being a big scaredy cat.'

'Well I'm sorry you had a wasted trip. You're welcome to stay for the carol singing, but if you want to get these two home to Dad…'

'Oh erm… no dad.'

'Sorry. Again.'

'You didn't know. He passed away.'

Emma seemed to be making things worse here every time she spoke, so she opted for silence.

'It's fine. Really. It was four years ago. This one doesn't even remember him.'

Emma sat down on the end of the bench next to the littlest boy's welly-clad feet. 'I'm sorry. I'm a matchmaker. I have to ask. Are you seeing anyone?'

The stranger shook her head. 'It's hard after you lose someone. People don't know what to say, and then they feel like they're competing with a ghost.'

'I understand that. My boyfriend lost his partner. It can be strange. For both of us.'

'But you make it work?' the woman asked.

'Yeah.' Apart from one little Atlantic Ocean-sized wrinkle that Emma was still determinedly pushing out of her mind. Her matchmaker instincts were tingling slightly though. 'So are you looking for someone?'

'Not actively, but if the right someone appeared...'

Emma heard that so often, and so often the right someone didn't appear, unless somebody, usually Emma, gave that someone a little shove in the right direction. 'Well fingers crossed for you then.' She caught Josh out of the corner of her eye, hovering slightly awkwardly a metre or two away. That must mean it was time for her to start the next part of the evening. Quickly, she dug her hand into the depth of her folder and closed her fingers around the square of cardboard that she was looking for. 'I was thinking. Erm... I've got this, but I probably won't use it.' She handed the card to the woman.

'Pottery Experience Days?' she read.

'Yeah. Try the wheel. Make a pot. All that stuff. Great for families. The kids might like it.'

'Right. Maybe.'

Oh for goodness' sake. Some people didn't seem to want to be fairy godmothered at all. 'Look. I think the kids would really enjoy it and you might meet somebody interesting. If you get my drift.'

The woman stared at the card. 'Are you matchmaking me? You know I'm not a client.'

Josh stepped forward. 'That won't stop her. It's a compulsion. We're lucky she's managed to make a business out of it really.'

'Ignore my brother.'

'No!' Josh objected. 'Don't ignore her brother. Listen to me when I say that if she's telling you it'll be worth your time to go to this place, then go. What have you got to lose?' He turned to Emma. 'I do need you now though.'

'Ok.' She stood. 'Sorry.' She pointed at the card. 'Ask for Philip. Tell him Emma Love sent you.'

The woman nodded.

'You're welcome to stay.'

'I don't really know anyone.' Then she looked around and her expression changed. 'Actually, I will. Thank you.'

–

Grace was having a surprisingly nice time. She'd assumed they'd lost Connie for the night when Morgan dragged her away, but actually she'd reappeared and seemed to be making a real effort to get along with Jackie. That meant that Dad was happy. And if everyone else was happy, Grace was, logically, happy too, she supposed.

'Erm, Grace?'

Grace saw the small boy in the blue duffel coat and the even smaller boy in the red duffel coat before she alighted properly on the owner of the voice. 'Sarah?'

Jon's sister-in-law. If she was here, then Jon must be here. Nobody came to a family event without their family member.

'Is Jon with you?'

Yes. That was the question. Grace stopped. But it wasn't her that had asked it. She glanced back at her family and took two steps away, angling her body so she could talk to Sarah slightly out of earshot, she hoped, of the rest of the group. 'No. I thought if you were here, he'd be with you. I haven't spoken to him this week. Not since the last Season thing.'

Technically not quite true. Not since she'd run out of his apartment a few hours after the last Season thing, but it was enough detail for now.

'Right. And did you?' Sarah sighed. 'Look, I don't want to pry, but was the thing between you getting serious?'

'No. Just a fling. We agreed.'

'What's a fling?' The larger little boy piped up.

'A type of Scottish dance,' his mother replied.

Grace stifled a giggle.

'I'm sure that is what you agreed, but was that what was actually happening?'

What was the point in lying? She'd probably never see Sarah again anyway. 'Not for me.'

'Look. I don't want to interfere.' Sarah pulled a face. 'I don't know why people say that. Obviously I'm about to interfere, so I must want to at least a bit. Jon's a good man. A really really good man, but losing Matt fucked him up. When somebody dies, you blame yourself. You think, what could I have done differently? How could I have changed things? Like I got up and changed this one's nappy that morning. What if I hadn't? What if I'd asked Matt to do it? Then he'd have gone out on his bike ten minutes later and he wouldn't have been on that bit of road at that moment and...'

'You can't do that. It wasn't your fault.'

'I know.' She sighed. 'I do know, but that's what your brain does. It tries to find a rhyme or a reason and when there isn't one you either accept that there isn't one and you try to carry on as best you can, or you let the fact that the world is random and scary and can break anything at any time terrify you so much that the only protection is to never get too close to anyone again. He could be so happy, but he's being a...' She glanced down at the child currently sucking his mitten thoughtfully. 'He's a big old scaredy cat, I'm afraid. And Matt was...' She smiled. 'Matt was great, but he struggled a bit when he came out of the army. Took a while to find his feet. Jon had to bail him out a couple of times. So I think he got used to taking responsibility for him.'

Grace's heart was literally breaking in two. Half of her wanted to run across London right now and wrap him up in her arms and tell him that everything was going to be all right. And the other half wanted to keep itself safe. 'Well I'm not sure he feels the same about me anyway.'

Sarah tilted her head. 'Jeez. If only there was some way of finding out, eh?'

Emma tapped on the microphone that was set up in the middle of the main part of the garden. Audio equipment outside in December felt like a risk, but there was something about being outside on a cold winter's night, all bundled up in coats and scarves and gloves, with mugs of hot gluhwein, that felt inescapably romantic. The opportunities for huddling up to your intended for warmth were reason enough for this event alone. 'Good evening and Merry Christmas, everybody. If you'd like to gather in, the actual carolling part of our carol evening is about to begin.'

She stepped back and let the choir leader they'd hired for the evening take her place at the microphone. She'd gone back and forth about whether to have religious music tonight. They'd be sure to mix in some more secular traditional songs but when it came down to it, there was something inescapably Christmassy about a proper carol. The first song was 'Good King Wenceslas', and as the band played a line by way of introduction she could see the ripple of smiles and exchanged looks and hand squeezes amongst the crowd in front of her. By the time the snow was laying round about, the group was already getting into the spirit of the thing. Emma made her way through the crowd and stood back to take in the scene.

It was these moments that reminded her that the Season was more than a series of singles' nights. It was a community. People had formed friendships as well as romantic relationships, and tonight people had brought their families along to join the community Emma had created. She could see dads with their arms around daughters and sons hold song sheets for their mums. Josh was to the side of the group, arms wrapped around Annie, who was standing in front of him, leaned back against his body, holding her song sheet up so he could see.

And Emma wished. Well, she wished Tom was here, of course, but he was sorting things out for his mum and she quite understood that he had a million things to get done. And she also wished. She wished that her own mum could see this. Her mum.

Emma Love senior. The true Queen of Matchmaking. Emma's superior in every area.

Emma made her way away from the carollers and around the side of the building next to the garden and pulled out her phone. It was an hour ahead in Spain, but that still made it before ten. And her mum lived on Spanish time now, so it would barely be dinner time for her. She hit her speed dial and waited for her mum to answer the call.

'Hello darling! How are you?'

'I'm ok. It's not too late to ring is it?'

'Not at all. I've just finished supper. What are you up to?'

'Erm… it's the seventh event tonight. Of the Season. It's the family night. Seeing all the parents made me think how nice it would be if you were here.'

'Oh, you don't want me cramping your style and picking fault. I know you've got everything under control.'

With the business certainly. But everything else? 'Well the business is good. Did Josh tell you about America?' Emma filled her mum in on the offer from the US.

'Well that's wonderful. What did Tom say? Will he go with you or is it a bit early for that?'

Emma stopped. This was why she'd called her mum. Of course it was. Her mum would understand. 'I haven't told him yet.'

There was a silence on the other end of the line.

'I said…'

'I heard what you said.' Her mother's tone was curt. 'Why on earth not?'

'Well nothing was certain and then his mum had a fall and she was in hospital and we were going back and forth from there, and now she's in a care home and he's still not sure if she's going to be able to go back to her house or not and, and so there was never really a good time.'

'Oh dear. Poor Tom. And Gloria. She won't like feeling like an invalid.'

'No. Not at all.'

'And you've been back and forth with him, sorting all that out.'

'Yeah.'

'And never once in any of those car journeys was there a two-minute lull in which you could have said, "By the way, darling, I've been offered the chance to work in New York"?'

Emma pulled a face, rather pointlessly, at the telephone. 'It's not that easy.'

'I think it is.'

'But…'

'But what? You don't want to upset him?'

'Of course not.'

'So don't go.'

'But…'

'But it's a brilliant opportunity and you want to go?'

'But I want to stay with Tom as well.'

'I'm not sure what you're expecting me to say. You know you have to talk to him about it, and you know that you've been putting it off, don't you?'

That wasn't fair. 'I wouldn't say putting off.'

'Emma darling, finding love is easy. We do that for people every single day. Making the relationship work is different. There's no magic formula. The only thing I know is that you have to talk. And you have to talk about the things that might upset them the most of all. While they're still little things, before they're bombs primed to blow the whole thing up.'

There was no arguing with that. 'You're right.'

Emma could picture her mother preening slightly at the other end of the line. 'Of course I'm right, darling. Now go and concentrate on your event. Phoning me in the middle of it. I don't know what's got into you.'

Emma let her mother harry her off the phone, and walked back towards the sound of singing.

'I'm sorry!' Grace Price almost knocked her over as she came back around the corner. Emma watched her race out of the gate and off down the street. Where on earth could she be going? Emma paused. And might it relate at all to a certain dater's non-appearance this evening? Interesting.

—

Grace was resolved. She wasn't going to wait and see if he contacted her. She wasn't going to apologise for coming on too strong. She wasn't going to tell him that she shouldn't have reneged on their deal not to grow feelings for one another.

She was going to take a different approach entirely.

The journey to Canary Wharf was much more hassle when a sleek black saloon didn't pull up alongside you within moments of you deciding on your destination. She couldn't. Could she? Why the hell not? If he was pleased to see her then everything would be fine, and if not then he'd have a charge on his account that was nothing to do with him, but that he could still very well afford to pay.

Grace dragged the business card from the bottom of her purse and dialled the number, requesting a car to Canary Wharf on Mr Rackham's account. Moments later – seriously, how did they do that? Were there cars hiding around every corner in the city? – she was leaning back on the cool grey leather, speeding through the night time traffic.

The next hurdle was how to get in to Jon's building. There was an automatic door that slid open and gave her access to the lobby, but the lift didn't appear to have anything as mundane as a call button. She tapped the touchscreen next to the lift doors, but it asked her for a fingerprint or a security code. She had neither. Well, she had loads of fingerprints, obviously, but none that could help her in this situation.

'45631.' Grace turned towards the voice. Carl was standing in the lobby behind her. 'But don't tell him I told you. He's been a right bastard this week. If you can cheer him up, it's worth risking my neck for.'

'Thank you. And I won't tell him. I'll say I saw him do it or something.'

'Have a good evening, Miss Price.'

The lift took her right up to the penthouse. She was half expecting to see Jon standing there as the doors slid open, all neat and pressed and in control, somehow expecting her. There was nobody there.

'Jon?' She called out as she moved into the apartment. 'Jon? Are you here?'

There was nobody in the open-plan kitchen living area. She stuck her head around the door of the study. Nobody there either. Bedroom then. Right. She'd marched right into his apartment without an invite, why shouldn't she march right into the bedroom? But still. She hesitated at the door. It swung open before she'd summoned the resolve to go in.

'What are you doing here? How did you get in?' Jon wasn't the perfectly pressed and presented man she was used to. Actually that wasn't quite true. He was dressed precisely as always, formal shirt, suit trousers, tie, even at home. It wasn't his clothes that looked wrong. It was him. His face was usually a shield – impassive and unreadable. Today it was etched with exhaustion. 'What are you doing here, Grace?'

'I came to see you.'

'I can see that much.' He moved past her and into the living room.

'You didn't come to the carol singing. Sarah was there. I think she was worried.'

'Yet Sarah didn't break into my home.'

'I didn't break in.' She hadn't, had she?

'But, nonetheless, here you are.' He sat down on the long L-shaped couch. 'Why are you here, Grace?'

She should have called. 'I nearly called. Lots of times.'

'To say?'

Right. Yes. 'Well I nearly called to say sorry, for being emotional and messing things up, and I was going to take it back and see if we could go back to how things were before.'

273

He was staring out of the floor-to-ceiling window into the night outside. 'Were going to?'

'What?'

'You said you *were* going to say all that, but you didn't.'

'No.' This was it. This was the last chance to step off the rollercoaster before everything turned upside down. 'And I'm not saying all that, because it wouldn't be honest.' For once in her life she wasn't going to make everything easy for the person she loved. For the first time in her life Grace was going to be more Connie. 'I'm sorry I freaked out you, but I'm not sorry for what I said. I fell in love with you. I know that's not what you wanted and not what we agreed, but it is what happened and it is how I feel. I love you. I love how you make me feel. I really love having sex with you. But I love how precise you are. I love how you give me permission to just be. And I won't pretend that all of that is nothing.'

'Grace, I can't...' He shook his head.

'Can't what?'

'I told you I wasn't going to be your boyfriend.'

She nodded. 'I know, and I'm not going to be the girl who thinks that if she holds on you'll change your mind. This isn't me clinging on. This is me letting go. I'm in love with you, but I'm not going to hang around and wait and see. I would really love to be with you. Properly. Fully. No pretending that it doesn't matter, but that's up to you now.'

'What are you saying?'

She exhaled hard. 'Just that. The last Season thing is on Christmas Eve. I'm going to go. I'd really like you to be there too, but as my date. As my partner. That's the deal. Shit or get off the pot, Mr Rackham.'

'Shit or...? That's your big romantic proposition?'

Grace nodded. She had no idea what had come over her but it was invigorating. She should be more Connie more often. Maybe she could go and see her boss and ask for a raise while she was on a roll? 'Yep. That's the best you're going to get.'

'And what if I can't?'

What if he couldn't? What if he didn't feel the same? That was the possibility Grace was refusing to allow herself to consider, but it was right there. Triumph or disaster were the two sides of the coin she'd flicked high into the air. 'Then that will probably break my heart.'

'So wouldn't it be easier to carry on as we were?'

It was so tempting, but no. 'I think that would break my heart too. Only slower.'

'I understand.'

'And?'

'And I'll consider your proposal.' He looked up at her. 'I'm sorry. That's all I can give you right now.'

This was the moment to walk away, but every fibre of her being wanted to slide onto the sofa next to him and pull him into her arms. 'Are you ok, Jon?'

'I don't think I am.'

'Is there anything I can do?' She could make it better. She could hold him, stroke his hair, make him some food. She could do something.

'I think you have done everything you can.'

Grace made her way back down in the lift, and across the lobby. Her stomach was tied in knots. Leaving him unhappy was the hardest thing to do, and she had no idea at all if it was the right thing.

Carl was leaning on the side of the car right outside. 'Can I take you home, Miss Price?'

She shook her head. 'I don't think Mr Rackham will be wanting to pay for that.'

Carl held up his phone. 'Well he requested the pick-up. I don't know what's gone on between you, but he must still care.'

'Perhaps.' She could only hope.

Chapter Twenty-two

The speed with which they'd cleared most of the old stuff out of the shop was almost frightening to Hope. A couple of days of hard work and the difference was unbelievable. She realised that even though she'd signed a lease and was paying rent, she still sort of saw the shop as something that was happening in the far distance. She looked around. The plasterer was coming between Christmas and New Year to deal with the damage to the walls where they'd knocked the partition out, but she was assured that that would only be a half-day job. And the plasterer was a friend of someone Theo 'knew', so would only be charging mate's rates, despite never having met Hope in his life, and he had another mate who would replace the missing glass in the door.

Theo came out of the tiny staff toilet at the back of the shop wiping his hands on an old tea towel. 'I think I've fixed that tap. It's still a bit spluttery but water does come out now.'

'Thank you.' Hope crossed 'plumber' off her list of immediately necessary expenses.

'No Callum tonight?'

'He's working. I think his boss is getting a bit pissed off with how much time he's been spending here.' Callum worked in a bar in the City, and was already testing his employer's patience with the number of days off he'd taken to attend the Season. 'He's only done like two shifts this week.'

'Just us then.'

'Yep.'

'So what's next?'

Hope looked around. They needed to wash down the wall for plastering, and take the last bits of the old Formica counter out to the skip, and clean up a bit. 'Mostly clearing up. Then it's shopping time!'

'Right. So my job is to stop you spending all the profit you haven't made yet.'

'Exactly.'

An hour later the last bits were in the skip, and Hope was sweeping the floor while Theo paid the pizza delivery girl. They sat cross-legged on the floor eating takeaway and drinking Coke from the can. 'Thank you,' said Hope.

'What for?'

'For encouraging me to do this.'

'I'm glad you went for it. I wasn't sure for a bit there. I thought I'd crapped up our relationship for nothing.'

'You're my best friend.' Hope smiled. 'You could never crap up our relationship.'

He closed his eyes. When he opened them again, he set his slice of pizza down in the box and rubbed his hands together. 'Don't be too sure about that.'

Hope giggled. 'Come on. You shagged my cousin and we're still mates.'

'I didn't…' He shook his head. 'It doesn't matter. Fuck. I can't believe I'm actually going to do this.'

'Do what?'

'Hope Lucas.'

He was making her nervous now. 'Yeah?'

'I love you.'

'Yeah. I love you too. You big soppy head.'

He winced slightly. 'No. Not "I love you, you're my best friend". I love you. I'm in love with you. I dream about you. I think about you pretty much constantly. And I know you're with Callum so this is horrible timing, but you're with Callum and what if that turns into something and in five years' time I'm playing the doting godfather to your perfect little mini-Callums and I still haven't told you?'

None of this was right. 'Don't be ridiculous.'

'What?'

'You're not in love with me. We're friends.' Hope's heart seemed suddenly keen to fight its way out of her chest. Her palms had gone all clammy. 'We're best friends.'

'Yeah. We are.' His face was utterly serious. 'And I will take that. If that's all that's on offer I will take that every single time, cos then I get to have you in my life, but on the very tiny chance that that's not all there is, I have to tell you.'

That was where he was wrong. He absolutely did not have to tell her. He didn't have to say anything. He could have carried on as they were. 'Why didn't you say anything before?'

'You were with Simon.'

'And after that?'

Theo sighed. 'You were so broken. I didn't want to be the rebound guy. I wanted you to get well, so you'd be ready.'

'And now I'm ready, and I'm with someone else.' She stood up. 'I need to go.'

'No. It's fine. I'll go.' Theo jumped up and gathered his coat and gloves from the floor. 'I'll call you?'

Hope shook her head. 'Just go.'

He had to go. She couldn't deal with this. Not right now. She had the shop and a million and one other things to think about. And Callum. Callum was good and kind and exactly the sort of person she wanted to be with. Hope slammed the door shut behind Theo and pushed the bolt across. He was gone. This whole conversation was over. It was an aberration. The best thing to do was to simply not think about it ever, ever again.

—

And she tried. She fervently didn't think about Theo while she picked out paint colours. She didn't pick up her phone a thousand times to ask him whether Heather Heights or Lavender Hush would be prettier for the wall behind the counter. She didn't think about him in the shower as she washed the dust of the shop out of her hair. She absolutely did not think about him at all while she talked to Callum on the phone.

But, in bed, alone that night, even Hope had to admit that her mind was filled with nothing else. Theo. Memories of Theo, which were one thing. All the countless times he'd taken care of her, or made her laugh, or shot her a look in the middle of a horrible moment that said that, whatever else went wrong, the two of them were in this together. Memories she could deal with. It was where her brain went when her imagination took over that was the worrying part. The thought of Theo's lips against her neck, Theo's hand on her thigh, Theo…

Hope checked the clock. Six thirty-five a.m. It was Sunday. Christmas Eve. She didn't need to go to the shop. There was nothing more she could do there until the new plaster was ready to paint. She didn't need to get up for work, but she couldn't stay in bed any longer. If she stayed in bed there was a risk she'd go back to sleep. Conscious daytime Hope was absolutely sure that she'd done the right thing, cutting Theo off, but dream Hope had her own ideas.

She pulled her slippers and dressing gown on and headed downstairs. Connie and Grace were already drinking coffee at the kitchen table. Connie looked up. 'You couldn't sleep either?'

Hope nodded, which was a lie. She could sleep. She just didn't like where her brain travelled to when she did. 'What's up with you two?'

She caught Connie's glance at her sister and Grace's tiny nod in response. 'We've both been screwed up by this Season thing. We kinda blame you for that to be honest.'

'It's not my fault.' Hope poured herself a coffee. 'How's it screwed you up?'

'Connie has to decide if she can do adulting,' Grace chipped in.

'And Grace has to wait patiently to find out what someone else decides.'

'I can do patience,' Grace protested.

'I can't,' Connie conceded.

Grace leaned back. 'So, there's this person I really like, but he says he doesn't want a relationship and I've told him I do and now... Now there's nothing I can do. I keep thinking of stuff I can try to make it better, but I can't, can I? I've told him the deal. It's up to him.' She drummed her fingers against the side of her mug. 'So I'm just sort of stuck.'

'Right.' So that was one romantic quandary Hope could definitely trump. 'What about you?'

'Morgan.'

'What about her?'

'She says she likes me but she wants to take things slow.'

That one didn't even sound like a problem. 'And?'

'And like get to know each other, not rush in to anything.'

'Still not clear what the problem is.'

Grace giggled at Hope's reaction.

'It's not that. It's...' Connie sipped her coffee. 'She's vulnerable. What if I fuck it up?'

'What if you don't?' asked Grace.

'But fucking stuff up is what I do,' Connie pointed out.

That wasn't fair. Connie was just a bit impulsive sometimes. 'No more than anyone else.'

'I do. I mess things up and Grace fixes them.'

'I can't fix things with Jon.'

'And I'm bound to mess them up with Morgan,' Connie added.

Oh for goodness' sake. 'Theo's in love with me,' Hope blurted out.

Both twins nodded.

'Maybe I could call Jon?' Grace suggested.

'Maybe we'd be better off just being friends?' said Connie.

Were these people not listening to her at all? 'I said, "Theo's in love with me."'

'Yeah.'

'Obviously.'

What? 'But he can't be in love with me.'

She finally had both her cousins' attention. Grace frowned. 'Why not?'

'Because he's my best friend.'

'Your straight male best friend who has had how many serious relationships since you've known him?'

Well that wasn't because of Hope. 'That's cos he doesn't want a relationship.'

'That's cos he won't let himself have a relationship,' Grace suggested.

'Right. So what was happening when you slept with him?'

'What?' Grace laughed. 'I didn't sleep with Theo.'

Connie nodded. 'She spent half the night listening to him whine about you while he got drunker and drunker and then passed out.'

Grace looked aghast. 'You really didn't know he had a thing for you?'

Hope shook her head. 'Not at all.'

'So how did you find out?' asked Connie.

'He told me. On Monday night. At the shop.'

'He told her!' Connie flung her arms in the air in a gesture of unbridled triumph. 'He told her!'

'Fuck,' muttered Grace.

'You owe me twenty quid.'

'I never thought he'd actually do it. Fine.' Grace picked her phone up from the table. 'I'll send you it now.'

Hope was reeling. Theo really was in love with her. Everybody knew. It was a whole big thing that everyone except her was party to. How could she be that oblivious? 'I don't want to lose him as a friend.'

She saw the look Connie and Grace exchanged. Had she already lost him? He'd said not. He'd said that if friendship was all she could offer he would take it, but how would that even work? Would she have to tell Callum? Would he want some other bloke who was in love with his girlfriend hanging around?

'I'm with Callum now,' Hope added. 'And he's great.'

Neither of her housemates disagreed.

'He's everything I wanted. He doesn't pressure me and he's straight down the line. He says how he feels and what he wants.' Something went thud inside her gut. 'Theo didn't do that. If he's felt like this for years why didn't he say anything?'

'Are you sure he didn't?' Connie asked.

Of course she was sure.

'I mean we both knew.'

'Cos he told you!'

Grace shrugged. 'It really wasn't news. You know how every single person you meet thinks you're a couple?'

'That's cos people are weird about man–woman friendships.'

'No,' Connie butted in. 'It's cos you're joined at the hip and he looks at you like you're some kind of angel falling from heaven. Look, I don't know if he actually said anything, but he told you how he felt one way or another every single day for God knows how long.'

'I don't know what to do,' Hope whispered.

'Me neither,' said Connie.

Grace folded her arms. 'Well it's all right for you two. You just have to make a decision. I made one and now I'm stuck in limbo waiting on someone else.'

'I don't have a decision to make. I'm with Callum.' That was how things were. 'I'm going to the ball with him tonight. That's that. Theo will have to accept that we're just friends.'

'Ok,' Grace didn't sound entirely convinced. 'What about you Con?'

'I don't know if I'm good enough for her.'

Hope grabbed her cousin's hand. 'You're good enough for anyone.'

Grace nodded. 'She's not asking you to be perfect. She's asking you to let her take things slow.'

'I don't know.'

'Well put it this way. Either you're with her at her pace or you're not with her at all. What ya gonna do?'

282

When Grace put it like that it wasn't really a decision at all, even though Connie's head was more full of doubt than it had ever been. She was absolutely sure she wasn't up to being the person Morgan needed her to be. She was fairly sure she'd mess things up within the very first conversation. She suspected she might have left having this conversation too late anyway. But she knew she had to try.

There was nobody in at Morgan's flat-cum-studio, so Connie grabbed the bus towards Highgate. She caught her knee twitching as she drummed her foot on the floor, willing the journey to go faster, and forced her heel to the ground and told herself to breathe. Slow and deep. In for four and out for six. Slow down. Enjoy the journey. Don't rush to the destination and miss the ride. She watched London rolling by outside the window. Families walking dogs. Teenagers striding, head down, hood up, ear buds in, lost in their own world. Runners slowing to a walk for a water break.

Finally she jumped off the bus and jogged round the corner. Highgate Library was on the far side of the road, but the entrance to the allotments was a few metres ahead. Connie forced herself to slow to a casual stroll as she pushed the gate open. The site was divided into plots with narrow grass pathways between each section. Connie couldn't see Morgan though.

There was a chap leaning on a spade surveying his domain not far from the entrance though.

'Excuse me.'

He looked up.

'Hi. I'm looking for Morgan Landy.' Connie held a hand up. 'About this high. Redhead.'

The man pointed to the far end of the site. 'Bottom corner.'

'Thank you.' Connie picked her way along the narrow grass pathway. There were three allotments along the furthest wall and on the corner one, to her right, Connie could see a familiar bright ginger head bent towards the earth. She moved closer and stopped at the corner of the plot. It felt like one ought to wait to be invited in rather than charging straight through. 'Hi.'

Morgan stood up and turned to face her. She smiled. 'Hi.'

So this was it. Connie took a breath. It was time to be less bull in china shop and more patient and gentle. It was time to be more Grace. 'I came to say yes.'

Morgan didn't move for a second. They stood, feet apart, gazing directly into one another's eyes. Sometimes it was impossible to say anything with a look, but this look spoke of an understanding between them that felt deep enough to last. 'Yes?' Morgan whispered.

'To what you said before. To giving it a go and taking things slow. To whatever you need. I want to give this a chance.'

She saw Morgan's shoulders drop slightly, as if a tension had physically left her body. She dropped her trowel onto the ground and stepped forward. She held up one hand. 'I'm all muddy.'

'That's ok.' Connie held out one hand and Morgan took it, and then moved closer and brushed Connie's lips, fleetingly, with her own. When Morgan stepped back Connie could see that she was smiling.

'Ok. So what do we do now? I can go, you know. We can meet up whenever. No pressure. No rush.'

'Stay.' Morgan looked around. 'If you want to. I was planting spring bulbs.'

'Isn't it a bit late for that?'

'It's not ideal, but what ever is? Better to plant them now and look after them as best we can and give them a chance, don't you think? Rather than tossing them away.'

Connie agreed. Definitely better to give things a chance.

Chapter Twenty-three

You are invited to a costumed ball to celebrate

Christmas Eve

and the end of the Festive Season.

Full Regency dress requested.

'Are you all ready?'

Hope heard Callum yelling from the hallway, closely followed by the sound of a housemate hurtling downstairs.

'Hope!' he yelled again. 'Taxi's two minutes away.'

She stopped and looked herself over in the mirror. She was slightly regretting not buying her final ball dress for the previous season, given how much she'd now spent on renting a Regency dress twice, but she did have to concede that there was something about the empire waist and the long dress and the astonishing boob scaffolding that made her feel like the heroine in a fairytale. Her dress this time was the palest of pale blues, with lace around her décolletage. She'd tied her hair up and managed to tease the remaining loose strands into pleasingly Regency-esque ringlets. She just had the shoes to deal with. She grabbed them from the box on the bed and ran downstairs barefoot.

The front door was already open and she could see Grace in the street, waving down the cab. Callum was standing in the hallway in breeches and tailcoat, his normally loose blond hair gelled back from his face. Not quite Mr Darcy perhaps, but a solid Bingley at least.

She held up her shoes. 'I need to...' She hopped one shoe onto her foot, and somehow managed to bend enough in her corsetry to tie the ribbon laces across the top of her foot. One more to go.

Callum reached past her and took the second shoe out of her hand. 'Allow me.'

She watched him kneel in front of her. 'Bit early for down on one knee,' she giggled.

He smiled. 'Don't worry. I'm not going to propose.'

She lifted her foot and he slid the shoe into place. 'It fits. I guess that means you're the girl I've been searching for.'

'Yep. I guess so.'

'Hope,' Callum reached up and took her hand.

He wasn't actually going to propose, was he?

'Don't look so scared,' he said. 'I wanted to tell you this evening, and well, now seems like as good a moment as any, that I think – well I know – I've fallen in love with you. I love you, Hope.'

Relief that this wasn't a proposal mixed with something else. What? Joy. It had to be joy. This was how relationships went. You met someone. You dated. You got to know each other. You fell in love. This was exactly right. 'Great. Well that's great,' she said.

'Taxi's here!'

Hope stepped back to give Callum space to get up. 'We'd better get going then.'

–

Emma walked the room with Josh jogging in her wake, as she snapped instructions at him.

'You know it all looks fine?'

She glared at him. 'I don't want fine. I want perfection.'

'Well I think we're pretty damn near it.'

She shot him another look.

'And you don't want near perfect. You want actual perfect. I know. Don't worry. I'm sure our new business associate will be impressed.'

Nina was coming tonight. She was in London. She'd arrived last night and described, to Emma over the phone, in very excited breathless detail, the lengths her assistant had gone to, to arrange, from New York, for her Regency dress to be waiting for her in her suite. Impressing her was important. Of course it was. The contracts for the US licensing deal weren't signed yet. A bad night tonight could still ruin the whole agreement.

Emma looked around. Having the final ball at a new venue wasn't ideal, but the summer ball had been outside, which wasn't going to cut it in Regency dresses in December, and the venue for the first ball was too small for the formal dance lines and squares of a period ball. Everything did look to be ready though, better than ready. The room had been decorated for Christmas but Emma's stipulation of no plastic decorations and no obviously twentieth-century materials had been followed. The candles adorning the Christmas tree were battery powered, but with the lighting low they gave off a golden flicker that gave Emma the same warm feeling as the real thing. Together with the tree itself and the swags of pine, holly and ivy that were slung from the ceiling, it really did feel as though you were walking into a Christmas ball from another age. She checked the time again. 'Five minutes to go.'

Annie arrived at Josh's side. 'The caterer said the extra waiting staff are here.'

Emma nodded. Christmas Eve. Obviously half of the booked waiters were going to flake out. That was one problem she'd been prepared for, with contacts from all her past events on standby for a last-minute call.

'Erm,' Annie and her husband exchanged a look. 'Is Tom coming tonight?'

'Yes.'

'And have you told him about America yet?' asked Josh.

'No. I only saw him once this week. At the care home. There wasn't a chance.'

'Right. Such a shame he doesn't have one of those, what are they called? Phone things that you could contact him on.'

Emma didn't meet her brother's eye. 'I'm going to tell him tonight.'

'Well hopefully before he meets Nina,' Josh pointed out.

'Definitely before he meets Nina. Which is why…?'

'Which is why me and Annie have to run interference when she gets here,' confirmed Josh.

'Just long enough for me to talk to Tom first.'

'Will and Lydia are definitely coming too,' Annie added.

Josh frowned. 'Are we still thinking about the country house idea as well then?'

'Yes. No.' Emma couldn't think about any of it. She had two hundred people about to come through the door. 'I don't know. Let's get this Season finished right and then we'll see.' She took a deep breath. It was time. 'Right then. Let's get this show on the road.'

There was something extra special about the moment the doors opened for the final event of the Season. The costumes made a huge difference of course. The guests carried themselves differently, but it was more than that. There was an air of celebration and anticipation, enhanced this time around because it wasn't only the last event of the Season, but also Christmas Eve. When the clock struck midnight and the ball came to a close they would also be ushering in Christmas. Hopefully the first Christmas together of many for Emma's many budding couples.

She watched people coming in. There were a good number of oohs and aaahs at the room. Moving venue to an even grander space had been a good decision. It was another thing that added a further sheen to the final night festivities.

Emma kept her eyes peeled for anyone who wasn't arriving on the arm of a partner. Theo Carter – the only surprise there really was that he was here at all. Emma had been half expecting him to cry off. Despite her very best efforts it was clear that he wasn't ready to move on.

Grace arrived with Hope and Callum, but without a partner on her arm. She'd been so sure Morgan was going to be a match for one of the twins. Maybe that was the problem. Maybe Emma was at fault for grouping the sisters together in her mind rather than seeing their individual needs.

At least Hope Lucas was with someone now. Emma's nemesis from the first Season had been slain. She watched Hope and Callum make their way towards the bar. It was possible there was the smallest hint of tension in Hope's expression. Emma discounted it. Probably just an over-tightened corset.

Emma's attention moved on to the tall dark-haired woman being greeted by Annie. Nina Elton, in a very impressive scarlet gown and feathers in her hair. If nothing else, you had to admire her commitment to fly in from New York and have such a perfect costume in place within twelve hours of arriving. It was a level of attention to detail Emma would aspire to.

And a second behind her, Tom. Something jumped inside Emma when she saw him in his tailcoat and neckcloth. That was how he'd been dressed the night they'd finally got together, the night they'd admitted that they were both utterly in love with the person they'd been fighting with constantly for the previous eight weeks, and the night she'd realised that the man who'd been infuriating her in real life and the man she'd been quietly falling for online were one and the same. She blinked back a tear as he walked towards her.

'Are you ok?'

She was. 'Seeing you dressed like that. It brought back some memories.'

'Good memories?'

'The best.'

He leaned forward to kiss her. 'So how's everything going?'

'It's good. How was your mum today?'

'Brighter. They think she should be ok to go home before New Year. We'll need to sort out extra care I think but she's pleased.' He sighed. 'I have no idea if it's the right thing, but it's what she wants.'

'Then I think it's the right thing.'

He looked around the room. 'Anyway, this all looks fantastic.'

'Thank you, Mr Knight.' She offered a little curtsy.

He laughed. 'And will you have time to dance with me later, do you think?'

'I'm sure we can squeeze one dance in.'

'There you are!' The strident New York drawl was unmistakable. Nina was bearing down on them.

Annie was half running after her. 'Nina, why don't we…? I was going to show you the…'

She was too slow. 'So this is your Mr Darcy then?'

'Yes. Erm, Tom this is Nina Elton.'

Tom nodded a greeting.

'I take it you're not going to be my biggest fan then?'

'I'm sorry?' Tom was confused. Emma felt, for what must have only been the briefest moment, as though time had slowed, as though she could see the lorry speeding towards her but had no power to step out of the way.

'When I steal this one away?'

He stared at Nina and then looked to Emma. 'Away?'

'Oh Jeez. Did I put my foot in something?' Nina shrugged theatrically. 'Well the truth will out. We're taking the Season to New York. Emma's coming over to act as our newest VP. We couldn't be more excited.'

'Right.' The hand holding Emma's dropped away. 'Well that's great news. Congratulations.' He stepped back. 'Excuse me a second, would you?'

–

'Would you like to…?'

'No. Thank you.' Grace batted away another invitation to dance. She wasn't here to have a nice time with some kind soul who was taking pity on her while their shiny new soulmate powdered their nose. She was here for one reason, and one reason only. To wait for Jon and to support Connie. She was here for two reasons. To wait for Jon, and to support Connie. And because the ticket was free. She was here for three reasons.

No. She was here for two reasons. Jon wasn't going to come. There was no reason to hope that he might come. Jon hadn't led her on or given her false hope. He'd been absolutely clear about what he wanted and who he was. And probably it was best that he wasn't here. He was all wrong for Grace. He was bossier than she was. They'd end up fighting constantly.

She was unable to suppress a smile at the thought of all the making up that could lead to.

'Grace.'

Part of her didn't want to turn towards the voice for fear that it was her imagination, but turn she did. And there he was. Not observing the dress code on any level, but dressed absolutely as Jon. Dark grey suit. Crisp white shirt. Silk tie. 'Why aren't you in costume?'

That perfectly unruffleable eyebrow shot up. 'Because I'm not eight years old, and this isn't a superhero birthday party.'

'It's a Regency ball,' she pointed out. 'You're supposed to...'

'Grace,' his tone was sharp.

She shut up.

'I'm here.'

Right. 'Why?'

'Because you asked me to be.'

Oh.

He stepped towards her. 'I missed you. I hadn't expected to miss you, but I did. There's a Grace-shaped space in my bed.'

'Just in your bed?'

He shook his head, gaze fixed down towards the floor.

'I know you're frightened. I'm not going to hurt you.'

He met her eye. 'That's not what I'm frightened of. That's not it at all.'

'So tell me.'

They were inch close now. In an instant she could press her body to his and kiss him and undo all of this tension. Maybe they didn't have to talk. Maybe they could carry on with the sex and the fun and avoid that whole 'being in love' question altogether. Grace stopped herself. She'd drawn her line in the sand. It was as much for her as for him.

'Sarah told you about my brother?'

'Yeah.'

'The night before he died we had an almighty row. It was about…' He paused. 'Weirdly it was about a 1962 copy of the *Beano* I was trying to sell.'

'What?'

'It doesn't matter. It wasn't about that really. It was about everything. We said things. He accused me of being controlling, which was probably fair, but I said that I wouldn't have to be controlling if he wasn't behaving like such a fuck-up, which wasn't fair at all, but I lost my temper, and twelve hours later he was dead. He died thinking I hated him.'

Grace took his hand. 'I'm sure he didn't.'

'You weren't there.'

'No, but I know brothers and sisters. Did you argue a lot?'

'Hardly ever.'

'Then he knew you didn't hate him. One argument after how many years? It was nothing. He knew that.' She thought about Connie. They fought every other day, but she knew with absolute certainty that the very last person in her corner when the whole world had abandoned her would be her sister.

'I was closer to Matt than anyone in the world and I did that though.' Jon shook his head. 'I never want to hurt you, Grace.'

Something warm flickered in Grace's heart. It was going to be ok. She could make this right. 'I love you. That means I'm gonna love all of you. The bits that sometimes lose their temper and say things they don't mean. And the bossiness. And the weirdly anal wardrobe.'

'It's efficient,' he protested.

'And I love it all, because it's part of you. And we probably will hurt each other, but we'll say sorry and we'll mean it and we'll

292

work it out. I'm not asking you anything more than if you love me back?'

She felt his breath on her neck before he answered. 'Yes, Grace. I do.'

That was enough. The rest of the conversation could wait. She pulled him against her, pressing her lips to his and felt his arms wrap tight around her waist.

'Oh my God, will you two get a room?' Connie's voice was, sadly, a guaranteed mood killer. Grace prised herself an inch or two away from Jon's body.

Connie was dressed in a purple velvet tailcoat and breeches and was, slightly sheepishly, holding Morgan's hand, but it was her hair that took Grace's attention. 'You shaved your head?'

'Yeah.' Connie ran her hand over her half inch of hair. 'I thought it was more me.'

'It's cool. I like it.' Grace looked from Jon to Morgan. 'You met already.'

'We did,' Jon confirmed. He smiled at Morgan. 'It looks like we might be meeting a whole lot more.'

Morgan nodded. 'Yeah. Like I was thinking maybe we could set up some kind of support group.'

Jon laughed. Grace wrapped both her arms tight around him.

'Are you a spy?' Connie's voice stomped all over Grace's moment of happy ever after.

'What?' Jon stared from sister to sister. 'You think I'm a spy?'

'No!' Grace insisted. 'I just wasn't quite sure what you actually do.'

Jon smiled. 'I'm not a spy.' He paused. 'Although a spy would say that.'

Grace steered him away from her sister. 'Seriously, what do you do?'

'I'm a dealer.'

Drugs. Shit. He was a mob boss after all. Grace's fear must have shown on her face.

'Not that sort of dealer,' he added. 'Essentially, if you are very, very rich and you want something that is very hard to come by, you contact me.'

Grace understood. 'Like a concierge.'

He pursed his lips. 'I tend to be called on for things slightly trickier to find than tickets to see *The Book of Mormon*. Art. Wine. Beyoncé singing live by your eighth wife's birthing pool.' He paused. 'Although this does seem like a conversation for before you declare undying devotion. What if I had been a drug dealer?'

'I knew you weren't a drug dealer.'

'How?'

How? 'Because you're a good man. Even though you try to hide it.'

His expression softened. 'I love you, Grace.'

'I know.' She'd known it before he admitted it. It had been there in all the small moments of attention. 'I love you too.'

—

Emma hurried through the crowd of bodies. Josh was rushing after her. 'Where are you going?'

'I have to find Tom.'

'Yeah. I got that.' Josh grabbed her arm. 'Will you slow down and listen, and for goodness' sake let somebody help you?'

'What?' She didn't have time for Josh being Josh.

'He went that way.' Josh pointed towards the main exit. 'Sorry. I was trying to tell you.'

Shit. She'd been hoping he'd have made his way to the bar for an angry shot of something, rather than actually walking out altogether. 'Thank you.'

She rushed towards the foyer. He wasn't there. She dashed to the doors. There he was, standing in the porchway. She shivered as she pulled open the door and stepped outside. 'I'm only still here because of the snow.' She looked out to the street for the first time. Fat white flakes were just threatening to cover the pavements. 'I wasn't waiting for you,' he insisted.

'Doesn't matter. You're still here. Still counts.'

She'd seen Tom pissed off before, when they'd rowed about her putting work first or when he got a bad beat at the poker table. His face now was something else. This wasn't irritation. This was fury. Pure cold fury. He didn't yell. He was perfectly calm. 'You're moving to America?'

'Nothing's definite.'

'But it's likely? Probable?'

Emma nodded.

'And you were going to tell me this when precisely? Text from the airport? Postcard when you arrived?'

'I was going to tell you. It just...' She knew she had no excuse. She had reasons, rationalisations, but no excuse at all. 'Your mum was ill and you were stressed out and I didn't want to add another thing.'

'Why not?'

She rubbed her arms in the biting cold of the December air. 'I didn't want you to think you were losing someone else.'

'But if we hide things and if we lie to each other, that's how we lose each other.' He stared at her. 'You told me not to hide how I was feeling.'

She had. 'I just didn't want to upset you.'

He took a very deep breath and rubbed the heel of his hand across his eye. 'And how do you think that's going?'

'I'm sorry.' For a moment they watched the snow fall in silence. This should be a perfect moment. Christmas Eve with snow falling around them, with the love of her life right there in front of it. All at once Emma could see everything that she'd risked throwing away. 'I'm so sorry.'

'I don't understand. Like how does that work? Something this exciting happens for you – how am I still not the first person you call? Worse than not the first person? Not top five? Not even on the list?'

'I thought you'd be upset.'

'Well I am now.'

'We committed to each other. And I meant it.' She caught the past tense. 'I mean it. And then the next time I talk to you I'm pissing off to New York. I thought you'd be angry.'

Tom shook his head. 'We promised we were committed. We didn't promise that nothing unexpected would ever happen. This is like a huge opportunity for you, right?'

'It is.'

'Then of course I'm sad about you going away, but I want you to have every single one of your dreams come true. I'm going to miss you horribly, but there's email and phones and aeroplanes.'

'I'm really shit at being a girlfriend, aren't I?'

Tom smiled ever so slightly. 'Frankly hopeless, yes.'

'I'm really, really sorry. I will do everything I can to make it up to you. It's not definite yet that I'm going.'

He took her hand. 'Again, I'm not cross about you going. I'm fucking livid that you didn't talk to me about it.'

'I'm sorry.'

'You said that already.'

'I don't know what else to say.'

'Maybe actually tell me what's going on?'

So she started. Whatever was going on inside the party, Josh and Annie could manage. If the deal with Nina went through they'd be running the Season in London on their own soon enough anyway. Tom stopped her. 'Indoors maybe. I'm not quite cross enough to want you to freeze to death.'

They moved into the foyer and Emma talked, properly, about everything she should have already told him. She told Tom about Nina and the US plan, and she told them about Will – sorry, the Earl of Hanborough – and Lydia's idea for a Country House Season. 'So I might not even go to New York. I can't do it all, can I?'

'Why not?'

'What?'

'Who says you can't do it all? You're brilliant. If anyone can find a way, you can.'

'What did I do to deserve you?'

'I don't know.' He looked her up and down. 'It's genuine mystery.'

'Oh that's nice. Very romantic.'

He shrugged. 'I'm still at ninety per cent supportive, ten per cent pissed off here. Don't push your luck.'

'I am sorry.'

'I know. And I will forgive you. Just give me an hour or two to process.'

'Emma?' Josh was standing in the doorway to the ballroom. 'Is everything ok?'

She looked at Tom. 'Yeah. Everything is ok.'

'Right. Well in that case, it's nearly time for your closing speechy bit.'

Emma checked her watch. He was right, but she couldn't leave Tom right now, could she? 'Right. Maybe you could...'

'It's fine. Go. Speechify. I'll be cheering you on.'

She kissed her boyfriend on the cheek. 'Thank you. I love you.'

'I love you too.'

Emma had spent a long time typing out her bullet points for the perfect closing words for the Festive Season. She had a whole extended motif about Christmas bringing people together and the Season being another version of that, and she wasn't going to say any of it. She stepped up to the microphone. 'Thank you everyone for coming this evening, and for being part of the Festive Season.'

She looked out over the crowded room. Tom was leaning on the doorframe being, as ever, more constant than she would ever deserve. Josh and Annie were together at the side of the stage. Further out amongst the daters she picked out the twins, standing together with Jon and Morgan at their sides. Morgan and Connie might have been worth a flutter at the start of the day,

Emma thought, but Jon and Grace were so far out of left field she couldn't even pretend to have seen that coming. Maybe she was losing her touch.

'I know that a lot of you have found what you came looking for during this Festive Season, and it would be easy for me to talk about that lovely bloom of new romance, but I want to say a little bit about what comes next, because a relationship, after the Season has ended, is about more than parties and romantic gestures. It's about being with someone day to day and letting them into your real life. It's about trusting the person you're with to care as much about your hopes and dreams as you do. It's about being more than just two individuals, but forming one team, where you know that whatever life throws your way that other person has your back. And sometimes it's about letting all your ideas about what a relationship is fall apart, and hoping that whatever is left is strong enough to be the foundation for something wonderful. What I've learned for myself recently is that there's no template for that something wonderful. There's no matchmaker who can tell you what to do. You have to find what works for both of you. But if you've got the right person beside you, the one who gives you permission to be your bravest, most brilliant self, then you will be ok. Right back at our second event I invited you all to make a wish. I hope that tonight, at least some of those wishes have come true.'

Emma held her champagne glass aloft. 'We'll be back to the dancing in a second but first, I'd like to propose a toast. To finding the one!'

—

Callum squeezed Hope's shoulder as he raised his glass. It was a small gesture of affection. Hope's whole body tensed. If Emma hadn't mentioned the wishes, if Callum hadn't said he loved her, then everything might still be ok.

Across the room Theo was raising his glass. He looked towards her. Hope looked away. She wasn't watching Theo. She was here with Callum. She was supposed to be happy about that, but something wasn't right. She knew that. She was telling herself it was because it was a new relationship and she was still learning to trust herself again.

But that wasn't it. It wasn't that Simon had left her unable to trust her feelings for Callum. It was that she had finally healed enough that she did trust her feelings. She knew absolutely how she felt and how she ought to be feeling. She knew what it was to love without fear. Without even realising, she'd been doing it for years. She stepped out of Callum's embrace and took his hand. 'Shall we?'

She led him away from the dance floor to a quiet corner to the side of the stage. This was horrible. 'We need to talk.'

He laughed. 'Sounds ominous.'

What was she supposed to say? Everything was a cliché. 'It's not you.'

He stopped laughed. 'Seriously?'

'It's really not you.' Still a cliché, but also true. 'You're great. I really like you.'

'Hope, I love you.'

'Yeah. I, I do really like you.'

'It's fine. I rushed things. We can slow down.'

It wasn't that. 'It's really not you. You're brilliant.' And he was. 'You're everything I would have said I wanted or needed. You're basically everything I did say I wanted when I filled in the registration form for this thing.'

'So what's the problem?'

Ultimately there was only one problem, but it was insurmountable. 'I'm in love with somebody else.'

Callum closed his eyes for a moment. 'Shoulda guessed.'

Hope shook her head. 'I only just worked it out myself.'

'Right. Well, I hope he's good to you.'

'He is.' He always had been, even when Hope hadn't been able to see it.

'I'm going to go.'

'You don't have to. I'll go. You stay and have fun.'

'Hope, I wanted to come to this thing with you. That's not how it's worked out. You have to let me go now.'

'But I want to know you're all right.'

'Not at the moment. No.'

Hope watched him leave. It was the right thing. She couldn't pretend to be in love just because Callum was so decent and she'd believed for so long that that was all she was allowed to want.

Emma Love appeared at her shoulder. 'Are you ok? I saw Callum...' She pointed towards the exit.

'We broke up.'

She winced. 'I'm sorry. I'll give you a free pass next time.'

'I don't think it would help.'

'Really?' Emma looked uncharacteristically defeated.

'Not your fault, but I'm in love with my best friend.'

Emma frowned. 'Theo?'

Hope nodded.

The matchmaker's expression changed. 'Of course Theo.' She shook her head. 'I'm an idiot. It was always because of Hope...' she muttered.

'What?'

'Nothing. Just trust me. You need to go and tell him.'

'What if it doesn't work out?'

'And what if it does? Go! Go on. Right now.'

Hope felt herself physically pushed onto the dance floor. Theo was standing alone at the head of a longways set at the far side of the room. She took her place opposite him. 'Could I have this dance?'

'Always.' He glanced down the length of the set. 'Although we don't seem to get to dance yet.'

'We start when the top couple get up to us. Haven't you been listening?'

'I wasn't really taking it in. Bit preoccupied.'

'Callum left.'

'I saw.'

300

Hope balled up her courage. 'Because I told him I wasn't in love with him.'

The wave of dancing bodies moved up the set to reach them, and Hope found herself turning away from him, before moving back to take his hand at the centre of a square. She raised her eyes to Theo's face. He met her gaze. 'Why did you tell him that?'

The dance pulled them apart again. Hope had a second to think about her answer. It wasn't too late to back out. She could say that things just weren't right with Callum, and her and Theo could go back to being friends and… she spun towards him. He took her arm in a promenade. It was now or never. It was say what she really wanted or forever live in fear. 'It was because I'm in love with somebody else.'

Theo dropped her hand and turned to walk up the far side of the step. Hope followed his lead, parading up the outside of the opposite line of dancers. Between each body she caught a glimpse of him, his gaze darting towards her. Finally they arrived at the head of the set, and retook their starting positions opposite one another, exactly as they'd been a few moments ago, and yet, surely, something had changed.

Her very best friend in the world looked wary. 'Who are you in love with, Hope?'

'I…' The fear was still there, but she was stronger. Together her and Theo were stronger.

'Please. Just tell me what you want.'

'I want you.' It was that easy. 'I love you.'

And in a second he had closed the gap between them. Hope jumped back. 'Ew!'

'What?'

'You were going to kiss me.'

'Well yes.'

'But we're friends. We don't do that.'

He took her hand, leading her out of the ballroom and into the cool of the lobby, where he stopped, and traced his fingers down her cheek and along the line of her jaw, bending his head just slightly towards her. 'Tell me when,' he whispered.

It was crazy. It would definitely ruin their friendship. It made no sense at all. You couldn't fall in love with someone without even noticing. And yet she had. Utterly and completely. For the first time in what seemed like forever, Hope knew exactly what she wanted. 'Now.'

Once upon a time...

As the clock at the end of the ballroom struck midnight, the netting that covered the ceiling was released and hundreds of balloons drifted slowly downwards onto the dance floor and the band moved from their earlier repertoire of country dance tunes to a chorus of 'We Wish You a Merry Christmas'.

Emma felt Tom's arm snake around her waist. 'Happy Christmas,' he whispered.

'Happy Christmas.'

She looked around the room. Everyone seemed to have someone to kiss and share season's greetings with. A hundred different happy ever afters, all forming the beginning of their own brand new stories.

'Are you happy?' Tom asked.

'I am.'

'So what next?'

'I don't know.' Nina Elton had been pursuing her to pin down the details of their arrangement all evening, but Emma's gaze landed on Will and Lydia giggling together under the cascade of balloons. 'I've got some decisions to make.' She stopped herself. 'We've got some decisions to make.'

'You know I'll support whatever you want to do?' Tom checked. 'Whatever you decide, it's going to be awesome.'

And when she looked into her partner's eyes, she believed it absolutely was. The future was unknown and utterly certain all at the same time. 'Even if I decide to go away?' she asked. 'We'll make it work?'

'We'll make it work.'

A letter from Ally

Hello!

Welcome to the Festive Season. I'm delighted that you've decided to join me and Emma for this adventure in dating. I hope you fall just as much in love with all our hopeful romantics as I did while I was writing about them.

There's a famous quote that happy families are all alike, but every unhappy family is unhappy in its own way. I believe it's from Leo Tolstoy – get me being all fancy! And writers often take that to imply that the unhappiness is where the writing gold can be found. Well, I've been thinking a lot, while writing this book, about happy relationships, and – with apologies to Leo – I really don't think they are all alike at all.

In this novel we get to spy on lots of romances, but also sibling relationships, friendships, and parents and children, and happy looks different for everyone. My biggest hope as a writer is that one day somebody out there might read one of my stories and decide that they are going to seek their own joy, whether that's romantic, personal, professional or anything else.

If that reader is you, then hi. I see you. Go for it. You absolutely deserve your own unique happy ever after. Good luck.

I always love to hear from readers so do feel welcome to get in touch. You can find me on:

Instagram: https://www.instagram.com/msallysinclair/

TikTok: https://www.tiktok.com/@msallysinclair

Twitter: https://twitter.com/MsAllySinclair

Facebook: https://www.facebook.com/allysinclairauthor/

YouTube: https://www.youtube.com/@alallyalison

And on my website: allysinclair.com

Or you can email allysinclairauthor@gmail.com

Thank you so much for reading *The Christmas Season*.
  Lots of love,
  Ally

Acknowledgments

Writing a novel is an incredibly solitary experience in a lot of ways, but also a hugely collaborative one so there are lots of people to thank. Firstly, huge thanks to everyone at Hera – editors, publicists, cover designers (seriously, this cover is just so pretty!), copy editors, proof readers. You are all absolutely Top People. Special thanks to Keshini and Jennie for their faith in this book and their brilliant and wisdomous editorial advice.

Thanks too, as always, to Julia Silk, the Queen of Literary Agenting. Thanks for letting me outsource having confidence in my own ability to you, when internal reserves of self-belief run low.

Having said writing can be very solitary, I also need to thank the writer buddy support crew who hold me together when the words don't behave. Annie O'Neil, Daisy Tate, Imogen Howson, Janet Gover, Jeevani Charika, Jessica Thorne, Kate Johnson, Rhoda Baxter, Ruth Long and Sheila McClure – thank you. If it takes a village to raise a book baby, then you are my village, and I salute you all.

As ever, thank you EngineerBoy, continuing in his role as provider of tech support, cuddles and emergency toast.

And finally, thank you, dear reader. You're awesome.